"Nicholas!" Angel whispered, holding

her arms to him. "My darling!"

He was like a boy in love for the first time. Gone was his cynical caution, his cool reserve. His lips touched her hair, her face, her eyes, her breasts, the throbbing hollow in her throat. His fingers caressed her, sending little shocks of delight through her trembling body. She sobbed out his name, her body responding eagerly to his. "Oh, Nicholas, Nicholas, I love you!"

Later, as he lay sleeping beside her, she put an arm about him and held him close. The candlelight, left to burn, showed her the thick black semicircles of his lashes, the clustering of the dark curls upon his forehead, and the shadowed hollows beneath his high cheekbones.

She had feared that he would be exhausted, but he did not seem to be. She noted, with relief, that his breathing was even, his sleep deep and natural. For the first time she allowed herself to hope.

He shivered in his sleep. She covered him quickly and snuggled down beside him. *"You'll not die, Nicholas, I won't let you! You must live for me!"*

Novels by Constance Gluyas

MY LADY BENBROOK
THE KING'S BRAT

Published by
WARNER BOOKS

My Lady Benbrook

By
Constance Gluyas

WARNER BOOKS

A Warner Communications Company

For my husband Don
Always with love

My Lady
Benbrook

MANY OF THE TALL TIMBERED AND PLAStered houses leaned forward until they all but touched their neighbors on the other side of the narrow, cobblepaved street. They provided a welcome patch of shade to the two gentlemen who had been sauntering leisurely along.

"Gad!" the taller man said, drawing a white handkerchief from his sleeve. " 'Tis plaguey hot today." He sat down on the crumbling front steps of a house and thrust his long legs out before him. "Come," he said, indicating the place beside him. "Rest yourself, Christopher."

Christopher Wren hesitated for a moment, then, drawing his cloak tighter about him, he obeyed with a shudder of distaste. "I could think of better resting place, Sire," he observed dryly.

Charles Stuart laughed. "And I. But a little dirt won't do you any harm, man." He began mopping his neck and forehead vigorously. "I am persuaded that you must hate me," he went on, his dark eyes on his companion's pale face. " 'Else would you not have cajoled me into this monstrous unpleasant walk."

" 'Tis not unseasonably hot for July, Sire," Wren replied. "And walking is good for you."

"I walk every day, as well you know."

"Aye, Sire, but never before have you walked as a simple man of the people."

"And 'twas the contrast you were after, was it not?" Charles said thoughtfully. "The contrast between my pleasant walks and these streets?" He put a hand to his broad-brimmed, unadorned black hat. "Hence the disguise, you damned sly fellow."

Wren smiled. Charles II of England, in his plain black garments unrelieved by the slightest suggestion of lace, his own short dark hair beneath the hat, his long thin fingers bare of rings, was hardly the jeweled, bewigged, perfumed, satin-clad, and beplumed personage Wren was used to beholding. " 'Twould scarcely have been wise for the King of England to display himself openly, would it, Sire?" he replied.

Why?" Charles shot the question at him sharply. "Am I so hated, then?"

"You know well that you are beloved of the people, Sire. But if a king wishes to walk in peace, he must needs adopt a disguise."

"And I have not seen these streets before, I suppose?"

"You have passed through them, but in a carriage, Sire, attended by a group of your gentlemen and the ladies of the Court. The streets were adorned against your coming. You did not see the filth and decay."

Charles Stuart studied him thoughtfully. "London is a warm and friendly place; my people are content. Why must you be forever seeking to tear it apart brick by brick, and—if your wild words are to be believed—raise a new London in its stead?"

"Because it is time, Sire," Wren said quietly. "I might be discouraged by your words. But I know the project is one dear to your own heart." Wren's pale face flushed. "I have drawn plans, Sire. I could show them to you. We could build clean, upright houses. We could find new methods of sanitation, and we could educate the people to—"

"I know, I know," the King interrupted. "I have heard it all before, damn you for an importuning scoundrel! But, Christopher, where is the money to come from? Parliament controls the finances with a tight hand. King I may be, but I have to go before them, cap in hand, and beseech them for every coin." He shrugged. "Nay, the time is not yet."

"I understand, Sire. But perhaps if you showed them my plans? If you reminded them that the disaster of the plague might well have been averted had the people had cleaner living conditions, they might see the wisdom of granting monies for this particular project."

"Thou art a dreamer, Chris," Charles answered. "As for the plague, it is still not entirely subdued."

"All the more reason, Sire, to—"

"*Nay.*" Charles stood up. "Some day, perhaps, but not now."

Christopher Wren rose too. "And if a further disaster should strike the people, Sire, what then?"

"We must pray 'twill not. Now come along."

Wren knew that the King's seemingly casual attitude hid a deep concern for his people and the conditions in which they were forced to live. But nonetheless, Wren told himself, he would renew the attack later. Bit by bit he would break the King down, until Charles, by the sheer force of his personality and belief, would go before the Parliament and force them to comply.

Dane Street was a fairly quiet area, but now, as they turned a corner, they came upon a hubbub of sound. Carriages, sedan chairs, carts, were all hopelessly tangled together, some with their wheels barely avoiding the filthy refuse-choked gutter that ran along the middle of the street. The occupants and drivers were shouting and cursing each other as they demanded the right of way.

The King winced and put his handkerchief to his nose as they passed several laystalls heaped with the accumulated filth of weeks. There was a strong stench of human excrement, mingled with the even stronger stench of animal offal, urine, rotting fish, and waste of all kinds, waiting a chance to be piled in the street gutter. The gutter was already overflowing and would remain that way until the rain came and flushed the swirling mess further along; only then would the laystalls be emptied of

11

their noisome burden. Housewives, either too lazy or too tired to take their refuse to the laystalls, had thrown the night's collection out of their windows, where it spattered the middle of the street.

The King stepped carefully over a pile of excrement mixed with orange rind, bones, and pieces of cabbage leaf. "Od's Fish!" he exclaimed. " 'Tis enough to turn the stomach!"

"Aye, it is, Sire," Wren replied quietly. "And might not something be done about it?"

The King did not answer. He was well aware that Wren's plan for building a strong and clean London was a good, even an inspired idea. But he felt hot and irritated, and Wren, good fellow though he was, did keep on so. Was it his fault if his miserly Parliament refused to countenance the idea?

"What do ye lack?" hawkers cried from their positions before the shops. "What do ye lack, madam, good sir? We got fresh fish. We got sweet milk as'll slide nice down a parched throat. We got ol' clothes, fit you a fair treat, they will. Come on, almos' like new, they are. We got nice spiced custards. Fine Newcastle coals to warm your backsides. Don' be cold, gents, when you can cuddle up to your wench all nice an' warm like. We got oysters, 'errings, 'addock an' cod. Over 'ere, lady, over 'ere. Try a bunch o' me nice sweet lavender. Scent your clothes, it will, an' if you was to put it in your bed, it'll cover up the smell o' the bugs. Try a bunch, jus' try. 'Ere, ladies an' gents, buy me nice fruits an' veg. Picked only this mornin' they was, an' you can' get no better 'an that. What do ye lack, ladies an' gents? What do ye lack?"

One hawker, his face red and earnest, thrust a bloody tray of fly-swarmed meat beneath the King's nose. "Try me meats, good sir," he shouted. "Beef, I got. Pork, I got. An' 'ens what's nice an' plump an' fresh as the day when they was 'atched. Eat nice, they do."

"No, thank you," the King shuddered. "Move aside, if you please, and let us pass."

The hawker retreated into the shadow of his doorway. "Bleedin' swells!" he shouted after them. "Me good 'earty meats ain't good enough for the likes o' you, I s'ppose. Fines' in the whole o' London, they be. I takes me perishin' oath on it." Glaring belligerently about him, he resumed his cries. "What do ye lack? Come on ladies an' gents, what do ye lack?"

Hiding a smile, Wren turned in the direction of Covent Garden. The King, his feet aching, his frown increasing, followed after him down Longacre Street and turned into St. Martin's Lane. Here Wren stopped, pointing with his finger at the ancient spire of St. Paul's dominating the tangle of brothels, shops, and ale houses.

Wren's dark blue eyes, the eyes of a visionary, turned to the King. "My dreams go on and on, Sire. I would give London dignity and beauty. I would give it pride in itself, to become the finest city in the world." He looked at the spire of St. Paul's again. "And I would give old St. Paul's a new façade, a new interior."

"If you live long enough."

"Then, Sire, I must contrive to do so."

They walked on, past the lodging houses and the broken down grimed wooden shacks that housed London's poor. When they came within distance of the murky Thames, the King rebelled. "I will walk no further," he said firmly. "You may call me a chair, you cursed persistent rogue."

Seated in the chair beside the unchastened Wren, the King tried to divert the conversation to lighter topics. "My lord Benbrook is just such another dreamer as yourself," he said casually, "but he disguises it beneath a harshness of manner. The dinner tonight, as you know, is in celebration of his forthcoming wedding. Mayhap you can expound to him." He put his hands in his pockets and regarded Wren with a lazy smile. "God knows he has plenty of money."

"I have not seen my lord Benbrook in a long time," Wren said quickly. "I trust he is fully recovered."

13

The King moved uneasily, shifting his long legs to a more comfortable position. "But that's the devil of it, Chris. I am not sure."

"Your pardon, Sire?"

"The plague seems to have left him with a condition of the heart," the King frowned. "It disturbs me greatly."

"Is it so very serious, then?"

"Plague take it, I don't know! I have no doubt that it was the strain of all those long months, when he believed Mistress Dawson dead, that aggravated his condition." Charles recalled finding Mistress Dawson in the Convent of the Angels. "When I restored Mistress Dawson to him, I had hoped that the condition would abate," he went on unhappily. "It has not done so. His housekeeper tells me that since that time he has had one or two quite serious attacks. The poor soul is all but demented with worry."

"Aye," Wren nodded. "She would be. Mrs. Sampson is devoted to him, I believe."

"Since the day he was born. As for Mistress Dawson, I verily believe no one else is alive for her." Charles sighed. "Od's Fish, Chris, to be loved like that! What would I not give to experience it!"

Christopher Wren gave him a quick glance. "I am sure that your Majesty has experienced the pleasant emotion of love on a great many occasions," said Wren, his voice carefully colorless. Wisely, he forbore to remind him that the love of his Queen, little Catherine of Braganza, was equally all-encompassing. Like Mistress Dawson, the Queen saw only one man, lived for only one man, and that man was her charming and graceless scamp of a husband, the ugly but fascinating Charles Stuart.

Charles drew the curtain back from the window and stared moodily at the passing scene. He saw a fat woman resting her enormous weight upon a small stool, her ragged purple gown hitched high over her great blue-veined legs; her eyes were incurious as she stolidly munched upon a hunk of coarse bread. He saw the flirtatious and beguiling smiles of the prostitutes leaning from the windows of the bawdy houses lining the street, their white breasts exposed to view, the nipples painted a glaring red. He saw the concentrated expression of an orange girl hawking her wares, the brutal ferocity of a small boy kicking at a fallen comrade. The unfortunate victim lay with the back of his head in the maggot-ridden gutter, his mouth opened wide in a cry of anguish. A passing coach sent up a spray of mud, and Charles hastily let the curtain drop.

Settling back in his corner, Charles thought of Catherine. What a fool Wren must think him, he thought, bewailing his lack of love. But to know the full wonder of love, one must love in return. He was fond of Catherine, very fond. He trusted her, confided in her, could go to her with all his troubles, as he had never before done to any woman, and she would soothe and cheer him. But it was not love he felt for her.

Charles glanced at Wren's absorbed profile. Wren, he smiled to himself, was no doubt thinking of Mistress Angel Dawson. At one time Wren had fancied himself in love with her; perhaps he still did. When Angel had been lost, it had been left to Charles Stuart himself to find her, and that only by chance.

Love, Charles thought, his fingers plucking restlessly at the leather curtain. Apart from his sister Minette, who must be forever denied to him, had he ever truly known love? At one time he had believed himself deeply and sincerely in love with Barbara Castlemaine, and yet, now he could scarcely endure her. There was Angel Dawson, whom he could never quite manage to banish from his thoughts. But 'twas useless to lavish affection on Angel, for she was bound mind and heart and soul to Nicholas. The King's love, the splendor of the Court, the expensive gifts he would like to have given her, appealed not at all.

"Sire," Wren's voice broke in. "What of Mistress Dawson?"

"She is blooming, quite radiant in fact. But tonight you will see for yourself, will you not?"

Wren turned upon him an expression so woebegone, that Charles had great difficulty in restraining laughter.

But he was essentially kindhearted. " 'Tis your love of beauty that has brought you to this pass," he said softly. "You do not so much love Mistress Dawson as you are enthralled with her façade. She is indeed a miracle of beauty to delight the eye, but you will recover, Chris. After all, you have seen her but half a dozen times."

"Once was enough, Sire."

"And you will never recover. I know, Chris, I know. But love, if it has nothing to feed upon, cannot warm itself at a cold fire."

His thoughts turned to the blonde and lovely Frances Stuart. She tickled his jaded senses with a subtle appeal, and what he felt for her was perhaps a *form* of love. Frances had once been in attendance upon his sister, and she had picked up many of Minette's ways and expressions, including her graceful manner of walking; perhaps this was what drew him so strongly to her. But if Minette was beyond him, so too was Frances, armored in her almost aggressive virginity.

"We are approaching our destination, Sire. Shall I tell the men to stop a little distance from the Palace? We can walk the rest of the way."

"Confound you and your walking! Have them take us to the plaguey door," he smiled. "I can then limp the rest of the way."

The chairmen were somewhat confused when, setting down their burden, they heard the short blond gentleman address his companion as "Sire." They had believed that they were perhaps carrying superior palace servants.

"They have run a swift race," the dark man said, smiling upon them. "I would have you reward them well, Chris."

"Most certainly, Sire. 'Twill be my pleasure to do so."

The chairmen doubted no longer. There was something about this dark man—an elegance of manner, something that they could not put into words. But they knew they stood before the King.

"Your Majesty!" Almost simultaneously they fell to their knees.

Charles looked down into their faces, then a smile of extraordinary charm lit his dark features. "Rise, please, gentlemen," he said.

They clambered awkwardly to their feet and stood before him, mute.

Charles held out his hand. "You will do me the honor, gentlemen?"

The two men looked at each other, then, in another simultaneous action, they wiped their hands on their mud-spattered breeches.

"It's—it's you what's adoin' us the honor, Your Majesty," the first man stammered, putting his hand in the King's. "Why, me ol' woman ain't never goin' to believe this!"

"Nay," Charles said gently, taking the other man's hand, "the shoe is on the other foot. As to your wives, if you find they do not believe you, you must take my advice—ignore them. Women must ever be kept in their places, do you not agree with me?"

They smiled, wide delighted smiles. "Aye, Your Majesty," the first man said boldly, "I do an' all."

His companion could find nothing to say for himself. "Here is a man of little words," Charles declared, clapping him on the shoulder, "but of much thought."

The two men seemed loath to leave the royal presence, but as the King made an almost imperceptible movement toward the door, they remembered their manners and bowed hastily. One of them, in his zeal to outdo the other, backed into a short clipped hedge and went sprawling to his knees.

Seeing his crestfallen expression, Charles called, "I have ever detested that hedge. A buffet or two won't hurt it. And now," he went on, shooting a glance at Wren, "I pray that you gentlemen will excuse me, for I have been an unconscionable time awalking and am wearied to my very bones."

He raised his hand in farewell. Grinning, they waved back heartily. "God save the King!" they shouted, as they disappeared from sight.

Wren bowed and took his leave of the King. It was no wonder, he thought as he went on his way, that Charles Stuart was so beloved of the people. He could adapt himself to each and every one of them. This was not hypocrisy on his part, but simply a sincere wish to put them at their ease. "God save the King," Wren muttered under his breath. "Aye, may God spare him to us for many long years to come!"

CHARLES STUART STROLLED SLOWLY ALONG the red-carpeted corridor, one of his numerous spaniels held in the crook of his arm. He paused by an opened window, his eyes examining with pleasure the pointed glossy leaves of the tall tree outside; the heavily garlanded branches swayed in the slight wind, tapping lightly against the rose-tinted windowpane. Nature, at least, had taken little heed of the plague that had killed so many of his people and had crippled the city of London.

"It seems long, long ago, does it not, Charlotte?" the King murmured, stroking the spaniel's silky ears. "And yet it is not so very long ago that the plague left us."

Aye, he thought, frowning. Not so very long ago and yet, as he had told Wren, there were still the isolated cases. The people, believing the danger entirely over, had come flocking back to London. Shops had opened again, resuming their trade as though nothing had happened; ships sailed in and out of the harbor. The fast-growing grass that had sprouted high between the cobbles during that time of terror had been hacked away. London was itself again. Or was it? But so many dead! So many that it haunted his nights.

Outside the door of the Queen's sitting room, he heard the little silver clock that Catherine had brought with her from Portugal, chiming the hour of three. Opening the door, Charles entered the room wih his long lazy stride.

The Queen was seated upon a crimson velvet-covered couch, her head bent, her slim fingers drawing a gold thread through her embroidery. She had been replying somewhat absentmindedly to a remark made to her by Mary Thaxter, the youngest of her maids of honor, but her words broke off abruptly. As always, at first sight of the King, she felt the quick leaping of her joy. She stared at the tall figure in the plain black garments. "Why, Sire," she said breathlessly, the delicate color staining her cheeks, "this is indeed an unexpected pleasure. I had not thought to see you back so soon."

The smile Charles directed at her was warmly intimate. There were times when his Queen appeared quite plain, but today she was a pleasing sight. Her cheeks were flushed, her eyes bright, and her thick, dark-brown hair fell to her shoulders in glossy ringlets. Aye, she was very pretty today, he thought, looking into her eyes, but why must she love me so damned much? She should not look at an unsatisfactory husband in that way. Little Catherine deserved better than Charles Stuart.

"Had you been in Wren's company, Madam, I vow you would have returned ere this," Charles said softly. "My legs are longer, but he can outdistance me." He laughed. "But for the fact that I enjoy his company so much, I'd forbid him the Palace, damned if I wouldn't." His eyes turned to Frances Stuart, who stood demurely in the background, her fingers nervously pleating the folds of her blue skirts. "Good day to *you*, Mistress Stuart."

She started. "Good day to you, Sire," she said, curtsying.

Catherine saw the desire in her husband's sleepy-lidded eyes as they rested upon Frances, but she forced herself to ignore it. Pain stirred as she asked herself the familiar question: Why was her love not enough for him? "You—you found the walk boring, Sire?"

"Nay, not boring. It was, in fact, extremely instructive. Wren is right. 'Tis time some of the old buildings were pulled down." His expression became thoughtful. " 'Tis little use hammering at Parliament, scurvy dogs that they are. But I will try again, if only to please Chris."

"And to please yourself, Sire, I am sure."

"You do me too much credit, Madam, as always. But in this one thing, at least, you are right."

"I know it." The Queen nodded a smiling dismissal to her ladies.

Wistfully, Charles' eyes followed Frances Stuart as she moved gracefully after her companions. A plague on the elusive wench. What did she desire of him? He had already given her jewels, and the many little costly trifles that appealed to her will-o'-the-wisp spirit. Frances had accepted them all gracefully, but she would suffer no more than a chaste kiss upon her cheek.

He stared broodingly at the closed door. Of late he had heard of a serious love affair between Frances and the Duke of Richmond and Lennox, a distant cousin of his, but he was inclined to discount the rumors. Lovely Frances and that boor Richmond? Nay, unthinkable!

Remembering the presence of the Queen, Charles stretched his arms above his head, yawning widely. "Faith, Catherine," he remarked, as he strolled over and seated himself beside her, "but I am most damnably tired." He glanced at her quickly. "Art excited about the ball tonight, Cat?"

"I am indeed." Catherine put her embroidery to one side, smoothing out the skirts of her white gown. "I have seen Mistress Dawson only twice since her return. 'Twill be pleasant to see her again, and to celebrate the happy occasion of her forthcoming marriage. 'Tis exciting, is it not, Charles? Angel and my lord Benbrook!" She clasped her small ringed hands together and smiled mischievously. "Though I must confess that I had not thought the grim-faced Benbrook had it in him to love so utterly and so completely."

Charles snapped his fingers at the little dog, and she, obedient to his unspoken command, settled herself comfortably upon the blue and silver carpet, her liquid brown eyes fixed adoringly upon him. Her eyes reminded him of

Catherine's, Charles thought, they held the same expression. He was immediately ashamed. Catherine loved him truly and sincerely. It was not for him to criticize, he should be grateful.

"Charlotte is my very own dog," Catherine said, laughing. "Yet she loves only you. 'Tis because she is a lady, I'll vow."

Charles ignored the faint sting in her words. "Dost remember when I gave her to you, Catherine?"

"Ah, yes, Charles. How could I forget!"

He frowned at the ardency of her tone. That look in her eyes again made him uncomfortable that he could not return her love. Plague take him for a selfish swine! To make up for it, he put his arm about her and drew her close. "We were talking of Benbrook, were we not? My lord Benbrook, I would have you know, is very much in love. Though, like you, I had not thought to see him so completely enslaved."

Catherine of Braganza trembled at his touch. She thought of the dark, sternly handsome Earl of Benbrook, in love for the first time, and she felt a pang of sympathy with him. Ever since she had left her native Portugal to become the bride of Charles II of England, had not she been in like case? Aye, she had found herself helpless to resist Charles' warm dark eyes, his brilliant smile, and his overpowering charm, and so she had tumbled hopelessly into love.

Catherine's soft mouth tightened to a bitter line. 'Twas true that she could no more help loving Charles than she could help breathing. But because she knew well that he did not return that love, she had sometimes wished that it might be possible to find a cure for herself. Charles was always good-natured, unfailingly kind and thoughtful, but he would never love her as she desired, and she had long ago faced that dismal truth.

She looked at him. His short dark hair was ruffled untidily over his head, his lined faced looked weary, his eyes, as always, mournful and disillusioned. Feeling a rush of tenderness, she put her hand over his. But dear God!

she thought, sometimes Charles and his never-ending procession of women were a little more than she could bear!

There was the hateful Barbara Castlemaine, of the fiery red hair and the beautiful face that hid a corrupt nature. Would she ever forget her devastating grief, her humiliation when Charles, ignoring all her tears and protestations, had forced her to accept the Castlemaine into her household? Charles had seemed like a different man at that time. Gone was all his warmth. He had been stern and cold toward her, so cold that she could no longer stand out against him. She had given way, and the triumphant Barbara had become a member of her household.

Catherine sighed. If she had wanted revenge over her enemy, she had it now. Though Barbara for a long time had been Charles' favorite mistress, her influence over the king was rapidly waning. At last Charles had sickened of Barbara's greed, of her perpetual demands, the screaming scenes she created when thwarted. But his loss of interest in Barbara made no difference, Catherine thought, for now his roving eyes had fallen upon Frances Stuart. Aye, Barbara was still at Court, still had her circle of admirers, but Charles was no longer one of them. The hard line of Catherine's mouth softened into a smile. She remembered Barbara's almost ludicrous fury and dismay when she found that the King could no longer be commanded to her bed. 'Twas a hollow victory, though. Barbara had been effectively routed, but what good was that since Charles now imagined himself in love with Frances Stuart?

But Catherine knew there was a difference between the two women, and she had little to fear from a girl who was not swayed by the King's attentions. 'Twas true she accepted the gifts and honors he heaped upon her, but she returned him no particular interest. Even when Frances had posed for Jan Roettier's etching of Britannia, her likeness to be stamped on the coin of the realm at Charles' request, still she had proved impervious to the charms of Charles Stuart. Frances, or so it was said, was showing a decided interest in the Duke of Richmond and Lennox, favoring him above her many suitors. Catherine could not help being fond of the girl, and she found herself hoping that this particular rumor might not be true. The Duke had been twice widowed and, in her opinion, was a most unsuitable husband.

Catherine's thoughts turned naturally to Angel Dawson —another who had been proof against the King. She loved Angel, but not for that reason alone. She hoped very much that she would be happy with her Nicholas.

Catherine glanced again at Charles. He was smiling faintly, and for once his attention seemed to be wholly concentrated upon her. But she would not allow herself to be deceived. It might be that he had heard of the rumors concerning Frances and the Duke and had come to her for consolation. Beneath his smiling affability, he was probably hurt and angry.

Nay, she was being absurd. The feeling he had for Frances would pass. She knew Charles was fickle, he could not help being so, but if 'twere not Frances, 'twould be another. He was showing an interest in various play actresses of late. Chief among them was Moll Davis of the Duke's Theatre, and her rival at the King's Theatre, Nell Gwynne. He had not yet sent for the actresses, Catherine knew, but in the case of Moll Davis, it might be that his interest was not yet sufficiently stirred.

His hesitation over Nell Gwynne might be due in part to the girl's extreme youth. Charles, when he wished to recognize the fact, was possessed of a conscience and certain scruples. However, 'twould be only a matter of time before he overcame them. Nell Gwynne was disturbingly lovely. In the small roles she had acted she had a gamine charm, which had brought her quick popularity in the newly opened King's Theatre. The gutter actress, as Barbara Castlemaine had dubbed her, was beloved of the people, and "our Nellie" was loudly cheered whenever her carriage drove by.

24

"Well, Catherine, why so pensive, eh? What were you thinking about?"

Startled out of her reverie, she said the first thing that came into her mind. "Of my lord Benbrook. You have not spoken of him of late. I—I had thought his condition to be improved."

Charles frowned. "It has not, I have it on a reliable authority. I remember once, when he was in attendance upon me, he was suddenly taken with these pains. He lost consciousness. We were alone at the time, so I tended him myself. But it was quite some time before he came to himself. The pains are significant of a grave illness." Charles hunched his shoulders together, repressing a shudder. "I cannot help but feel that I shall be powerless to do anything to help him."

Catherine placed a consoling hand on his arm. "Charles, does—does Angel know?"

"Nay. The fool refuses to tell her. Mayhap he fears to lose her. Who can see into Benbrook's subtle mind?"

"But Angel would never leave him, you know that, Charles. She loves him!"

He smiled at her indignant expression. "I know it, and you know it, but does Benbrook?"

"Then he must be made to realize it!"

Charles laughed. "Oh, Catherine, Catherine," he said, shaking his head. "No one, to the best of my knowledge, has ever moved friend Nicholas into doing that which he does not wish to do."

Catherine shook a perplexed head, and Charles, seeing her so flushed and pretty, felt the first faint stirrings of the desire she could sometimes inspire in him. "But at this moment, I would rather talk of ourselves," he said huskily. His lips touched her cheek, tracing feather-light kisses downward. "Dost agree, little Catherine?"

His lips were against her breast, and she responded with a quivering eagerness. "Dear Charles!" she whispered, stroking his dark hair. "Oh my dearest, dearest Charles! I love you so very much!"

Charles rose slowly to his feet, drawing her up with him. "I would be alone with you, dear Madam," he said in a low voice.

"But—but we *are* al—alone."

His ardent eyes gazed deeply into hers. "And do you deny me an invitation to your bedroom?"

"Nay, Charles. Never!"

"Then, sweet Catherine, I feel that there is pleasant work ahead for the Stuart."

She clung to him tightly, her body trembling violently. "If only you loved me, Charles. Me alone!"

Impatiently, he swept her up into his arms. "Wouldst prattle at a time like this? Od's Fish, Catherine, I love you in my own way. Is that not enough for you?"

Nay, she thought, as Charles bore her to her bedroom. *'Tis not enough, not nearly enough. I would have your whole heart, as you have mine!*

Charles laid Catherine gently on the bed. She made no move at first, contenting herself with looking at him as he began to disrobe. She lived for these times, for only then could she feel that Charles truly belonged to her. It was an illusion, she knew, but in her eager response, and the pleasure he took in their union, she could tell herself that he was hers alone.

She saw the slumberous look in his eyes, his lazy, half-teasing sensuous smile. But that smile was not for Catherine of Braganza alone, it was the smile he turned upon all women who pleased him, as she did now.

With trembling fingers she began to unbutton her bodice, but Charles brushed her hand aside. He undressed her, his thin, cool fingers lingering on her breasts. She could feel her body turning fluid, beginning to throb and burn with the urgent force of her desire.

"Charles," Catherine whispered, holding out her arms. "Come to me. Come quickly!"

"Catherine," Charles said, his experienced lips sending little shocks of ecstasy through her body. "You ever pleasure me as no other woman is capable of doing. You ever surprise me, small one."

The words meant nothing. Her body arched upward to meet his. Yet she would treasure his words, and later, when she was alone, would repeat them over and over again, with the fervency she applied to telling the beads of her rosary.

Some time later, lying by her side on the big bed, Charles inquired of her, "Dost really love thy graceless Charles Stuart so very much, then?"

He raised himself up on an elbow and looked at her, a faintly puzzled expression in his eyes. Catherine, usually so meek and pliable in her daily life, had a force and a driving hunger that surpassed even that of the Castlemaine.

Shrugging, he lay down again. Why then did he need other women? No one woman, it seemed, could satisfy him. No one woman? Minette, Minette! The little nickname he had given her mourned deeply inside him. Would to God I were not your brother!

Catherine's voice startled him. "Do I love you?" she said. "I do, Charles, never doubt it, please. I shall love you always and forever!"

"Ah, Cat, I am not worthy of you. But if you will have patience, I will try to be."

She smiled. At moments like this the cynical man disappeared. He was like a child then, defiant, half ashamed. She put an arm about him and drew him close. He made a sleepy protesting mumble, his head burrowing against her breast. " 'Tis I who am not worthy of you, dear love," she murmured.

Charles started at the sound of her voice. "What was that?" he said sleepily. "What did you say, Catherine?"

"It was of no importance. Forgive me for disturbing you." She shivered, and Charles opened his eyes fully. "I was afraid suddenly, afraid that my happiness will not last."

"Are you really happy, Catherine?"

"Yes, yes! For me it is a great happiness to be your wife." Her pretty lisping accent was more in evidence now. "But sometimes I have the great fear that I will lose you. Oh, Charles, don't ever leave me! Promise!"

27

Women and their infernal hysterical scenes, Charles thought wearily. But if one wished to enjoy their company, then one had best be prepared for times like these. "Leave you?" he said in a voice that he strove to make casual and yet sincere. "Why, Catherine, you know I'll never leave you unless the good Lord wills that it shall be so."

She nodded as if convinced, and after a moment his eyes closed again. Catherine's head moved restlessly on the pillow. Frances Stuart, Castlemaine, Angel Dawson . . . and she, Catherine of Braganza, so small and insignificant beside them. What chance had she against such beauties?

She bit her lip. "I'll never leave you unless the good Lord wills . . ." Nay, the man she loved was in excellent fettle; his very wenching was proof of that. Would that her "little friend," as she called Mistress Angel Dawson, could say the same, for it might be that the Earl of Benbrook's illness would result in yet another tragedy.

And there had already been too many in Angel's life. Catherine sighed as she recalled Angel's past, related to her so vividly by the girl herself. Sometimes she still found it hard to believe that the poised and elegant Mistress Dawson had once been a homeless and uneducated waif of the streets. Yet just before King Charles' triumphal progress through London on the occasion of his Restoration, seventeen-year-old Angel Dawson had been taken up by the Watch for the crime of theft, and was on her way to incarceration in Newgate Prison.

In Newgate, she had received frequent and savage beatings, and, indeed, her back still bore the scars. Catherine shuddered, thinking of the sufferings the poor child had undergone. The experience might well have broken a lesser person, but Angel, that child of the London gutters, had somehow managed to come through. In that sordid atmosphere, exposed to ugly scenes of violence, penned in with prostitutes, hardened criminals, and others like herself, guilty of lesser crimes, she had not sunk into uncaring degradation, as had so many of them.

Strangely, it was her very incarceration in the infamous prison that had led her to my lord Benbrook. Marianne Tavington, taken up by the Watch as a vagrant after an accident that had brought about her loss of memory, had been unable to establish her identity. And so, like so many unfortunates before her, her plight had been dismissed by an uncaring society and she had been thrown into Newgate. Slowly dying, she had regained her memory, and she had begged Angel to go to her brother, Nicholas Tavington, and in the name of his sister, ask for his protection. Angel had found it easy to make that promise to Marianne, for she had no hope of ever being set free.

The Queen looked down at the King with tender eyes. It was Charles' Restoration that had accomplished the miracle for Angel. One of the King's first acts had been to pardon all first offenders, of which Angel was one.

Delighting in her freedom, Angel nevertheless remembered her promise to Marianne Tavington. After watching the Royal Parade with her only other friend, Nell Gwynne, she presented herself at the big house in St. Bernard's Square. Not unnaturally, she was terrified to find that the dead girl had been *Lady* Marianne Tavington, and Nicholas Tavington the great Earl of Benbrook himself.

The Queen smiled to herself as she pictured that encounter between the uneducated, half-starved street waif and the haughty Earl.

"There he stood, Madam," Angel had told her, "a tall man, forbidding of expression, dark of complexion, and incredibly handsome. I knew, even before he spoke to me, that he disbelieved me. He gripped me by the shoulders, shook me, called me 'liar.' I was so afraid, Madam, for how could I dream that the 'vanishing Earl,' the man riding beside the King in the Royal Parade, would turn out to be the Nicholas Tavington I sought?"

But Benbrook went to Newgate and made inquiries. Mrs. Sampson had taken pity on Angel and given her a position in the house, the first home she had ever known. The Earl, even when he found her story to be true, addressed no further word to her.

What followed then had always seemed to the Queen to be the most romantic part of the strange story. For when the Earl roused himself from his grief, he remembered that Marianne had wished him to do something to aid the girl. Discovering that Angel had always wished to become a "fine lady," as she put it, he decided to educate and groom her and give her her dream.

"I knew then, Madam," Angel told her, "that he had accepted the truth and held me to be blameless. He seemed most harsh and severe, and he drove me so mercilessly that I thought I would surely go insane. In my desperation, I begged him many a time to let me go free. I swore at him, used the language of the gutter, but his only reply was to drive me yet harder at my studies, until, finally, I became as you see me now.

"Though I did not know it myself then, I was in love with him long before my education ceased. I thought the feeling that so constantly burned me was one of hatred. How could I be in love with this aloof and embittered man?—he, who though indulging in many light love affairs, could not be brought to put his trust in the love and fidelity of any woman?

"It was after the Honors Ball that lord Benbrook came to my room. At first he sat there, very stiff and silent, as was his wont. Something had surely occurred to upset him, I thought. His attire was disordered, a most unusual circumstance for my lord, and he was flushed as though suffering from a fever, I myself knew now, beyond any doubt, that I was in love with him, but I was terrified. He had redeemed his promise, he had made me into a lady, and now, I felt sure, he would no longer wish me to be part of his household.

"But he had come to forbid me to leave his house under any circumstances. Oh, Madam, the expression in those somber dark eyes of his! Though he sought to hide it from himself, even as I had done, I knew that he loved me.

But still he could not bring himself to put his trust in a female. If I wished to hear a declaration of love from him, I would have to force it. So I—so I told him that I loved him.

"He did not actually deny that he loved me. He said that he knew not what he felt. He asked me to be patient, to give him time to think. He said these words so gently that I could hardly believe that it was my awesome lord who spoke. Later, when he told me he must go to Benbrook Manor for a while, I was desolated. It was pity he felt for me, nothing more. He was gone for several weeks. I had no word or sign from him, and then he came back."

Catherine frowned. It was Charles who had parted them, though not intentionally. He knew nothing of the Earl's love for Angel. Charles had ever wanted the maddeningly elusive Angel, and so he gave her the special ring worn by all his mistresses, hoping to claim his reward later. That the ring branded her the property of the King, he had carefully refrained from telling her. When my lord Benbrook saw the ring on her finger, in contempt and anger he left her. When he did return, he was suffering from the plague that was to kill so many thousands. Against my lord Benbrook's wish, Angel remained in stricken London, determined that she would not lose him again.

Much later, when Nicholas seemed to be showing signs of recovery, she left the house on an important errand. She had been feeling ill all day, and walking along those pestilence-ridden streets, she collapsed. The death cart came rumbling through the streets, the men giving their gruesome cry, "Bring out your dead! Bring out your dead." Believing Angel to be another plague victim, the men threw her on the death cart. In a frenzy of terror, she roused herself sufficiently to slide from the pile of stiff corpses. She might have died had she not been discovered by the nuns of the Convent of the Angels, who nursed her back to health. But the horror of her experience had been too much for her. She could not remember her name, or where she came from. She was content to believe herself

31

to be the girl Mary, as the nuns had christened her. That way lay peace, but in her buried memories there was fear.

Catherine looked at the King tenderly. Charles, though perhaps he did not deserve it, had been given the chance to right the wrong he had done his friend. He it was who had discovered Angel in the Convent and restored her to my lord Benbrook.

"It would seem, Cat," Charles had smiled, "that it was the unexpected sight of me that restored Angel's memory. She could scarcely wait to reach Benbrook's side. Od's Fish, never have I seen friend Nicholas so moved!"

My lord Benbrook and his Angel were to be married soon. *Gracious God,* Catherine began to pray fervently, *let my Lord Benbrook be restored to his full health.*

"Catherine," Charles' sleepily complaining voice broke in on her prayer, "I'm cold." Snuggling down beside him, she drew up the covers, enclosing them both in a warm and private world. For these moments Charles belonged to her alone. "I love you," she said, putting an arm about his waist. "My dear Charles."

"And I love you, Cat," Charles mumbled, settling his head against her breast. After a moment his breathing deepened.

His response had been automatic; there had been no real feeling behind it. Sighing, Catherine kissed the top of his head. "Mayhap you do, my darling," she whispered. "But 'tis not the same love as my lord Benbrook gives to his Angel. Would to God that it were."

ANGEL DAWSON STOOD TWISTING AND turning before the long gilt-edged mirror, her eyes anxious as she examined her appearance. She wore her long red-gold hair loose, held away from her face by a wide jeweled band. It was not entirely sophisticated, perhaps, but Nicholas liked it that way. Her gown was of white satin, with a filmy overskirt; the front hem was caught up by a cluster of artificial scarlet rosebuds, revealing lacy, pale blue petticoats bound with silver ribbon. About her neck, suspended on a thin silver chain, was the diamond heart Nicholas had given her.

She held out her left hand, admiring the emerald and diamond ring that Nicholas had placed upon her finger. It was an heirloom, and since his mother had worn it last, he had been hesitant about passing it on to Angel. She had poisoned his youth, he hated anything even remotely connected with the notorious Lady Catherine Tavington.

She turned once more to the mirror for a final appraisal. Yes, she decided, she looked very different from the draggled gutter brat who had first faced the Earl of Benbrook, nor did she bear any resemblance to the gray-clad Sister Mary. Angel laughed softly. The past was behind her. She was to marry Nicholas on the thirtieth of August. It was the ending to her stormy life, and the beginning of a new and happy era.

She sat down upon the padded bench before the mirror, seized with a sudden doubt. Nicholas had been cold of late, remote. It was almost as if he had tired of her and was seeking to find the words to tell her so.

She stared down at her small, white-slippered feet, her eyes momentarily held by the glitter of the diamond buckles adorning them. Nay, it was not only Nicholas's changed attitude toward her—if changed he had—it was the whole dark and ominous atmosphere of the house, an atmosphere that seemed to hold secrets that dare not be revealed.

The housekeeper, Mrs. Sampson, had always liked her in her brisk, unemotional way. But even she seemed to go out of her way to avoid speaking to Angel. And Pip, or M'Zeli, as he now insisted upon being called. The boy had proved his devotion to her in a number of ways, yet he too seemed to avoid her. On the one or two occasions when he had been forced to address her directly, she could swear she had seen pity in his large, soft brown eyes. What was wrong in this house that was being so carefully kept from her?

She was so lost in her thoughts that she did not hear the tap upon the door. "My lady Angel," M'Zeli's voice said softly, "the lord awaits you."

She started violently, but the boy came further into the room. "You are looking very beautiful tonight," he said, picking up her silver tissue cloak and holding it out. Angel rose, allowing him to drape it about her shoulders. The white fur lining was cool and silkily soft.

"My lady Angel," Pip touched her arm. "Will you do something for me?"

She looked down at the black hand. "Yes, M'Zeli, if I can."

"The man called King, he who holds these festivities tonight for you and the lord. Will you say to him that I, M'Zeli, render unto him my sincere homage?"

" 'Tis scarcely necessary," Angel smiled, "I am sure he already knows."

34

"Ah, but homage should be rendered anew, should it not? Lest, if your skin be black like mine, it is forgotten."

She was struck by the note of bitterness in his voice. " 'Tis unworthy of you, M'Zeli, to think that the King could forget. Why do you speak so? Has anybody been unkind to you?"

"Nay, lady. King has not been unkind, nor has anybody in this house. It is others who are unkind." He looked at her, his eyes fathomless. "I also am unkind to myself, in wanting that which I cannot have."

"And what is that?"

"I would be a man of medicine, lady. I would discover great cures for vile diseases. I would—" his voice faltered and his eyes turned away. "I w—would seek a cure for hearts that—are tired and c—cannot much longer go on beating."

"Do you know of such a one with a tired heart?"

He looked at her again. "Aye, lady. He is close to me, and to him I give the love of a brother."

"Who, M'Zeli?" Her heart began to beat suffocatingly. She felt cold suddenly, frightened.

But M'Zeli too seemed to have caught her fear, for he retreated a few paces. "The lord awaits," he said. Clasping his hands before him, he bowed.

"Who, M'Zeli?" she repeated.

His eyes flickered. " 'Tis no one you know, lady." Gone was his solemn gravity, the impression of age and wisdom beyond his years.

"M'Zeli," she said impulsively, "forgive me. For a moment you frightened me." She hesitated. "If you wish to be a man of medicine, mayhap my lord Benbrook can help you. I will speak to him."

"My lord has offered to help me." Again, that touch of bitterness in his voice—" 'Twould be useless, lady. White people would not allow black hands to touch them, no matter how great the cure those hands offered."

So that was the reason for his strange attitude. For a moment, she had thought— Nay, she was a fool. It was not Nicholas of whom he spoke, of course not. "I know how you must feel," she said gently, "but there are the people of your own race. Mayhap, if you study long and diligently, you can help them."

"Mayhap, lady," M'Zeli shrugged. "But they too are ignorant, and wary of new ways." He looked at her consideringly. "If you needed help, lady, would you turn from M'Zeli?"

"Of course not!" She looked at him indignantly. "How can you even ask?"

"Thank you. I am happy to say that neither would King, or the lord."

She drew the cloak about her. "I must not keep my lord waiting, must I?"

"Nay." M'Zeli's lips softened into a smile. "The lord is a man of a very impatient nature."

She smiled back at him. "But he is also a man of kindness and generosity."

"This I know." M'Zeli stood to one side as she passed through the door. "Lady," he said, "will you request also of King that he visit this house more often? My lord is his friend, and I think perhaps he is sometimes lonely for King's companionship. They—they should see each other often."

She stopped short, turning to him swiftly. "What is it you would tell me, M'Zeli?"

"I would tell you nothing, lady, that your heart does not already know."

"I don't understand you," she said impatiently. "Is it my lord, M'Zeli? Is—is he ill?"

"If he were," the boy said, shrugging, "he would tell you so, would he not?"

Her hand gripped a fold of the cloak between tense fingers. "Look well upon the one you love," he said, moving closer to her. "Allow the eyes of the heart to open."

"M'Zeli, please!"

The boy shook his head stubbornly. "The lord awaits you."

Her legs trembled beneath her as she descended the stairs.

In the foyer below, Nicholas awaited her, garbed in his usual impeccable black. Jet beads glittered upon his wide cuffs and edged the lapels of his jacket with a somber splendor. White lace fell over his hands, and his white lace cravat was pinned with a diamond and ruby bar. His hair, as usual, was his own, drawn back and tied at the nape of the neck with a black ribbon.

Allow the eyes of the heart to open M'Zeli had said. He had grown thin, she thought, or was she imagining it? The deep bronze of his skin seemed to have faded to a paler hue; his cheekbones were prominent in a drawn face, and there were shadows beneath his dark eyes.

"Nicholas!"

He looked up sharply as she hurried toward him. "What is it, brat? Is something amiss?"

She shook her head. "You—you look very splendid, m—my lord."

"Do I so?" A smile made his face seem younger, less gaunt. "You also. You are very beautiful, Angel."

He took her hand, leading her across the foyer and out through the front door.

"Nicholas," she said, as they approached the waiting carriage. "Do you l—love me?"

His dark brows rose. "What a question! Are we not on our way to celebrate our forthcoming wedding?"

"Yes, but—"

His cool fingers fastened firmly about her wrist. "Not now, if you please. Unless, of course, it pleasures you to have Bateson listening to our more intimate conversation."

She flinched before his sarcasm. "You know that it does not," she retorted coldly. She glanced quickly at the coachman seated on his high perch, his eyes staring straight ahead, his ruddy face blank.

On the way to the palace, Angel's voice was all but drowned out by the drumming of the horses' hooves. "If

37

I have displeased you in some way, my lord, I pray you to tell me my fault, that I may correct it."

He moved impatiently, "Oh, Angel, you were ever a silly chit. You are, as usual, allowing your imagination to run away with you."

Was she? Then why was he so cold, so removed from her? "You will admit, my lord, that your behavior has scarcely been that of a lover."

He was silent for a moment. "What do you want of me, Angel? There are many things that command my attention. I have no time to be forever kissing in corners."

Hot tears stung her eyes, but she blinked them back. "And yet, my lord, when first I returned from the convent, you were vastly different. Why have you changed toward me?"

"I have not changed. Pray do not be ridiculous!"

She edged closer to him and put her hand over his. "Nicholas, darling, you are not looking well. Are you ill?"

"Certainly not!" he snapped. Deliberately, he removed his hand. "Where did you get such an idea?"

"I don't know." She twisted her hands together, "It—it is something I feel. Won't you tell me, darling!"

"I fail to understand you. There is nothing to tell."

Angel sat back, her shoulders drooping. It was of little use talking to him now, she decided. Something was wrong, she knew it now. But what? Later, when they were alone, she would try again.

Nicholas clenched his hands tightly on his lap. How could he have spoken to her in that way? His darling, his beloved little guttersnipe! Was he too stubborn and proud to tell her the truth or was he still afraid of losing her? His lips tightened. It didn't matter what his reason might be. He must be fair to her, he must let her go, and soon. His attacks were more frequent now, and only Sampson and M'Zeli, and possibly the King, had guessed how far along the road to death he was. Would it be fair to marry Angel, only to leave her widowed within the space of a few short months? But how could he be sure?

He swallowed hard against the choking lump in his throat and smiled mirthlessly. Or did Angel love him enough to marry him, no matter what the consequences might be to herself? If he still could not wholly trust her, not even now, then he deserved to lose her, didn't he? But he was torturing himself to no purpose. It was not a question of trust, but one of fairness. She was so lovely, so glowing! He wanted to pull her into his arms, press his lips to hers, beg her not to leave him! Fool, fool!

He became conscious of the uneven beating of his heart. Not now! he prayed inwardly. Don't let me be struck down before her! Leave me at least that much dignity!

"Nicholas." He felt Angel's soft lips touch his cheek in a fleeting caress. "Pray do not look so grim, my lord," she said in a light voice, "else will you offend the King."

He had not even noticed that they had stopped. He heard the babble of voices and laughter now. Playing for time, he drew the curtain aside and looked out at the scene before him. Green-liveried servants, their flaring torches held high above their heads, were assisting the guests to alight, then turning them over to others, who led them with slow majestic stride into the Palace.

The glimmering lamps of carriages, as still more approached, looked like fireflies in the night. Nicholas noticed Samuel Pepys, resplendent in bright red velvet, silver lace at his throat and wrists, his wig askew as usual, escorting a lady dressed in pink. Her yellow curls were piled high and threaded through with jewels. Her voice, as she replied to some remark of Pepys, was fluting and gay. Behind Pepys was William Penn, clad in gray. Nicholas wondered idly if Penn still clung to his dream of going to America and founding the colony that was to be named after himself, Pennsylvania, as he had announced he would. If he continued in his persistence, he would doubtless obtain his grant from the King. Following after Penn was Peter Lely, the renowned artist.

Nicholas had not trusted himself to capture Angel's beauty, and so he had commissioned Lely to paint her portrait.

Nicholas saw a servant approaching, and he let the curtain drop. The beating of his heart seemed to have settled into a fairly steady rhythm, and he felt reasonably confident that he could carry the evening through.

Angel was watching him, her eyes intent, her hands clasped tightly together. "Do not watch me so closely, my dear. 'Tis unnecessary."

"I am sorry." She put her hand on his extended arm. "I did not mean to embarrass you, my lord."

How cold and icily formal she sounded. It should not surprise him, he thought ruefully, since his own harshness, his stubborn refusal to tell her the truth about himself, had brought it about. Tonight, after this ball, which he would not have attended save at the King's express command, he would tell her everything. Either that, or find some other excuse to sever their relationship.

"Nay, love," he said gently, " 'tis I who should beg your pardon. I know that I am an impossible boor. Pray forgive me."

She brightened immediately at the trace of warmth in his voice. "So you are at times, my lord. And will you now admit, my darling, that this is a very special and wonderful occasion?"

"Very wonderful," he said, his eyes on her face. He stood aside to allow her to descend. Angel put her hand into that of the servant, and the white-gloved hand gripped hers firmly. "This way, Madam," he said in a deep voice. "This way, my lord."

Following after a tall, stately footman, they passed along wide, red-carpeted corridors bright with banked flowers and redolent with the mingled perfumes of the ladies, and the heavier ones of the gentlemen. Angel looked up at Nicholas, glad that he stood out from the painted, befrilled, and scented fops of the Court. She was reminded of the first time she had entered the Palace. How frightened she had been, though she had done her best not to show it. How tightly she had clung to Nicholas's arm! And when she had taken the King's hand and curtsied to him, how awed she had felt. But it was different now, she thought. She was poised and assured, and not even the most critical eye could find fault with her. Her sternly critical mentor had made sure of that.

Angel glanced quickly over her shoulder, half expecting to see the same lady and gentleman who had followed after them on the occasion of the Honors Ball. She had been to the Palace many times since then, and had once resided there for a number of months, and yet it seemed as if she had been thrown back in time.

The footman led them into the anteroom and, from there, into the great ballroom.

Hidden musicians made soft music from behind the flower-bedecked gallery. Nicholas led her forward over the shining expanse of floor, and Angel found her feet wanting to trip to the measure.

Smiling eyes watched them as they made their way toward the King. Ladies in low-cut gowns, their white arms bare, their bodices lavishly embroidered with jewels and exposing most of their bosom, waved painted and lace-trimmed fans in greeting. Men, bright as a peacock's tail, in their vividly hued silks, satins, and fur-trimmed velvets, cheeks decorated with black patches cut into various shapes, bowed bewigged heads as they passed.

Even knowing that the ball was in their honor, Angel was dazzled. This must surely be how the King and Queen felt when they moved among their subjects.

The King was seated in a gilded and carved chair upon the red and gold draped dais. Beside him, Queen Catherine looked flushed and pretty in a gown of golden lace with a vivid green underskirt. Diamonds flashed rainbows of color from her small coronet, from her long earrings, and from the diamond and sapphire collar about her slender throat. But radiant though she was, the King surpassed her. He was clad in pale-lavender velvet; the lapels of his long jacket were edged with scarlet ribbon, upon which were sewn rubies, diamonds, emeralds, and pearls, in rounded patterns. Silver lace, decorated with diamonds, fell from the knees of his breeches in fantastic flounces; the same diamond-sparked lace half covered his jeweled hands and gleamed at his throat. His black wig, though elaborately curled, was bare of the ribbon bows that tied the love locks of the other gentlemen.

Angel curtsied, receiving a look of admiration from the King and a warm friendly smile from the Queen.

"Mistress Dawson, my lord Benbrook." The King leaned toward them, his black locks falling forward. "Plague take you, Nicholas," he said in a laughing undertone, "could you not have dressed suitably for this one occasion, to celebrate your forthcoming wedding? You are a dull dog, and so I tell you."

Nicholas smiled. "I regret that I do not please your eyes, Sire, but, with all respect for your opinion, I am dressed suitably. 'Tis simply that I prefer plainer apparel."

"So you have told me before," Charles laughed. "And damned if I don't think you look smarter than the others. With the exception of myself, of course."

"If Your Majesty wishes me to swoon at your feet, I will willingly do so."

"You, sir, are a liar." Charles looked at him, laughter gleaming in his eyes. "Though I must admit that I'd give my crown to see it."

"Would you, Sire? Your crown would be a prize well worth winning. 'Twould look well on me, I'll wager. Shall I go down on my knees now, Your Majesty?"

"Oh curse you Nicholas! Why must I ever seek to get the better of you? I know well 'tis a hopeless task."

"Mayhap, one day, Your Majesty will manage to accomplish it."

Charles looked at Angel. "Do you hear how this fellow addresses his King, Mistress Dawson?"

"I hear, Sire," she answered, smiling at him. " 'Tis *lèse majesté,* is it not?"

Charles took her hand and held it tightly in his. "You are sure you wish to marry the scurvy dog?"

Angel's eyes lingered on Nicholas. "Quite sure, Sire," she said softly.

Charles sighed. " 'Tis like Benbrook to make away with the most beautiful woman I ever did see. For friend Nicholas, as usual, nothing but the best."

"And for Your Majesty," Angel said, her eyes on the Queen's face, "nothing but the best."

Catherine flushed at the compliment, and looked shyly at Charles, who caught her glance. "Madam," he said, holding out his hand to her, "the lady is quite right."

All through the long and elaborate dinner that followed, Angel felt she moved in a dream. Nicholas's satin cuff brushed her arm now and again, and when she turned to address a remark to him, his dark eyes smiled into hers. Gone were all her doubts and fears. He was not ill, of course he was not. And he did love her, it was there in his eyes for her to see.

Seated opposite Angel was Peter Lely, whose light-blue eyes studied her intently, as though he sought to impress her features on the canvas of his mind. Angel wondered for a moment why Nicholas had chosen to commission Lely. Why could he not paint her himself? Lely was a great artist, but not, in her opinion, better than Nicholas. She turned to him, her mouth opening for speech.

"Nonsense, brat," Nicholas said, forestalling her. "Lely is the greater painter."

She stared at him blankly. "And has my lord Benbrook now taken to reading my mind?"

" 'Twas not very difficult, you were staring at him so. Have I not told you about staring, Mistress Dawson? 'Tis ill-mannered and unladylike."

The remark was made lightly, and she smiled at him. "Well, 'tis as you say, ill-mannered and unladylike, but he has been staring at me."

"But with a purpose, brat. He is doubtless planning

how best to paint you." His hand sought hers, squeezing her fingers briefly. "As to your mind, I know every twist and turn of it, my little one." He squeezed her fingers again. "Sit up, you infernal brat. Your shoulders are hunched."

Angel was so happy that not even the sight of Barbara Castlemaine, dressed tonight in a cream gown, her flaming hair piled high and glinting with emeralds, could dampen it. She returned Barbara's faintly malicious smile with a polite inclination of her head.

Further down the table was John Evelyn, one of the founders of the Royal Society, in earnest conversation with Isaac Newton, a Fellow of that same society. They appeared to be arguing, though apparently with perfect amiability, for there were smiles on both faces.

Samuel Pepys, seated on Nicholas's other side, said in his deep rumbling bass, "What a cursed fellow Newton is. He is no doubt trying to convince Evelyn that his theory is right." He laughed and shrugged his burly shoulders. "The theory of gravitation indeed! What rubbish!"

"No doubt there is something in it," Nicholas answered. "I for one believe there is."

"My dear Benbrook! The place for Newton is in Bedlam. I had far rather talk of John Milton," Pepys said, his face lighting up with enthusiasm. "He has completed his poem, though doubtless he will redo it many times yet. Now there, Benbrook, is a real genius. His words are pearls, sheer beauty! It is far from being published yet, but he has favored Lely and myself with a first draft. He is calling it 'Paradise Lost.' "

"Indeed, but if you have an enthusiasm for words, then let me commend you to John Bunyan."

"That traitorous rogue! Why, damn, the Bunyan fellow is naught but a traveling tinker. Fought for Cromwell, didn't he? The blasted scoundrel! Deserves to be in prison!"

"He is. But I might remind you that Milton is thought by many to be the bigger traitor of the two. He too worked in Cromwell's cause. As for Bunyan, no doubt he has expiated his sin by now."

Pepys turned his head away, but his curiosity won. "What's the rogue Bunyan done that he can be called a genius?"

Nicholas smiled. "Why, Mr. Pepys, you surprise me. I had thought you had knowledge of every happening, no matter how great or small."

Pepys colored at the sarcasm. "I don't spend my time scouring around prisons, my lord."

"Nor do I. But word of an extraordinary thing is bound to get out, is it not, Mr. Pepys?"

Pepys stared at him, goggle-eyed. "What thing, eh, what thing?" He laughed his loud, somewhat coarse laugh. "What's Bunyan up to, eh, eh? Training soldiers to fight against the King, I suppose, eh?"

Nicholas immersed his fingers in a golden bowl scented with rose petals. He dried them carefully before answering. "Nay," he said. "Not this year, I believe."

Pepys clicked his tongue impatiently. "You're a plaguey fellow, Benbrook. Now, will you not satisfy my curiosity and tell me what the rogue has done?"

"He has written a work while in prison. I am told by those who have read it that it is quite magnificent."

"Eh? You read it?"

"Naturally not, else could I give you a fuller account."

"Then howd' you know it's any good, eh?" Pepys said triumphantly.

"My informants are reliable, I believe," Nicholas answered. "Doubtless, Mr. Pepys, were you to visit Bunyan in prison, he would allow you to read it."

"I'll not read a word the traitor has written. Probably rubbish anyway." He was silent for a moment. "What did you say it's called?"

Nicholas looked down at his hands, hiding a smile. *"Pilgrim's Progress.* 'Tis an easy title to remember."

"Aye, so 'tis. Well, I don't believe in pampering scoundrels, but I might as well have a look at his writings, I suppose. 'Tis one's Christian duty to lift the fellow's spirit, eh?"

Nicholas smiled openly. "Mr. Pepys, I knew I could rely upon you to do your duty."

Pepys bridled indignantly. Angel thought he looked rather like the fat pouter pigeons who waddled pompously over the cobbles in St. Bernard's Square. "Very clever, my lord," Pepys spluttered. "But good words are good words, no matter who writes 'em, eh? Not that I'm prepared to say the fellow's good."

"Of course not," Nicholas said. "I will leave the judgment entirely to you."

"Laughing at me, are you, my lord?" Pepys scratched at his wig again. "Time I had the cursed thing deloused, I suppose," he grumbled, pulling at one of the long yellow curls. "It appears to be growing quite active."

"It might be as well," Nicholas agreed gravely, his eyes on the towering wig. "I distinctly observed it to move."

"Said it was active, didn't I?" Pepys small blue eyes twinkled. "Just because you wear your own hair, my lord, there's no need to be sneering at fellows who wish to be in high fashion."

Nicholas looked at the wig again. "High indeed," he said quietly. "But I stand reproved."

"I know you too well, Benbrook. And why in damnation don't you call me Sam? Are you my friend, or are you not?"

"I believe you may count me a friend, Sam. Though I must confess that there are times when your infernal curiosity can prove somewhat daunting."

Pepys glanced at Angel. "Can't imagine what you see in the fellow, Mistress Dawson."

"I have often wondered." Nicholas said in a low voice.

Ignoring this aside, Angel smiled upon the plump little man. Pepys, for all his fiery words and his insatiable curiosity, was good-natured and sweet-tempered. "Nor I," she answered him. "But if you will give me a month or two to think, I can doubtless produce a reason."

Nicholas's eyes met hers, and Pepys snorted disgustedly at Angel's expression. "Well here's a fine thing! No need to let the whole Court know how much you're in love with the plaguey fellow, is there, eh? 'Pon my word, I never saw anything like it before. The rogue's not worth it."

"Mr. Pepys," Angel answered demurely, "you and I must agree to differ."

"Mr. Pepys! Don't those pretty lips of yours know how to form the word Sam, eh?"

"And that, Samuel," Nicholas said firmly, "will be all."

Pepys winked at Angel. "Devilish fellow's jealous, plagued if he's not." He straightened his wig to a more becoming angle. "Prefer me, don't you, little Mistress Dawson?"

"But naturally."

Pepys sighed. "A real little beauty is your Angel, Benbrook. Wish I could say as much for my own choice."

A laugh came from the King's end of the table. "I see my lord Benbrook has involved himself with Mr. Pepys. Both gentlemen being expert at parry and thrust, neither can hope to win." Charles rose to his feet, raising his wine glass. "Gentlemen and ladies, I give you a toast to my lord Benbrook and his lady."

The King drained his glass, and the guests followed suit. "Well, my lord," he called, setting the glass back on the table, "have you anything to say in response?"

"Aye," Nicholas said, getting to his feet and raising his own glass. "I have this to say, God save the King!"

"God save the King!" The cry was taken up enthusiastically.

Charles waited for the hubbub to subside. "I thank you," he said. "I promise I will not take issue with that. Anything more, my lord?"

"Most certainly." Nicholas looked at the Queen. "God save the Queen!"

Angel, drinking with the rest, noticed that though Barbara Castlemaine had lifted the glass to her lips, she did not drink. She was a frighteningly malignant creature,

Angel thought, as was her cousin, the Duke of Buckingham, lolling indolently in his chair on Barbara's left. The Castlemaine had tried to humiliate her before, but now that she was to be lady Benbrook, surely— She met Barbara's hard, bold glance, and noticed that the eyes that instantly dismissed her as unimportant went to Nicholas's face, softening as she gazed.

The King called for silence. "Very prettily. put, my lord Benbrook," he said, laughing. "However, think not to deceive me. I know well 'tis your way of avoiding a speech."

Nicholas smiled. "Your Majesty sees through me, I fear."

"Only when you allow me to do so, scoundrel." He rose to his feet again. "If you are all replete, let us hie ourselves to the dancing. Come, Madam," he said, looking at the Queen. "Let us show them a perfect example."

Chairs scraped back from the table. As the King led the way into the ballroom, the fiddlers broke into a lively French air.

Charles, dancing first with the Queen, then with Angel and Frances Stuart, and—reluctantly, it seemed—with Barbara Castlemaine, seemed tireless.

Watching him jig to the lively tune of a country dance with Maria Huntington, the latest popularly acclaimed Court beauty, Angel felt a resumption of her earlier anxiety. In contrast with the King, Nicholas was pale and looked very tired. He had danced with the Queen earlier, with herself and Lady Mary Carew, but after that he had quietly excused himself from further dancing, on the plea that he did not care overmuch for the popular pastime. She noticed he appeared to have some difficulty in breathing.

"My lord," Angel heard the Queen say softly, "you seem tired. Will you not sit beside me for a while?"

"I am—am honored, M—Madam." Nicholas bowed, then sat down rather heavily. "B—but I assure you that I am not tired."

"Nonetheless I am happy that you indulge me, my

lord." The Queen's eyes met Angel's. "The hour grows late, and I myself am very tired." She paused significantly. "Are not you, Mistress Dawson?"

"Indeed, Madam." Angel answered quickly. " 'Tis a wonderful ball, but I must confess that I am wearied."

The Queen nodded her head—approvingly, Angel thought. "You are luckier than I, child," she said. "Though the ball was held in your honor, I must stay until the end. His Majesty will not, I am sure, object if you now take your farewell."

"You are kind, Madam," Nicholas said, getting hastily to his feet. He bowed. "As you have said, the hour grows late."

Catherine held out her hand to be kissed. "You might intimate that to His Majesty," she said, laughing.

Nicholas kissed her fingers. "Madam," he said in an undertone that only she could hear. "You are a very gracious lady, but you are a poor liar."

"My lord!"

"Nay, dear Madam," he said, gently squeezing her fingers. "Forgive me the impertinence. 'Tis my way of thanking you for your consideration."

Catherine stared at him for a moment. " 'Twas a poor ruse, I do admit. Promise me that you will take care of yourself."

Nicholas dropped her hand. "Madam, I will do my best."

ANGEL SAT VERY CLOSE TO NICHOLAS IN THE carriage, her hand in his. His breathing was less labored, but what had caused his distress in the first place? Had M'Zeli lied to her? She could see Nicholas's eyes studying her in the half gloom.

"You are very silent," he said. "What ails you, brat?"

Angel took a deep breath. "If I might reverse the question," she said clearly, "I would ask, what ails you, my lord?"

"Nothing. Don't be absurd."

"Do you take me for a complete fool, Nicholas? There is something wrong with you. I demand to know what it might be."

The carriage stopped. "We are home," Nicholas said. "Come, brat, you will oblige me by lowering your voice. I pray you to control yourself."

"I will not be snubbed," she cried resentfully, "or—or patronized as though I were an imbecile! And 'twould be as well were you to remember that."

"I might be induced to do so," Nicholas said dryly, "were we within the house." He descended from the carriage and lifted his arms to help her to alight. "No more now, brat," he said, swinging her to the ground.

"But you will talk to me?"

"Yes," he said curtly. He turned to the coachman.

"Bateson, see that the horses are well fed and bedded down in clean straw."

A faint look of indignation came into Bateson's face. "Yes, m'lord. I always do, m'lord."

Nicholas's brows rose. "If my vision is indeed failing me, my man, then I trust you will forgive me? But it did seem to me that the straw in which they were bedded last night was far from clean."

"M—my l—lord," Bateson stammered. "It—it might be I overlooked changing the straw last night."

"So it might. I trust, too, that you will remember in future that I am not easily hoodwinked. Where the comfort of my animals is concerned, you will find that I hold very strong opinions. That will be all. Goodnight."

"Goodnight, m'lord, Mistress Dawson. I'm—I'm sorry, m'lord."

Listening to Nicholas's freezing rebuke, Angel was reminded that he had once spoken to her in much the same way. Her hand tightened on his arm as he led the way to the house. Her dear ogre! It had taken her a long time to realize that the surface coldness belied the inner man. At least where she was concerned, oddly enough, Nicholas was shy, and he had attempted to cover it with icy sarcasm. But no more. Nicholas, to quote his own words, would find that she was not easily hoodwinked.

Despite the hour, Mrs. Sampson greeted them at the door.

"Why, Sampson," Nicholas said, "you should have been in bed long since."

"I'm not tired, Master Nickey."

His smile held a touch of amusement. "You have always told me that you needed at least eight hours of uninterrupted sleep."

Mrs. Sampson drew herself to her full height. "I hope I know my duty, which is to see that you and Mistress Dawson are comfortable before I retire."

"We are perfectly comfortable, thank you." He smiled at her. "I am going to bed myself."

"Nicholas!" Angel cried. "You can't go to bed now."

"Can I not?"

"No. We were going to talk, remember?"

He turned from her. "I have changed my mind."

"Nicholas, I won't be treated like this! If you are ill, you must tell me about it."

"Go to bed!"

Angel's face flushed red. "No, Nicholas," she said quietly. "I could not sleep anyway."

Mrs. Sampson looked from one to the other, her sharp blue eyes anxious. "The child is right, Master Nickey. There now, lad, take her into the library, and I'll bring you some warm wine and sandwiches."

"I require nothing, thank you."

"I'll bring it just the same. Just you do as I say, lad. It's for the best, you know."

"Oh confound you, Sampson. Confound the pair of you, meddling females that you are! I require time. I must request you not to bedevil me. I—I—" His words broke off in a gasp. "G—g—go now!"

"Master Nickey!"

"I said leave me! P—please, Sampson." He looked at her almost pleadingly. "It w—will pass."

"That's as may be. But I'll be within earshot, Master Nickey."

"Mrs. Sampson!" Angel's eyes were huge and frightened in her white face. "Wh—what is—"

"Not now, child. Go with him. Call me if you need me."

The housekeeper bustled away. After a moment's hesitation, Nicholas led the way to the library, his back stiff. He flung the door open. "Very well," he said savagely, "if you will not be denied. What is it you wish to—to know?"

"Are you ill, Nicholas?"

He waited until she had seated herself, before walking over to the big chair behind his desk. "Yes," he said at last.

"W—what is the nature of your illness?"

"So calm, Mistress Dawson, so practical?" A quiver

53

passed over his face. "I must confess that I am disappointed in your reactions."

Her nails dug into her palms. *I am not calm!* she wanted to shout at him, *and I am not in the least practical where you are concerned. Can't you realize that I'm afraid?* Aloud, she said, "I am not a stranger that you must address me so."

His mouth twisted into a wry smile. "I seem to have developed something that, for want of a better name, I will call a—a failing heart."

She rose from her chair and ran to his side.

"Ah, that is better. I knew you would not fail me."

"Ah, don't, dear m'lord, don't talk to me so!"

His mouth tightened. "Pray, Angel, oblige me by going to bed. I don't want you here."

"But I want to be here. Oh, Nicholas, you have been so unkind of late. I thought—I thought it was because you no longer loved me. Oh, darling, my darling!" She put her arm about his shoulders. "There is nothing we cannot face if we are together."

He clenched his trembling hands together. He must finish things now. He could not expect her to undergo the torment their life would inevitably become. The thought of her watching him and fearfully waiting for the moment when his heart would fail him altogether! She was young, and so lovely; in time she would forget him. His eyes misted, but he must be strong, for her sake.

He looked up at her. "But we will *not* be together, Angel."

She stared at him. "What mean you, my lord?"

"Y—you were right in your first assumption, Angel. I—I have found that I no longer love you." He looked down. "If, as seems likely, I am going to die, then I would prefer to do so in peace."

Angel's mouth trembled. "P—pray do not jest, my lord," she faltered. "I—I know that you love m—me."

He closed his eyes momentarily. "Mistress Dawson," he said with an effort. "Forgive me, please, if you can. You will want for nothing, I do assure you." His eyes were so cold. He sat there so unmoved, so very calm she could almost believe him.

"I want nothing, Nicholas, and I want no one, save you."

The pain about his heart was stabbing savagely; he could scarcely breathe. He must be rid of her, and now. "H—h—hysteria ill becomes you, Angel. You m—must be calm."

She fell to her knees beside him. "Think you that you can command yourself not to love me, and it will be so? Think you to command me in the same way? Nay, there is only one truth I recognize, my dear love. You love me, even as I love you."

Oh dear God! he struggled against the pain, forcing himself to breathe deeply and slowly. "A—Angel, don't insist!" He could scarcely see her through the swirling mist before his eyes. "Don't. Go now, leave me. At—at once!" His hand clutched at his chest. "P—please."

She saw the grayness of his face, his features twisted by the agony he could no longer conceal. "Nicholas!"

His eyes held the expression of a tortured animal, his breath came in great sobbing gasps, and his face was glazed with perspiration. "P—p—please," he gasped out. "H—h—help m—m—me." He slumped forward over the desk, his outflung hands gripping the edge, his knuckles showing white. Terrified, she pried his fingers loose and pushed him back against the chair. He slumped down again. His mouth was half open, his chest heaving as he fought for air.

"G—get S—S—Samp—son," he begged her. His head fell heavily sideways.

"Mrs. Sampson!" she shouted. Lifting up her skirts she ran to the door.

Even as she approached it, it opened abruptly, and Mrs. Sampson stepped into the room. "Now you know, Angel," she said, hastening toward Nicholas, and bending over his slumped form. "I've wanted to tell you, but my foolish stubborn lad wouldn't hear of it."

"Never mind. Help him!"

"That's what I am trying to do, girl." Mrs. Sampson undid the buttons of Nicholas's shirt. Sliding her hand inside, she began to massage his chest vigorously. "It will be all right, Master Nickey. You just leave everything to your old Sampson."

Nicholas made a convulsive movement, his face contorting with a fresh spasm of agony.

"No, lad, no," Mrs. Sampson said in a soft, cajoling voice. "Don't struggle against me. I want to help you. The pain will ease soon, I promise."

Angel's voice broke. "Oh, Mrs. Sampson, he doesn't hear you!"

"Girl! You've got to be strong for his sake. He knows we're both with him. You stay calm, that's much the best way." Her hands moved harder, determinedly. "He's as proud as Lucifer, is Master Nickey. But this is one battle he can't fight for himself, poor lad."

Angel knelt at Nicholas's other side. She smoothed back his damp disordered hair with a loving hand. "We'll both help him, won't we?" she said, taking his icy hand in her firm clasp.

"If he'll let us, child." She bit down hard on her trembling lip. "But I—I fear he is going to die."

"No!" Angel gasped. "In the name of Christ, how can you say such a thing? He's not going to die. I—I won't let him!"

"I'm sorry." The slow painful tears seeped from the housekeeper's eyes and slid down her furrowed cheeks. "I'm so sorry, my dear, but, unless we can work a miracle, I fear 'twill happen. 'Tis scarcely up to you and I, Angel. 'Twill be as the good Lord wills."

"Then He must will him better!" Angel caught at Nicholas's hand and pressed it fiercely to her lips. "My dear, m'lord! My dearest!"

Mrs. Sampson's hands continued their brisk massage. "Angel, don't look at me like that! Dear Lord, do you think I want my lad to die? I've known him from the moment of his birth."

"I saved him once from death with the help of M'Zeli,

56

and, by God, I'll do it again!" She broke off as she felt the weak pressure of Nicholas's fingers. "Mrs. Sampson, he hears us!" she exclaimed. "See! See! He's clasping my hand!"

"Aye, Angel. It helps him to know that you are with him." She was silent, listening to his harsh, rattling breathing. "I do believe he's coming out of it!" She looked at Angel, an unusual color tinging her face. "It was the effects of the plague, and his continual grieving for you, that brought him to this. I'm convinced of it."

Angel bent her head over Nicholas's hand. "He—he tried to tell me that he no longer loved me."

"Aye," Mrs. Sampson nodded her white-capped head, "that would be his way of sparing you. The lad was ever harsh with himself."

"Sparing *me?*" Angel cried out. "How could he think for one moment that I would ever leave him?"

Mrs. Sampson smiled. "I daresay he knew you'd not go, so don't go fretting yourself about that. But, being Master Nickey, he had to try. He loves you all right, and there's an end on it."

As if Nicholas took in the sense of her last words, he gave a faint protesting moan, his head turning restlessly.

"Aye, you hear me lad," Mrs. Sampson scolded gently. " 'Twas rubbish he told you, and he knows it. But when you're yourself again, you can tell me I'm quite mistaken. Not that I'll listen to a word you have to say." She bent her head and kissed his brow. "He's easing nicely now, Angel. Slide your arm beneath his head. That's right. I'll warrant he'll find your shoulder comfortable."

"Will he be all right?"

Mrs. Sampson drew the shirt together, then straightened her aching back. "He'll do for now. 'Tis a milder attack than usual."

Angel looked at her with horror. "This—this is *milder?*"

"I've known him to be much worse." Mrs. Sampson turned and made her way over to the door, her eyes

57

carefully avoiding Angel's. "I'll be getting to my bed."
She took a handkerchief from her capacious pocket and
blew her nose—to cover her emotion, Angel knew. "You
take care of him, girl, no matter what he says. I doubt
I'll sleep, so if you need me I'll come at once."

"Thank you. Will he be safe with me?"

"Of course," Mrs. Sampson said tartly. "Perhaps he's
forgotten how you managed all on your own that time,
and him lying there suffering from the plague. It takes
courage and plenty of love to do what you did." She
chuckled. "You're a rare one, Angel. You were that
set on having your own way, remember?"

"I remember." Angel's mouth firmed to a straight
line. "I didn't let him die then, and I won't now!"

Nicholas was moving in the chair, his mouth opening.
Angel bent her head closer to catch his halting words.
"W—w—*will* n—not, brat. I dis—dislike con—con-
tractions."

"I know it, dear m'lord." The withheld tears spilled
from her eyes. "I know how very much you dislike
contractions, ev—even though you are oft times guilty of
using them yourself. I *will* try to do better."

"As—as y—you should, saucy w—wench."

Mrs. Sampson left the room, closing the door gently
behind her.

It was some time before Nicholas spoke again. Angel
held him close to her and listened with satisfaction to the
rapid easing of his breath.

"Well, wench," Nicholas said in a stronger voice.
" 'Twould seem that I—I cannot r—rid myself of you."
She saw his faint smile. "For you have ever been a cursed
st—stubborn and troublesome brat."

"Nay, dearest." She pressed her lips to his forehead.
"I regret to tell you, my lord Benbrook, that 'tis impossible
to rid yourself of me. Here I am, and here do I stay."

"Angel—" He broke off, and then his hands were
clinging to hers. "Nay, love, you cannot help me, but—
oh blast you, Angel, for a stubborn foolish wench, stay
with me! Aye, stay, even though I should send you

away for your own good. Don't leave me! Don't leave me ever!"

She was taken aback by this extraordinary outburst from the cool, controlled, reserved Nicholas.

"There," Nicholas said, "are you satisfied to know that you've made a weak fool of me? But you—have not answered me. Will y—you stay?"

"Does it really need an answer, my darling? I'll not leave, though you commanded me to do so a thousand times a day."

"But I will leave you, and soon, I think."

"What of M'Zeli?" she said sharply. "We know well that his herbs can work miracles. You were dying, yet he saved you. I will go to him—"

"M'Zeli can do nothing, love. He has tried." He touched his chest. "His herbs are powerless to replace a heart." He smiled wryly. "M'Zeli told me he had had a dream, and the dream told him that men would one day find a way. But not in my lifetime," he sighed. "Mayhap 'twould be better for us not to marry. I cannot bear to think of you so soon bereaved."

Angel rested her face against his. "Do not talk to me of bereavement, my lord, for you have such little patience with tears." Her fingers curled about his hand. "Though you, my lord Benbrook, once indulged in them yourself. Dost remember?"

"Yes," he said hastily. "But we will not dwell on that, will we? I was sickening of the plague. And that," he concluded firmly, "was the reason for such foolishness on my part."

"My lord, will you marry me? For if you do not, I fear the King would not approve of you."

He laughed. "Charles? Aye, he is the perfect example of moral conduct, is he not?" His laughter died. "But have you thought well, brat? 'Tis inevitable that I will become something of a liability. Oh, Angel! Why will you not go and leave me in peace?"

"For three reasons. One, because I love you. Two, because you asked me to stay, though—"

" 'Twas in a weak moment, and you know it. I meant it not."

"Though," Angel resumed, "I would have stayed anyway. And three, because we are to be wed."

"You command it, I suppose?"

She considered this, her head on one side. "Aye, my lord, I am afraid I must insist. And there is a fourth reason," she said softly. "Would you care to hear it? Very simple, and yet very important. I would die without you."

"Nonsense!" He caught her hand and held it tightly in his. "Angel, use your eyes, your sense! I am not usually given to dramatics, and who should know that better than yourself, but I am dying. Accept it, realize it!"

"Oh, Nicholas, you shall not say so! I w—would that you might live forever. B—but if it is not to be, then grant me the happiness, however brief, of being your wife!"

"Angel. Let me see your face."

She drew back, lifting her face to his. "There, what do you read in it?"

"That you love me well."

"Then seek not to turn me away. For indeed, sweetheart, I will not go!"

His fingers stroked the tears from her face. "What am I to do about you, brat? Is there to be no escape for me, then?"

She took his hand and held it against her cheek. "Nay, dear m'lord, none at all."

"A pretty thing for me to hear, is it not, you bold jade! Then, if you insist, I will marry you. What have you to say to that?"

"Only that I love you, love you!"

"Aye, you do, don't you? God knows why." He patted his knee. "Sit here." Gingerly, she seated herself, fearful of hurting him in his still weakened condition.

"Angel," he said, his lips against her hair. "I would have you know that I will try to be all you desire in a husband."

"I pray you not to put yourself to the trouble. I love having your own way."

you exactly as you are. Arrogant, overbearing, and set on

"I?" he seemed genuinely astonished. "I am not arrogant or set on having my own way."

"You have left out overbearing. You have been so all along. Why, on the first occasion that we met, you shook me and called me a liar. Dost remember?"

Her words brought back unpleasant memories of his sister Marianne, who had been brutally beaten to death in the infamous Newgate Prison. "I remember," he said briefly. "But that was not the first occasion that we met."

"Of course it was."

"Nay. I saw you for the very first time on the day of the Royal Parade."

"Of course! I remember the way you looked at me, as though I was a—a nothing. How I hated you for that look!"

"On the contrary. I found you an extremely interesting object. How reprehensibly dirty you were, and how outlandishly dressed."

"That was not my fault," she said, laughing. "I would have you know I considered myself to be quite in the mode."

"And you dare to call me arrogant and overbearing? Hast listened to yourself of late?"

"If I am to be Lady Benbrook, I will dare anything. I had a very able teacher, did I not? You taught me my manners and my lord has ever known best. But if I am an object merely, then why does my lord trouble with me?"

"I have often asked myself that same question. The answer, I suppose, is that I love you."

"In that case, my lord, may I urge upon you the distasteful task of kissing me?"

"You may." He pulled her closer, lifting her face with his right hand. "Doubtless I will survive it."

"You will," she said, fastening her lips hungrily to his. "You will survive that, and more. Much, much more."

Nicholas's eyes regarded the lengthening shadows on

the lawn just outside the window. "I could almost believe you, brat. How like you to threaten fate, Angel. You know, underneath, you have not really changed from the little savage I worked so hard to tame."

"Nicholas, is—" Her face sobered. "Is the pain as severe as it seemed to me to be?"

"Nay, not now, brat," he said, deliberately misunderstanding her. He took her hand and pressed his lips to her palm. " 'Tis gone."

"Nicholas! I know you do not wish to talk about it. But you know well my meaning."

"Discussion is pointless," he said, frowning. "Aye, the pain is quite severe. Let us go on to another subject, if you please."

"Oh, Nicholas, pray do not shut me out. Hast forgotten that I am to be your wife? I have nursed you before," she reminded him.

"So you have." He grimaced. "I could scarcely forget that, either. You saw me stripped of all dignity. But, I suppose, a man cannot expect to be dignified when he is suffering from the plague."

"Can he not? Somehow you managed to retain yours."

"What a liar you are."

"I am not. But perhaps it was because I was much too tired to notice one way or the other."

"You are still with me, are you not?" He looked into her eyes. "I know how difficult I can be, Angel, how demanding, but though I cannot visualize how you can bring yourself to love me, I am grateful that you do."

She laughed softly. "Oh, Nicholas, do you now seek to show me yourself in a humble and diffident light? Nay, love, as I told you before, the role is not suited to your personality."

She felt his arm tighten about her, but he did not answer. She found herself remembering how he had been in earlier days, this handsome dark-browed man of whom, thought she had sought not to show it, she had been so afraid. Cold-eyed, he had been, cynical and unapproachable; his mocking smile freezing her, holding her at arm's length, and forbidding even the slightest intimacy on her part.

"But then, you see, you do not know me at my worst," he said finally.

She winked at him. "Beggin' your lordship's bleedin' pardon," she said, slipping easily into the cockney twang that had once been her only means of expressing herself, "an' hopin' as I ain't offendin' yer, but you're a bloody great bully, tha's what yer are."

"Nonsense! I am nothing of the sort. And, Angel," he went on, laughing, "I will not have such atrocious speech coming from such lips. I forbid it, do you hear?"

"I hear." She put her hands on either side of his face. "But I'm glad as yer now inten's ter marry the perishin' wench."

He looked at her for a long moment. "Aye," he said, grave-faced, "But tha's only 'cause the perishin' wench is so bleedin' beautiful, an' 'cause she won't let me go."

"Nicholas!" she said after an astonished moment. "I would not have believed it possible!" She broke into laughter. "Did I actually hear it coming from your lips, my dear and so correct Nicholas?"

"Is it not obvious why? You have succeeded at long last in corrupting me."

"Not I, my lord Benbrook. Such a feat is quite clearly beyond me."

"You will be silent," he answered her calmly, "and pay more attention to your lessons. Now then, Mistress Dawson, pray keep your eyes on me, for I am about to teach you the correct way to kiss your husband to be."

"Yes, my lord." She flung her arms about his neck. "Pray tutor me. 'Tis my favorite lesson, I would have you know."

SIR PETER LELY'S EYES WERE WARM WITH admiration as he watched Angel seat herself upon the dais. He had painted many beautiful women in his time, but this one had a glow to her, a warm and lovely glow. She was like—like— Lely's thoughts roamed fancifully, as they were apt to do. She was like a sun-ripened peach.

Angel was wearing a gown of yellow silk. The front of the gown, caught up with a diamond brooch, showed frothy green petticoats threaded through with golden ribbon. Her hair was piled high on her head, but one long ringlet had been allowed to trail upon her white shoulder. Fire against snow, the dazzled Lely thought, looking into her violet-blue eyes.

He turned abruptly to Mrs. Sampson, who was hovering disapprovingly in the background. "That will be all. Yes, Madam, you may safely leave Mistress Dawson in my hands."

Mrs. Sampson sniffed. "Since Master Nickey is not at home, sir, I feel sure he would prefer me to stay."

The painter lifted a blond eyebrow. "Do you mean my lord Benbrook?"

"I do, sir."

"My lord Benbrook has given to me his confidence, is it not so? I assure you that he would wish you to go and leave me in peace."

Angel looked at the housekeeper's grimly implacable

face. "Mrs. Sampson," she said, laughing, "I believe you may trust Sir Peter."

Mrs. Sampson glanced at the untidy clutter of paint-stiffened brushes on the long wooden table, the glittering heaps of pigment already ground for use. Stooping, she picked up a brush from the floor. "Is this yours, sir?" she said, holding it out.

"Yes, yes, it is mine." He snatched it from her impatiently. "What is it? I am not allowed to drop the brush, eh?"

"Of course you are allowed to drop it, sir, if you wish to do so. It surprised me to see it lying there, because Master Nickey is himself always so tidy."

Tidy? Angel hid a smile. When Nicholas was painting, he was anything but. She looked down at the paint-spattered floor. Mrs. Sampson resented the fact that Nicholas was allowing Sir Peter to use this room that, hitherto, had been sacred to himself. Even more bitterly did she resent the painter's presence. The fact that Sir Peter Lely had painted the Queen and many of the Court beauties, including Barbara Castlemaine, Frances Stuart, and Lady Mary Squires, meant nothing to her. She had looked at the beautiful glowing canvases so amiably offered by Lely for her inspection, with a disparaging eye. In her opinion, Nicholas was the only painter worthy of note.

Who could forget, for instance, his masterly execution of the King? The King had been depicted kneeling in prayer, his eyes closed, his long hair blown by a Dover wind. Nicholas had called the painting, "A Stuart for England." But for all his undoubted genius, it seemed now that he did not trust himself to paint her. She did not doubt he had his reasons, but he had painted her a number of times before, and she had been flattered and delighted by the results. Nevertheless, he stubbornly refused to do so again, and, when pressed, declined to explain.

"Shall I go, Mistress Dawson?" Mrs. Sampson said.

"Please." Angel smiled at her. "Sir Peter cannot be expected to concentrate, if you are standing there."

"This is quite right, yes." Lely stuck the brush in his thick mop of graying blond hair. " 'Tis my favorite brush," he explained, beaming upon the housekeeper. He quailed as he met her eyes. "It will be safe so, yes?"

"If you say so, sir," Mrs. Sampson said stiffly. Her cold glance traveled over his tall burly figure, the paint-stained smock, the rosy cheeks in his round face, and locked for an instant with his smiling blue eyes. "Very well, Mistress Dawson," she said at last, "I will go. But if you need me, I will be quite close by."

"Thank you, Mrs. Sampson," Angel answered.

"Well," Lely said blankly, after the door had closed behind her. "What is it I do that she does not trust me? She thinks me a bad man, yes?"

Angel laughed. "No indeed, Sir Peter. It is simply that she is jealous of my lord Benbrook's reputation as a painter. She cannot understand why he has commissioned you."

"Ah, I see." Lely nodded wisely. He looked at her consideringly. "Mayhap he feels he cannot do you justice." His blue eyes twinkled at her. "Looking at you, mistress, I can sympathize with the feeling. For now I begin to doubt my own powers."

Angel said nothing. She was a poor sitter, and already her back was feeling the strain. Surreptitiously she moved her position.

"Mistress Dawson," Lely bawled, "I have arranged you. You must not make the move, eh?"

"But my back is aching."

"You have only just sat down, yes? How can you be aching? Anyway, I care not about the ache. You will please not to make the move again, eh?"

He advanced upon her, his small, round mouth pursed in indignation. "The hands just so, yes." His plump fingers prodded them irritably into position. "The feet so, the curl dropping over the shoulder like so. Ah, that is better."

Hasty words rose to her lips, but she thought better of them, and submitted in silence. She had heard that

67

Lely, while amiability itself in his private life, was exceedingly temperamental where his art was concerned. She could believe it now.

After swirling his brush lavishly in the paint, Lely beamed brightly upon her and began to quote—

> *Thus Satan, talking to his nearest Mate,*
> *With head uplift above the wave, and eyes*
> *That sparkling blazed—*

"What is that, Sir Peter?" Angel interrupted. "What are you quoting?"

"You like, eh? Always I make the poetry for my sitters while I am painting, so that they will not grow weary and make the move. 'Tis from an epic by John Milton. You like?" he said again.

"Yes. Very much."

"Good. I say more?"

"Please."

"I know not all of it. I pick pieces at random, yes?"

"Do."

Lely continued,

> *The tyrant's plea, excused his devilish deeds,*
> *Then from his lofty stand on that high tree*
> *Down he alights among the sportful herd*
> *Of those four-footed kinds, himself now one,*
> *Now other, as their shape served best his end*
> *Nearer to view his prey, and unespied*
> *To mark what of their state he more might learn—*

Angel listend to him droning on and on, his deep voice with its slight foreign accent all but lulling her to sleep. She concentrated her thoughts on him, willing herself to stay awake. Lely, she thought, was much easier to pronounce than his real name, Pieter van der Faes. The Dutch painter, so Nicholas had told her, had been born in Soest. Nicholas now seemed to be in good health. She had watched him covertly, but she had detected no sign

68

of pain. He was with the King at present, attending the ceremony of The King's Evil, or, as it was more commonly known to the people, Touching for Scrofula. The King, who hated this ceremony, had called upon all his friends for support. Not that they could aid him in any way, but he liked to have them near.

Angel shivered, bringing a further reproof from Lely. She herself would not care to be forced to touch these people who suffered from all sorts of terrible ailments. But it was the King's duty to take part in the ancient ceremony. When the King went walking, she had heard, he was quite often approached by these diseased people, who, in their misery, would attempt to grasp at his hand and guide it to their open and running sores in the hope that his touch might cure them.

"Mistress Dawson," Lely thundered, "your head is drooping! This I will not have. Up with your chin!"

Nicholas was thinking of Angel, too, wondering with some amusement what she was making of Lely. He himself was not easy upon his clients, having very little patience and, so he was told, an acid tongue. But if they did not respond to his every word or whim, Lely had been known to reduce his feminine sitters to tears. While posing for him, the Duke of Orminster had become so incensed that he had challenged the painter to a duel. Fortunately, for the Duke was known to be a deadly swordsman, Lely had declined. He had done so without shame or embarrassment, merely recommending the Duke to pose as he had arranged him. If he did not do so, he had added menacingly, he would paint his nose a bright red, so that all who passed him would know that they looked upon a buffoon.

Nicholas smiled to himself. But Mistress Angel Dawson was not a fragile flower who easily dissolved into tears, as Lely would find out should he drive her too far. When Lely had been introduced to her, he had called her an angel both in name and appearance. He had yet to learn that she could oft times be possessed of the very devil of a temper.

It pleased the King to see Nicholas smile, but at this moment he was feeling very sorry for himself. "You might, if only for decency's sake, preserve a sober mien." Scowling, the King picked up an emerald ring from the table and thrust it with unnecessary force upon the middle finger of his right hand. "I see that my misery means nothing to you."

"Hardly," Nicholas said. "As for my countenance, you have, unless memory plays me false, oft times lectured me upon its grimness."

"But must you choose this occasion to become cheerful?" Charles snapped. "If I must suffer, then so, too, must you."

Nicholas gave a short laugh. "I sympathize with you, Sire. But 'twill soon be over."

"Will it so! You might call me Charles now and again," the King said, finding a fresh grievance. "May the devil take you for a formal scoundrel! The ceremony goes on for hours."

"Only in your imagination."

" 'Tis not my imagination, and you know it." The King picked up a scarlet fur-lined cloak and draped it about his shoulders. "It comes to something, does it not, Benbrook," he grumbled, "that I now am forced to dress myself."

" 'Tis a pity, I will admit," Nicholas said dryly, "that a grown man must dress himself." He shrugged. "But if Your Majesty will send his gentlemen away, what else can be expected? You might call me Nicholas now and again," he added.

"Nicholas," Charles said, abruptly changing the subject, "how is your health these days?"

"I am quite well, Sire. Thank you for inquiring."

"I recognize your delicate way of telling me to mind my own business."

Nicholas's face softened. "Nay, you are mistaken. If— if I do not respond as I should, it is perhaps less resentment than an inability to gentle my tongue."

70

"Od's Fish, Nicholas! Can you not see that I am concerned? Tell me!"

"If you insist. I am much better of late." He hesitated. "Charles, Angel knows of my condition. She happened to be with me when I—when I—"

"When you had one of your attacks? 'Tis not a shameful thing to be ill, you know."

Nicholas averted his eyes. "She was, I must admit, a little upset."

"A *little?*" Charles laughed. "You're a plaguey liar, Nicholas. 'Tis obvious to all who have eyes to see, that the chit adores you. Will the wedding still be taking place at the end of this month?"

"Naturally."

"Ah, I thought so, for Mistress Dawson, of course, refused to be sent away?"

"She did," Nicholas said, smiling. "Aye, she did, most decidedly and emphatically. 'Tis selfish in me, I know, to be so pleased."

"'Tis *human,*" Charles said, striding toward him. "Friend Nicholas," he laid his hand upon Nicholas's shoulder, "never before have I taken you for a fool, but now I am by no means sure. What the devil possessed you to try such a thing? Are you still not certain she is in love with you?"

Nicholas raised his hand; for a brief moment he clasped the King's fingers warmly. "Nay, Charles, fool I may be, but not that much of a fool. I have always known of her affection." He caught the King's quizzing smile. "Shall we say, *almost* always. And now, if Your Majesty's curiosity is quite sated, 'tis time for the ceremony."

"Plague take the ceremony! Can you not answer a simple question? Are you happy, man?"

"I am."

"Benbrook, you cursed chatterbox! Why the devil do I put up with you?"

"I cannot imagine."

"Neither can I. Well—" The King stopped. Nicholas,

71

in his well-cut dark blue jacket and breeches, a small frill of lace at his throat, and a slightly more extravagant fall at his wrists, had contrived his usual air of casual elegance; his caped cloak touched the top of his shining boots, and upon his middle finger he wore one ring of heavy, plain gold. The King, though he professed to scorn such lack of frills, felt suddenly dissatisfied with his own appearance.

"Sire?"

"Eh? Oh yes, I was about to ask you how I look."

Nicholas stepped back a few paces. He surveyed the cut of the King's scarlet velvet tunic and breeches, both of which were lavishly decorated with flounces of silver lace, each flounce edged with a band of diamonds. Diamond and ruby buckles gleamed from his square-toed silver shoes with their high red heels, and his long slender fingers were loaded with rings which, when he moved his hands, shot out dazzling prisms of light.

"Er—very elegant, Sire."

The King's eyes gleamed suspiciously. "Which is your way of saying, you scurvy rogue, that you don't approve?"

"Would I say such a thing, Sire?"

The King grinned. "Yes, damn your hide, you would."

"It is merely that it is a little ornate for my taste, Sire."

"Well, we can't all expect to dress like cursed Puritans. Come, man, attend me."

In the Banqueting Hall a long procession of the sick and lame awaited the King's ministering touch. A wild cheer arose as the King entered, followed by the Earl of Benbrook and several other gentlemen. Then the cheering was quickly stifled as the sufferers began shuffling for position.

Hopeful eyes in sick, wasted faces followed the King as he took his place in the gilded chair beneath a red canopy.

Nicholas stood behind the King, to his left, holding a large bag of gold coins in his hand.

In the gallery, Alex Barrymore, seated in the front

72

row, smiled down at Nicholas. The King looked up. "Is that Barrymore?" he said in an undertone.

"It is, Sire. He will be returning home with me. He has not yet met Mistress Dawson."

"I'll wager he'll be dazzled by her."

Nicholas's dark brows rose. "Most men are, it would seem. Including yourself, as I remember."

Color mounted in the King's cheeks as he remembered his determined pursuit of Angel. But he had put things right, hadn't he? " 'Tis scurvy of you to bring that up now," he burst out, "knowing full well that I cannot respond."

"The people are looking at you," Nicholas warned. "As for myself, Sire, may I pray your forgiveness that I have so inconvenienced you?"

"No, you may not, devil take you!"

Nicholas smiled. The king was always uncomfortable when reminded of Angel and the incident of the ring. Dismissing the thought, Nicholas watched as the King lifted his jeweled hands, calling for prayers for the sick.

Charles' clear, carrying voice led the prayers, and the eager mumbling response of the sufferers followed after.

Eyes that should have been closed watched the King's dark head bent over his clasped hands. He was their own Charlie, and 'twas certain that his touch would cure them. Some of them looked furtively at the tall Earl of Benbrook, known to be England's foremost hero and the King's greatest friend. It was rumored that the Earl was to be married soon to a Mistress Angel Dawson. The King and Queen would be attending the ceremony, so mayhap there would be feasting and free wine for all.

Charles' voice ceased, and immediately an air of excitement pervaded the hall. The King's dark, friendly eyes looked at the assembled people. "Come ye forward one by one, please," he called. Listening to his warm, charming voice, Nicholas thought, one might almost be persuaded that he was enjoying the ceremony.

Charles laid his hands on the first head, the white lace at his wrists in startling contrast to the grimy blond hair.

The suppliant lifted his face, his sore-encrusted eyes beseeching. "Get well, friend," the King said, his hands gently touching the blotched cheeks.

The stench of soiled clothing and perspiration grew thicker as the men and women shuffled ever nearer, endlessly on and on, until the last face had been touched. Then the procession re-formed as each man and woman came forward to receive a golden coin from the King's hands.

Nicholas tipped the bag and poured a further stream of gold angels into the King's cupped hands.

"Bless you," the King murmured, as he rapidly distributed the coins. He had a ready smile for all, and none there could guess that his flesh crawled at contact with the diseased people.

At last the King rose to his feet, and to the ringing cries of "God save the King," he walked among his people, stopping to chat here, to exchange a joke there, or to take an outstretched hand in his.

Nicholas's heart warmed as he followed after him. It was typical of Charles. He might complain bitterly about the ceremony, but he was not now forced to mingle with the afflicted. This was the real Charles, breaking with tradition, carried away by compassion.

"Unbend, can't you?" Nicholas heard the King mutter. "It won't hurt to give them a smile or a handclasp."

Nicholas was genuinely surprised. He had always felt for the suffering of the poor, but it had not occurred to him that it was necessary to demonstrate it. Such actions might be typical of the King, but not of himself.

Stiffly, Nicholas held out his hand to a woman with sore and running eyes, her head afflicted by a palsy. "I pray, Madam," he said in his deep serious voice, "that you will find yourself much improved on the morrow."

The woman looked into his unsmiling face, evidently a little frightened. Then something in the dark, grave eyes reassured her. She wiped her hands on her patched black skirt, bobbed him a little curtsy, then shyly placed her hand

74

in his. "God bless you, me lord," she said, as his cool firm fingers closed about her hand.

"God bless you, Madam."

She smiled, showing toothless gums. "You're smiling, me lord. You've a bonny face when you smile."

Nicholas inclined his head. "My thanks."

The woman turned about. " 'Ere," she called, "all o' you come an' shake the 'and o' our 'vanishing Earl.' 'E's frien'ly, 'e is, jus' like our gran' King."

Nicholas saw the King's wide grin, and he flushed faintly. "There, friend Nicholas," the King whispered. " 'Tis not so terrible after all, is it?"

Nicholas shook his head. "Nay," he said in a soft voice. "Though had I remarked Your Majesty's earlier complaints, I might well have thought so."

Sighing, Charles took an outstretched hand in his. "You impudent jackanapes, will I ever manage to outwit you?"

The man whose hand the King had taken looked startled. "Pardon, Yere Majesty?"

"Not you, my man," the King said, laughing. "I was addressing my lord Benbrook."

The man's eyes blinked. "The—the 'vanishin' Earl?' " he whispered.

"Why, yes." the King answered. "Do you find the Earl so very formidable then?"

"Wha's that mean, Yere Majesty?"

"Frightening." Charles said. "Do you find him so?"

"Well, 'e is a bit, ain't 'e, Yere Majesty." The man smiled weakly, his eyes avoiding Nicholas.

"I am nothing of the sort," Nicholas said, his abrupt voice causing the man to start. "Do me the honor of shaking hands with me."

"Thank you, me lord," the man said. He shook Nicholas's hand heartily. "Yer'e a good soul, a'ter all." The man scampered back into the crowd.

"Proving something, Nicholas?" the King said.

"Indeed yes. Sire. Proving that one does not always need to be charming to gain a response.'

75

"A thrust which I am determined to ignore. But tell me, do you not consider yourself charming?"

Nicholas shrugged. "Not particularly, Sire."

"Ah, but the ladies would take issue with you on that, and Mistress Dawson in particular."

Nicholas's rare smile showed. "There is no accounting for taste, Sire."

Lord Millington, his rubicund face slightly alarmed, pushed his way toward the King. "Sire," he said in a high tremulous voice. "You have forgotten to make your speech."

Charles grimaced. "So I have, my lord. Do you think it necessary?"

"Sire, it is part of the ceremony."

"Very well. But it always seems to me to be a little insulting, and I have no wish to antagonize the people."

"Sire, they will not be insulted. They expect it of you."

"In that case, I pray you, call for silence."

Charles faced the hushed people. "My good friends," he said in a loud voice. "I must tell you that cleanliness is essential to good health. Therefore, if you would recover and become whole again, you must keep yourselves scrupulously clean and wash your sores as many times as you can."

There was a pause. Charles looked into the serious faces surrounding him. "Though why in plague you need *me* to tell you that," he went on, grinning, "I'll never know. Mayhap I should pass on that bit of advice to some of the gentlemen of my Court. They could do with it."

Lord Millington's face was agonized. "Your Majesty," he said, trying to make himself heard above the ensuing waves of laughter. "You must not, indeed you must not! 'Tis not—not traditional."

"Or royal, I suppose you would say?" Charles answered him, cocking a quizzing eyebrow.

Millington blushed scarlet. "I—I did not say that, Sire. But—but the people do not expect you to—to behave as one of themselves."

"Do they not?" Charles turned to Nicholas. "What say you, friend?"

Nicholas bowed. "Sire, for once I believe we are in accord."

Charles' eyes gleamed with laughter, "Then a plague on you, my lord Millington, and a plague on tradition!"

"Sire!"

"Well done, Charles," Nicholas said, as they left the hall together. "I have long been aware that I may count on Your Majesty for the unusual."

"Aye, friend." Charles linked his arm in Nicholas's. "Now shall we wash ourselves? 'Twould be unpleasant, were we to wake on the morrow and find ourselves festooned with sores, would it not?"

"Distinctly daunting," Nicholas agreed.

"Will you try scented water?" the King asked, his eyes twinkling. "Or is it, perhaps, a little frivolous for one of your spartan tastes?"

"A little, Sire," Nicholas said gravely. "But I am willing to overlook it."

"Rogue! You know, the thing I like best about you is your cursed servility."

"I am happy to have pleased Your Majesty in some small way."

"Then a plague on you."

Nicholas turned smiling eyes on the King. "I have already indulged, Sire, dost recall? But I thank Your Majesty for the kindly thought."

"Not at all, my lord Benbrook, not at all."

NICHOLAS ENTERED THE HOUSE IN ST. Bernard's Square, Alex Barrymore following him, to find Mrs. Sampson awaiting him in the hall. Her white cap was askew on her neat gray hair, always a sign that she was laboring under some strong emotion. "Master Nickey," she began immediately, "you'll never guess what your fine painter has done now."

"I decline to listen to complaints of Sir Peter's conduct in this drafty hall." Nicholas looked at her quellingly. "It may have escaped your notice, Sampson, but we have a guest."

"Oh yes, Master Nickey, I noticed. A very good day to you, Mr. Barrymore."

Alex Barrymore smiled. "Mrs. Sampson and I are old friends." He turned to Nicholas. "Is Lely up to his tricks again?"

"Yes, sir," Mrs. Sampson broke in. " 'Tis disgraceful how he goes on. I—"

"That will be all for now," Nicholas said coldly. "Mr. Barrymore and I will be in the green room. Send one of the wenches with some wine and biscuits. By the way, in an hour or two we are to have another guest, a Mr. Milton. The gentleman is blind. Pray watch for his carriage."

"Very well, Master Nickey." She turned away, offended. "When you hear how Sir Peter treated Mistress Dawson, you'll think differently."

"What's this?" Nicholas's voice was suddenly sharp.

"You don't wish to hear, Master Nickey. I quite understand."

"Sampson, do you wish to be pensioned off?"

"No, Master Nickey."

"Then you will bring the wine yourself, and I will then listen to your story."

"Yes, Master Nickey." Mrs. Sampson hurried away, her black gown rustling crisply.

"That poor woman," Alex Barrymore said lightly, his dark blue eyes twinkling. "You have quite crushed her spirit."

Nicholas led the way to the green room. "To answer your comment, Alex," he said, seating himself and stretching his legs out comfortably, "that poor woman is quite uncrushable; at least, I have never yet managed that particular feat."

"I see." Alex gave an amused laugh. "You do not think you should seek Mistress Dawson out? Mayhap she is upset and would welcome your concern."

Nicholas laughed. "You are thinking I should play the concerned lover, Alex? I will do so, should there be any need for concern. But whatever may have occurred, I am reasonably sure that Mistress Dawson had a hand in bringing it about. And you will find her well able to take care of herself."

Mrs. Sampson came into the room and set down the silver tray upon a small side table. She had straightened her cap, but she still looked ruffled and indignant. "Now, Master Nickey," she began.

"Pray pour the wine, Sampson."

Fuming, she did so. Tight-lipped, she handed a glass to each man. "Now may I speak, Master Nickey?"

"You may, Sampson."

"Sir Peter lost his temper with Mistress Angel."

"Why?"

"Because she was sleepy, and did not pose as he requested. No wonder she was sleepy, the way he kept quoting poetry to her. I was outside the door, and I heard him."

"Eavesdropping, Sampson?"

"Nothing of the sort, Master Nickey! I was guarding her."

"From what?"

"From him and his nasty temper."

"Then pray accept my apologies. Go on."

"Well, he shouted at her." Mrs. Sampson folded her hands beneath her apron and looked at him defiantly. "I wasn't having that, so I opened the door. Well there he stood, Master Nickey, his face quite purple with rage, and to make matters worse, he'd splashed paint all over the floor—"

"A little extra paint on the floor will scarcely be noticed, Sampson."

"No, Master Nickey, if you say so. But then you always were sweet-tempered."

Alex Barrymore grinned. Careless of its arrangement, he rumpled his dark blond hair with his finger, a habit of his when he was amused. "You, Nicholas? Do I hear aright?"

Mrs. Sampson turned to Alex indignantly. "I would have you know, Mr. Barrymore, that Master Nickey is a very good boy."

"Sampson," Nicholas drawled, "we will leave my many undoubted virtues to another and more suitable time."

"I stood there in the doorway transfixed, as you might say, and while I stood there, he strode across to Mistress Angel, and laid his hands upon her."

Nicholas stiffened, his eyes narrowing. "Interesting."

"Well, he did, Master Nickey. And then he—he shook her."

"Ah!" Nicholas said softly, visibly relaxing, "and what did Mistress Dawson have to say to this?"

"She said, 'Remove your hands at once, Sir Peter.' But he continued to shake her. It was then that Mistress Angel lifted her hand and struck him full in the face. I daresay you'll not approve, lad, but I for one did not blame her a bit. And Sir Peter called her a she-devil, Master Nickey. Then he packed up his things and stalked out of the room. Swearing, he was, in that outlandish Dutch. At least, I think he was swearing. He vowed he'd never return to this house again, and I was to tell you so."

Nicholas laced his fingers together and rested his chin upon them. "He will return," he said, smiling faintly, "when his rage has spent itself."

"Not to this house, Master Nickey! I'll not have it!"

"You, Sampson, will do exactly as you are told. Where is Mistress Dawson now?"

"She's in her room. She said to tell you that, if you'll not lecture and scold her for unladylike behavior, she'll come down."

"Good of her. Tell her I make no promises, Sampson. She is to present herself at once."

"But, lad, she was provoked. That Sir Peter is enough to try the patience of a saint, let alone Mistress Angel."

"Give her the message, Sampson."

She inclined her head, and left the room reluctantly.

Alex laughed. Rising from his chair, he walked over to the fireplace. "Doubtless," he said, stirring the logs to life with his elegantly booted foot, "she is very beautiful?"

"No indeed. The word would be plain, I think."

"You surprise me, Nicholas. Hitherto you have only gone in for the most beautiful of women."

"True. That is why ugliness can sometimes be restful to the eyes."

"Ugliness? Come, Nicholas! I don't believe you."

"Do you not? Well, I will leave you to judge for yourself."

Angel came slowly down the stairs. She decided Nicholas was bound to be angry, thinking that his careful tuition of her manners, speech, and deportment had all been for nothing. But to defend herself, she had dressed carefully in a green gown, with ruffled white petticoats, threaded through with green and silver ribbons. The gown was high at the back, for she still bore the scars of the floggings she had endured in Newgate Prison, but cut low in the front, half exposing her white bosom. To soften him further, she had loosened her hair, tying it back with a huge bow of green satin ribbon. Her only jewels were the emerald ring and a double string of pearls. She looked very demure, but she did not delude herself that Nicholas would be moved by her appearance. Try though she might, he usually managed to see through all of her pretenses.

Approaching the half-opened door of the green room, she was agreeably surprised to hear the murmur of voices. If Nicholas was entertaining a guest, the lecture would be postponed, and, if she were lucky, perhaps indefinitely.

She peered through the crack in the door. Nicholas was seated. He looked handsome as ever in his impeccably cut dark blue apparel. The other gentleman was standing by the fireplace, his back to it. He was handsome, too, Angel decided, though not as strikingly as Nicholas.

He was wearing silver-gray jacket and breeches, a black, red-lined half-cape swinging carelessly from his broad shoulders. Lace foamed at his throat and wrists, and as he moved his hand to drink his wine, she saw a sapphire ring glow with a subdued blue fire upon his right hand. Like Nicholas, he chose to wear his own hair rather than a wig. It was nice hair, crisp and dark blond, waving slightly in the front, held back with a narrow black ribbon.

Without turning his head toward the door, Nicholas said clearly, "Pray to enter, Angel. Do not linger there."

Angel jumped violently. "How did you know I was there, m'lord?" she answered, stepping into the room.

"As always, I sensed your presence." Nicholas rose from his chair and held out his hand to her. "Come here, brat."

She went to him quickly. "This is Alex Barrymore, Angel," Nicholas said, "a friend of mine. Alex, may I present Mistress Dawson." Nicholas paused, looking with amusement at Alex's astonished face. "Mr. Barrymore owns the neighboring estate to Elm Park Manor."

Angel flushed as she met Alex's fascinated dark blue eyes. What possessed him to stare at her like that? Self-consciously, she adjusted the bow of green ribbon, then extended her hand to him.

He bowed over her hand and pressed his lips to her fingers. "Mistress Dawson," he murmured. " 'Tis an honor."

Over his bowed head. Angel's eyes met Nicholas's. He was regarding her with his faint enigmatic smile, his fingers idly twisting the gold ring he wore.

"Thank you, Mr. Barrymore," Angel said, drawing her hand gently away.

Surely she must be the most beautiful girl in existence, Alex thought confusedly. He thought of others he had known. None of them came near to matching Mistress Dawson. He turned back to Nicholas. "Your sense of humor is undoubtedly keen," he said reproachfully.

"I thought you would think so," Nicholas answered composedly. "Sit down Angel, Alex. Angel, you will take a glass of wine?"

It was more a statement than a question. "Thank you." She seated herself on a small brocaded sofa, curling her legs beneath her. A frown from Nicholas caused her to hastily lower them and to place her feet together.

Nicholas handed her a glass of wine. "If your business is concluded, Alex," he said, returning to his chair by the fire, "I suppose you will be settling once more in Edgehill Manor?"

"Unfortunately, it will entail several trips. I shall be going backward and forward for quite a bit yet."

"Your business is in London?"

"Yes, curse it! 'Tis a damned nuisance too. I am not a city person." Suddenly remembering his manners, Alex started, and looked apologetically at Angel. "I beg your pardon, Mistress Dawson."

"You are pardoned, Mr. Barrymore," she answered him serenely.

She became aware of Nicholas's amused eyes. He was no doubt recalling that she had been used to hearing far stronger language than Mr. Barrymore's mild oath. She stared defiantly back at him.

Sipping her wine, Angel listened with interest to the talk between the two men. Her eyes studied Alex Barrymore with an equally frank interest. He was as tall as Nicholas, broad-shouldered, and of a slender and elegant build. She found herself liking his warm, slightly shy smile, the way he had of running his long tapering fingers through his hair. He had a long straight nose; well-shaped, thin, and sensitively curved lips. And when he looked over at her, which he did increasingly often, his blue eyes seemed to hold a perpetual smile. He had a way of narrowing them, she noticed, as though he might be slightly shortsighted and sought to focus her within the range of his vision. Comparing them, she thought of the two men as day and night. Nicholas, dark-browed, handsome, was the night, and Alex, fair-complexioned, blond of hair, was the day.

"Dreaming, brat?" Nicholas said. "Your usually ready tongue seems to have quite deserted you."

"I was listening to your interesting conversation, my lord."

Nicholas laughed. "Do you tell me you are interested in the problems of drainage and the subduing of the rats that infest the city?" He put his hand on Angel's shoulder. "Mr. Barrymore is about to take his leave."

"Oh come," Alex protested, as Angel rose to her feet and extended her hand to him, "may I not be Alex to you, Mistress Dawson? With Nicholas's permission, of course."

"You have my permission," Nicholas said, watching him bow over Angel's hand.

"Excellent," Alex said, retaining Angel's hand in his. "Do I also have the permission of the lady to call her Angel?"

She smiled at him, feeling the color rise in her cheeks at his look of admiration. "You do, Alex."

"It sounds delightful, coming from your lips." He carried her hand to his lips. "Beauty is ever a delight to the eye." He regarded her with that slightly narrowed gaze, which added to his charm. "And you, Mistress Dawson, are exceedingly beautiful."

"Thank you."

Nicholas turned to the door. "You have my permission to call her Angel. However, I do not recall giving you permission to linger over her hand." His slight smile took the sting from his words.

There was something pointed in his polite opening of the door. Alex grinned, his eyes crinkling at the outer corners. "Do I detect a note of rebuke in your voice, Nicholas?"

"Not at all."

"Mistress Dawson is a poem, Nicholas."

"I gathered that you thought so. Take care you do not flatter her overmuch, for the young baggage is monstrously conceited."

"I am not!" Angel exclaimed.

"Were I you," Alex said seriously, "I would be."

Alex bowed himself from the room, Nicholas following after him. Waiting for Nicholas to return, Angel wondered if he would show displeasure over the incident with Sir Peter Lely. After all, she was but human, and he had shaken her. Even a genuine lady would have taken offense.

Nicholas re-entered the room. "You liked Alex?" he asked.

"Very much. I thought him charming."

"Hmm!" He regarded her with critical eyes. "Methought your eyes were overbold. They licked over him like a candle flame."

She stared at him. "Nicholas! Can you possibly be jealous?"

"Would that be so very strange?"

"Think you there is a man to compare to my dear m'lord?" She twined her arms about his neck.

He bent his head and kissed her lips. "However, brat, think not to cajole me into forgetting your behavior toward Sir Peter."

"Nicholas, he shook me. What else could I have done but strike him?"

He laughed suddenly. "Many things, brat."

She looked at him rebelliously. "I could not think of any other course of action. If I did wrong, my lord, I crave your pardon. I cannot always be right, you know."

Nicholas raised a mocking eyebrow. "But you are seldom right. Have I not proved this in the past?"

"Oh, Nicholas!"

His arms tightened about her. "I would remind you, Mistress Dawson, that you are wasting my time."

"I am?"

"Your arms are already about my neck, are they not? You are talking when you could be kissing me. You do not consider that a waste of time, Mistress Dawson?"

"I do, my lord Benbrook. Assuredly I do."

She kissed him several times, on his lips, his eyes, his cheeks. "There. You cannot call that a waste of time, can you?"

"Nay, love." His dark eyes were tender. "Indeed I cannot call it that."

"But I was right once, was I not?" Angel went on, pursuing the previous subject.

"Tell me of it, so that I may record the occasion for posterity."

"Very well, laugh if you wish. It was when I told you that I loved you, and forced you to tell me that you loved me in return."

The smile died from his face. "That, my darling, may well have been your greatest mistake."

"If mistake it was, my lord, then may I make many such."

He put an arm about her shoulders and led her over to the couch, drawing her down with him. "I have never mentioned this before, Angel, but I would like a son, and a daughter who will look like yourself. Things being as they are, though, I very much doubt that this could be managed."

"Well, I do not." She put her head against his shoulder. "You will have your son, your daughter, too. I believe that you are much better, my dearest."

"Would you like children, Angel?"

"If they are yours, my lord, I would adore them."

"They had best be mine, had they not?" he said dryly.

She laughed. "For shame, my lord. You know well my meaning."

"Aye, I do." He looked at her uncertainly for a moment. "Then shall we drink a toast to our son and daughter?"

" 'Tis a little previous, but let us do it." She raised her head and looked at him, her eyes twinkling. "But I must regretfully remind you, my lord, that before I can present you with your heir, you will first have to marry me."

She saw his slight smile. "You are asking me to make an honest woman of you, is that it, brat?"

"Aye, love."

He made a wry face. "Must I indeed marry you? 'Tis a big step. I will ponder the matter. But you have my leave to kiss me."

"Have I so? You are most gracious, but perhaps 'twould be best if I first give it some thought."

He slid his arms about her. "You, Mistress Dawson, will do exactly as I tell you. I am glad that you recognize my graciousness. I have many other virtues also. Should you doubt this, then may I recommend that you speak to Sampson on the subject of myself. She, at least, or so she will tell you, sees me in my true light."

"Bah!"

His lips closed over hers, silencing the further words she would have uttered.

Some minutes later, he said, "Referring once more to this question of Lely. I—"

"Oh, Nicholas, *must* we refer to him again?"

88

"We must. I wish your portrait to be completed. You will apologize to him."

"I will not!"

"You will," he assured her calmly.

"Oh very well, if you will have it so. But he is an impatient bully."

"He is also a genius."

"I think your talent is the greater."

"Nonsense! You see me through the eyes of love, I am happy to say."

"But, Nicholas—"

"Talking of genius," he said, cutting her short firmly, "we are shortly to have a visit from Mr. Milton."

"Are we? Now there is a coincidence. Only today Sir Peter was quoting some lines from Milton's new poem."

"It is not yet published."

"Yet he quoted from it."

Nicholas's forehead wrinkled. "Ah yes, Pepys told me that Milton had given him and Lely a first draft. He was undoubtedly quoting from that. Though, if I know John, he will alter it several times before he can bear to let the printer see it."

Angel put her hand to his cheek. "Nicholas," she said, her fingers stroking gently, "might I ask you a question? You will not be angry with me?"

He looked at her with guarded eyes. "Until I know the nature of the question, I cannot say."

"Ah, darling, always so cautious! But I wondered why you associate with a man who spoke out so openly against Charles I? Here is my Nicholas, that staunch Royalist, inviting the equally staunch Cromwellian into his home." She paused to give him a triumphant look, then went on, a smile in her voice. "Hast read Mr. Milton's sonnet celebrating the triumph of General Fairfax during the Civil War? If so, you will remember that in that sonnet he begged the General to rid England of fraud and avarice and sundry other evils. Those words, however stirring, were an indictment against our late King, were they not?"

"They were, obviously. But the Civil War has been over these many years, brat."

She went on quickly. "Then too there was Mr. Milton's work, 'The Tenure of Kings and Magistrates.' Those words, too, were against the King. Indeed, Nicholas, I would say that they encouraged tyrannicide, wouldn't you?"

Nicholas put his hands on her shoulders and held her away from him, studying her face. "What now, brat? Do you seek to parade your learning before the tutor, or have you determined to build up a case against our guest?"

"Oh no. The case was built up against him by those in support of the King. I cannot say that I like his politics, but other than that I have nothing against him." She flushed faintly. "But 'tis true, love, that I did seek to impress you a little."

"You have ever impressed me, Angel, and you continue to do so. Like you, I did not approve of his views, and I still do not. But Charles is restored to the throne, England is at peace, and surely there must come a time when we lay censure aside. Sins must be forgiven at some time, must they not, my darling? The King has forgiven Milton, so why should not I?"

She laughed. "Speaking strictly for myself, in the past you have not shown yourself to be the most forgiving man."

"I applaud the thrust, but I would say quite to the contrary. I forgave you many times, did I not? For a multitude of things," he said softly. Gently his hand stroked her hair. "For insolence, for defiance, bad language. For tormenting me, turning my life upside down, and for making me love you against my will. Therefore it must follow that I have a very forgiving spirit."

"Was it a very painful process when you found yourself becoming human, my darling?"

"Indeed, but it brought with it plentiful rewards."

Angel's mood veered at this acceptance of her teasing. "Nay, love," she said indignantly, "you shall not speak so of yourself. You have ever been human. I only meant that you held yourself so aloof. But it is as though in loving me, you have softened toward all."

"Then may I not forget Milton's politics and concentrate on the man himself?"

"Of course. Have I not told you that I have nothing against him?"

"I feel sure that he will be relieved to know that," he said with drawling sarcasm. "You say Sir Peter quoted line from Milton's epic? What thought you of them?"

She hesitated. "Sir Peter asked me that same question. I told him that I liked them."

Nicholas studied her face. "You did not, did you?"

"Well," she answered him defensively, "I am sure that the words are very grand and inspiring. But in all truth, no, I did not."

"Come, look not so downcast. 'Twould be a dull world indeed were we all to have a like taste. I have met Mr. Milton on several occasions. He is a gentle man, and not at all like the fire-eater I had half expected to meet. I found myself liking him. I think perhaps you will be of the same opinion."

"Will I?"

"I think so, yes. I believe too that he is a very unhappy man. Having been unhappy myself, I can sense it in another. He is blind, as you know. It is said that he has never recovered from the loss of his second wife, the one woman he truly loved. I know not her true name. Milton used only the name he bestowed upon her. He called her Serena, because of the serenity of her nature. She died after fifteen months of marriage."

"Poor man!"

"His first wife, Mary, presented him with four children. The three daughters appear to be in excellent health."

"You have also met his daughters?"

"Aye, briefly. But then too, he had to contend with the loss of his son."

Angel felt a coldness creeping over her as her mind

dwelt on Milton's loss. Instinctively, her fingers gripped Nicholas's arm and she moved closer to him. "How terrible to lose those you love. He married again, though. Is he happy with her?"

"Really, brat, the questions you ask me! How can I know that? I was told, though I know not the truth of it, that he had married again in an attempt to alleviate his loneliness."

"Were I to die, I would not like you to marry again. I am very selfish, you see."

Nicholas saw the clouding of her face, and he said quietly, "Nay, love, let us not dwell on possible tragedy. You must not wince from hurt before that hurt has been inflicted, else will your life become quite unbearable."

Tears sprang into her eyes. "Nicholas, my darling, I love you so much!" She put her arms about him and rested her cheek against his. "I know you are much improved, but sometimes I cannot help being afraid."

She felt the beating of his heart against her body, and she wondered if her words had distressed him, but he said calmly enough, "I know, brat. I have seen your fear in your eyes, though you seek to hide it."

A knock sounded on the door. Nicholas put Angel gently from him. "Mr. Milton's hearing is very acute, and I would not have him hear tears in your voice. Enter," he called.

The door opened. "Master Nickey," Mrs. Sampson said, coming into the room. "Mr. Milton's carriage has arrived."

"Thank you, Sampson." Nicholas rose to his feet. "I will be back shortly," he said to Angel.

Mrs. Sampson gave her a sympathetic look before leaving the room.

Angel was calm again by the time Nicholas returned. The man he led into the room was of medium height, with broad shoulders and a thick waist. His plum-colored cloth jacket and breeches were plainly cut, though the jacket was adorned with a bright yellow velvet collar and cuffs, and two rows of brass buttons. His face beneath a small black wig was pale of complexion, the lips thin, and the clouded eyes showed a faint trace of blue. It was a severe face, but his expression at the moment was one of gentle expectancy.

"Angel," Nicholas said, "may I present Mr. John Milton. John, Mistress Angel Dawson."

Angel came forward quickly. "Mr. Milton," she said. Her gown rustled as she curtsied before him.

Milton smiled. "I have heard much of you from Nicholas," he said. "I am happy to make your acquaintance, Mistress Dawson."

"And I yours, sir."

Milton held out his hands. "Your perfume, mistress, and the silken rustle of your gown create a picture in my mind. Will you allow me to touch your face so that I may also know your features?"

Angel glanced at Nicholas, who nodded encouragingly. "Yes, sir," she said in a low voice.

She stood very still as Milton's long thin fingers traced their delicate way over her forehead, her nose, the contours of her cheeks, her chin, and lastly her mouth. His fingers felt like the fluttering of wings.

"I know that your hair is red-gold," Milton said at last, "and that your eyes are of a violet-blue. And now I know that you have beautiful bones. Nicholas, your lady is indeed lovely."

"Will you sit down, John?" Nicholas drew a chair forward.

"Thank you." Milton nodded gratefully as Nicholas assisted him into the chair. "I have been blind for some time, Mistress Dawson," he said, his head turning in her direction, "but still I have not yet managed to reconcile myself to it."

"I am indeed sorry, sir. But will you not call me Angel?"

"A nice child, Nicholas. Aye, mistress, I'll call you Angel, if you in turn will promise to call me John."

"Then I will, John, and thank you."

She listened attentively to the conversation of the two men, occasionally contributing a remark of her own. When

93

Mrs. Sampson arrived with wine, Milton took his glass and sipped absentmindedly, for he was deep in a discussion of his work. The glass tilted, and a few drops of wine splashed on the green and silver carpet. Mrs. Sampson compressed her lips. Nicholas sent her a warning glance, and she sniffed and left the room.

"Sir Peter Lely quoted some lines from 'Paradise Lost' to Angel," Nicholas said. "Is it finished, then?"

"Nay, I am not yet satisfied. 'Twas a first draft I gave Sir Peter. But there are many alterations I wish to make." Again his head turned. "Did you like the lines Sir Peter quoted, Angel?" He sounded like an eager boy.

Angel looked away from Nicholas's amused eyes. "Aye, John," she said with every evidence of sincerity, "I thought 'twas beautiful."

Nicholas's lips formed the silent word, "Liar!"

"But the underlying sadness," Milton prompted. "Did you feel the horror of the revelations?"

She looked at Nicholas indignantly. "I vow that your words made me turn quite cold."

"Indeed." Milton looked so pleased that Nicholas rewarded her with an approving smile. "Your lady has great discernment, Nicholas. But there, I fear I must sound most conceited."

"Nay," Angel protested. "You have every right to be proud of your work. This is a very exciting moment for me, John, 'tis not often I meet with a genius."

"Aye, they call me that." His face clouded. "The blind genius."

Angel rose from her chair. Seating herself on a padded stool beside him, she took his hand in hers. "You see with the eyes of the soul," she said softly. "And beside that, our vision alone can have no importance and meaning."

Milton's lips trembled slightly. "You have a kind heart and a gentle manner, Mistress Angel. Your lord is to be congratulated on such a prize."

"Thank you, John." Nicholas rose to his feet. "I pray

you to excuse me, there is a message I must give to my groom. I will return in a few moments."

Angel looked after Nicholas in some bewilderment. Then, glancing at Milton, she saw that his eyes were bright with tears. Now she understood. Nicholas, deeply sensitive himself, with that exquisite tact of his, was giving the poet time to recover.

Now that Nicholas was gone, Milton did not try to hide his emotion. "I ask you to forgive me, Angel," he said in a low voice. " 'Tis your tone, your manner that stirs me so painfully. 'Tis so extraordinarily reminiscent of my wife Serena. She too was a gentle soul. She died very soon after we were married. I had less than a year and a half of happiness with her. It seems strange to think I have never seen my Serena's face, for I see her so vividly in my dreams. I remember the clutch of her hand when she was dying, the sound of her voice saying my name for the last time. That voice of hers, so faint, so lost to hope, and yet full of love. Aye, blind and helpless though I was then, she loved me!"

This last was said so triumphantly that Angel felt her own eyes sting. She drew her kerchief from her sleeve and pressed it into his hand. "And loves you still, I make no doubt, John," she murmured.

Milton dabbed at his eyes with the wisp of silk and lace. "If you're thinking me a fool, Mistress Angel, then let me tell you that 'tis your own fault. 'Twas the tenderness in your voice, that gentle manner that made me think of Serena, and thereby unmanned me."

Angel smiled. "I thank you for the compliment, but I was not always gentle."

"No? What mean you?"

Nicholas would not mind, she thought, if she told this man her story to distract him. Touching lightly on her grim experience in Newgate Prison, she told him as briefly as possible of her former life, of the King's timely pardon, and of her meeting with Nicholas and the events that had followed. Only one thing did she leave out, and that was the misunderstanding that had parted her from Nicholas for so long. "So you see," she concluded, "I was a gutter brat, and, at that time, far from a gentlewoman."

Milton was silent for so long that she began to wonder if she had bored him with her tale. "My dear child," he said at last, "what a story!" He turned to her a face that was bright with eagerness.

Angel's heart fluttered in alarm as the door opened and Nicholas entered the room. "Is that you, Nicholas?" Milton cried.

"Aye." Nicholas crossed the room. "What has you so excited?" he said, seating himself.

"The story Mistress Angel has been relating," Milton cried. "The story of your meeting, your love affair. 'Tis true that she told me so that she might take my mind from my own tragedy, but I find it quite inspiring. With your permission, I would make the attempt to put it into verse."

Meeting Angel's pleading eyes, Nicholas smiled faintly. She relaxed. He was not angry, then. "You might try, John," Nicholas said quietly. "Though I vow that even you will find it difficult to accomplish. What will you call it, 'Benbrook's Folly'?"

"Nicholas!" Angel said in a stifled voice. Her dismay died as she saw his smile.

"Heed him not," Milton said. "When first I met my lord Benbrook, his dry comments took me quite aback. I told myself that his stiff manner showed a great dislike of me. But then I came to know him better. 'Tis only his way. You must not let him distress you, Mistress Angel."

Angel's eyes were very tender as they met Nicholas's. "I won't let him distress me," she said softly. "I promise."

Some time later, when Milton rose to leave, he asked if Angel would take the time to visit him now and again. "I live in Artillery Walk. 'Tis not far, and easy to find."

"I will," she promised, giving him her hand. " 'Twill pleasure me greatly to visit you, sir."

"And you will come, too, Nicholas?"

"I will. 'Tis a promise," Nicholas assured him.

When Milton had driven away in his carriage, Nicholas took Angel in his arms. "You do not care for the title of 'Benbrook's Folly'?"

"Nay."

"Then what say you to 'The Earl and the Guttersnipe'?"

"I do not care for it."

"Then what shall it be, my darling?"

"It must be called "Angel's Love,' because that is what you are, my dear and eternal Love."

ALEX BARRYMORE STOOD BY THE LONG window in the Banqueting Hall. He watched the ladies, their gowns brilliant patches of color, their eyes sparkling over the lavishly ornamented and lacy fans made popular by Catherine of Braganza, laughing and flirting with gentlemen who were even more gorgeously arrayed.

He listened to the busy clinking of glasses, he smelled the heavy richness of wine mingling with the perfumes of the ladies. Musicians played from the flower-smothered gallery. Many of the couples were growing impatient for the King to open the dance. A general air of festivity prevailed, but Alex, in his frozen misery, could not feel himself a part of it.

Outside, there was more festivity. The people feasted on great hunks of beef and pork, drinking the free wine that flowed from the conduits in the street, and toasting the health of the "vanishing Earl" and his lady on this, the occasion of his marriage to Mistress Angel Dawson.

Alex's fingers clenched about the fragile stem of the glass he was holding. He was a fool! He had seen Mistress Dawson but four times since that first meeting in St. Bernard's Square, and now he could not get her out of his mind. In that short space of time he had fallen hopelessly and irrevocably in love with her. And yet, he asked himself bitterly, why was he surprised? How much time did it really take to fall in love? Perhaps Nicholas had guessed at his feelings; now and again Alex had surprised an expression in his eyes that might be one of pity.

In the twenty-nine years of life, he had had many light affairs. For some of the women he had felt such a sincere affection that he had oft times mistaken it for love. Well, he knew the difference now, God help him!

At the long involved ceremony that had united them, Alex had not been able to take his eyes from Angel. She was so very beautiful in her gown of white and silver. The skirts, flaring out gracefully, were embroidered in intricate patterns, sewn with sapphires and pearls. Her lovely hair gleamed beneath a small, pearl-embroidered cap. Watching her face as she looked at Nicholas, Alex had felt a lump choking his throat.

In that moment he had almost hated Nicholas, standing at her side, clad in midnight blue satin jacket and breeches, lace ruffling at his throat and about his wrists, his usually tidy hair falling in thick black curls over his forehead. Nicholas, who now possessed her entirely.

Behind the couple had stood the King and Queen: Charles, magnificent in wine red, splashed with jewels; Catherine, small and pretty in a gold-shot green silk gown with a lacy overskirt of petunia-red. Alex watched Angel now, as she moved gracefully toward the King.

The King was reminded of the first time he had ever seen her. She had held her head high in just that way. But then her eyes had been both frightened and defiant; now they were serene. It had been on the occasion of the Honors Ball, and Charles had not known just how severe was the test imposed on her. From guttersnipe to lady! Yet she had curtsied before him with what had seemed perfect composure, and three had been nothing in her manner to suggest that she was ill at ease.

Charles smiled to himself, his fingers smoothing his thin mustache. He remembered that time with pleasure. *Od's Fish, but what a magnificent job Nicholas had made of the wench! She had been lovely then, but today she was radiant.*

100

"My lady Benbrook," Charles said, as Angel paused before him and swept a low curtsy.

He put out his hand and assisted her to rise, his sensuous lips parting in a brilliant smile. "I am glad to have you to myself for a few moments." He bent toward her, adding in a hissing whisper, "Where is your cursed jealous husband?"

Angel laughed, returning the slight but insistent pressure of his fingers. "Doubtless he is even now glowering at Your Majesty," she answered.

"By Gad, but he'd not dare!" He looked down into Angel's face, his dark eyes frankly amorous. "Benbrook is a handsome brute, I'll not deny. But I, my lady Angel, am the more skillful lover. Have you not begun to regret your choice?"

Angel shot an apprehensive look at the Queen, who was standing a few paces from them, and was relieved to find her smiling. "I doubt not your ability, Sire," she answered in a low voice. "But, if Your Majesty will forgive me, my lord Benbrook has ever been my first and only choice."

"Aye, so he has, curse him."

Charles surveyed the people thronging the hall, all of them gathered in celebration. "Barrymore is looking cursed gloomy, Angel," he said, his eyes teasing. "What think you can be the matter with him?"

"I know not, Your Majesty."

"No, I really think you don't." His smile faded, and he added in a more serious voice. "Now is not the moment to talk of it, but I know of the problem facing friend Nicholas. I would have you know that you may rely upon me in all circumstances." His fingers tightened about her hand. "In *all* circumstances, Angel, do you understand?"

Some of the color had left Angel's cheeks. "Aye," she said quietly. "I thank Your Majesty for your graciousness."

"I am his friend. Yours too, I hope?"

"Indeed, Your Majesty."

"My lady Angel, may we not dispense with the formalities on this occasion?"

"If it pleases Your Majesty."

"It does please me. Will you not let me hear you say Charles? I vow the name would trip quite prettily from your tongue."

"But—but, Your Majesty," Angel stammered, trying to draw her hand away. "I would not s—so presume."

"'Tis not persumption if I command it." His eyes laughed into hers. "Say it, my lady. Say Charles."

"Ch—Charles."

"Ah, I was right. You make a lovely sound of that very simple name."

Angel found herself responding to the warmth of his smile. *Libertine* he was called, *rake*. He was doubtless all that and more. But despite his lined, almost ugly face, he had an incredible fascination for women. A magnetism that, had she not already known and loved Nicholas, would have brought from her an immediate response.

"Charles," Angel said softly. "Dear Majesty."

"You know that I would be more to you, my lady," he said caressingly, his finger stroking her palm. "But, since you have made it abundantly clear that it is not to be, then I am proud to stand your friend."

"Thank you, Sire."

The Queen waved her fan in front of her flushed face. Despite Charles' openly amorous attitude, she was not jealous. Angel, she knew, had eyes only for her lord.

Catherine's eyes singled out the Earl of Benbrook. He was standing by a table, sipping a glass of wine and replying with what, from this distance, seemed to be absent courtesy, to the remarks made to him by the garrulous Lady Twining. His eyes, Catherine noticed, were on Angel.

My lord Benbrook in love! the Queen thought. She would not have thought it possible for the controlled Earl to show such depths of emotion. She noticed, too, that he did not seem to be at all disturbed that the King was still holding Angel's hand. Another triumph for Angel, who had apparently laid to rest, once and for all, the ghost of that lovely and immoral woman, his mother, who had poisoned and haunted his past.

The Queen looked at Angel fondly. They were a perfect pair. Angel, the most beautiful woman in the room, and Nicholas, surely the handsomest man. Gone for the moment was my lord Benbrook's coldly austere expression. His dark face had taken on a glow of happiness that matched Angel's. His hair was ruffled, and he looked almost as young as his bride.

Remembering Charles' concern for the Earl's health, Catherine felt a twinge of apprehension. She put the thought firmly from her. It might be that Charles had exaggerated. He sometimes did, she knew.

A loud laugh from the opposite corner of the room distracted her attention. Catherine's soft mouth hardened. Barbara, Countess of Castlemaine, was flauntingly beautiful in her gown of lavender silk. Diamonds flashed from her ears and from the necklace about her long slender throat. She was, as usual, holding sway over a little group of admirers.

Despite her hatred of the woman, the Queen strove to be fair. Barbara's figure, though a little fuller than once it had been, was still perfectly shaped. There were lightly etched lines of dissipation in her face, but her hair flamed as brightly as ever, and she was still breathtaking to behold.

Catherine's hands clenched, remembering that the King still sent for my lady Castlemaine on the odd occasion. Though it was becoming increasingly rare for him to do so, Catherine nonetheless would have him finished with the woman once and for all. If she must share her husband, as it seemed she was fated to do, she would rather it be with any other than the hated Castlemaine.

Catherine looked at the King, her anger fading. He was not as handsome as my lord Benbrook and the blond Alex Barrymore, but for all that, his personality seemed to dominate the room. His dark curling wig touched his velvet-clad shoulders, and his sleepy-lidded eyes were still fixed upon Angel.

So intent was his regard, Catherine thought with a touch of satisfaction, that he did not even notice Frances Stuart, who was passing by, vividly lovely in her gown of rustling violet-blue silk. Frances curtsied to the King and Queen, then went on her way.

"Your Majesty does me too much honor," Catherine heard Angel say. "But, Sire, before I keep such an assignation, may I first request you to obtain the permission of my lord Benbrook."

"Think you he would give it, my lady?"

"He would not, Sire."

Charles chuckled. "Minx! Though I be the King, God pity me were I to ask my lord Benbrook's permission to bed his wife. Why, the arrogant rogue would think nothing of running me through, and well do you know it."

Angel joined in his laughter. "I fear 'tis all too true, Sire. Therefore would it be better to say nothing and to do nothing." Angel bit her lip as the King's fingers touched her face, traveling lightly downward and coming to rest upon her shoulders. "'Twould be England's loss," she added lightly, "were she to lose her most charming King."

There was a smoldering look in his dark eyes as he answered her. "And am I charming to you, my lady?"

"Indeed, Sire. And, I would imagine, to most women."

Charles shook his head sadly. "Well said, my lady. But I perceive that I am not yet charming enough. So I must bow my head in defeat, must I, my lady?"

"In this instance, yes, Sire. But for you there are many glorious victories ahead."

"Perhaps," he said gloomily. "But for me, the unobtainable has ever held the greatest fascination."

Charles looked away from her, turning his smiling eyes on the Queen. "Has it not, Madam?"

"I do believe it has, Sire."

"Come, Catherine," he said, holding out his hand to her. "Be not so aloof. I would have you by my side."

Catherine placed her hand in his, her heartbeat quickening as his lean fingers curled about her own. Someday, she thought, smiling up at him, if God be good, he will love only me.

Barbara Castlemaine's eyes narrowed as she viewed the scene from across the room. "Will you look at the King holding the Queen's hand," she said, nudging the man standing to her right. " 'Tis the perfect domestic picture. It quite touches the heart, does it not, Laurence?"

Sir Laurence Payne's pale gray eyes twinkled with frosty malice. "So it does. Are you jealous, my dear?"

"I pray you not to talk nonsense!" Barbara snapped open her white fan. "I declare you are as bad as Buckingham," she said coldly, fanning herself with brisk angry strokes. "Surely you will agree that it is laughable to see our Charles endeavor to play the epitome of the loving husband."

Sir Laurence's eyes lingered on Frances Stuart, laughing and gay, talking to the Duke of Richmond and Lennox. "You have many rivals, have you not, my poor Barbara?" he jibed. "But I think you need not fear the Queen, though I vow that she is quite radiant tonight."

Barbara's lips curled into a sneer. "For my part, I can only see that, as usual, she is dowdily dressed. Why in the name of the saints will she wear that particular shade of green? It makes her look so unpleasantly sallow."

"Nay." Sir Laurence hid a smile. "It seems to me to suit her quite well. As for the new Lady Benbrook, even you must agree that she is in excellent looks."

"That guttersnipe!" Barbara spoke venomously. She could never look at Angel without recalling that terrible time when, touring Newgate Prison, Angel had thrust her in with the screaming women prisoners. It was the fate she had privately reserved for Mistress Dawson. Had it not been for the interference of the black page, Pip, all would have gone well. Instead it had been she, not Angel, who had suffered. Aye, it was she who had all but been torn to pieces by the maddened women.

"The guttersnipe, if you must insist on calling her so," Sir Laurence murmured, "is very lovely." He shot a swift glance at Barbara's furious face. "Benbrook is a lucky man. Would that I were in his place."

Despite her beauty, Barbara was, as Buckingham had once told her, really very stupid. She did not discern that Sir Laurence was deliberately goading her into indiscreet speech. She tapped her foot impatiently. "I confess, Sir Laurence, that I cannot admire your taste. But the wench will get what she deserves. Benbrook is a cold man, he will undoubtedly freeze her to death. I would not care to be married to him."

"Would you not, my pet? Then 'tis strange indeed that the whole Court, including the King himself, knows of your consuming desire to bed yourself with that same cold Earl."

"Nay!" she lied, eyeing the little man resentfully. "You are a newcomer to Court, how come you to hear of this?" She snapped the fan closed. "I think I know. Buckingham has been spreading his malicious and lying gossip again."

Sir Laurence shook his head. " 'Tis common knowledge, though in your case, I would say that Benbrook is more elusive than aloof."

Barbara's fingers gripped the fan so hard that Sir Laurence distinctly heard the snapping of the delicate sticks. "If you are implying that I am in love with my lord Benbrook," she said in a low thick voice, "then you, sir, are quite mistaken!"

"But I would imply nothing so ludicrous. The tender emotion is not for such as you, dear Barbara. I have learned that the Countess of Castlemaine, though often the prey of her passions, loves only her very delectable self."

"How dare you, you impudent upstart! Buck will hear of this, and so I warn you! Be not surprised if he calls you out. 'Twould pleasure me to see you run through!"

"I have no doubt of that," Sir Laurence laughed. "But the Duke is much too lazy to concern himelf with his cousin's affairs. Like you, you see, he is concerned only with his own sacred person." Sir Laurence lifted his hand, stemming the tide of angry words she was about to pour forth. "Speaking of Buckingham," he said, nodding toward the double doors, "here he is now. And escorting a very pretty wench, I see."

Barbara stared at the girl clinging tightly to the Duke of Buckingham's arm, and her eyes widened incredulously. "Why, that damned fool!" she exclaimed. She whirled on Sir Laurence. "By God, does Buck really have the infernal insolence to present that slut to the King!"

" 'Twould seem so, would it not?" Sir Laurence eyed the girl appreciatively and gave vent to a low whistle. " 'Tis the darling of the boards. Little Nell Gwynne in person!"

Mistress Gwynne, as Sir Laurence had remarked, was very pretty. She had bright honey-colored curls that framed a piquant face. At this moment her large, bright blue eyes were gleaming with excitement, and her full ripe-looking mouth parted in a smile, showing deep dimples in delicately pink cheeks. She was dressed badly, however, in a startlingly green gown embellished with scallops of black lace.

Barbara's jaw dropped as she watched Buckingham making his leisurely way toward the King and Queen. Buckingham, to bring a play actress into the royal presence! He must have run mad. Unconsciously, Barbara was casting the licentious King in the role of a saint, and Buckingham, who was undoubtedly deserving of the name, as the devil.

Catherine became aware of the uneasiness in the room. She moved uneasily as she heard the murmurings all about her. She had not the slightest doubt that it had to do with Buckingham. What had the despicable man done now? She looked hard at the girl on the Duke's arm. A pretty creature, she decided, though execrably dressed.

From somewhere near at hand, a man's voice rose excitedly, "I tell you 'tis Nellie Gwynne! Aye, by God's teeth, 'tis the gutter actress!"

This, then, was Nell Gwynne? Catherine wondered. But what was she doing here? Was this Charles' way of sending for her, through the Duke? She looked quickly at the King. He was looking startled. Then he hadn't been party to this!

Catherine waited for the cold anger of which the good-natured Charles was sometimes capable. It did not come. She saw his lips curl into his familiar lazy smile. She should have known better. He would never allow a guest to be slighted; it was not his way.

"My lord Buckingham," Charles said, as they paused before him, "Mistress Gwynne. We are happy to see you here."

The Duke bowed, his expression faintly bored. But Nell Gwynne, unable to contain her simmering excitement, sank into a deep rustling curtsy.

The King's eyes lingered on her thrusting bosom, almost entirely revealed by her low-cut bodice. "Pray rise, Mistress Gwynne," he said at last, holding out his hand to her. "Allow me to assist you."

Enthusiastically, Nell grasped his hand. Bounding to her feet, she smiled brightly upon the Queen. Taking her stiffly extended hand, she bestowed upon her fingers a loud smacking kiss.

Catherine drew her hand away quickly. Then, against her will, she found herself responding to Mistress Gwynne's infectious smile.

"You are welcome here, Mistress Gwynne," Catherine said slowly and clearly.

Charles gave a quick start at her words. He had expected her displeasure, not her welcome to the actress. Her magnanimity was rewarded by Charles' approving nod.

Nell glanced round at her fascinated audience, her smile embracing them all. Here I am, she thought. *Me, Nell Gwynne, where I've always longed to be, with the bonny King! As for the rest of you, you can like me as I am, or a plague on you all!*

Nell's eyes were caught by one young woman who was staring at her in startled amazement. Was this the bride? Nell wondered. Lovely, she was, in her splendid white and silver gown, her shining hair peeping from beneath her pearl-embroidered cap. Aye, lovely, and somehow familiar. Where had she seen this great lady before? At the theater maybe? Walking on the street perhaps?

Nell looked back at the King. He was staring at her with his intensely dark and sleepy eyes. Her mouth went dry as she recalled her vow to become the mistress of Charles II of England. Perhaps the tide of her fortune was about to turn. Perhaps—exciting thought—she would shortly achieve her dearest dream. 'Twould be so easy to fall in love with the charming royal Stuart.

When Nell had made her entrance, Angel had not at first recognized her. Then, when the King had spoken her name aloud, her impulse had been to rush forward and make herself known. It was because of Nicholas that she had restrained herself. What would he say were she to do such a thing? Would his sense of correctness be offended if she claimed acquaintance? Would he be coldly displeased?

"Well, my lady wife," Nicholas said from behind her. "Do you not wish to bid Mistress Gwynne welcome?"

She turned quickly to face him. "I thought—thought perhaps you would object."

He took her hand in his. "I would prefer that you cease to regard me as an ogre, my love. For indeed, where you are concerned, I am nothing of the sort."

"Oh, darling, I have never thought of you as an ogre."

"But of course you have. And there will no doubt be occasions when you will revert to your previous belief. A man cannot change too quickly, I fear."

Angel glanced across at Nell Gwynne. "Then you really will not mind if I speak with Nell?"

Nicholas sighed and shook his head reprovingly. "My

darling, I have been accused of many things in my time, but never yet of snobbery."

"Oh, Nicholas, my dearest, I'm ashamed. I should have known that for myself."

"Aye, you should. But I must pray you not to look at me in quite that way, brat. Else will our wedding celebration end before it has properly begun."

"It cannot be too soon for me," she whispered. "I love you!"

He eyed her with a sternness that was belied by the look in his eyes. "Aye, Mistress Immodesty, I know that you do, but you must be content to wait for tonight." He pressed her hand. "When, you may be sure, I will amply demonstrate how very much I return that love." Smiling, Nicholas extended his arm. "Shall we greet Mistress Gwynne? Our wedding would not be complete without her felicitations, would it?"

She looked at him quickly, suspecting sarcasm. "Nay, brat," Nicholas said softly, reading her mind as he so often did. "Mistress Gwynne helped you when you needed help, therefore is she also my friend."

"Yes, my lord." Her fingers tightened on his arm. "Your pardon, husband, but did I remember to tell you how much I love you?"

"You did, my lady. Not once, but many times."

The boyish smile that Angel had come to look for warmed his austere face. "Such conversation on your part," he went on lightly, "based as it is on your idolatry of myself, could never grow dull."

He was laughing at her just a little, she knew. When others were present, he must ever seek to hide his true self behind a slightly mocking façade. But tonight, when they were alone, she would rediscover the warm and loving Nicholas. She had found that he could sometimes be highly emotional where his deeper feelings were concerned. He was tender, too, deeply sensitive and sincere. Aye, he was very different from the man others knew, from the man whom she had once thought she knew.

"Buckingham, I fear," Nicholas said, leading her

110

forward, "will be vastly disappointed with our reactions. If I read him aright, Mistress Gwynne's presence was intended to cause us acute embarrassment. But it will do nothing of the sort, will it, my lady?"

Angel's eyes sparkled. "Quite the contrary."

Buckingham bowed as they came to a standstill before him. "Ah, my lord Benbrook," he said silkily, "my lady Benbrook. May I offer to you my sincere congratulations. I wish you happy indeed."

"We thank you for your good wishes," Nicholas said, unsmiling, "and we accept your congratulations."

With a polite inclination of his head, Nicholas took a step forward.

"My lord," the Duke said hastily, placing a restraining hand on his arm. "I would introduce a dear friend of mine." Lifting his hand, the Duke beckoned Nell forward.

Nicholas looked into Nell Gwynne's flushed and excited face, his eyes faintly smiling.

"My lord Benbrook, my lady," the Duke said. "May I present Mistress Nell Gwynne."

"Mistress Gwynne," Nicholas bowed over her hand. " 'Tis an honor."

Staring into the Earl's dark, haughty face, Nell was momentarily disconcerted. Then, seeing the soft look in the dark eyes regarding her, she brightened.

"Thank you, m'lord," Nell said. She looked at Angel intently. "Begging your pardon for staring, m'lady, but I thought perhaps I knew you. I see now that I was mistaken." Nell turned her sparkling smile on Nicholas. "But I know you, m'lord, as who doesn't. I seen you lots of times. You're the 'vanishing Earl,' ain't—I—I mean aren't you?"

"I have been called so, Mistress Gwynne."

"There!" Nell exclaimed, "Fancy that! I never thought as I'd meet you, m'lord."

Angel was fascinated by Nell. Her rough voice had gentled with the years, but there were still unmistakable traces of the little cockney girl who had been her only

111

friend. What had happened to Rose, she wondered, and Madam Gwynne?

Feeling Nicholas's fingers on her arm, prompting her to speech, Angel said quickly, "Have you forgotten me, then, Nell? I'm Angel, Angel Dawson." She smiled into Buckingham's incredulous face. "Mistress Gwynne and I have been friends these many years, Your Grace."

Nell appeared to be struck dumb. "A—Angel," she stammered at last, the shrill note in her voice attracting the attention of those about them. "Why it ain't never you, is it?"

"It is, Nell. I am so happy to see you here."

"And I, Mistress Gwynne," Nicholas said. "May I hope that my wife's friend will also consider herself to be mine?"

"But—but—but—" Nell looked at them helplessly. "Go on, 'tain't so! How could it be? If you're Angel Dawson, how come you to be married to *him?*" Nell stopped short, struck by a sudden thought. "But then again, if you ain't Angel Dawson, how'd you know about 'er?"

"Exactly." Nicholas said. "She is—or was—Angel Dawson. She is now my lady Benbrook."

"Well I never!" Nell's eyes softened appreciatively as she stared into the Earl's handsome face.

Angel became aware of the shocked glances about them, of amused eyes, malicious eyes, and the babbling of many tongues. She was suddenly very happy. She was Nicholas's Angel, and if he made nothing of it, why should they? She was about to address a further remark to Nell, but restrained herself as she saw the people parting to make way for the King. He came slowly toward them through the lane of curtsying women and bowing men.

"Well done, my lady," the King said, as Angel rose from her curtsy. He turned to Nicholas. "There are many sides to you," he said in a low voice, placing his arm about the Earl's shoulders, "but this one, I confess, I much appreciate."

Nicholas's brows rose quizzically. "I thank Your Majesty. But I had dared to hope that you had discovered this side of me long since."

Charles laughed. "Well so I did, curse you. But how can I give recognition when you so earnestly seek to hide your finer points? I would have you know, my lord Benbrook, that you are generally looked upon to be a sullen and damnably icy fellow."

"Hardly sullen, Your Majesty," Nicholas murmured. "Disagreeable perhaps, but sullen I cannot accept."

"Have it your own way, my lord." The King's eyes gleamed as he saw Angel's face. "My lady is looking indignant," he laughed, pinching her cheek. "I fear I have offended her, friend Nicholas. Wilt forgive me, my lady Angel?"

"Indeed, Your Majesty."

"Ah," Charles exclaimed. "But I see by the flash in your eyes that you resent this slur upon your lord. Is it not so?"

"Did I truly believe it to be a slur, I would resent it," Angel answered him. "But knowing Your Majesty's affection for my lord, I cannot believe you meant it as such."

"Baggage!" The King stroked her cheek with gentle fingers. Then, his smile disappearing, he turned to the discomfited Duke of Buckingham. "We read your mind all too easily, my lord," the King said coldly. "Therefore, since we know you have been forced to neglect your many duties in order to attend this wedding celebration, we are ashamed to have so discommoded you. You are excused, my lord of Buckingham."

The King waited, unmoved, as Buckingham made his bow. His face resentful, the Duke walked away, his shoulders squared defiantly. Then Charles turned on his high red heels to face Nell Gwynne. "Come, Mistress Gwynne," the King said, holding out his arm, "you may talk to Lady Benbrook later. But in the meantime there is something I would show you." He patted the small hand she had placed on his arm. "You know, Mistress Gwynne," he said, walking away, "the Queen and I have oft times enjoyed you in your delicious farces."

Nell's blue eyes worshipped him. "But as yet, Your Majesty, I am only allowed to play minor roles."

"Small parts can grow amazingly large," the King said softly.

Nell sent him a mischievous glance. "Your Majesty has not forgotten Nell Gwynne, I see."

"Have I not said that you intrigued me?"

"Oh, I don't mean in the theater, Your Majesty. I seen you there many times o' course, and I've often wished you'd speak to me. Like you was interested, I mean. Same as what you are in Moll Davis of the Duke's Theatre."

The King choked. Hurriedly, he drew his lace kerchief from his sleeve and pressed it to his lips. He was amazed at the frankness of her speech, but at the same time, amused and diverted.

"Y—you do not care for Mistress Davis?" he said in a voice that quivered on the edge of laughter. " 'Twould seem that I detected a disparaging note when you spoke her name."

"No," Nell said instantly. "I don't care nothing for her at all. Begging Your Majesty's pardon, and hoping as you'll excuse me if I speaks me mind about Moll. But she's a clumsy great cow, that's what she is!"

"I see." The King struggled to compose his features. "But if you did not mean the theater, sweet Nell," he said, changing the subject, "where did we meet?"

"Don't you remember, Your Majesty?"

"Gallantry prompts me to tell you that I could never forget you, Mistress Gwynne, but—" His fingers traced little patterns on her arm, and Nell's susceptible heart jumped in response—"but," he went on, "I must confess myself puzzled. Pray explain yourself, Nell."

"It was on the day of the parade," Nell burst out. "The Royal Parade, Your Majesty."

She saw his eyes narrow in thought, and she went on quickly. " 'Twas the day that me and Angel—I mean my lady Benbrook, stopped the parade." She stopped short again. "I just can't get over her being my lady Benbrook. How'd it happen, Your Majesty? About Angel, I mean?"

" 'Tis a long story," Charles said, his finger absently stroking his mustache. He looked at her intently. "I make no doubt that my lady Benbrook will explain all to you."

"Aye, Majesty. Me and Angel stopped the parade, all right. We spoke to you, too. But there, I don't suppose you'd remember."

Charles' mind went back to that warm May day of six years before. He saw the soldiers standing stiffly at attention, ringing two slight figures. One, a child with tangled honey-gold curls and a dimpled smiling face. The other, taller, her face yellowed as if from a long illness. Lovely, he had thought the taller girl. Aye, he remembered now. 'Twas strange, but with all the incidents crowding his life one would have supposed he would have forgotten that small incident. But oddly enough, perhaps because it had been part of his welcome back to England he had not.

Charles snapped his fingers. "You!" he cried, his face lighting up. "You were that child! And the other girl was—no, by God! I don't believe it."

Nell giggled delightedly. "But 'tis true, Your Majesty. The other girl was Angel."

" 'Pon my soul! That is one thing friend Nicholas omitted to mention."

"Aye, Majesty. I said to you—"

"Wait!" Charles grasped her arm tightly. "You said—Aye, you said 'Don't forget Nell Gwynne.' Am I right?"

The irrepressible Nell spun round on her toes, her wide green skirts ballooning about her. "That's exactly what I said, Majesty. How ever did you remember? I never really expected you to."

"I don't know." Charles shook his head. "But I did, Mistress Gwynne, I did. You know, Nell, I have the feeling you'll be good for me. I must see more of you."

Gazing into his dark eyes, fringed by thick, short, black lashes, Nell said impulsively, "Good for you, and good to you, Majesty. And it won't be just because you're the King, neither."

Charles' cynical smile showed briefly, then he said softly, "I think I believe you, Mistress Gwynne. 'Tis strange indeed that I should do so, for I have rarely found the protestations of females to be truthful."

Charles had the oddest feeling that he had known her for a long time. She was a child in years, barely seventeen, he guessed correctly, yet she seemed older. There was something about her that was—aye, was almost motherly. Nell would be different, he was sure of it. She would not be greedily demanding as was the Castlemaine and his various other mistresses. She would not, when displeased, plague him with a shrill and ugly voice. Nell's concern, he felt hopefully, would be for the man, not for the king strewing gifts.

Charles smiled with a hint of self-derision. He must be mad. After all, what did he really know of Mistress Gwynne? Nevertheless, he decided firmly, he would see her again. He thought of the elusive Frances Stuart; of Angel, who had placed herself beyond his reach, for he could not in honor pursue her now; and of that other blonde and golden-skinned beauty, Mary Foxfield, in whom he was increasingly interested. He'd send for Mistress Gwynne, of course, but not yet. Perhaps at some time in the future.

Nell looked at him with dazzled eyes. Was this really she, Nell Gwynne, walking with her arm entwined in that of the King? Her eyes traveled over his tall, velvet-clad and jeweled person, at the foam of lace at his wrists that caressed her thin childlike arm; his strong, gem-laden fingers were gripping hers, and her heart began to beat high in her throat. Charles, she said silently, Charles, Charles Stuart. Oh, I could love you! I could really love you, you magnificent Stuart!

Charles stopped walking. "Sir Peter," he called, beckoning to a tall burly man clad unsuitably for one of his bulk, in pale blue satin trimmed with beige lace.

Sir Peter Lely's heavy face lighted up as he came swiftly toward them. "Your Majesty," he said, bowing to the King. Even as he made the obeisance, his eyes were on Nell Gwynne's face.

Noting the look, the King said, "Charming, is she not, Sir Peter?"

"Charming indeed, Sire."

Sir Peter placed a pudgy finger beneath Nell's chin, tilting her face. "She is to me different," he pronounced. He stuck out his full lower lip. "Aye, she is to me paintable."

The King laughed. "You must forgive him, Mistress Gwynne. Sir Peter at this moment is concerned only with your hues and tints. Ah, Lely, methinks you view people as paintable or unpaintable. Do you never think of anything else?"

Lely beamed. "But of course, Sire. Sometimes I think of the good food and the wine. Sometimes I think of women for the making of love." He paused, shaking his head. "But perhaps you are right, Sire, for mostly do I think of the painting."

"I must congratulate you again on your portrait of my lady Benbrook. It is quite, quite brilliant."

Sir Peter smiled. "It is, is it not," he said, without the smallest attempt at modesty. "Sometimes I have to wonder, Sire, how I managed to make of the portrait the finish. My lady Benbrook was difficult." He drew in his breath sharply. "She was the she-devil, who would not listen and obey."

"A pity," Charles said gravely. " 'Twas a revolt against tyranny, do you think?"

Sir Peter's eyes opened wide. "But me, I am not the tyrant, Sire! No, no, I am a man of the great kindliness."

"Until thwarted." Charles laughed. "Fence not with me, Sir Peter. I know your reputation."

"As you say, Sire." The big man's eyes clouded, and

he looked like a hurt child. "I do the best I can," he said, "but when my lady loses the temper with me, I am determined not to finish the portrait. But I am fair, so I go back."

"And the result is beautiful," Charles said consolingly. "We would like to view the portrait, Sir Peter." He glanced at Nell. "And perhaps in time, we will arrange for Mistress Gwynne to sit for you."

"Me!" Nell's eyes went round. "Me sit for Sir Peter Lely! Oh, Sire, 'twould be wonderful! Why him and my lord Benbrook are the ones what paint all the great ladies!"

Lely, completely mollified by this artless admiration, smiled upon her. "You I will love to paint, Mistress Gwynne." He turned to the King. "This way, if you please, Sire. The painting has been placed in the anteroom."

"All have viewed it?" the King said, moving forward.

"All, Sire, save Mistress Gwynne. My lord Benbrook was warm in his congratulations. He said of me that I am the greater painter. But of the two, I believe that he is the greater. Do you not agree, Sire?"

This inquiry was accompanied by a side glance, and Charles instantly perceived the danger. "I confess that I am not qualified to judge," he said smoothly. "It is a question you must ask of a learned man of the arts. By his decision you must stand or fall."

Lely seemed about to argue this, but by the time he had marshalled his thoughts, they had reached the anteroom. Bowing, Lely stepped to one side.

For a long time Nell stood before the canvas, saying nothing. She gazed at the portrait, a rapt expression on her face. "Oh!" she breathed once. "Oh!"

It was almost as though Angel were present in the room. She sat serenely on the velvet-covered dais, her yellow skirts frothing about small, yellow-slippered feet. The portrait seemed to Nell to breathe and move. There was vivid life in the sidelong glance of her smiling violet-blue eyes, in the mouth that, half parted, trembled on the verge of laughter. Her piled-up hair gleamed with fiery lights, and the single curl that lay upon her shoulder appeared to rise and fall with the movements of her breathing.

"Oh!" Nell said again, turning to Lely. "It's so beautiful!"

"I am glad you like." He patted her blonde curls. "One day, I think, I will show to the world Mistress Gwynne. You would like, eh?"

Nell clasped her hands together in an ecstasy that had nothing of affectation in it. "Oh, Sire," she said, looking at the King, "if I could be painted by Sir Peter Lely, I believe I—I really believe I would die of happiness!"

"But I wish you to live, little Nellie," Charles teased. "Therefore would it be better not to record your looks, charming though they are."

Nell looked crestfallen. "But 'tis only a saying, Your Majesty. I would not really die."

"Of course you would not." Laughing, Charles put his arm about her drooping shoulders. "Lely shall paint you, Nell. But I make no promises as to when."

"Oh, thank you!"

"Wilt give me a kiss, Nell?"

Nell's cheeks dimpled. "I am willing, Majesty. But he who would kiss Nell Gwynne must claim that kiss for himself."

She did not see Lely go quietly from the room. She was only conscious of feeling. Charles' arms were about her, his lips, urgent and demanding, were on her own. And what she felt was a tingling in her body, a singing in her veins, and a breathless happiness that made her wish to surrender herself completely to this man—now, this very instant.

When Charles finally let her go, she was dizzy and trembling.

"Oh, yes," Charles said, taking her hand and leading her from the room. "Oh yes, Nell, you generous little soul, I would see more of you. Much, much more!"

The Queen's eyes were shadowed and unhappy as she watched them approach. She knew that look on her husband's face meant that he had plans for Mistress Nellie. And she, if one could go by the look on the girl's face, would eagerly anticipate and enjoy her seduction.

Catherine looked about her. She saw the flower-banked room, the hundreds of candles, flickering frail yellow tongues of flame, ensconced in their silver holders; the colorful turning figures of the dancers proceeding to the graceful measure of a minuette, and across the room the Earl of Benbrook, believing himself to be unobserved, was holding Lady Benbrook's hand.

Catherine felt a painful lump in her throat. If only Charles would look at her as the Earl was looking at his lady!

"Madam, you look sad." Charles' voice caused Catherine to start. "Is aught amiss?"

Catherine smiled at him. "Nothing, Sire."

"Good. Then, Madam, here is Mistress Gwynne to bear us company."

Only Catherine's dark eyes showed her hurt. "How pleasant, Sire," she said quietly. "I am happy to have the opportunity of speaking with Mistress Gwynne."

Nell's smile was wide and friendly. "Thank you, Your Majesty. 'Tis kind of you."

"Will you not be seated, Mistress Gwynne?"

Nell obeyed with alacrity, settling herself in the chair beside the Queen. She was very conscious of Charles' tall figure standing before them, but she did her best to concentrate on the Queen's voice.

"I have seen you on the stage," the Queen was saying, "but I did not immediately recognize you when you entered with the Duke. Pray forgive me."

"Why bless you, Madam," Nell said heartily, "that's all right. We all look different on the stage."

"I particularly like your little dances," Catherine said in her soft voice.

"If Your Majesty wishes, I will perform especially for you."

"Thank you."

Nell's wise eyes studied the Queen's face. *Poor little*

120

lady, she thought, *she loves him so much. Well, even if I become the King's mistress, I'll try never to hurt her. I'll not make her too much aware of it, as some of the others probably do. I don't want to hurt anyone, and least of all her, I just want to be loved by Charles. It was meant to be. I was born just to love him, and I knew it from the first moment I set my eyes on him.*

Angel watched Nell talking to the Queen, her face eager, her honey-gold head held proudly high.

"Look, my lord," Angel said, smiling at Nicholas. "The King shows much interest in Nell. I believe she will make a place for herself at Court."

"Aye, Charles would not have it any other way. And this time, if he presents Mistress Gwynne with his ring, it will have the true meaning."

"You mean it will not have the innocence it did when worn upon my finger?"

"Exactly. Though there are times when I still wonder."

"Nicholas!"

"Nay, love, I do but tease."

"With so grave and unsmiling a face?"

"What, art not used to my looks by now?"

"Nay, how could I be? One moment you look like a winter's storm, and the next moment, as now, like a pleasant summer's day."

"Is it so? Pray forgive me for such a bewildering climate."

"I forgive you, my lord. For in all your seasons, you are always so very handsome."

"Pshaw!" Nicholas took her by the arm and drew her into the shadows cast by the banked flowers. "Prattle not of looks, my lady Benbrook. 'Tis time to kiss your husband."

She put her arms about his neck. "Is it a command?"

"You may make of it anything you wish, as long as you kiss me instantly."

"A small kiss, perhaps."

"I fear, my lady, that a small kiss will not suffice."

He drew her into his arms, pressing his lips to hers.

"Angel!" he said, raising his head. "I love you, my little one!"

"And I love you, my dearest." She frowned faintly. "Oh, Nicholas, are we never to be alone?"

"Such impatience, madam, is scarce seemly." He touched her cheek gently with his finger. "For shame, brat!"

"I am not in the least ashamed." She caught his hand in hers and pressed her lips to it. "I remember, Nicholas, in those days when you were teaching me to be a lady, how you used to touch my cheek if I had done something worthy of praise. I didn't know then if I loved or hated you, but I do know how I felt when you touched me."

"And how did you feel?"

"As if—as if I were melting inside. I wanted to do more and more to please you, so that you would touch me again." She hesitated then added almost shyly, "When —when you smiled at me, and you so rarely did, it was as if the sun was shining inside me."

"Oh, Angel!" His arms tightened. "I have so much love to give you!"

She could feel the trembling of his body against her own. She said softly, "I accept your love, my lord. Providing you will give back to me all the love you once denied me. Will you?"

"I will. But it works both ways, you know, brat. What of yourself? You should have made known your feelings for me, should you not?"

"How could I, when I did not know what was causing me to be so disturbed that I trembled in your presence?"

"Nonetheless, you should have known."

She laughed. "And if I had said to you, 'I love you, my dear lord Benbrook,' you would have frowned at me, and said, 'Pray do not be ridiculous, Mistress Dawson; resume your studies at once.'"

"Perhaps. But let us talk of the future, not the past."

Her lips touched his mouth softly, lingeringly. "Yes, dear m'lord."

ELM PARK MANOR, A PROPERTY OWNED BY Nicholas but little used, was the place where Angel had decided they should spend the first four weeks of their married life. London was crowded with people whom they knew. But here at the Manor they would be undisturbed. Only Mrs. Sampson and two of the more trusted servants were now in residence.

"We do not need more servants." Angel had told Nicholas, boldly overriding his protests. Her firmness had brought an involuntary smile to his lips. "We will not wish to be inundated with callers at this very special time, will we, my lord?"

"Nay," he had answered her gravely. "Elm Park Manor is quite suitable for the purpose I have in mind. If I desire to beat my wife, as seems likely in view of the rebellious spirit she is displaying of late, I may do so in a decent privacy."

"Indeed! If my lord wishes a poor and spiritless person for a wife, why does he not say so?"

The Manor House, lying just outside London, was situated in rolling parklike grounds. It was the haunt of wild game; birds plundered its orchards undisturbed. Deer, their wild soft eyes tranquil and free from fear, wandered there freely. In the days before the Restoration, the house was said to have sheltered the wounded

Prince Charles. For three long weeks he had taken refuge there, while outside, Cromwell's soldiers, believing the house to be empty, had passed by frequently. Sometimes they had drilled in the grounds, shouting rough friendly epithets at one another. But not once, doubtless because it was reputed to be haunted, had Cromwell's superstitious soldiers attempted to enter the quiet and seemingly deserted manor.

During those tense weeks, so the story went, the Prince had been tended by the Earl of Benbrook, himself wounded and more than half delirious. Adam Nichols, a loyal Royalist supporter, was said to have smuggled food in to them.

Nicholas, when Angel inquired, had promptly discounted the story. "Nonsense!" he had said. " 'Tis but the usual gossip that has ever surrounded the King and myself. We are but human, brat, and were we to have done half 'tis said we have done, 'twould surely be miraculous."

Smiling, Angel had nodded her head in agreement. But privately she believed the house had sheltered Nicholas and the Prince. Nicholas, she firmly believed, could accomplish miracles. Had he not proved it in the case of herself?

The sprawling place was dear to Angel's heart. It was ivy-hung with unexpected curves and oddly angled wings. Flowers clustered close against its sun-faded red bricks, bright splashes of color that sent a mingled subtle fragrance into the deserted rooms. Tonight, as the carriage stopped before its heavy oaken doors, the house was bright with candlelight, blooming yellow through its many windows. It looked friendly, Angel thought, warm and intimately welcoming.

Mrs. Sampson waited to greet them on the broad marble torchlit steps. She seemed to be shaken out of her customary composure. Her white lace cap was askew on her severely brushed iron-gray hair, and her usually dour face wore a beaming smile.

124

"My lord Benbrook, my lady Benbrook," Mrs. Sampson said in a muffled voice.

Her black gown rustling, she attempted a small dignified curtsy. Then, to Nicholas's amusement, casting dignity aside, she flew at Angel. " 'Tis a wonderful day, dear child!" She embraced her fiercely, holding her with thin trembling arms. "A wonderful, wonderful day! I know you will make my lad happy."

"Sampson." Nicholas tapped her arm lightly with the small swagger stick he was carrying. "I am loathe to remind you of my presence, but I would point out that I am here, too. And since when have I become my lord Benbrook to you?"

Mrs. Sampson turned to him. "I was about to greet you, Master Nickey. And may I say," she went on, with a slight return to her old brisk manner, "that I hope I know when to observe the formalities."

"Oh, is that what you were doing?" Nicholas laughed. "You are a fraud, Sampson. You have nursed me, punished me, poured your vile concoctions down my throat until I retched at the taste. You have, in general, exerted a formidable tyranny over my blameless and innocent self. So shall I now be to you my lord Benbrook?"

She touched his shoulder with a fond hand. " 'Twas all done for your own good, Master Nickey. You were that stubborn when you were a little lad, and that set on having your own way." She nodded at Angel. "Aye, and he hasn't changed much, has he?" She smiled. "But you've met your match now, Master Nickey. My lady will keep you in order, I'm thinking."

Angel gave a mock shudder. "Never believe it, Mrs. Sampson," she said, laughing across at Nicholas. " 'Twould be sacrilege should I so far forget myself as to attempt to tame my lord. I would not dare to do so, unless I wished to bring down on my head the most dire punishment."

"It is so," Nicholas answered calmly. "And furthermore, Sampson, I intend to remain as evil and as stubborn as ever. Also, should I deem it to be necessary for the proper humbling of my wife's soul, I shall chastise her brutally and regularly."

Disregarding the rest of his words, Mrs. Sampson shot Angel a sharp, suspicious look. "Who said you were evil? I'm sure that I never did."

Consideringly, Nicholas rubbed his chin with the silver tip of the swagger stick. "On a great many occasions you have referred to me as a young limb of Satan."

"I'm sure I never did!" Mrs. Sampson said indignantly. "Oh, all right, Master Nickey, if you say. But I've no doubt you deserved it."

"Oh, I did." Nicholas's rare smile touched his lips. "But have you no greeting for the unhappy bridegroom?"

She took his hands in hers, then, releasing them, suddenly threw her arms about his neck. "I wish you happy, my dear, dear boy! I know well that you dislike sentiment, lad, so do I, as a rule, but I take this opportunity to tell you that I love you very much."

"Nay, Sampson, you wrong me. If it be sincere sentiment, then I like it very much."

He put both arms about her, holding her close. "I know you love me, Sampson, and I, in case I have forgotten to mention it, love you in return." He touched her cheek with the back of his hand. "What's this? Tears? Plague take you, woman! Would you ruin my jacket with your infernal sniffling!"

"Ah, that's more like my Master Nickey." Grateful to him for the intervention, she drew away from him, hurriedly composing her features. "And I am not crying," she said acidly. "You know that I never cry."

"Do you not? What a damned odd creature you are, then!"

"No swearing, Master Nickey. I simply cannot abide it."

"I beg your pardon." Nicholas caught Angel's hand in his. "You are smiling, I see, brat. But lest my unwonted

126

meekness go to your head, I would remind you that I will still be master in my home."

"Did I need such a reminder, my lord," Angel answered, "then I would indeed be the dull head you have so often called me."

"But you are a dull head, and to prove it, you have married me."

"Then," Angel said demurely, "I pray I may ever remain so."

"And I, my dear," he said, a shadow touching his face. "And I."

Majestically, the housekeeper led the way to the door, her keys clinking at her belt.

"Master Nickey," Mrs. Sampson said in a low voice, as he entered the wide hall. "You're not tired, are you, lad?"

Nicholas saw Angel's anxious eyes on him, and he shook his head in reassurance. "Nay, Sampson," he answered, regarding the woman's face with faintly smiling eyes, "I wish you would get rid of this abominable conviction of yours that I am a small boy who must be comforted and cosseted. Just for this once, Sampson, oblige me by bridling that clucking tongue of yours. I am tired, but pleasantly so."

"I'm sure I'm very glad to hear it, my lord," Mrs. Sampson answered loftily. "And now, if you will excuse me, I'll be seeing about the dinner."

Nicholas ran exasperated fingers through his thick black hair. "Sampson, if you call me my lord again, you will soon be seeking another situation. Do you hear me?"

Mrs. Sampson smiled at him. "At my age? For shame, lad!" She moved slowly toward the door at the back of the hall. "If I may borrow words from my lady Benbrook," she said, "yes dear m'lord, I hear you."

When the door had closed behind her, Angel laughed. "She means well. You mustn't be unkind to her."

"Ah, but you see, brat, she expects little else from me.

Were I to start cooing and smiling at her, she would think me suffering from a fever."

Nicholas took her by the hand and led her into a large bright room on the right of the hall. The room was bright with firelight, and redolent with the mingled scents of crackling apple logs and the flowers with which the room was lavishly decorated.

Nicholas seated himself upon the sofa and pulled Angel down beside him. She had already discarded her blue cloak, and in the coach she had loosened her hair, knowing that he liked it that way.

She was so beautiful, Nicholas thought, regarding her with a touch of wonder, and unspoiled, despite the example of the avarice and insatiable ambition that prevailed at Court. Firelight touched her hair, bringing out its fiery glints. She was looking at him, and one half of her face was in shadow, but he could see her eyes clearly. The look in them moved him unbearably, so soft they were, so wide and bright with love.

"Come here, my brat," he said huskily. He put his arms about her. "My darling, must we really eat this dinner that Sampson has prepared?"

"I fear so."

"Another fault of mine," he said, kissing her softly on the mouth, "is that I am cursed impatient."

She returned the kiss, then drew his head down to rest against her shoulder. "For myself," she said, her hand caressing his hair, "I could not eat a morsel. But we must make the effort, else will Mrs. Sampson be sorely disappointed."

"I suppose so," he said resignedly. "But you must make me a promise, Madam." Nicholas picked up her left hand, examining the wide gold band on her marriage finger. "That ring makes you all mine, you know. Forget it not, wench. As to the promise, it is only that you will not dally unduly over the meal."

"I promise faithfully, love."

He sat up straight. Taking her hand in his, he held it

very tightly. "And what of the other promises you made this day? Will you always love me, Angel?"

She looked at him searchingly. The habit of mistrust had grown up with him; it could not be lightly dismissed. "Always," she said very gently. "Hast looked into the mirror of late, love? If you have done so, you will see the handsome Lord Benbrook looking back at you. Why, I vow you could have any woman at the lifting of your finger."

"I see only Lady Benbrook. And she is far too beautiful for my peace of mind." He put his head back against her shoulder. "Oh, Angel!" he said in a choked voice. "Life can be so damnably unfair. Once I had so much to offer you, but now there is so little time! So very little!"

Her arms cradled him close. "You must not say that, I won't let you. We have an infinity of time, my darling!"

"Aye, perhaps we have, who knows?" He kissed her neck, his breathing quickening. "Oh, brat, I love you so!"

She stirred uneasily at the note in his voice. "Then tell me so in your old manner," she demanded. "In the way that is usual to my Nicholas. Abruptly, dear m'lord, as if you were conferring a favor on me to tell me so at all. Arrogantly, in the way that once caused me to bridle in outrage."

He laughed. "I understand you not."

"Sometimes," she said, looking into the fire, "when you are very tender, it hurts me in my heart. I do not know why, my lord, save that in you tenderness seems always to be mingled with an underlying sadness."

"I had not noticed it. Do you tell me, then, that you are content to spend your life without tenderness?"

She shook her head. "By no means, dear m'lord. Tonight, in our bedchamber, you may be as tender as you please."

"Enough." He put a hand over her mouth, cutting off her words. "I would be loathe to start off our married life by giving you the sound trouncing that you deserve."

He took his hand away, smiling at her. "When my only intention is to love you, brat. To love you as passionately as ever you may desire."

"Oh do, Nicholas! Do!"

A tap sounded on the door. " 'Tis Sampson come to announce dinner," Nicholas said, frowning. "Confound her!"

He rose to his feet. "One hour," he said meaningly. "Remember it, my lady, else will you be sorry."

When Angel finally entered the bedchamber, Nicholas was standing by the window, his back toward her. He seemed to be completely engrossed with the darkness outside.

She studied his tall straight figure in his plain black dressing robe, and remembered another time when she had seen him thus. Only then he had been facing her, and she but a servant in his house. Her duty had been to make his bed. The Earl of Benbrook had stood there, looming above her and frowning at her efforts to pick up the bedsheets which she had dropped in her alarm at coming upon him so unexpectedly. He had seemed, then, to be as far above her as the stars in the heavens.

"Nicholas," she said softly, smiling at the memory.

He did not turn. "Come here," he said, holding out his hand. "Do you hear that owl?" he asked. " 'Tis loud in its hooting, is it not?"

"Aye." Angel studied his profile with loving eyes. 'Twas strange that he, always so calm and sure of himself, should exhibit this shyness when it came to herself. "But, dear m'lord," she said, touching his arm. "I am not interested in owls."

His eyes studied her. The candlelight was behind her, and her body in the tissue-thin negligee was clearly outlined. He felt a constriction in his throat. "You do not prefer the subject of owls?"

"Nay, my lord. Do you? If so, I will discuss them with you at great length. The owl, in its mating season, will always—"

He swept her up in his arms and held her fiercely close.

"Curse the owl and its mating season, you impudent little guttersnipe. Angel, damn you, I love you! I love you, do you hear me, wench? And I care not if you refuse my tenderness!"

He made an inarticulate sound, then he was carrying her to the wide bed. He laid her down gently.

When he disrobed, it was her turn to be shy. She flushed, conscious of her own nakedness, then her small attack of modesty was swallowed up in a surge of love.

"Nicholas!" she whispered, holding out her arms to him. "My darling!"

He was like a boy in love for the first time. Gone was his cynical caution, his cool reserve. His lips touched her hair, her face, her eyes, her breasts, the throbbing hollow in her throat. His fingers caressed her, sending little shocks of delight through her trembling body. She sobbed out his name, her body responding eagerly to his. "Oh, Nicholas, Nicholas, I love you!"

Later, as he lay sleeping beside her, she put an arm about him and held him close. The candlelight, left to burn, showed her the thick black semicircles of his lashes, the clustering of the dark curls upon his forehead, and the shadowed hollows beneath his high cheekbones.

She had feared that he would be exhausted, but he did not seem to be. She noted, with relief, that his breathing was even, his sleep deep and natural. For the first time she allowed herself to hope.

He shivered in his sleep. She covered him quickly and snuggled down beside him. *You'll not die, Nicholas. I won't let you! You must live for me!*

He turned over on his side, muttering something beneath his breath. Fearful of waking him, she held herself very still.

Dawn came, and Angel still had not slept. She lay on her back, watching the gray sky flush with a soft rose-pink circled with an edging of light green. Flaming colors came trailing across the sky, until the whole met and merged in a burst of vivid breathtaking beauty.

"Angel." Nicholas stirred restlessly, putting out a

groping hand. "W—where are you?" There was a break in his voice. "Don't leave me. I need you, brat!"

She looked at his closed eyes, the frown between his brows, then she took his hand and held it tightly in hers. "You do but dream, dear m'lord," she soothed. "I'm here beside you."

PUDDING LANE WAS QUIET AT ONE O'CLOCK in the morning. The hawkers who, in the daytime, ran over the dirty cobbles raucously crying their wares, were all in bed, seeking a well-earned rest. Save for one skinny cat, who was busily engaged in scratching the lice from its dingy gray fur, the silence and emptiness were complete.

A full moon silvered the tall houses edging both sides of the narrow alley. In the moonlight, they seemed to lean forward even more precariously, their eaves almost touching their neighbors across the street. They made an ominously frowning picture etched against the star-spattered sky.

The occupants of the houses slept. Some, having laid their cares aside for a few hours, slept serenely; others, who had taken their worries to bed with them, uneasily, moaning below their breath, their bodies twitching. Fortunately, though, they were unconscious of the urgent scrabbling of the rats and the piercing cries of children which, now and again, sundered the silence of the night. A few lay awake; they were concerned with sad thoughts, happy thoughts, the blossoming of a romance, with tragedy, with death, with hope for the future; or, more rarely, with a simple happiness and a contentment with their lot in life.

Farynor, the King's baker, was one of those who lay

awake. He heard the rats, but with only part of his mind, and so they did not disturb him unduly. Once, when a large rat scampered across the floor and ran under the bed, he swore at it, but in an absentminded way.

He was not concerned with rats, but only with the cake he was planning to make as soon as it was light enough to see. The cake was to be his masterpiece. It would stand a good four feet in height, and it would require the services of four boys to carry it to the King, with himself bringing up the rear. In shape, the cake was to be a replica of the King himself. The complexion of the face would be composed of a pale pink cream, soft and nutty to the taste. It would have sugar plums for eyes, and the new imported chocolate for hair and mustache.

Farynor frowned down at his wife, who lay sleeping by his side. She was a simple woman, content to live from day to day and let the future take care of itself, untroubled by her husband's soaring ambitions. It was honor enough that her husband had gained the illustrious position of baker to the King. She was content.

Her snoring annoyed Farynor, making him wonder, as he often did, why he had married this uncouth and ignorant woman. As baker to the King, he could have married nearer to his heart's desire. He dug her sharply in the ribs. She mumbled crossly, kicking out at him sleepily, but her snoring did not cease, there was only a temporary break in its rhythm.

Farynor allowed himself to relax, shutting his ears to the sound. He resumed his dreaming. The clothes for his masterpiece troubled him briefly, then he smiled and nodded his head. He would mix his most brilliant colors to tint the royal robes. Why should he worry about such small details? With the mixing of colors, he had a cunning and clever hand. The body of the cake would be stuffed with rich fruits, interspersed with layers of marzipan. The King would almost certainly be intrigued and flattered, and would doubtless reward him well. Perhaps, who could tell, he would bestow upon him a title. Should the figure have a hat, he wondered, or should he perhaps leave the head bare? Should he—

Farynor's thoughts broke off. Mother o' God, but it was uncomfortable warm. His heavy nightshirt was sticking to his body. Even the bedclothes, he thought, exploring them with a tentative hand, felt hot to the touch. A sound impinged on his ears. For a long time, he realized now, his mind had been unconsciously registering that rumbling, crackling sound.

His heart leaping with apprehension, Farynor shook his wife roughly awake. "Woman!" he bawled. "Woman, did you remember to damp down the fires?"

"What's that?" she mumbled. "Oh shut up, do. Le' me sleep!"

Something fell heavily. Light leaped upward, filling the room with an eerie flickering glow.

Farynor wondered no more. "Fire!" he screamed. Springing from the bed, he grabbed at his breeches, pulling them on with trembling hands. "Fire! Fire! The shop's afire, you stupid woman! Get up!"

The doorlatch felt hot as he lifted it and flung the door open. From the burning staircase, the flames that sprang at him almost seared his face before he managed to slam the door shut.

His wife was out of bed now, a lumpy trembling figure, clutching her nightgown about her and whimpering softly to herself.

"Shut up!" Farynor snarled. " 'Tis all your fault, you lazy, selfish sow!"

"But I damped the fires down! I did, I remember!"

"It's too late. The stairs are ablaze. We'll have to get out of the window."

"I can't!" she squealed. "I can't, I'd fall!"

For answer, Farynor lifted a heavy chair and smashed it against the window. "Get out there!" He grabbed the protesting woman and pushed her through the window. "Crawl along the roof edge until you reach Tom Billington's house. You can get down his outside stairs."

"Oh! Oh!" the woman shrieked. "My knee's cut. It's bleeding!"

"Curse your knee! Get along, I tell you, I'll be right behind you."

"I'm falling!"

"Then fall, and be damned to you!"

Farynor flung a heavy leg over the sill. He winced as shards of glass pierced his flesh. He felt the rough slates of the roof, and he opened his mouth and bawled at the top of his voice, "Fire! Wake up everybody! Fire, fire!"

Moments later, though it seemed hours to him, figures came pouring from the houses like so many scurrying ants, swearing, pushing at each other, clutching wailing children.

"Christ's body," a woman's voice screamed. "Look at that!"

Farynor paused in his crawling. He saw that a sheet of flame had leaped from his house to the house across the street. Panicking, his heart hammering heavily, he pushed his wife forward. Down below it looked like an archway of flame as more and more flames ribboned out and caught at houses opposite. In another moment, the whole street would be ablaze.

Thames Street lay the space of ten houses from his, Farynor thought. What if the fire should reach the warehouses in Thames Street? Moaning softly to himself, he remembered that the warehouses were stacked with tallow, hemp and oil. And these warehouses led directly to wharves which held mountains of hay, coal and timber.

"Get water!" Farynor screamed, trying to make himself heard about the hubbub of sound.

Only screams answered him, the high-pitched shrieking of terrified children and the hoarse cursing of men. Some, realizing their danger, began a sudden scramble further down the alley. The flames seemed to pursue them, leaping out, clutching, trying to gather them up in a fiery embrace. The others, sheeplike, followed after them.

The heat was terrible. Great beads of sweat dripped from Farynor's forehead into his eyes. For a fleeting moment he thought of the masterpiece he had intended to make. Oh God! What would happen to him when it became known that the fire had started in his baker's shop in Pudding Land? He would be ruined, and especially with the King. Who could be expected to put their trust in a man who allowed his shop to catch afire? It was his wife's fault! Everything bad that had ever happened to him was always her fault.

He saw her scrambling down the rickety outer steps of Billington's house, and he followed quickly after her. Just as they reached the ground, a dull booming sound was followed by a great wall of flame that seemed to reach to the very heavens. The warehouses had caught. God's precious thumbs! What had started as a little fire was now a roaring, ungovernable monster!

Across the city, Samuel Pepys stirred in his sleep. After a moment he opened his eyes and looked toward the window. What was that glow in the sky? It was filling the room with red light.

Grumbling to himself, Pepys rose from his bed and padded across to the window. *Fire somewhere,* he thought. Yawning, he rubbed at his eyes, then, turning, he made for the snug security of his bed again. Huddled beneath the bedclothes, he wondered to himself what explanation Sir James Trent was going to offer to his wife, who had found out he had been keeping an actress. Pepys grinned to himself. The old fox had really got himself caught this time. Sleepily, Pepys reached out and patted his wife's buttocks. Trent should have known better than to get caught. He himself had had many a narrow escape, but he had always managed to keep things from his wife. It was a man's duty to keep things from his wife, if he intended to go on enjoying life. Pepys' thoughts drifted to the fire. Some fool had been careless, he supposed. Doubtless it was nothing much anyway. Pepy's eyes closed, and he drifted into a deep, dreamless slumber.

THE KING TURNED IN THE BED. WHY THE devil couldn't he sleep? He looked at Catherine curled up in a ball, her back toward him, her hair a dark splash against the white pillow. It must be close to three in the morning, he thought, judging the time roughly. It had been gone two o' the clock when he had left Lady Mary Trevor's bed.

He frowned into the sultry darkness, feeling suddenly and unreasonably annoyed. He had hoped that Catherine might be awake and would talk to him for a while. Sometimes the life he led began to pall on him, but his jaded senses could always be revived to a new life under the flow of Catherine's innocent, though increasingly barbed conversation.

Charles put his hand on Catherine's waist, willing her to awake. She did not stir, and he experienced a sudden surge of desolation. He did not love her, true, but without his quite knowing how, she had become essential to him. In her own quiet way, his gentle and loving Queen had managed to twine herself about his life. She would always be here waiting for him to return to her when he had tired of his latest affair, even if the look in her soft brown eyes would fill him with a sense of shame. Why could he not be faithful to her? He had tried, but his spasmodic attempts always came to naught. His sensuous nature, seek to stifle it though he may, always responded to a pair of alluring eyes, a neat ankle, a shapely leg, or a soft mouth raised in ardent invitation. Od's Fish! He could not help it. He was Charles Stuart, and he was as God had made him. Never had one woman been enough for him. And yet without Catherine, he felt, he would be lost indeed.

Charles turned again in the bed. By Christ, but it was hot! His throat irritated, and he coughed. Now he came to think of it, there was a damned odd odor in the room. He thought for a moment of investigating, then, changing his mind, he settled back against the pillows. He was too tired. His throat felt dry, his lungs cramped, and his eyes were watering. Could he be coming down with an illness? A fresh attack of the pox? Oft times it had started in just this way. He had survived each attack, and doubtless would do so again. One must expect such things, it was all part of the life he led.

He coughed again. Turning on his left side, he drew the bedclothes away from his hot legs and tried to get his body to relax.

His mind drifted after a while, recalling a memory of Lucy Walters. Lucy had been his first true love, and to her he had given a boy's passion. Lucy of the lush body, the dark and slumberous eyes. Their passion had resulted in the conception of his son Jamie. What had happened to Lucy after he had left her, he wondered. She was dead now, of course. He felt a faint pang. She had been so vibrant, so willing. But why would people keep circulating the infernal story that he had married her in a secret ceremony. Even Jamie seemed to believe it, and had grown very arrogant. Nay, it had not been necessary to marry Lucy, though often she had urged the step upon him. But he had tired of her quickly and would not have married her, even had such an act been possible. Jamie, he knew, longed to think that he had been conceived in wedlock. But, not even for the sake of this much-loved son, would he lie.

A fresh attack of coughing overcome him, and he had the horrible conviction that he was about to vomit. He gritted his teeth together, deliberately conjuring up a picture of Barbara Castlemaine. The woman, with her flaming red hair, her vivid blue eyes, and her full provocative mouth, had turned out to be an intolerable bitch. Yet once he had wanted her with an almost insatiable passion that could only be temporarily assuaged within the deepest recesses of her body. Her cold and calculating nature, her vile temper, and her greed had managed to kill all feeling. There was the lovely and innocent Frances Stuart. She who prattled like a six-year-old child, who built her card houses and invited her admirers to participate in the infantile game, laughing and clapping her hands together when the cards collapsed into a heap—Frances, who had recently been heard to declare her love for the Duke of Richmond and Lennox! Charles felt a familiar anger and desire at the thought of her. Catherine saw Frances as a calm and sensible girl, but he saw her as a lovely, stupid, flighty piece whom he must possess. Then there was Angel Dawson, or my lady Benbrook, as he must think of her now. He could have loved Angel, but she had always been exasperatingly faithful to her lord. The King sighed. He was glad for Nicholas. He loved him like a brother, and he deserved to be happy.

He buried his face in the pillow, finding solace in the thought of Nell Gwynne. Why was he still hesitating? He'd send for her soon, he resolved. His thoughts drifted inevitably to his sister Minette. Minette, haunting as a dream, moved like a piece of thistledown across the corridors of his mind. She had been akin to a strain of music throughout his stormy and troubled life.

Charles choked, retching a little. Aggrieved, he touched Catherine's leg with his foot. He was feeling damned ill. He needed her. Why didn't she awaken?

But Catherine was awake, and had been from the moment Charles had entered the room. Lying perfectly still, her lips pressed together against the cough that sought to emerge, she had been absorbed in her misery. Why was Charles always so faithless, so light of character where women were concerned?

Charles retched again, and she turned to him quickly, misery was swallowed up by alarm. "What is it, Charles? Are you feeling ill?"

"Aye," he said shortly.

Now that she was awake, he felt remorse for having disturbed her. He touched her hair with a gentle hand. " 'Tis nothing, Catherine. 'Twill pass. 'Tis this cursed heat, I think."

"It may be. But I think in the morning, 'twould be advisable to consult your physicians. It might be that—" she broke off, the cough betraying her.

Charles sat up in bed. "What, you too, Catherine?"

He fumbled for his tinderbox, swearing beneath his breath as it slid from the table to the floor. Recovering it, he lit the candles. "Catherine!" he exclaimed. " 'Tis no wonder we cough. The damned room is full of smoke!"

Charles slid from the bed, reaching for his robe. Tying it about his waist, he strode over to the window and drew the heavy red drapes aside. "Fiends seize me! The sky looks to be on fire!"

Catherine sat bolt upright in the bed. In the lurid light, her face was anxious. "What—what can it be, Charles?"

" 'Tis evidently quite near." He turned from the window. "But have no fear, 'twill be dealt with in due course."

Catherine turned her head as the babbling of many voices came to her from beyond the door.

"Sire! Madam!!" a woman's voice called. " 'Tis I, Frances Stuart. Sir Mortimer Fenn desires to have speech with His Majesty."

"Enter," Charles called.

Sir Mortimer came in hastily, followed by Frances Stuart. Behind her peered the frightened faces of the Queen's ladies. Only Barbara Castlemaine stood aloof from the rest, her face expressing amusement rather than fear. She had made nothing of Sir Mortimer's story. He was known to drink heavily, and she believed it to be the babblings of a drunken idiot.

"Sire!" Sir Mortimer knelt before the King. "Samuel

Pepys is below. He would have urgent speech with Your Majesty."

Charles looked at the man closely. He saw the smudges on his face and his red-rimmed eyes. He felt the first stirring of alarm.

"You look exhausted, man," he said. "Here, get up and sit in that chair."

Sir Mortimer rose to his feet. "I thank Your Majesty, but I dare not delay."

"Very well. What does Mr. Pepys wish to discuss with me?"

Sir Mortimer's eyes shifted to the Queen, and he made her a small jerky bow. "It would be better if Mr. Pepys saw you alone, Sire."

Charles waved an impatient hand. "I will see him, of course. But it is evident you know of the matter which brings him."

Sir Mortimer swallowed unhappily. "Sir, I have no wish to alarm the Queen, or—or the other ladies. But London is burning!"

"What!" Charles drew back from him. "Are you mad?"

"Nay, Sire." Sir Mortimer swallowed again. "The fire is already raging out of control, consuming whole streets of houses. But Mr. Pepys can tell you more. He first witnessed it from his bed, but believing the glow to be nothing, he went back to sleep. Something awakened him again, and he knew then that the matter was serious."

Charles walked rapidly to the door. "Come with me, Sir Mortimer."

Sir Mortimer Fenn stumbled after him. He was ashamed of the prodigious yawns of strain and fatigue that now attacked him, and he sought to hide them behind his hand. Charles strode past the women. Automatically, they curtsied before him.

Frances Stuart looked at the Queen. "Madam," she said, her voice trembling. "Sir Mortimer tells me it is like hell's inferno outside."

Catherine got out of bed. "Sir Mortimer doubtless exaggerates," she said as calmly as she was able.

Frances knelt before her to fit on her slippers.

"Come, Mistress Stuart, you must be strong, you know. Else will you have the other ladies falling into hysterics." The Queen summoned a smile. "How can the whole of London be burning? You know well 'tis impossible."

Impossible? Frances thought of the closely leaning houses, the wooden hovels of the poor, of the shops clustered tightly together, and she felt the blood draining from her face.

"Madam," she said, "Sir Mortimer says that already the fire has gained a terrible hold. There is an east wind, and it is driving the sparks before it. Thames Street is aflame, and many of the surrounding areas."

Catherine clenched her hands tightly together. "Thames Street? Is that not where the wharfingers are?"

"Aye, Madam. The fire has been fed by the oil and spirits stored there, and the timber and coal."

"No!" Catherine said. "Oh no, Frances!" Her eyes turned to the sullenly red sky, and she felt the clutch of a terrible fear. It was typical of Catherine that, in that moment, she thought only of her husband. The agony that thousands of others must undergo if this devastation continued had not yet penetrated her usually clear thinking mind. She knew Charles so well. He would insist upon going out there and helping to fight the flames. He would insist upon being with his people, helping them, encouraging them. But he must not. Somehow she must contrive to stop him!

The smoke came belching through the opened window in a thick, yellow acrid cloud. "The window, Frances," Catherine gasped. "Close it."

She clutched her blue velvet robe about her. "The King," she said, her pretense of courage forgotten, "I—I must go to him."

"Yes, Madam." Curtsying, Frances drew to one side. Walking over to stand by the door, she watched the Queen's hurrying figure. Her robe was clutched in both hands, so that it might not impede her progress along the marble inlaid corridor. The banners on the wall fluttered as she sped past. Her long dark hair bobbed on her shoulders. She scarce looked like a Queen, Frances thought. She looked like a woman in love, a woman who was terribly afraid for her lover.

Frances' head throbbed dully as her thoughts followed much the same pattern as the Queen's. Only it was not of the King she thought, but of her own Charles Stuart, the Duke of Richmond and Lennox.

Charles looked up sharply as Catherine burst into the room. "Catherine," Charles said quietly. "I pray you to return to your apartments, my dear. There is nothing you can do here, and you will become chilled."

Chilled! Catherine looked at the robust and serious-faced Samuel Pepys, at Charles, whose face had taken on a grim strained look, and she felt hysteria bubbling inside her. Looking at him, she realized that his words had been said not so much in concern for her, but as a wish to rid himself of a troublesome female.

Catherine advanced further into the room. "I am the Queen, am I not?" She laid her hand on her husband's rigid arm. "It is my right to be here. The well-being of the people concerns me also."

"Well spoken, Catherine." He frowned. "But nonetheless, Madam, pray leave us now. I will come to you later."

"No!" It was the first time she had openly defied him since the episode of my lady Castlemaine, and she trembled a little. "I will sit quietly in that corner," she said, "and I will speak no word. But, Sire, I wish to remain."

"Very well." Charles turned from her impatiently. "Pray to continue, Mr. Pepys."

Nervously, Pepys straightened his blond wig, which he had evidently donned in great haste, for it now sat askew on his closely shaven head. Blinking his eyes rapidly, a tic pulsing at the side of his mouth, he said hoarsely, "St. Magnus is on fire, Sire, and it is feared that the flames will soon reach London Bridge. The people are too terrified to aid themselves, they run around screaming and clutching their children and those household possessions they have managed to salvage. Some have even gone so far as to throw their goods in the river, in the hope, presumably, that they will float and thus be recovered later."

"They are entitled to hope," Charles spoke sharply. "What of the Lord Mayor?"

Pepys face flushed to an even deeper red. "I fear that the fat fool will do nothing," he said contemptuously. "He is afraid to act."

"But I am not," Charles said, his eyes gleaming with the light of purpose. "Return, please, and seek out the Lord Mayor. Tell him he must demolish the houses and make a break between the flames, for only thus can they be subdued. He is to spare no houses in the path of the fire. All must come down, else will they serve as fresh fodder."

"But the man is a coward, Sire."

"Sometimes those whom we believe to be cowards surprise us, by turning overnight into brave men. Find him. Tell him what I have said."

"I will, Sire. What if he should refuse?"

Charles thought for a moment. "York!" he cried, snapping his fingers. "Between us, York and I will rally the people. They'll help us, and with a good heart, I'll vow."

"Sire!" Pepys exclaimed in alarm. "You cannot be thinking of demolishing the houses yourself?"

"With the aid of the people, of course. Why not?"

"But, Sire, forgive me," Pepys swallowed. "Undoubtedly your presence and that of your brother the Duke will hearten the people. But Your Majesty must not even think of placing yourself in such danger." Pepys looked at Catherine. "The Queen, I would imagine, agrees with me."

Released from her silence, Catherine ran to the King. "I pray you, Sire, to take heed of Mr. Pepys. After this is over the people will need you."

Frowning, Charles stared into her pleading eyes. "And of what use a King, Madam," he answered quietly, "if he cannot take his place beside his people when they are sorely beset? Should he remain snug in his palace and leave them to burn alone? Were he to do so, then I vow that he would not deserve, or be fitted to rule." Charles glanced at the flushed and uncomfortable Pepys. "You mean well, I know," he said. "I will remain here until first light. After that, I take my place with my people. The matter is settled. You may go, Mr. Pepys, but in the meantime, I pray you do what you can."

"I will, Sire." He bowed, then hastily left the room.

"Well," Charles said, putting his hand against Catherine's cheek, "and what have you to say, small one?"

"Only that I wish you would not go."

"I wonder if you really wish that. Come, Catherine, take courage. You know well 'tis my duty."

She nodded gloomily. "I suppose so." She looked at him from beneath her eyelashes. "But it seems to me that you enjoy that duty well."

Charles laughed. "So you see through me, do you? I could not stay here, Catherine, you know that," he said soothingly. "Not that there will be that much danger. So think not to rid yourself of Charles Stuart quite yet."

"I am not quite a fool, and I know better."

Charles saw the tears she was unsuccessfully trying to hide, and his face became grave. "Didst not remind me that you were the Queen?" he said gently. "Very well then, Madam, you must act like a Queen. I will return unharmed, sweetheart, have no fear."

She looked into his dark eyes. "You do well to remind me, Sire," she answered, her lips quivering. "But, Charles, may I not go with you?"

He shook his head firmly. "Nay, Catherine. What then, wouldst become a man in petticoats?"

A tap on the door interrupted him. "Come in," Charles called.

The door opened, and James, Duke of York, strode into the room.

James' fair-complexioned face was flushed, his shirt was

buttoned into the wrong holes, and his wig tilted rakishly over one eye. "Have you thought of the soldiers under my command?" James burst out. "They are trained for any emergency, I have seen to that. They will obey without question any order given to them. Unlike the people," James added, his full lips sneering, "who run before the flames like a bunch of panic-stricken dolts."

"The people are not trained soldiers, James," Charles rebuked him softly. "As is natural, they fear for the safety of their children and other loved ones."

James ignored the rebuke. "I repeat, Sire, my soldiers stand ready. You have but to say the word."

"Then I will say it. See to it, James."

"I will indeed, Sire." James' face took on the eager boyish glow that had but lately transformed Charles' own features. "I would wish to go myself, Sire, with your permission."

"You have my permission, James. I, too, am going."

"Splendid! By God, Charles, I wish we could have Benbrook by our side, and a dozen more like him."

"The wish is in vain. Benbrook is ill, and I, for one, would not wish to subject him to such a strain."

Catherine watched, fascinated, as James' blond wig, moving, tilted itself further over the Duke's eyes. "Charles," Catherine said, turning to the King, "would you care to make a small wager that my lord Benbrook, as soon as he hears of the calamity, will be riding in all haste to your side?"

"That is one wager I would hope to lose," Charles answered her. "But I fear you are right. I know how Benbrook thinks."

Bored with what he thought of as trivialities, James shuffled his feet impatiently. "I'll give the order then, shall I, Charles? The sooner the better, I think. Pepys tells me that the rabble are already fighting among themselves. There has already been some looting." He frowned. "They are like cornered rats, snarling at each other, and raging and adding to the confusion."

Charles put his hand upon James' heavy shoulder. "You will not refer to them as rabble, James, nor yet as cornered rats. They are our people, and as such they are entitled to our respect."

A note in his voice told James it was the King who spoke, not his careless easy-going brother. "Then let them *earn* respect," James said sullenly. "Have you forgotten what they did to our father?"

Charles' hand dropped. "Nay, I forget nothing. But the people are easily misled, which should tell you how much they have need of us now."

James bowed. "With your permission, Sire," he added stiffly, "I beg leave to retire. There is much to be done."

Charles stopped him at the door. "James," he said softly, "you are as yet my only heir. I would wish you had more charity and understanding in your heart. A king, if he is to rule wisely and well, needs both of these qualities."

James grinned, his ill humor immediately forgotten. "But God send that I may not be put to the test for some time to come. I happen to be excessively fond of you."

"Which is your misfortune," Charles answered. "I preach to you, James, but I myself am a very graceless fellow, and hardly the model you should follow."

James' grin widened. "But nonetheless you have the charity and understanding of which you spoke. Forget it not, brother." He left the room, closing the door behind him with a resounding bang.

Charles turned to Catherine. "York is not at all a bad fellow. You have to know him to appreciate him." He put a hand to his mouth, stifling a yawn. The gesture was made, she guessed, to cover his emotion. Charles was easily moved, and especially by members of his own family.

"Charles," she said, touched. "I would have you know that I pray often to the Holy Virgin. It may be that She will heed my prayers. If that should happen, then James will not be your only heir."

Charles' dark, mournful eyes held a soft light. He stooped to kiss her. "Will he not? Then, little Catherine, I pray you will intensify your prayers."

She clung to him, her hands caressing his face. "You will take care of yourself, my darling?" she entreated. "Promise me that you will."

"I will promise you something else," he said, opening the door for her. "I will come more often to your bed, Madam." He dropped a light kiss on her brow. "I must do, if I intend to father that heir, must I not?"

After he had closed the door upon her, Catherine stood there for a moment.

"Benson!" she heard the King shout to his personal attendant. "Get out here, you plaguey lazy hound! I have been waiting for you this past hour or more."

Smiling to herself, Catherine listened to the body-servant's raised indignant voice.

"Begging Your Majesty's pardon, and trusting you'll not be offended if I give you the lie. But I have been ready and waiting this long time, as Your Majesty well knows."

"You are calling me a liar, Benson?"

"I am, Your Majesty." Benson's voice changed. "Nay, Sire, you'll not be putting on that shirt. 'Tis not properly aired."

"Damnation, Benson! Am I a child that you must treat me thus? Where the devil have you put my boots? Hurry, hurry! I'll stand for no more of this dallying."

"If Your Majesty would but contrive to remain calm, much could be accomplished. Did I not teach you this lesson when you were but a lad? Aye, and won you into taking the physic Her Majesty prescribed for you."

"Speak not to me of my mother, or of her infernal physic. It was enough to sicken a full-grown man. You have quite obviously lost my boots and my clothes."

"Nothing of the sort, Sire. Your boots are beside you, and here are your clothes."

Catherine went on her way. She had heard the old friendly wrangle between master and servant many times before. Each was devoted to the other, but neither man would dream of showing it.

Frances Stuart met the Queen in the corridor. Catherine saw that she was very frightened. She curtsied quickly. "Madam," she said, rising.

"What now?" Catherine said wearily.

"They say that the fire is swallowing up whole streets," Frances wailed, wringing her hands. " 'Tis doubtful if they can save the houses on London Bridge, nor yet St. Paul's, which lies in the path of the fire. Oh, Madam! What if the fire should reach the Palace?"

"It will not." Catherine spoke consolingly, but with no belief in her own words.

Frances hesitated. "I have heard that His Grace, the Duke of York, has issued orders that stocks of gunpowder be brought forth."

"Nonsense, Frances! How can the Duke's plans be known to you?"

"His—His Grace was overheard discussing it with another."

Gunpowder! Despite her renewed terror, Catherine answered the girl steadily enough. "Mayhap His Grace has given such an order. But I feel sure that the King would not countenance the use of gunpowder for the blowing up of the houses. 'Tis too dangerous."

Frances curtsied and went on her way. Catherine stared after her. The King *would* countenance it, she knew. He would do anything to save his beloved city. He would doubtless insist on setting the charges with his own hands. Charles would never demand of others that which he was not prepared to do himself. But surely he would try the old and tried method of pulling down the houses first?

Feeling incredibly weary, Catherine entered her apartments. Her ladies stood in a huddled group at the window. They were silent, but their faces were strained and fearful.

Catherine stayed them when they would have curtsied

before her. "Nay," she said, smiling at them. "No ceremony, I pray you." She took little lady Mary Howard's cold hand in hers. "Come," she said, pressing her fingers reassuringly, "we will all keep watch together."

Barbara Castlemaine, in the forefront nearest to the window, detached herself from the group and turned to speak to the Queen. "There are certain matters which require my immediate attention, Madam," she smiled, her blue eyes hard and bold. "Perhaps if Your Majesty intends to keep watch, you will not require my services for a while?"

All Catherine's dislike of the brazen Countess of Castlemaine was evident in her face. "You are excused, my lady. We do not require your services now, or at any time."

Barbara's arched bronze brows rose mockingly. "Your Majesty does not require me for this particular period of time, do you mean?"

Catherine colored. If only it were possible to order the creature from her presence permanently. "Naturally, my lady Castlemaine," Catherine said coldly, turning her back. "What else did you suppose us to mean?"

Barbara curtsied to the Queen's back. "I have no idea, dear Majesty," she answered demurely.

Going toward the door, Barbara was furiously angry. It might be true that Charles came less and less to her bed, but that did not mean that her power was ended. If the Queen knew what was good for her, she had best remember that. Catherine, with her great soft cow's eyes, had not won. Nor, if Barbara had her way, would she ever win.

Barbara's hand clenched on the latch. *I would the Queen were dead. She, and Frances Stuart!*

Catherine heard the door close behind Barbara. Her heart was aching, as only the Castlemaine could make it ache. She stared blindly out of the window. The red glow in the sky seemed to have deepened. Great gusts of smoke, driven by a fierce wind, billowed before the windows, sometimes finding a crack and managing to filter through.

There was a heavy sickening stench in the room, and the ladies were stifling their coughs behind dainty kerchiefs.

Catherine crossed herself hastily. "Have mercy on the King," she whispered.

Lady Mary Howard regarded her with tear-filled eyes. "Madam! I am so afraid!"

"We are all afraid, Mary," Catherine said gently. "But those who face the flames—the many who are suffering—have need of our prayers, do they not?"

With a sudden swift movement, Mary hid her face against the Queen's shoulder. "I will pray, Madam. We will all pray!"

LONDON WAS BURNING! IT WAS A DEVASTATing foretaste of hell! Sir Thomas Bludworth, the Lord Mayor of London, stared with appalled eyes at the raging flames, at the screaming people who ran past him. Some of them fell, wriggling on the ground as they tried to dodge the showers of sparks raining down from the burning buildings.

Sir Thomas lifted up an old woman who lay directly in his path sobbing hysterically. Her hair had come loose, and her few poor possessions were scattered on the ground. "There, mother," he said soothingly, smothering the smoldering sparks with his hands, "You'll be all right. Let me help you along."

But the woman hit out at him with clenched fists, her face contorted into a mask of fury. "Don' you touch me!" she cried. "I knows who you are, I do. Some fine bleedin' Mayor, you are! Why'nt you to do somethin', eh? I los' me 'ome, me cloes, and me cat, what was me only comfort, an' 'ere you are jus' standin' aroun'. Ought to be ashamed o' yourself, that you ought!"

Still shouting accusations, she went stumblingly on her way.

Sir Thomas looked after her despairingly. They were all the same, all ungrateful. He had made many suggestions, some of them quite practical, too, but the people just would not listen to him. They clung to their burning homes until the very last minute. He had heard the cries of the bereaved, and again, when he had attempted to offer comfort, he had been rejected. His stomach had turned at the streams of squealing rats that had issued forth from the burning buildings. He was a well-meaning man, he really was. Was it his fault that his duties took him often from London? So that now, when he attempted to bring them some comfort, they all but spat in his face.

Sir Thomas's weak blue eyes filled with tears, and he wallowed in self-pity. The injustice of it! Why would they not listen to him? He put up his hand, wincing, as he felt the great bruise on his forehead, the result of a stone flung at him by an infuriated youth. Doubtless, if the fire was not put out soon, they would hang him from the nearest post.

Trembling, Sir Thomas turned away. Why, he had only returned to London on the Saturday. Did they think *he* had gone out in the small hours and fired the buildings? How could they call him such names! Shouting at him, brandishing their fists under his nose, until he had grown confused and scarcely knew what to do next. He was a good man, why could they not see it?

He was so lost in his thoughts that he all but walked into a plump little man, who glared at him indignantly.

"Pepys!" Sir Thomas exclaimed.

Samuel Pepys was an odd sight. The singed curls of his wig hung limp and shortened. As the Lord Mayor continued to stare at him, one curl dropped to the ground. His fine brocaded waistcoat had a large jagged hole in the front, and the tails of his long jacket were burned and frayed.

"I've been looking for you everywhere," Pepys barked. He plucked a handkerchief from his sleeve and began to mop at his sweaty begrimed face. " 'Twas a damned bit of luck that I managed to find you, and here you are staring at me like a dolt!"

Two more curls detached themselves and fell at his feet. "Look at that!" he shouted, beside himself. "Best wig

I ever had, and now the cursed thing's falling to pieces! Had to douse my head in water, or my pate would have been aflame. It's your fault, Bludworth, hiding yourself from view like a common criminal. Why can't you be where you're supposed to be?"

Sir Thomas wilted. " 'Tis hardly the time to talk of the loss of a wig," he ventured.

For a moment he thought the infuriated Pepys meant to strike him. But the man tore the wig from his head, flung it to the ground, and trampled it beneath his feet.

"I have a command from the King, Sir Thomas," Pepys snapped. "You are to pull down all of the houses in the path of the flames. Do you hear?"

Sir Thomas stared at him. "P—pull down all the h—houses?" he stammered.

"That's what I said, isn't it, eh?" Pepys gave the wig a kick. " 'Tis the King's command."

"But it cannot be!" Fresh tears started into Sir Thomas's eyes. He placed a trembling hand on Pepys's plump arm. "Sir," he whispered, "I am in fear of my life. The people blame me."

"And so they should," Pepys shook off his hand. "A poorer excuse for a Lord Mayor I never did see."

Sir Thomas staggered back a pace. "Lord!" he cried out in a trembling voice. "What can I do? I am spent, do you hear me? The people will not obey me!" He touched the bruise on his forehead.

Unmoved, Pepys said, "Am I to tell the King that you choose to disregard his command?"

"Nay, nay! Tell His Majesty that I will try. But that in doing so, I take my life in my hands."

"Pah!" Pepys turned on his heel, colliding with a woman carrying a bucket of water full of live, wriggling eels.

"Out of my way, madam," Pepys cried, glaring at her.

"Ain't no swell goin' ter talk ter me that way!" she shouted. With a swift movement of her brawny arms, she lifted the bucket and dashed the contents in his face. "If anyone's goin' ter get o' the way, it's you!" Picking up her bucket in one hand, her ragged skirts in the other, she swept past him.

Dazed, Pepys blinked water out of his eyes. "I never would have believed it," he muttered. He picked an eel from his coat front and flung it to the ground with a shudder of distaste. "They've all gone mad, Bludworth."

"I told you, I told you!" Sir Thomas whimpered.

Pepys pushed him to one side. "You'd better do your best now," he shouted, stalking away, "or 'twill be the worst for you!"

A flaming timber crashed down near Sir Thomas, and for one wild moment he thought his coat was afire. With an incoherent cry, he bounded away from the danger. "Attention!" he shouted. "Attention! I have an announcement to make!"

Nobody took the slightest notice of him. They continued to surge past him, eyes wild, trembling hands clutching bundles, swearing, crying, laughing hysterically. A dog, trying to fight his way out of the mob, rolled near Sir Thomas's feet.

"Poor old fellow," Sir Thomas said, stooping to pat him. "I know just how you feel."

The dog's hackles rose, and he bared yellow teeth. Snarling, he snapped at Sir Thomas's ankle.

It was too much! Whimpering beneath his breath, the Lord Mayor went on his way. "Attention!" he cried every now and again, wringing his hands like a despairing woman. "Stay calm, I entreat you! Stay calm!"

Alex Barrymore, pausing for a moment in his self-imposed task of directing the women and children to areas which were not yet burning, saw the Lord Mayor stagger past. He stared after him for a moment, then, shrugging his shoulders, he concentrated on his problem. The fire was ringing them around. Very soon, if the holocaust continued, there would be no escape.

Alex shook his head to clear it and wiped his grimed face on the tail of his shirt. There was grit between his teeth, his blond hair was blackened with flying smuts; he was wet through from handling endless buckets of water, and he was weary to his very bones. He felt as though he stood in the very heart of an oven. He laughed, the sound without mirth. It was true, London was falling in red ruins before his very eyes.

A small child, crying helplessly, her knuckles in her eyes, came blundering toward him.

"Wait!" Straightening his aching back, Alex put out a detaining hand. "Tell me the trouble, little lass." He put his hand on her matted hair. "Hast lost your father and mother?"

The child stared at him for a moment, then her face creased and she wailed afresh.

Alex stooped down to the child's level. "If I am to help you, you must tell me all about it, must you not?"

The little girl stared into the kind blue eyes in the soot-blackened face. "M—m—my Ma was over there with my dad," she sobbed. She pointed her finger at the people crowding near the Thames embankment. "An'—an' now I can't find 'em!"

Alex pulled her into her arms. "I'll help you," he said, rising to his feet with his small burden. "But you must not cry any more, else will you not be able to see them, eh?"

A woman came bursting from the midst of the crowd. Catching sight of the child in Alex's arms, she came running toward them. "Jane!" she cried, tugging at the little girl's arm, "wherever 'ave you been, you bad, bad lass!" She paused in her tugging to look at Alex. "Sorry, sir, but what wi' one thing an' another, I been nigh frantic."

Alex handed the child to her mother. "I pray you not to scold her. She, too, has been very badly frightened, you know."

Listening to his low, beautifully modulated voice, the woman gave a hasty bob. "It's all very well for you to say, sir, but she ain't the on'y one what's frightened. Take Ned Jorkins, not as you'd know 'im, sir, but he was atryin' to get 'is wife out o' the house, an' the whole thing collapsed on 'im. All burnt to death, they was, Ned, 'is wife, an' their four little 'un's."

"I'm sorry," Alex said gently. "And what of yourself, madam, how do you fare?"

"I los' me 'ome an' all me linen." The woman darted a quick fierce kiss at the child's wet cheek. "But I got this un' an', thanks be to God, me 'usband!"

She turned away, hugging the child tightly to her thin breast, and, as Alex watched, once more lost herself among the crowd.

Alex Barrymore swayed on his feet. He was stupefied with fatigue, and he had a great longing to lie down and rest, just close his eyes for a moment. But he must be insane to think of sleep. There was so much to do, so very much! For a moment he thought of Angel. Thank God that she was safe.

He stared into the waters of the Thames. Its rolling swells flared crimson. It was crammed with boats, all tightly packed with people, frantically trying to make their way down river. Some clutched household possessions and wire coops filled with squawking chickens. In one boat, a man, an iron pot partially enveloping his head, sat high on a pile of goods, using his feet to kick away those who were trying to lay claim to his hard-won space. In another boat, a woman, holding her child in one arm, a struggling duck in the other, sat there as if frozen into position, her eyes staring straight ahead. She seemed indifferent to the struggles of the duck, the piercing screams of her child, and the cries and pandemonium all about her.

Another scream, pitched higher than the others, caused Alex to start violently.

"Look!" somebody was shouting. "The houses on the bridge have caught!"

There was a mad scramble away from the embankment. The fire, proceeding sluggishly for the space of a few seconds, caught firm hold. A roaring fury ignited the flimsy dwellings like torches against the sulphurous sky.

Alex stared with haunted eyes. Merciful God! He

could only hope the people within had had the sense to vacate. There was nothing he could do for them, nothing that anybody could do. Watching the spectacular hoop of flame on London Bridge, he realized, with a sinking heart, that the occupants had clung to their hearths until the very last minute.

He heard the screams of the victims, he saw them trying to scramble to safety through the small windows, many of them with their clothing already alight. He saw others hanging to the sill, fingers desperately clutching, their mouths wide-open black holes of agony as they plunged headlong into the scarlet waters below.

Sickened, Alex turned his eyes in another direction. Burdened men and women, children clinging to them, plodded heavily along an already gutted street. Horses, their eyes rolling and wild, dragged laden carts, neighing pitifully, plunging and struggling in an effort to free themselves from tangled traces and to escape the whips wielded by terrified owners. One horse screamed, a high piercing sound, as unable to keep its feet, it fell forward in a shower of boxes, pots and pans, plates and beakers.

The moving people stopped for a moment to stare at the terrible sight of the flaming bridge, then they began a frantic rush to reach the narrow city gates. They fought each other with flailing fists and hard-kicking feet. Hair was pulled, faces were scratched, but still they fought, a solid, swaying, frantic mass. Some were wedged in the space between the gates. Feet trampled over their helpless bodies, grinding them into the mud, dust and sharp-edged stones. Still others were kicked to death by the flying hooves of the frightened horses.

Alex saw one woman, her face mashed to a bloody pulp, kicked to one side. She rolled down the slight incline and lay still. She looked like a broken doll, her legs and arms at grotesque angles.

Alex knew that it was too late but he started toward her, only to be pushed back again by the surging people.

A man with a bandaged head, his light blue eyes blazing fanatically from his blackened face, fell to his knees and clasped his hands together in prayer. "Our Father," he shouted, "save us! Save us from this hell and damnation that Thine enemy, the Devil, has inflicted upon us!"

Still mouthing his prayers, he was kicked aside by the trampling feet and he rolled straight into the filthy gutter. Sobbing, his hands still raised in prayer, he fell face down into the scum.

Alex turned blindly away and managed to fight his way toward a wall. He sagged heavily against it, his hands clawing at the rough bricks for support. In the lurid light, his face looked drawn and ghastly, and his eyes had the appearance of being sunk deeply into his head.

Recovering, he began to move again. Gasping still, his eyes stinging with the smoke, he turned a corner and walked along a street choked with people. The street was lined on both sides with blazing houses. He could hear the snapping of timbers, the full-bellied belching roar of the flames, and the hissing sound as useless buckets of water were thrown into the conflagration. Men tore past him, pushing him to one side, their buckets grasped in their hands as they made for the street pump.

Alex stumbled over the hot ground, trying to evade the flaring showers of sparks. His lungs were filled with smoke, and, like the people about him, he was torn with helpless fits of coughing. He must work, he must do something to help! But he was so tired, too tired to think for himself!

At the corner of River Street, he saw a long line of people passing buckets of water from hand to hand, their efforts somewhat impeded by the jostling of those behind them. The flaming buildings, ignoring the water thrown against them, sent the flames leaping upward toward the sky, mocking their puny attempts.

In the center of this human chain, Alex made out the figures of Lord John Halsey, and Sir Montague Jermyn, an unfamiliar figure without his wig, his short red hair shining in the light.

"That's right, my lads," Lord John was shouting. "Put your backs into it. Don't flag!"

His brain feeling thick and heavy, his body weaving from side to side, Alex made his way toward them.

Sir Montague, happening to glance round at that moment, saw him approach. Whispering to a man beside him, he relinquished his bucket and stepped out of the line.

"Alex," he said, grasping his hands. "I'm glad to see you safe. By God, we can use every man!"

"Yes, I know. Give me something to do."

Sir Montague examined him closely. "How long since you slept?"

Alex laughed unsteadily. "When the fire broke out, I hadn't slept for two nights. I was—was transacting some important business, and—oh, I don't know. I can't really remember clearly. What does it matter anyway?"

Sir Montague's rich jovial laugh rang out. "Well, lad, 'tis no use bidding you to rest, for there is no place where you may lie in safety."

He is enjoying all this, Alex thought dully. Not the sufferings of the people, but the perilous adventure of it all. "How may I help?" he asked.

"Are you up to riding a horse, Alex? You will not fall asleep in the saddle, eh?"

"I think not."

"Good, I want you to ride out and acquaint Benbrook with our dilemma."

" 'Twould be hardly fair, Monty, would it? He has but recently been married."

"I know," Sir Montague said impatiently. "I would not disturb him, had the King not given orders that demolition must be started. We must pull down the houses if we are to stop the fire, and already we have delayed overlong. The Duke plans to use gunpowder, and Benbrook, he tells me, is the best man for the job."

"Powder! The King will never permit it."

"It's simple enough if you know what you're about. And

Benbrook has blown up quite a few buildings in his time, expecially those housing the King's enemies." He smiled. "Come, Alex, 'tis not much to ask of you. Ride out and tell him."

Alex looked up at the sky. "I would imagine that he must have guessed. Elm Park is not that far from London."

"Then it could be that he's already on his way," Sir Montague said eagerly. "But you'll go, just in case, eh?" Sir Montague pointed to a gray horse tethered to a post. The animal was straining to break away, his shrill terrified neighing mingling with the commotion all about him. "Take my horse, Alex. Poor old Thunder will be only too happy to get away. Take the old Post Road. 'Tis never used now; confoundedly overgrown and somewhat hazardous for the horse, but you'll get through."

"I will go if you feel you really need him."

"I do, or rather, the Duke does."

Sir Montague felt a sense of shame as he watched him go. Alex knew nothing of Benbrook's illness, and he dare not tell him, else he would have refused the mission. He himself had been against calling on Benbrook, but the Duke had assured him that Benbrook was quite recovered, and had promised in any case, to keep an eye on him and see that he came to no harm.

Sir Montague could not help smiling at the thought of the austere Earl Benbrook allowing anyone to watch over him and to guide his efforts. Nay, Nicholas had never, to his knowledge, allowed anyone to dictate to him, not even the King. Least of all would he take orders from the Duke of York. He'd go his own quiet cool and competent way. The "vanishing Earl" would do all within his power to aid them, and he'd not whine.

Sir Montague rejoined the line.

"Was that Alex I saw with you?" Lord John Halsey inquired.

"Aye." Sir Montague avoided his eyes. "He'll be with us again soon."

Lord John sighed. "If only this damnable wind would calm, Monty, we might have a chance. Where has Alex gone?"

"Oh, I sent him off to another street."

"Why in thunder did you do that? We need him here."

Sir Montague did not answer. He just shook his head and reached for the bucket of water being passed to him by his neighbor.

THAT EARLY MORNING, WANDERING TOGETH-
er with Nicholas through the overgrown grounds surrounding the Manor, Angel felt that she had discovered
yet another man. He smiled often, and his old forbidding
frown seemed a thing of the past. He was wearing his
oldest clothes and, because Angel liked to see it so, he had
allowed his hair to fall in thick untidy curls over his forehead. Then Angel insisted that he help her to pick wild-
flowers. "God's teeth," Nicholas remarked, "but you go
too far, madam!" Nevertheless he consented to help her.
"Is this truly I?" he said, placing the flowers he had
picked into a basket, rubbing his sap-stained fingers on
his breeches. "I must indeed be mazed in the head.
'Twould entirely ruin my reputation were I to be seen
indulging in such tomfoolery."

Angel smiled at him. "What you really mean," she
said lightly, "is that people would no longer go in awe of
the great Lord Benbrook. Why, they might even gain the
impression that he was human."

"Can you imagine Charles, for instance, picking wild-
flowers to please a pesky wench?"

"Aye, I can," she answered promptly. "The King is
generous and kindhearted. You know well that he would
do anything to please a lady."

"And I am not generous and kindhearted, is that what
you would say?"

167

She hesitated. "Well, let me say that sometimes you were less than kind."

"Exactly." He seated himself upon a fallen log and pulled her down beside him. "I am not by nature a patient man, as you know, but I believed myself to be reasonable. And then you came."

"And?" she prompted.

"You provoked me, you goaded me. You turned me from a reasonable man into a savage."

"How did I do that?"

"You made me fall in love with you, very much against my will, I may add. That says it all, does it not?"

She did not answer this. "My lord, I have been studying the sky. It looks strange, does it not?"

Nicholas glanced upward. The sun seemed to be obscured by a gray veil, and as far as the eye could see, the sky was tinged with red.

"I noticed it at first light," he answered. "Something is wrong in London. They have a fire I believe, and it must be a big one, else we would have noticed nothing."

"Do you think so? But I am sure they will manage to put it out."

"Perhaps. Nevertheless, I am riding for London after lunch."

"Nicholas! Whatever it is, I am sure they can manage without you." She stared at his set mouth, and she knew that he had made up his mind.

"But I must find that out for myself, must I not? And if it proves to be a very serious fire, the King will need help."

Angel felt a coldness at her heart, a sudden sense of forboding. "If there is danger, I would not have you walk into it." She clung to him tightly. "I would have you stay here."

His arm dropped away from her. "Nay, Angel," he said curtly, "in this life nothing lasts forever, especially those things that are good and warm, beautiful, precious and right. 'Tis a lesson you would do well to learn, but I must tell you that I have provided for you in my will. You need not fear, dearest."

"Don't!" she cried. "I care nothing for whatever provisions you may have made! I will not talk about it! I want only you, only you!"

He looked at her reprovingly. "Then I will say nothing more." He stroked her hair. "Come, brat, I didn't mean to hurt you, you must know that."

She looked up at him. "I know, of course I know. But Nicholas, it will hurt me if you go to London."

"It may be that I will find nothing serious," he said firmly. "In that case, you may expect me back before dark."

"Then I will go with you."

"You will stay here. I would not have you in the midst of what may well be a disaster. I ask you to stay here. I d—do more. I—I command you to s—stay here."

She heard the slight catch in his breathing, one of the danger signs Mrs. Sampson had warned her to look for. "Very well, Nicholas, if you command it." Relieved, she felt the tension go from his body. Privately, however, she was resolved to follow him.

His eyes searched her face suspiciously. "I must ask you to give me your word."

"I will do nothing of the sort. You must trust me or not, just as you please."

"Angel—" His words broke off as he heard the sound of footsteps crackling among the fallen leaves.

"Master Nickey!" Mrs. Sampson appeared between a clearing in the trees. "The gardener has—has just found Mr. Barrymore."

"*Found* him? What the devil are you talking about, Sampson?"

"He was lying near the gates. Evidently his horse had wandered off, for we could see no sign of it."

Nicholas rose to his feet. "Is he badly hurt?"

"I don't know. He's got numerous cuts and bruises, and from the look of him, he must have gone in for sweeping chimneys."

"Go, then, Sampson. We will follow you."

Angel hung back a little. "Nicholas, what can be wrong?"

He looked up at the sky, his mouth tightening. "I think that I have a very good idea."

Alex Barrymore struggled to open his eyes. There seemed to be a great weight pressing down on his lids. He put an exploring hand to his jaw. It felt stiff and swollen and it hurt when he moved his mouth.

"Alex," a deep voice said. "How are you feeling?"

He felt the cool smoothness of pewter against his bruised lips, and he swallowed the wine automatically.

"*Alex!*" the voice said again.

"I'm all right," Alex muttered. "J—just let me rest, please." "If you will but answer some questions," the deep voice said with a trace of impatience, "then you may rest for as long as you please."

Nicholas's voice? Unwillingly, Alex began the struggle again, and through a wavering blur, he made out the figure of Nicholas standing before him, looming tall and straight, the goblet still in his hand. He appeared to be dressed for riding, for he was clad in plain black, with bands of white edging the high neck and the wide cuffs of his jacket. A black cloak swung from his shoulders, and a broad-brimmed black hat embellished with a curling white feather shadowed his face.

"The black earl in—in person," Alex said weakly, managing a smile. "Don't rear above me like that. I v—vow that you look positively satanic."

"Hast seen yourself, Alex?" Nicholas said, returning the smile. "I would imagine, from your general appearance, that you have but recently come from the city. But how came you by your cuts and bruises?"

"Nicholas!" Alex attempted to sit up. "I must tell you about the fire."

"I am more interested in your injuries. I will find out for myself about the fire."

Alex nodded. "It happened when I began riding out for Elm Park. I was just outside the city. Some men sprang

170

out from the bushes. Like me," he shrugged, "they had just come from the city. Escaped through the gates, I suppose. I was mounted, they on foot. They dragged me from my horse and—er—used their cudgels upon me quite effectively. I was, I must confess, too spent to defend myself. I recall them shouting," Alex said slowly, his brow wrinkling in thought, " 'here's a Dutchy, boys. Let's give him something he'll long remember for firing our city.' "

"By that they meant a Dutchman, I presume?" Nicholas said, his black brows drawing together.

"Aye. Hysteria is mounting as the fire rages on. I managed to catch enough of their conversation to gather that a general idea is going around that the Dutch are responsible for the firing of London."

"The people must ever seek a scapegoat."

"Nevertheless there is such talk throughout the city. The rumor is that the Dutch are in a plot to destroy us, and will shortly begin an invasion. I saw many foreigners set upon and badly injured."

"And what do you here, Alex?"

"I came at the behest of Sir Montague Jermyn."

Alex explained the situation rapidly. He had just reached the word "gunpowder," when a stifled exclamation caused him to turn his head sharply. He had not noticed that Angel was present. Beside her, wringing out a cloth in a basin, stood Mrs. Sampson.

"Your pardon, my lady," Alex said quickly. He nodded and smiled at Mrs. Sampson. "My head is still rather muddled, I fear."

"Mr. Barrymore," Angel acknowledged him. She walked toward Nicholas. "Will you not reconsider, my lord?" she said, putting a pleading hand on his arm.

Nicholas put his hand under her chin, tipping up her head until her eyes met his. "I am not a child, brat," he said softly. "Hast forgotten that I am known as the 'vanishing Earl?' If danger threatens, I promise you that I shall live up to the title."

Angel did not smile. "I know better, Nicholas."

"I was about to depart for London," Nicholas said, turning back to Alex, "when you made your dramatic appearance. And how are you feeling now?"

"Much better, thank you." Alex's eyes turned to Angel. The delicate skin about her eyes was puffy and red, and her face was blotched as though she had been crying for a long time. He looked away hastily, unable to bear the accusation he thought he read in her eyes. "I will go with you, Nicholas," he added quietly.

"Nonsense. Those cuts need attention. After you are rested, you may ride for London, not before."

"I am glad you have such a care for Mr. Barrymore," Angel cried out bitterly. "But what of yourself, my lord?"

Nicholas slapped his riding gloves sharply against the palm of his hand. "That will be enough, Angel!"

" 'Twill be too much for you!" Angel's voice rose hysterically.

"You will be silent!"

"I will not!" Baffled by her vehemence, Nicholas stared at her for a long moment, then shrugged. "We will not discuss it further. I will return to you unharmed. That is all that need concern you."

Mrs. Sampson sighed. "You know that Angel is right, Master Nickey. I pray you to listen to her."

"Sampson!" Nicholas said in a low goaded voice. "You will oblige me by minding your own business!"

Alex looked at Angel's drawn face, the distress in the housekeeper's eyes. Mrs. Sampson, the most stoic of women as a rule, was crying, and the hand holding the wet cloth trembled. What could be wrong? Was Nicholas ill? He looked healthy enough, but still one could never tell.

"Nicholas," Alex began hesitatingly. "If there is some reason why you should not go, then I pray you to pay heed to the ladies."

"I thank you for your concern," Nicholas said curtly.

"Nicholas!" Angel cried.

"Come, brat," Nicholas said, turning to the door. He held out his hand. "Will you not see me off?"

He waited until Angel had taken his hand, then he said calmly, "I will look for you in London, Alex. As for you, Sampson, come over here."

"Don't go, Master Nickey, please don't!"

"Shut your prattling mouth, woman, and give me a kiss."

"A kiss!" Mrs. Sampson's alarm intensified. "Why do you ask me for a kiss, Master Nickey? You have never done so before."

"Have I not? 'Twas most remiss of me, then."

Mrs. Sampson kissed him on both cheeks. "Oh, lad lad, have a care for yourself, and may God walk with you!"

For some moments after the door had closed behind them, Mrs. Sampson stood there, her back toward Alex, her arms hanging heavily at her sides.

"Mrs. Sampson," Alex said, breaking the silence. " 'Tis not like you to create a scene. What is wrong with Lord Benbrook?"

"Why did you have to come here, Mr. Barrymore?" Mrs. Sampson whirled to face him. "Why did you have to encourage him in his folly? You don't know what you have done!"

"And what exactly have I done?"

Mrs. Sampson's face changed. "Nay, sir, forgive me, you have done nothing. Even had you not come, he'd have gone anyway. He would have it that he was quite recovered." Mrs. Sampson bustled forward. "Best let me have another look at those cuts, sir."

"I asked you a question, Mrs. Sampson. What is wrong with Lord Benbrook?"

"He—he—" Her mouth trembled. "It's his heart, sir."

"Damnation, that fool!" Alex struggled to rise from the couch. "I must stop him."

" 'Twill do no good, sir. 'Tis already too late. Can't you hear his horse's hooves?"

"Run after him!"

"If my lady cannot change his mind, sir, be sure that

you'll not be able to manage it. I—" She broke off, seeing the blue eyes regarding her turn cold. "I'll do it, sir, if you insist," she added lamely.

The door opened just as Mrs. Sampson reached it, and Angel came into the room. "He's gone, Mrs. Sampson," Angel said in a low voice, not looking at Alex.

"I know," Mrs. Sampson said soothingly. "But he'll be back, child."

"Do you really believe that?" Mrs. Sampson flinched from the burning eyes in the white bleak face. "Think you I would let him ride into danger, and I remain safely behind? Nay, you know better than that. Tell Bateson to saddle a horse at once."

"Very well." Her shoulders drooping, Mrs. Sampson left the room.

Alex looked at Angel's rigid back. "My lady," he began, "I would have you know that I had no knowledge of my lord Benbrook's illness. Had I known, I would have refused to carry the message."

She started, then turned quickly to face him. He knew, from the look on her face, that she had forgotten his presence. "I—I beg your pardon, Mr. Barrymore. What did you say, please?"

He felt absurdly hurt that she could so easily have dismissed him from her thoughts. But he answered her gently enough.

"Oh." Her eyes turned blank and her forehead wrinkled as though she sought to make sense of his words. " 'Twas no fault of yours, sir," she said at last. "Either way, you could not have stopped him."

She dropped him a quick curtsy, then turned to the door. "Mrs. Sampson will return shortly. Be sure that she will care for your injuries."

He wanted to shout at her, *I care nothing for my injuries. I care only for you!* " 'Tis not good to be in London at this time, my lady. Won't you at least wait until I am able to accompany you?"

"Wait?" She shook her head. "My lord is on his way to London. Where my lord goes, I go."

Without another word or a glance in his direction, she left the room.

Alex lay perfectly still, her last words echoing in his ears. *"Where my lord goes, I go."* Suddenly he found himself recalling his Bible, and the poignant speech made by Ruth. *"For whither thou goest, I will go!"* Alex quoted softly.

He could not get her white face, the feverish brilliance of her eyes, out of his mind. When Mrs. Sampson returned, he was still thinking of her, the beautiful Lady Benbrook, with her golden skin, her bright hair, her lovely mouth, and her consuming love for Nicholas, made so transparently obvious by her every word and gesture. Alex found himself shivering. Nothing must happen to Nicholas, for if it did it would surely destroy her.

"You're not listening to me, sir." Mrs. Sampson said sharply. "I think you'll find your ankle more comfortable now. I have bound it quite tightly. 'Twill give you more support."

"Thank you," he answered vaguely. "It feels much better."

"You need not worry about Angel, sir. She'll survive this, just as she has survived other things."

"Why do you call her Angel?"

"Because it is her name, sir."

Alex frowned. "I know it's her name. I wondered why you addressed her as Angel, rather than my lady Benbrook. Have you known her for a long time?"

Mrs. Sampson looked at him, her eyes unreadable, a faint smile curling her lips. "Aye, sir, I've known her for a very long time." Her smile deepened. "I was present at her rebirth."

"Rebirth? My lord Benbrook spoke of a story in connection with his wife," Alex said slowly. "What is it, Mrs. Sampson?"

" 'Tis not for me to say. If Master Nickey returns, he will tell you about it, if he's of a mind to." Mrs. Sampson's eyes clouded. "He must return, sir, for if aught happens to him, my lady could not go on living!"

175

Alex stirred uneasily. "People do not die of grief," he said abruptly.

Mrs. Sampson stooped to pick up the bowl of water, and again she regarded him with that unreadable expression. "My lady would," she said simply. "Perhaps not physically," she went on quickly, seeing his startled face, "but inside she would die. Master Nickey is her life. Without him there would be no Angel."

"What do you mean?" Alex waited, knowing how she would continue.

"I mean that there would be a stranger who spoke with her voice, who would be possessed of the same face and figure, but it wouldn't be Angel, sir. Not the Angel that I have known." Mrs. Sampson moved slowly and heavily toward the door. In that moment she looked every year of her age. " 'Tis by her own request that I call her Angel."

The door closed gently behind her. Alex lay still, surprised to find that his eyes were wet. Again he remembered the words of Ruth: *For whither thou goest, I will go, and there will I be buried!*

THE RIVER THAMES WAS CONGESTED WITH small craft, each one crammed to capacity with people who sought the river lane to escape the roaring fury. Pots and pans could be seen floating on the water, articles of clothing, small toys, wooden cages, many of them containing squawking birds; dotted here and there was the dark sleek bobbing of heads as some tried to swim to safety. Yet others, unable to find room, clung desperately to the sides of boats, their fingers whitening with the strain as they were swept along. Men cursed aloud as they wielded the clumsy oars; sobbing women tried to hold on to screaming, squirming children and to keep their balance in the craft at the same time. Behind them rose a macabre background, as the sky flared crimson and yellow with great pillars of fire that rent the dense billowing clouds of smoke.

That marching wall of fire meant the inevitable destruction of their homes, their hopes and dreams for a safe and secure future. And yet the people's tired grimed faces still lit up as they saw the King's barge proceeding downriver. The King, with his brother the Duke of York, and his friend the Earl of Benbrook beside him, were going into the heart of it.

Charles was touched by the wild cheering that greeted his appearance. There were tears in his eyes as he snatched off his plumed hat and responded vigorously.

The Duke of York, the curls of his long blond wig blowing in the fierce wind that swept the riverfront, gave his own hearty response, but his thoughts were only with the job that faced him. Charles had finally given his consent for the use of gunpowder in leveling the buildings in the path of the fire. James sighed. He was genuinely fond of his brother, and the King had turned on him a look of cold rebuke when the Earl of Benbrook had put in an appearance. In vain had he explained that Benbrook was an expert in the use of gunpowder, and that they needed an expert if they were not to court fresh disaster. To all of this, Charles had said firmly, "My lord Benbrook is ill, James. You know he should not be subjected to this."

Benbrook, as was his way, had said nothing. He had stood by with that look of faint amusement in his eyes that had always managed to exasperate James in the past.

Charles' anger had finally cooled. "My lord," he had said, turning to Nicholas. "You will return at once to Elm Park Manor."

"Nay," Nicholas said, shaking his head. "Here do I stay until the danger has been averted."

"You forget yourself, my lord." Charles' eyes had flashed imperiously. "I have given you a command."

"If I forget myself, Sire," Nicholas said, " 'Tis in your interest, as it has always been."

Charles, as usual, had been unable to withstand Benbrook's own particular blend of cool arrogance and determination. "All right," he had grinned reluctantly, "and curse you for an insolent rogue." Turning to James, he added, "I shall hold you accountable for my lord Benbrook's safety."

"Oh come, Sire," Nicholas said quickly. "I am accountable only to myself."

James looked at Benbrook now. He was lounging in a corner of the barge, apparently unmoved by the fury and destruction all about him. Yet James was not deceived by his air of indolence. He had seen the look in

Benbrook's eyes when a child's broken toy had swept past the barge. He had seen the shaking of his hands before he had clasped them firmly in his lap. Nay, Benbrook was as he had always been in the field of battle, so touched by the suffering that confronted him that he needs must put on his iciest and most remote expression to hide it. Not for the first time, James found himself wondering why Benbrook was so afraid to display emotion. Poor little Angel, James thought. Would all her fire and spirit be quenched by Benbrook's coldness, or would she manage to find that other Benbrook, the one so rarely glimpsed, that hid beneath the stiff exterior? One never knew with Benbrook, mayhap he had grown too used to concealing his deeper feelings.

Nicholas coughed as an incautiously drawn breath drove the smoke bitingly into his lungs. Then as he saw Charles glance at him, he stifled the cough against his cloak.

"Sire," Nicholas said, rising to his feet and approaching Charles, "let me once again assure you that I am flattered by your anxiety, but I am well able to take care of myself."

"I was not aware that I had mentioned anxiety, my lord Benbrook."

Nicholas shrugged. " 'Tis true, Sire, that you have not done so for the last fifteen minutes. But 'tis when the look you turn on me becomes that of a brooding mother rather than a King, that one tends to wonder."

Charles flushed. "Friend Nicholas! Why the devil do I put up with you?"

Nicholas surveyed him with his dark grave eyes. "Perhaps, Sire," he said slowly, "it is because of the title with which you have gifted me."

"Title? What title?"

"Friend Nicholas."

At that moment the barge grounded to a halt. Refugees, laden with children and bundles, surged past them as they stepped ashore. In their panic, they jostled the King roughly to one side, not even recognizing him.

Sir Thomas Bludworth, who had been expecting the arrival of the royal barge, ran forward and fell to his knees. "Sire!" he wailed, raising a face streaked with soot and tears. "Sire, I have done my best to carry out your command, and let no man tell you differently!"

Charles had some difficulty in recognizing the Lord Mayor, so begrimed was he, so ragged and wild of aspect.

"Get to your feet, Bludworth."

The unfortunate Sir Thomas managed to lumber to his feet. He stood there swaying, his eyes glaring in panic. "I set the men to pulling down the houses, Sire, but the flames will not be stopped. No, Sire, no gap will stop them, they just go on and on, destroying everything in their way!" In the flickering light, the man looked ghastly. There were bruises on his face, his clothes were dripping wet, he had lost his wig, and blackish slime clung to his bald head. "Sire," he said in a quivering voice, breaking into tears. "The people blame me for the disaster. They have attacked me like wild beasts, and have twice flung me into the Thames. And, Sire, I c—c—cannot s—swim. Had it not been for the good offices of two little lads, I might well have drowned!"

Despite the gravity of the situation, Charles had some difficulty in suppressing a laugh. "You have done your duty, Lord Mayor. There, man, try to rest, if it be possible." He placed his hand on the man's quivering shoulder. "I am here now, so if blame there be, it will be attached to me."

"But, Sire!" Sir Thomas wrung his hands together. "You must not dream of venturing among the people."

"Worry not, Sir Thomas," Nicholas's calm voice put in. "His Majesty is a very strong swimmer."

The Lord Mayor did not see the smile in the eyes regarding him. "Then is my mind at rest," he said seriously. "For I assure you, Sire, when the waters met over my head, I thought that my last hour had come."

Charles, after a rebuking glance at Nicholas, was about to reply, when a messenger broke through the crowd surrounding them. The man's clothing was singed, his eyebrows and his beard charred. "Your Majesty," the man gasped out. "The Royal Exchange has been destroyed. Cheapside has gone up in flames, and the fire in Thames Street has spread outward to Billingsgate and the docks!"

Charles stared at him, stunned, but recovering, he saw the messenger's frightened eyes fixed upon his face. "There, laddie," he said bracingly, "all will be well. We have a plan to stop the fire." He looked at the Duke of York. "Od's Fish, James, the plan must work, else will all London be in ashes!"

He turned back to the messenger. "Take word to all the Stations," Charles said abruptly. "Evacuation must begin at once. Tell the councillors that when this has been done we will start the demolition."

"I will do as you bid me, Sire," the messenger said, heaving a deep sigh, "but 'twill take some time." He hesitated. "Your Majesty, there have been many deaths. Not only from the flames, but from the panic. Some of the people were kicked to death, others were suffocated by bodies piling on top of them."

The King turned stricken dark eyes upon him. "May God forgive me for my helplessness!"

"Nay, Your Majesty," the man protested, " 'tis no fault of yours. You have done all that may be done."

"Not quite. But with the gunpowder, we hope, God willing, to make a considerable impression. There, lad, off with you now. See that you visit all of the Stations."

"At once, Your Majesty." The man hurried away.

"Bludworth!" the King shouted, glancing about him. "Bludworth! Where i' plague has the man gone?" A faint whistling whine from behind him caused him to swing round sharply. "So there you are, Bludworth."

Again Sir Thomas wrung his hands together. "Your Majesty will forgive me that I stepped back a pace or two, but almost did I feel myself sliding into a swoon. Gunpowder! We will be destroyed, Sire. It will blow up the whole city and lay it in waste."

The King frowned impatiently. "And what do you

think the flames are doing now? I requested horses. Where are they?"

"They are tethered nearby, Sire. I will—I will fetch them."

"No need. Just point out the way." Charles strode forward, Bludworth struggling feebly after him.

Just before they mounted the frantically pawing horses, Nicholas laid his hand on the Lord Mayor's arm and said kindly, "You may swoon now, Sir Thomas. From the look of you, I doubt not you have need of the rest."

Struggling to control his frightened horse, the King grumbled, "That infernal sense of humor will get you into trouble one day, friend Nicholas."

Hands soothing on the reins, but at the same time in iron control, Nicholas lifted a mocking eyebrow. "Humor, Sire? How can you so accuse me? I have been told that I have none."

"Fools who cannot see beyond their noses may have said so, but I know better."

A bark of laughter came from James. "Charles, did you see Bludworth's face? I vow that the poor devil looked like a stag at the end of the chase."

" 'Tis hardly the time or place to sit upon our horses laughing like loons, James. The man is decidedly unfortunate in that he is unpopular with the people."

Any small inclination they may have had toward laughter left them as they rode into the city. With a few exceptions, they were ringed about by a solid wall of flame.

All the rest of that day the King, with his brother and his friend beside him, toiled with unknown men. Weary after a few hours, but unflagging, the King, his coat and wig flung aside, his lace ruffles scorched, burns on his hands and face, rallied them to further efforts. He made his small jokes, listened to theirs, and encouraged them to go on creating the gap which might temporarily turn the flames aside until the evacuation of the city had been completed and the gunpowder could be safely used.

Once he and Nicholas, with James running behind,

rushed to the assistance of a woman who seemed to be in imminent danger of receiving a deluge of bricks on her head. Panting, her eyes wild, she stood directly beneath the jutting roof of a church which was already beginning to blaze at the back. Despite the havoc all about her, she was grandly dressed, as though in defiance of the fate that might conceivably await her. She wore her hair dressed high on her round head, her ample form was clad in a gown of violent pink, and her tremendous bosom enclosed in a foam of yellowing, singed lace.

"Don' you lay one bleedin' finger on me," she screamed, resisting the King's efforts to pull her from her dangerous shelter. "I 'eard as the King's acomin', an' I ain't movin' from this spot till 'e do."

"Madam," the King panted, taking hold of one flabby arm, and signaling to Nicholas to take the other, "the King is already present."

"No 'e ain't then. I'd 'ave seen 'im if 'e was." She wrenched one arm free. "Leave me be. I got ter see 'im, I tell you!"

"Why?" Nicholas said gently. "Why is it so important to you?"

The woman's mouth worked. "I wan' ter see 'ow 'e looks. 'Cause if bonny Charlie ain't afraid, it'll 'elp me." Her voice dropped to a whisper. "Can' very well be afraid if the King ain't, you see?"

Avoiding the eyes of the others, Charles said in a shaken voice, "Have no fear, the King is with you."

" 'Is he," the woman said eagerly. "You seen 'im, 'ave you?"

"Madam, you are looking at him."

The woman stared for a moment, then she gave a shriek of laughter. "What, dearie, you? You tryin' ter tell me as you're the King? Makes me laugh, that do. You talks like a swell, an' you're tall an' skinny like 'im, but you ain't nothin' but a bleedin' scarecrow." She jerked a thumb at the two men standing silently beside him. "If you're the King," she said, winking, "who's these 'ere others, then?"

Grave-faced, Charles made the introduction. "The Duke of York, madam," he said, indicating James, "and the Earl of Benbrook."

"Oh my! Now we got a Dook an' an Earl." The woman bobbed a mock curtsy. "If you're them, then I'm that bleedin' 'igh class whore, me lady Castlemaine. It's nice ter meet up wi' you, gents."

"Your Majesty!"

Charles turned sharply. "What is it?" he said, to the man running toward him.

Trembling, the man stopped before him. "The flames have leaped the fire gaps at Cripplegate. Fleet Street is under fire, and the flames are threatening to destroy the Temple."

Charles' mouth went dry. "And what of the houses in the Fleet Valley?"

"Gone, Your Majesty, so I heard. Christ Church, too, and Newgate Prison."

"Newgate Prison?" Nicholas said in a low voice.

"Aye, my lord."

"Od's Fish!" Charles turned to James. "You are in charge of the demolition, brother. See the evacuation completed, then do what you must. Nicholas, you come with me." At James' exclamation, he added quickly, "Friend Nicholas will be with you before long, but at this moment I need him."

They had forgotten the woman. She stood staring at them, her mouth half open. "Why," she said in a faint voice, "you're the King, ain't you!"

Charles frowned impatiently. "I am sorry if my appearance disappoints you."

"Workin'," the woman said in a dazed voice, "Workin' just like my man an' my brother Tom!" She continued to stare at him, then, remembering her manners, she swept him a curtsy. "Always wan'ed ter do that, I did," she said, straightening. "An' you ain't disappointed me, Your Majesty. You're gran', you are, an' I won' 'ear different from no one, see."

"My thanks, madam."

"I met the King," she whispered, drawing herself to her full height, " 'an the Dook an' the 'vanishin' Earl,' fancy that!" She peered closely at Charles. "An' you ain't afraid, are you?"

"Madam, we are all afraid. But 'tis best if we do not show it." He looked at the Duke. "James, since you are leaving us, pray escort the lady to safety."

" 'Twould pleasure me to do so." Sober-faced, James extended his arm.

Beaming, the woman took it. "Me on the arm o' a Dook! I never would 'ave believed it!" Her happiness was completed when Charles, on a whim, took her hand and carried it to his lips.

Quite beside herself now, the woman gave her hand to Nicholas. "I 'ad me 'and kissed by the King an' the 'vanishin' Earl,' " she shrieked, as she waddled away. "I ain't afraid no more. We're all goin' ter come through to saf'ty."

"Amen to that," Charles said below his breath. He glanced at Nicholas. "What the devil are you smiling about?"

"Even in the midst of this holocaust you do not forget your manners. The Stuart will be charming, even though it kills him."

"Naturally," Charles answered, grinning. "I am an ugly devil and charm is my only asset." His smile faded. "Name of God, Nicholas, my poor people! Those hovels in the Fleet Valley, all destroyed, and there is nothing I can do to help! London, my London is burning before my very eyes!"

"I remind you that you are the King!" There was a sharply rebuking note in Nicholas's voice. "Do not let others hear you speak so." On an impulse, Nicholas put his arm about the bowed shoulders. "Come, Charles, take heart. The people look to you. You help them by being here when they need you, by working with them. I believe, as the lady recently remarked, that we'll win through."

"But London—"

"London can be rebuilt. A better, stronger, cleaner London."

"Aye, you're right," Charles said huskily. The ghost of his old smile flashed out. "Though only God can know where the money's to come from. As for you, your presence helps me, friend Nicholas, as it has ever done. Now come, you lazy hound, there's work for us to do."

Laboring tirelessly, Nicholas beside him, Charles' spirits rose. Up to his knees in mud, deluged by water, and several times struck by falling bricks, his red satin breeches now indistinguishable from the rougher clothing of the other men, he gave a fresh fountain of energy to all who worked with him. Other men, coming to aid the little group, and not knowing that they worked beside the King, cursed him when his flying shovel sent mud into their eyes, but all worked with a will, and with a comradeship brought about by a common danger.

Only twice did the King's spirits fail him, once, when Nicholas, attacked by a sudden spasm of pain, fell against him, gasping. Alarmed by his white lips, the spasmodic clenching of his hands, the King had sharply ordered him to rest. For the space of ten minutes Nicholas had obeyed this command, and then, to the King's great relief, he had seemed quite recovered.

The second time, Charles, his little group of workers staring in awe and fright, had watched the burning of St. Paul's, the great dome blazed like a torch against the sky, rising high above the burning houses surrounding it. Its leaden roof bubbled in the fierce heat, sending molten streams splashing down to the cobbles below. Hot lead struck the fleeing people, and the air was filled with screams of agony.

"My God!" Charles whispered to Nicholas. "Oh, my God!" He put his hand to his shaking mouth. "I think I'm going to vomit."

"No, you're not," Nicholas said firmly. "You are going to work, Sire, as you have been doing these many hours."

Charles' hand dropped. "So I am," he said coolly.

186

"You, my lord Benbrook, are nothing but a cursed slave driver. Are you the King, or am I?"

"You are, Sire," Nicholas's faint smile appeared. "I thank my Creator that it is not I."

Some time later, the Duke of York appeared, his broad face reddened with the heat; he was panting as though he had run a long way. "Sire," he said, stopping before the King. "I have need of the services of my lord Benbrook."

With a wry smile, Charles took the shovel from Nicholas's hand.

"We begin, Sire," York cried, "and may God aid our efforts."

"Friend Nicholas," the King said impulsively. "You will take care?"

"I will, Sire. Else will my lady never forgive me."

Charles gazed deeply into the dark eyes. "And neither will I, my lord. Remember that, please."

James cleared his throat loudly. "I'll look to him, brother."

"You are well meaning, James, I know," Charles said, smiling. "But your remark is not acceptable to him."

"Wrong, Sire," Nicholas put in quietly. "Friendship is always acceptable."

Charles sighed. "Ah, even now you must have the last word. There, get you gone, and remember to have a care of yourselves."

Charles gazed after them. He did not notice the curious look directed at him by the tall thin youth beside him. When he turned again, he met the lad's eyes. They were a light gray in color and very penetrating. For no reason that he could think of, Charles felt a cold aversion toward him. Charles summoned a smile. "Well, friend," he said, "shall we dig?"

"Yes indeed, Sire. The city needs all the help she can get."

The voice was high and nasal. Looking at the broad freckled hands grasping the shovel, Charles realized that never before had he taken such an instant dislike.

Ashamed, he said in a friendly tone, "Are you a citizen of London?"

"On the odd occasion, Sire. I do much traveling. I have seen many places, and I have been many things."

Charles smiled. "You have been many things, you say. But you are very young, are you not?"

"Young in years, Sire. I am seventeen. But I am, I assure you, old in knowledge."

"What do you mean?"

"I know many things, Sire. Look at the inferno about you." The high voice dropped to a whisper. "I know, for instance, that the fire of London is the result of a Popish plot. All things that are evil result from Popery."

The lad was raving. "Nonsense!" Charles spoke more sharply than he had intended. "I do not appreciate that kind of talk. In times like these, it is dangerous to spread such gossip."

"Popery is dangerous, Sire."

The hot-headed young fanatic! "I believe in freedom of religion," Charles said. "I have ever held this view."

The youth's blotched face creased into an unpleasant smile. "So I have heard, Sire."

"This is no time for idle chatter. Let us to our work."

"Would you like to know my name, Sire? One day you will remember me, for I intend to make myself known in England, and in all other countries where Popery flourishes."

"Fanaticism is dangerous, lad. You are young yet, and no doubt ambitious to make a name for yourself, but you would do well to heed my words."

"You are the King, and the King is always right."

At this barely veiled insolence, Charles' temper overcame him. "Aye," he said shortly, "I accept your words."

"I am glad, Sire. But I have not told you my name."

"Very well, young sir." Charles summoned his smile again. "I am listening."

With his eyes fixed dreamily on the blazing buildings a short distance away, the youth said slowly, "My name, Sire, is Titus Oates."

"Doubtless I will find it an easy one to remember."

"You will remember it, Sire, I promise you." The cold gray eyes rested thoughtfully on the King's face. "Aye, you will remember."

Titus Oates, Charles repeated to himself, as he piled his shovel. He was annoyed to find that his hands were trembling. What was the matter with him? His nerves must be in a perilous state if he could allow a foolish, big-mouthed young cub to so upset him. He worked on, but though the youth was shortly directed to another site, he could not rid his memory of those gray eyes, the high nasal voice, and, it seemed, the underlying threat in his words.

A stout man, who seemed to have taken over the role of the King's guardian, said cheerfully, "Nas'y creature, that one, Your Majesty, ain't 'e. Them eyes o' 'is is enough to give a soul a bleedin' nightmare."

"Aye, my friend, they are indeed."

ANGEL HAD LOST HER HORSE SOME FIVE MILES back. The animal, stumbling over a half-submerged moss-covered stone, had thrown her heavily to the ground. Then, snorting, whinnying loudly, he had wheeled about and bolted in the direction of Elm Park Manor.

Bruised and shaken, Angel managed to rise to her feet. Leaning against a tree for support, she tried whistling to the horse, calling to him in a soft cajoling voice. But the minutes went by, and still he did not appear.

Angel's mouth tightened into a line of determination. She would walk, then. Looking about her, she felt suddenly frightened. The woods bordering the road on either side were heavy with silence. Without the familiar rustlings and callings of the birds, everything seemed strangely dark and brooding. Shivering in the chill wind, she drew her cloak tightly about her and walked on steadily, her footsteps sounding unnaturally loud as she trod over carpets of dry dead leaves.

No wonder the horse had been nervous. Even from this distance she could smell the smoke from burning London. Doubtless the birds and the animals were terrified by the heavy choking smell.

As she drew nearer to her destination her eyes began to sting and water. It was as though she walked in a blue-black wavering haze, and several times she was actually uncertain of her footsteps. Her green hood had fallen back, her hair blew wildly in the driving wind. There were blisters on her heels, and, as the smoke became thicker, she was shaken with periodic fits of coughing.

The daylight had begun to fade when she came in sight of the city gates. Now she could see great showers of sparks flaring upward, the fierce flickering glare of flames against the clouded skyline. The air was filled with roar and fury. For some time now, she had been painfully aware of the rumbles that shook the earth. With each successive rumble, her heart beat a little faster. Gunpowder! 'Twould take but a chance spark to ignite it. Where was Nicholas, what had happened to him?

— She began to run toward the narrow gates, her eyes widening at the scene of human misery before her. Men and women, crying children, were huddled near the wall, their household goods and what small possessions they had managed to save strewn about them. As she drew nearer, she could hear the sound of singing, as some, in an obvious effort to raise their flagging spirits, joined their voices. Still others were quarreling among themselves, and the snarl of their voices rose above the singing.

As Angel approached, a woman, her eyes red-rimmed and fierce in her smoke-smudged face, rose to her feet and stood there staring. "Jus' look at what's acomin'," she cried.

"You're in a mighty 'urry, ain't you," the woman went on, grabbing at Angel's flying cloak. She fingered the material. "Tha's velvet, that is. Look good on me, it would. Hey, lads and lasses, ere's a fine lady come avistin'."

"Let go!" Angel shouted, pushing at the woman. "Stand aside, please. I must get through!"

"She mus' get through. You 'ear her, lads and lasses? Speaks English 'n' all. Ain't no foreigner, this un'."

"Maybe she's English, an' then again maybe she ain't," a man growled. He elbowed his way through the crowd. " 'Ere, le's 'ave a good look at you, then."

With dirty fingers, he tipped up Angel's face, and was somewhat taken aback when he met the fierce glare of her eyes. "Don' look like no foreigner. Still, one can't never tell." He pinched her chin viciously. "You English, are you, wench?"

"Of course I am, you fool!" she cried. She stared at the faces about her. In their savagery, they reminded her sickeningly of the inmates of Newgate. In her mind, the man before her took on the aspect of Jim Gibbons. She kicked out at him, trying to pull free. "What's the matter with you all? Have you lost your reason?"

The man's hands descended on her shoulders, and he pulled her close to him, thrusting his face near hers. She gasped aloud, recoiling from the strong singed smell of his clothing. "Nay, wench," he said in a menacing voice, "ain't none o' us lost our reasons. We're jus' comin' to 'em, we are. A suspect, tha's what you are, if you wants to know. But maybe, if you ain't no foreigner, you might well be one o' them dirty thieving murderin' Papists. Be you one o' them, eh?"

"Idiot!" She jerked herself away. "If I were Papist or foreigner, think you I would admit it?"

Shaken by her spirited defiance, he said truculently, "I ain't no idiot! I'll jus' show you, me gran' lady, how much of an idiot I be!"

"Shut up!" the woman snapped. She still continued to finger the material of Angel's cloak, but her mood seemed to have softened. "It be nice material, dearie," she pronounced. "Did I mention as it'd look right well on me?"

Wearily, Angel untied the strings of the cloak. "Yes, you did mention it. Here," she went on, thrusting it at the woman, "you may have it. I care naught for anything, save that I must get through. My husband is in there. He is helping to set the gunpowder charges."

The woman's eyes rested upon her thoughtfully. "If that be the truth, you can go through. If your man's in there wi' the King atryin' to save our city, you can go wi' my blessin'. Wha's your man's name? Maybe I know him."

Angel was uncertain of their reactions, and for a moment she hesitated, then she said defiantly, "My husband is the Earl of Benbrook. There, now you know, and you may make of it what you will."

"Eh!" The woman gaped at her. "Benbrook, did you say, my dearie? You ain't tellin' me as you're the 'vanishin' Earl's' woman?"

"I am."

There was a murmur among the crowd, and Angel caught the name Benbrook as it was bandied from mouth to mouth.

"Did you 'ear?" someone cried. " 'Tis the wife o' our 'vanishin' Earl.' 'Tis not too long since that we drank to the 'ealth o' both o' 'em. Give the lady back 'er cloak, Peg, you bloody thief!"

The woman held out the cloak, " 'Ere," she muttered, shamefaced. "You 'ave it back, me lady."

Angel's lips felt stiff, but she managed a smile. How quick a crowd were to rend you, and, fired by a chance word, how quick to acclaim. "Nay. Pray keep it as—as a memento."

They were all smiling good-naturedly now. They could not get near enough to her. Jostling and pushing each other, they stared, smiled, and reached out their hands to touch her. "Touch me baby's 'and, m'lady," an old woman shouted. " 'E's me grandson, but 'e'll grow up to boast as the vanishin' Earl's woman touched 'im an' wished 'im good luck."

The first woman, now the lawful owner of the cloak, donned it proudly. "Ah, but your bleedin' grandson can' say as 'e wore a garment what belonged to 'er, can 'e."

A guffaw greeted this. "Nay," the old woman cried. " 'E'd look perishin' funny in a ladies' cloak, that 'e would."

The first woman ignored this. "Don' you look so worried, dearie," she said to Angel, "ain't nothin' goin' to 'appen to your man." She chuckled, "Nay, not to 'im, it won't. Didn't old Noll 'ave 'im fast many a time, an' didn't 'e always escape right under the very noses o' old Noll's soldiers? Take more'n a fire, even one o' the like o' this, to 'arm 'im.''

Beaming, she pushed Angel toward the gates. "There, get along in, me lady. An' min' you 'ave a care o' yourself.''

As Angel went through the gates, she could hear their voices raised in singing—"Oh, the 'vanishin' Earl' is Cromwell's curse, is Cromwell's curse—''

Angel stared, appalled, at the devastation before her. There were no people to be seen. Great piles of plaster, brick, and smoldering timbers marked the sites where houses had once been. But all along the riverfront the fire still raged, so near to her that she could feel the scorching heat on her face. To the left, St. Paul's still flamed, a gradually dwindling torch against a jagged leaping rim of fire.

As she stood there, another explosion thundered in her ears, shaking the ground. Wincing, feeling the heat searing through her thin shoes, she picked her way around piles of smoldering ashes. Here and there, when she could see no other way clear, she was forced to climb over them, using her hands to aid her. Her gloves split open with the heat, but she scarcely felt the pain. Her mind was obsessed with one thought—Nicholas! Somehow she must find him!

Where was he, where was the King, all the people? Her breath began to labor in her lungs as they filled with the acrid smoke. It was a ghost city, with only the monstrous ravaging fire to keep her company.

She began to run, as though in the running she would outdistance the horror, the horror! Deserted, all deserted! In one street, she was forced to jump quickly aside as the front of a drunkenly leaning house fell to the ground with a great splintering crash. For a moment she stood there staring, her hand pressed to her trembling mouth. *Nicholas, Nicholas, where are you? Where have all the people gone?* The words persisted in her brain like a mad refrain.

She ran on and on, drawing her breath in great sobbing gasps, the roar of the flames loud in her ears. Then, as she turned a corner, she saw people. How had she missed hearing their voices? They were yelling at each other, banging loudly on the buckets they held. "We're beating it!" she heard the triumphant yell. "We're beating the fire! Three cheers for the King, the 'vanishing Earl' and the Duke!"

She rushed toward them, following after them as they disappeared into Thames Street. O God, let Nicholas be all right! Oh please, God, please!

Thames Street was milling with people. In this street the houses still stood. She could see a long line of men passing buckets along, throwing the water against a flaming house. Angel stood still, her eyes darting from face to face. She saw the King first, and standing beside him, Nicholas; at the King's other side, the Duke of York.

"I'm proud of you, lads," the King cried out, a note of exultation in his voice. "I'm proud of the lot of you! You've done a grand job this day!"

The King looked strangely unlike himself without his wig. His short dark hair curled in damp tendrils over his head. His clothing was torn and filthy, and his face reddened with burns. "Nicholas," he said, turning to the Earl, "I would say that we have now gained control over the fire. Am I correct in this assumption?"

"You are, Sire." Nicholas smiled at him, his teeth flashing white against his blackened face. "Save for this street and one or two other troublesome places, the full fury has been blunted."

"Thank God for that!"

"I echo the sentiment, Sire. Further charges of gunpowder have been laid in Ponder Street and the surrounding district. You should be hearing the explosion soon."

No sooner were the words out of his mouth than they were followed by a tremendous earth-shaking roar.

Charles reeled, catching quickly at Nicholas's arm to

save himself. "Gad!" he exclaimed, raising his voice above the excited cheering that had broken out, "damned if that didn't catch me quite unprepared." He laughed. "But 'twas the prettiest report I have ever been privileged to hear."

"Glad to give satisfaction, Sire."

Charles' face sobered. "You have done well. As for me, 'tis not fit that I should be laughing, and my city laid waste."

"There are times when a man must laugh, Sire, even though it outrages his grief, else would he not be able to bear it."

Charles nodded. "Aye, I myself have seen men laughing while the tears still fell from their eyes. There are those who mourn that way. The laughing outer mask that conceals a never-ending flow of tears. But we must not dwell on such things. What of yourself, my friend?"

"I am feeling quite well, Sire," Nicholas answered shortly.

"Forgive me. I know you do not wish to discuss it. But I am your friend, and, as such, surely privileged to make comment?"

"Of course, Sire. As for forgiving you, who would not forgive the King?"

"Bah! Do you have enough men at your disposal?"

"More than enough. But the men have no further need of me now, for all is under control. So, Sire, with your permission, I will take my place in the line."

"You do not need to ask my permission." Ruefully, Charles looked down at his swollen and blistered hands, the blood oozing from his torn fingernails. "But if you feel you have need of it, then right heartily do I give it."

Angel found herself unable to move. She stood there, her eyes on Nicholas, indifferent to the uproar and the people who continually jostled past her. Nicholas, she thought, looked exhausted, but surely not more so than the others. Her eyes turned to the King. He looked ready to fall asleep where he stood. As for the burly Duke of

York, his eyes were half closed, and she could see his big capable hands trembling with the weariness that beset him.

"Nicholas!" As though released from a spell, Angel screamed out his name and began fighting her way toward him. Another burst of cheering drowned out her voice, but she managed to push her way through the crowd.

Nicholas was talking to the King, but suddenly, as though he sensed her presence, he stiffened. He turned slowly and saw her standing in the cleared space before him. He stared at her for a long moment. "Angel?"

"Aye. I had to come."

"You little fool!" He grabbed her hand and pulled her close to him. "Did I not bid you to remain at Elm Park Manor? How dare you defy me!"

"I am your wife, m'lord," Angel said, her eyes flashing, "not your slave. I do not take kindly to orders."

"I care not in what fashion you take my orders," he said ominously, "but you will take them! I have no need of a guardian angel, madam. You will return to Elm Park Manor at once. The fire, as you can see for yourself, is not yet contained."

Her mouth set stubbornly. "I refuse. You cannot make me leave you!"

"If you think that, you are much mistaken." His hands clamped heavily on her shoulders. He hesitated, then said impatiently, "Nay, perhaps I do not quite mean that. But in this instance you will obey me. 'Tis dangerous in the city, and I will not have you exposed to it."

"Gad, friends," the King's voice broke in, "think you that this is the time for a quarrel between you?"

"Your pardon Sire," Nicholas said stiffly. "I should not have spoken so in your presence."

"Why not? Never before has my presence stayed you from speaking your mind." The King smiled at Angel. "As you can see, Nicholas, the lass is not to be moved. Give in and let her stay. You will have to do so in the end, so why not now?"

"There is no place for her here, Sire."

"Come, friend Nicholas, most of the danger has passed, has it not?"

"It has, Sire. Nonetheless there could still be danger. I must repeat that there is no place for her here."

"There is," Angel broke in. "I can—I can help to pass the buckets of water along the line. Nay, m'lord, 'tis no use glowering at me. I am staying, and that is my final word."

Nicholas's head rose arrogantly. "How dare you, madam!"

"A woman must learn to dare, if she be wedded to my lord Benbrook, else would she be utterly crushed."

Nicholas's slow reluctant smile appeared. "Stay, then, and be damned to you for an obstinate little guttersnipe!"

"Know you not that the ladies only pretend to let us have our way?" the King said, laughing.

"Indeed, Sire. Not in my household."

"Then, my friend, you must be capable of working miracles. I would have you pass your secret on to me."

"No miracle, Sire, I do assure you. Be not misled by the fact that I have accepted temporary defeat." Nicholas's eyes, frankly smiling now, turned to Angel. "I have every intention of crushing all signs of defiance. Have I not, my lady?"

"But shall we call a truce? Will it satisfy you, dear m'lord, if I promise that in the future I will endeavor to obey your every command?"

"No, for I don't for one moment believe you, brat." Nicholas touched her hair with a gentle hand. "You will obey, you say. 'Twill be a new departure for you, will it not?"

"You have done enough work for ten men this day," Charles said, with an understanding smile, "and a few minutes will not make much difference now. Take the plaguey wench away from the line, Nicholas, and mind you kiss the insolence from her bold mouth."

With Angel's hand in his, Nicholas turned away. "Thank you. I will return shortly."

199

"Aye, see that you do." Charles dug the Duke of York sharply in the ribs. "James! Wake up. Wouldst fall asleep while your brother toils like a damned slave?"

Holding tightly to Angel's hand, Nicholas began to push his way through the crowd. When they saw who it was, a scramble began to clear a path for him. Some called greetings, to which Nicholas replied with an inclination of his head.

They stopped before a wall, half of it still standing, the other half lying in rubble about their feet. Beyond the wall, Angel could see blazing trees, and the scurrying figures of men dragging their useless buckets of water over the sodden ground.

"This is not exactly a private place, brat," Nicholas said, "but 'tis the best I have to offer. Now then, explain yourself."

Angel studied his face. In the leaping light it looked very tired, the cheekbones standing out sharply, the dark eyes buried in shadowed hollows. "But naturally, m'lord," she replied, swallowing a lump in her throat, "the explanation would depend on whether your intention is to punish or to kiss me."

"You do not imagine, wench, that I would kiss you in this very public place, do you?"

"And why not? 'Tis as good a place as any, dear m'lord. Come, love, the heavens will not fall if you kiss me."

His smiling eyes looked into hers. "Since it is my misfortune to be in love with you, I will confess that I would like very much to kiss you."

"Then pray do so. Besides, did not the King himself command it?"

Nicholas drew her slowly into his arms. "So he did." His arms tightened about her. "It behooves us all to obey the King."

His mouth closed over hers, firm and cool at first, then warm demanding, urgently hungry. "You say you love me, and I believe you," Nicholas said softly. "But how much? Tell me, little one."

" 'Tis impossible to measure. What if I say I love you more than all the world?"

"Come, would you disappoint me? Only one world?"

She twined her arms about his neck, clinging to him tightly, her body trembling. "More than the world then, dear m'lord. More, much more than anything that might lie beyond. Oh, my lord, my love, you are my world! You are everything to me!"

The trembling passion in her voice surprised him at first, then, understanding, he said soothingly, "Hush, my brat, I did but jest with you. Why so serious?"

She looked at him helplessly, trying to smile. "I know not. Save that this seems to be the right time, the right place."

"While there is love between us, and mine for you will never grow dim, it will always be the right time, the right place." His hand stroked the damp hair back from her forehead. "I would that you will always remember what I tell you now." He hesitated, a muscle beside his mouth twitching. "I would have you know that you have made me very happy, Angel. So very, very happy!"

She stared at him, and he saw the fear clouding her eyes. "It is as though you are placing our happiness in the past!"

"What? Nay, my darling, I did but make a simple statement." He stooped to kiss her cheek. "Is aught else addling that foolish head of yours? The worst is over, brat, and, as you can see, I am still whole. Tired, of course, but healthy enough." He smiled at her, his eyebrows rising in his old sardonic manner. "As for taking care of myself, I can do no other, since my shrew of a wife is here to guard me. But what of yourself? Will you be careful?"

"I?" She frowned impatiently. "I learned how to look after myself from hard experience, hast forgotten? Nay, dear m'lord, have no fear for me. 'Tis you who matter, for 'tis my opinion that you take too many risks with yourself."

"Come, brat, there is much work to be done."

She placed her hand in his and felt his fingers clasp it warmly. "I will come. But first, m'lord, you must kiss me."

He sighed, "Dost realize that we have collected a most interested audience?"

She turned her head and looked at the grinning faces, the sympathetic eyes regarding them. "But should they not be getting about their own work," she went on tartly, "instead of standing there and gaping at us? You will kiss me at once."

"Will I?" He pulled her into his arms, holding her tightly. "I like not your imperious tone, madam. 'Tis a fault in you that I will endeavor to correct, when we are once more at home."

"Aye, dear m'lord, you may do so, if you will but kiss me now." She smiled at him. "Or art too shy to do so?"

"Shy? What nonsense is this!" He bent his head and pressed his lips firmly to hers. "There," he said, releasing her abruptly, "you have had your kiss, madam. See that you remember it."

"How could I forget it, dear m'lord?"

She saw his slow, almost boyish smile light his face. "I would have you know, my guttersnipe, that Benbrook does not give his kisses lightly."

"Does he not? Ah, but there was a time when he gave them frequently, and most lightly. And to lips other than mine. Many of those kisses were given, I know, at a time when you did not know me."

"A handsome admittance."

"It is, is it not?" she agreed calmly. "Later, however, when you did know me, your kisses were given to others because you were determined to punish me for daring to arouse love in your heart. Knowing this, I think I will forgive you."

He touched her nose with the tip of his finger. "Behave yourself, baggage, else will it be the worst for you."

"Well done, m'lord!" a man cried, as they made their way back through the crowd. "Wenches ought to be kissed good, that they did. It shows 'em who's master."

Ribald laughter greeted this statement, but Nicholas,

stopping before him, answered calmly. "I agree with you in every respect. Man must remain master, else will our society be turned upside down. As for the kiss, 'twas rather well done. See that you profit by the lesson, fellow."

"On 'ow to tame a lass, m'lord?"

"Aye, if the lass be half tigress." Nicholas's eyes turned to Angel. "If she be half tigress," he repeated in a low voice, "then 'tis the only way to deal with the situation."

Good-natured laughter followed them, and several faces plainly showed an astonished pleasure that the great Earl of Benbrook had so far unbent as to converse like any ordinary man. To them he was a hero, but there was an arrogance about him, a cold and rigidly unbending manner, as though he held himself far above the common man. And too, there was his icy bleakness of expression that, even while they admired him, was vaguely frightening.

Angel guessed what they were thinking, and her eyes became brooding and tender. *They don't know you, my darling,* she thought. *They don't know your compassion, your kindness, and they never will, simply because you don't know how to express it.* Her fingers tightened about his. *But I know. I have seen you stripped of all pretense, and I love you more than I can ever tell you!*

The King greeted them with a smile. "Ah," he said, his eyes on Angel's face, "my lady is flushed, and not from the heat of the fire, I'll vow. Has this rogue managed to cure you of your insolence?"

"Nay, Sire," Angel answered, feeling a rush of affection for him, "though 'twere better to let him think so."

The King's smiling eyes turned to Nicholas. "Your wife, my lord Benbrook, is a shameless hussy."

"Very true, Sire, as she has always been. But we must not turn her head, Sire. Now what of the men?"

"Their spirits are rapidly rising, and so, I must confess, are my own." Charles' smile flashed. "I have just had another report, and it confirms that the worst is over. I shall not forget your part in this, Nicholas, I'll show you my gratitude."

"Your friendship will suffice, Sire, as it has ever done. My lady Benbrook is willing to work, so she assures us," Nicholas went on, resuming his place in the line. "Shall we see if she has the fortitude?"

"So you shall," Angel said quickly. "For I tell you now, my lord, that my intention is to outwork you."

The Duke of York, rousing from his state of lethargy, reached across to pat Angel's shoulder. "That's the right spirit, my lady. I like well to hear such words." He turned his sleepy eyes to the King. "If you are grateful to Benbrook, Charles, you should also be grateful to me. 'Twas I who sent Barrymore posting to Elm Park Manor."

"Indeed?" Charles' brows drew together ominously. "I was under the impression that Barrymore rode to Elm Park Manor at the instigation of Sir Montague Jermyn."

"So he did." James chuckled softly. "But it was my idea. I knew, you see, that Benbrook was the best man when it came to the use of gunpowder."

"I know not at whose instigation Barrymore came," Nicholas put in coolly, "but my own decision to return to London was made long before he arrived."

James smiled from one to the other. They had all but conquered the fire. For almost four days it had raged, and he had often been a prey to private moments of despair. "It turned out well, did it not, Charles?" he said, putting down his bucket. "Benbrook is still with us. He has not been felled, as you feared he might be."

"Be silent!" Charles said curtly.

Taken aback by the King's tone, the Duke said quickly, "Are you angry, Sire? But why? I sent for Benbrook because I believed it to be for the best. I would not have done so, had I not been assured in my heart that he was quite well."

"I repeat, Your Grace," Nicholas said, a cold edge to his voice, "that the decision was my own. Therefore you must not hold yourself in any way to blame."

The King saw the sudden grim set of Nicholas's lips. " 'Tis not fitting to discuss my lord Benbrook as though he were not here."

"Your pardon, my lord," the Duke said stiffly. "I would like to see how my men are faring, Sire. Might I be excused?"

"Go, James. Do not dally overlong, for I doubt not we will have further need of you."

"Very well, Sire." His lower lip thrust out petulantly, the Duke walked away.

"James," the King said, gazing after him, "does not always take the time and trouble to think things out clearly."

"Nay, Sire, it is of no great moment, is it? His Grace, I feel sure, acted with the best of intentions."

Nicholas turned to Angel, who had taken a brimming bucket from the man next to her and was now holding it out with arms that trembled slightly. "Here, Sire," Nicholas said, taking it from her and handing it to the King, "the brat seeks to show us her muscle."

Charles' mercurial spirits rose at once. "Od's Fish," he shouted, "but I'll not be outdone by a dainty slip of a female! Attention, lads, haul buckets!"

Laughter greeted this, and the men attacked the burning house with renewed energy, but it was some time before they at last managed to reduce it to a black and sullen ruin. A fresh line formed, and the King, taking his own men with him, moved on to another site.

When they reformed before another building, Angel's head was aching dully. Her arms felt so heavy that she was scarcely able to move them. She wanted to sit down and rest, if only for a few moments, but she could not bring herself to plead her sex as an excuse. The dogged endurance of those about her drove her on. Gritting her teeth together, she continued to pass the heavy buckets.

Nicholas bent his head and brought his mouth close to her ear. "You must not be foolish, my darling. I wish you to take a rest."

Angel pushed a lock of singed hair away from her

eyes. "Surely *you* have earned a rest? When you take one, I will also, and not before."

"Angel, you will listen to me. I will—" Nicholas's words broke off. He looked up, startled, as a rending noise came from the flaming house before them.

"Back!" the King shouted. "Back, I say. The beam is about to fall!"

Angel looked up. The charred beam was inclining slowly outward from the house. It had not yet detached itself, but she stood there fascinated, unable to bring her feet to move. Then, as Nicholas's hand grasped her and pulled her roughly away, fascination gave way to horror.

"What was the matter with you?" Nicholas snapped. "Why didn't you move?"

"I don't know. I just c—could not."

"It's falling!" somebody shouted.

Behind Angel, somebody stumbled, and she felt a violent push against her shoulder. Her hand was torn from Nicholas's, and she went sprawling forward, directly in the path of the falling beam.

She screamed loudly as a crushing weight pinned her to the ground. "Nicholas! Nicholas!"

"Angel!" Nicholas was on his knees beside her, his arms straining as he attempted to lift the beam. "Hold still. Don't struggle! You'll be free in a moment, darling!"

There was a swimming mist before her eyes, but Angel dimly made out the feet of the men surrounding her. "Easy, Nicholas," she heard the King say. "Don't try to do it all yourself. We'll all help. Heave, lads, heave!"

The weight was lifting. She heard the crash as the beam was flung to one side. She was free. She moved her legs experimentally. She was not seriously hurt, then, she decided, or she would not have been able to move them at all. "Nicholas?" she said faintly.

"I'm here, Angel." He was kneeling beside her, taking her in his arms and holding her tightly against him. She heard his shaken whisper. "Oh, my brat, my little one!"

"Hush, dear m'lord. I am not m—much hurt, truly I am not."

He held her away a little, staring anxiously into her face. "But 'twas a terrible weight across your legs."

Frightened by the convulsive shuddering of his body, she tried to make light of it. "If you insist that I be hurt, my lord, then I—I will try to accommodate you. I—I am bruised, and my back aches abominably, but other than that I am all right."

"Angel!" He cradled her close again, and she felt the tears on his cheeks. "Thank God!"

"Did I hear m'lady say that she was unhurt?" a light voice said.

Angel looked up into the King's face. " 'Tis a miracle, Sire, but nonetheless true."

The King glanced sharply at Nicholas, his eyes clouding as he saw the shuddering of his body. "Come, my friend, this will not do. You must take hold of yourself. I understand how you feel, but people are watching."

"Give—give me a moment, Sire," the reply came in a stifled voice.

"As many moments as you wish." The King hesitated, a worried frown creasing his forehead. "Look to your husband, my lady," he said softly, as he moved away.

Angel put her hand to Nicholas's wet cheek. "You must not," she said gently. "Indeed, dear m'lord, I cannot bear to see you cry. Come, Nicholas, this is not like you."

"Is—is it n—not? But you must know, since first you c—came into my life, that I am as—as unlike my old self as it is possible to be. I very much fear, b—brat, that you have—have brought me to my ruin."

"But you enjoy your ruination, do you not? Tell me you do, love."

"Aye, I do, you insolent baggage." He gasped, and his arms tightened bruisingly about her. "A—A—Angel!"

"Nicholas! What is it?"

"P—pain! C—cannot bear it!" His arms fell away from her. "An—Angel, I c—c—can't see y—you. Don't l—leave m—me!"

He fell back, his chest heaving as he labored to draw breath. "S—stay with—with m—me, b—brat."

207

"Nicholas!" she screamed out his name, her arms trying frantically to lift him. "I'm here with you, my darling! I'm here!"

"Attend to my lord!" the King's voice was a sudden explosion of sound. "Lift him higher, lads, let him get some air."

Air! Angel thought. There was no air in this stifling atmosphere. She tried to struggle free as the King's hands drew her to her feet. "Let me go! Let me go!"

"Take heart, Angel," the King whispered, holding her in his arms. "Friend Nicholas will recover."

"Will he?" She was still for a moment, her eyes lit with a sudden wild hope. Then she heard the gasping sounds that Nicholas made. She beat against the King's chest with doubled fists. "Let me go to him! He needs me!"

"Nay, Angel, be still. He is being helped. He will be all right, believe me!"

"Liar!" Her hand struck at his face, her feet kicked at his legs. "He's dying, you know it!" She tore herself free from his arms. "Damn you, you fool! How dare you try to keep me from him?"

She fought her way through the men surrounding Nicholas. "Darling!" She fell to her knees beside him. "I'm here, dear m'lord!"

His eyes were open, dark eyes that stared at her vaguely. She could see the shadow of death upon his face, the blue tinge about his mouth, the icy coldness of the hand she clasped in her own. Again she allowed herself to hope, for his breathing seemed to have eased and his clearing eyes recognized her. "Angel," he whispered. A smile of extraordinary sweetness lit his face.

She pressed his hand to her lips. "You will not leave me, my darling, say that you will not! Well do you know that I am—the empty-headed little fool, you have ev—ever called me so. I could not exist with—without you."

His hand tightened about her own, a weak grasp, yet curiously compelling. "There is no pain now, Angel, but I—I am spent." He gave a sudden deep sigh. "I am—am so very sorry."

"For what, my darling?"

"C—come closer, little one."

Stooping, she pressed her cheek to his. A tremor shook him, and she cried out wildly, "Don't do this! Don't leave me, oh don't, don't!"

"I'm sorry," he said again. "You will—will be a g—good girl, will y—you not?" His finger touched her cheek gently, caressingly. She felt him stiffen, his body jerking. "Angel!" it was a wild, desperate cry. "I—I will always love you. Remember it. Remember m—me." His head dropped sideways.

"No!" Angel said dully. "No, Nicholas, no, no, no!"

"He's dead, m'lady," a man's voice said.

She came to sudden, blazing, furious life. "You fool! You liar! How dare you say my lord is dead!" She crouched over Nicholas's still form, her arm sliding beneath his neck. "Help me to lift him, please."

Hands assisted her, placing him in her arms. She held him to her, rocking him gently. "Open your eyes, my lord," her voice was soft and cajoling. "I know that you do but sleep, my precious, my little boy!"

Somebody touched her shoulder, and she jerked away from the touch. Across the chasm of time she could hear Nicholas's voice. *You will straighten your shoulders, you little fool!*

"I will straighten my shoulders," she whispered. "I will do anything you say, if only you will not leave me!"

What did you hope to gain? Nicholas's voice again. *Why have you chosen to come here with your farrago of lies? Was it for money, was it?*

"But I didn't lie, my love."

You will sit down and pay attention, Mistress Dawson. We have a great deal of work to do. Plague take you, Angel. What do I want with you, damned insolent brat that you are! What do I want with a cheeky-faced guttersnipe who has ever defied me. You have ruined my peace of mind, you have made of me a bad-tempered wreck! But—oh devil take you, wench! I need you, I suppose.

209

"And I need you, dear m'lord. Oh, dear Christ! I need you!"

She strained to hear his voice. *I'll kiss you, aye, and I'll bed you too. What then? When shall we go shopping for those pretty baubles to adorn your person?*

"I love you, darling, I love you!"

You will not call me darling. I will tell you when and if 'tis time to call me so.

"I shall never betray you, Nicholas, therefore shall I live out my full time."

You slut! Nicholas's voice rough and hating. *You filthy little whore!*

"No, no! Don't leave me, don't go!"

"My lady!" Angel started out of her dream. She saw the King kneeling at Nicholas's other side. "Oh, my dear, I pray you to accept the truth."

Angel saw him signal to the two men standing behind him. She fought them as they took Nicholas from her arms. "Give him back to me!"

"Nicholas," the King said softly, his tears spilling on the still face. "I shall miss you, old friend."

Angel stared down at Nicholas's closed eyes, the thick lashes resting against his cheekbones, and knew that those eyes would never again look at her in mockery, in hate, or in love. She saw his shadowed mouth, the untidy black hair that fell curling over his forehead, the hand still stretched toward her as though in a mute appeal for help, and her heart broke.

The eyes she turned on the King resembled hard blue stones.

"I'm so sorry, Angel." The King put a hand to his mouth, trying to conceal the shaking of his lips. "I'm sorry for us both. He—he was my very good friend."

Hate leaped in her, that he could so easily, with a few words, consign her Nicholas to the past. *"Was* your friend?" She spat the words into his startled face. "Say *is!* Say that he *is* your friend!"

"Is, then, if it pleases you, my lady." He looked at her, his dark eyes soft with mingled grief and pity. "Angel,

mayhap for friend Nicholas, this is for the best. You would not want him to go on suffering such severe pain, would you?"

She did not answer him. She lifted her face to the sky, her hair blowing slightly in the dying wind. "Where are You, God?" She raised her arms and shook her clenched fists in a violent gesture of repudiation. "Where were You when my Nicholas had need of You? Damn You, damn You! I'll never believe in You again!" her voice rose to a scream. "I hate You, do You hear me!"

Faces blank with shock stared back at her. Her lip curled as she noticed a man hastily crossing himself. "You fools! Do you think there is someone there to hear you? Nay, there is nothing, nothing!"

The King rose quickly to his feet and went to her. "You must not, dear child!" He seized both her hands in his, holding them tightly. "Indeed you must not say such things!"

"I hate God!" she shouted.

"If, as you say, He does not exist, then there is nothing left to hate, is there? Come, I will take you home."

"Home! Where is home without Nicholas? He's left me forever, and without him I am nothing, no one!"

Charles flinched before the wildness in her eyes, but he forced himself to answer her steadily. "Nay, my lady, he will never be there again. But 'tis still your home."

She shook her head. "Nay, you are mistaken. I have no home, no life without my lord." She looked at him, a bewildered heartbroken woman, seeking to make him understand. "He is dead, therefore have I lived out my life, and it is best that I die too."

Charles knelt down beside her again and pulled her into his arms, holding her in a fierce embrace. "You shall not say so Angel, he would want you to live."

"Nay, Sire, you knew him not if you can say that. My Nicholas would want me to be with him."

"Stop it, Angel! Surely I am not wrong when I tell you that time will aid in softening your grief?"

"It will get better in time, Angel!" she mocked his

words savagely. "You will forget him, Angel! Time eases all sorrow! But I tell you now that I will never forget him. Not for a moment, a second!"

"Not forget, Angel, I did not say that." The King's voice was soothing, but there was a note of desperation in it. "This is hard for me too."

"For you, perhaps, Sire, it will soften, but for me, never! The last day of my life, which I devoutly hope will not be too long in coming, shall see me in this same bitter mourning."

"There are other kinds of love, Angel, other men who will wish to make you happy. Mayhap, if you wed again, 'twill not be the glorious experience you shared with Nicholas, but it will be love."

She stared at him as though he had taken leave of his senses. "Other loves!" she said in a breaking voice. "Nay, Sire, you do not understand. Please leave me now." She looked at the circle of silent men. "Go. Leave me alone with him!"

"A moment only, then," Charles said, rising to his feet. He turned to the men. "One of you go and seek the Duke of York. Tell him I wish to see him immediately. The rest of you join the others in the line."

Angel did not notice the King standing behind her. He stood there, his shoulders slumped, the slow painful tears coursing down his face.

"They know me not, love," Angel whispered to Nicholas, her hand smoothing back his hair. "I could as soon forget to breathe as to forget you. And, Nicholas, if there is a God who hears, pray for me. Ask him, beg him, to allow me to come to you!"

Kneeling there in that livid light, she saw no one but Nicholas, heard no voice but his. It was silent now, yet it seemed to echo in her ears louder than it had in life. *Angel, I love you, damn you, I love you!* Words he had spoken, words he would never speak again.

NELL GWYNNE APPROACHED BARBARA CAS-
tlemaine on silent feet. She was resplendent in a gown of
vivid green, her thick curls drawn up to the top of her
head and held in place with a green ribbon. She looked
vivid, charming, radiant with life. Her large blue eyes
sparkled and her mouth was curved into an urchin's grin.
Stopping a few paces from Barbara, she said in her
coarse, rather husky voice, "And how are you on this
fine day, m'lady?"

Barbara spun round, startled. "You!" She drew her
white skirts to one side, as though she feared contamina-
tion.

Nell swept her a low curtsy. "I, m'lady and none
other."

Barbara's nostrils flared in disgust as she continued to
stare at the girl. "What do you here at the Palace, Mistress Gwynne?"

Nell's eyes studied her with frank interest. "What is it,
m'lady? Do you smell something bad? 'Tis strange indeed, but just as I drew near to your ladyship, I seemed
to smell it too." She moved closer, her small nose wrinkling. "Ah, the smell doth seem to come from your person. Could your ladyship's skirts be concealing something unwholesome?"

Barbara's hands clenched. "By God, I'll not tolerate
your impudence, you filthy little gutter rat!" With some-

thing of an effort, she forced down her rising temper. "Pray have the goodness to tell me what you are doing here."

Nell walked slowly to a chair. Smiling, she sat down and carefully arranged the rustling folds of her gown. "If it pleases your ladyship, I will start from the beginning. I was in my lodgings in Drury Lane, preparing to go out, I was. When, to my surprise, there came a thundering on my door. The—".

"I do not need to hear all that, Mistress Gwynne."

"Oh, but m'lady," Nell smiled demurely, "I always tell things in my own way. Like I was saying, the King had sent for me."

"I don't believe even His Majesty would sink so low."

Nell's laugh rang out. "He bedded you, didn't he?"

"You—you—!"

"That's right, that's me. Nell Gwynne, at your service." She folded her hands in her lap, her smile demure. "Traveled to the Palace in a sedan chair, I did, though 'tis but a hop, skip and a jump from Drury Lane to the Palace. A lovely chair, it was, all of a sparkle and glitter." She turned innocent eyes on Barbara. "That's what I'm doing here, m'lady. Why else would I come?"

Barbara's lip curled. "I thought, mayhap, you had come to console your friend in her grief."

The sneer in Barbara's voice brought an angry flash to Nell's eyes. "Aye," she said in a tight voice, "m'lady Angel is one of the reasons the King sent for me, bless his kind heart."

" 'Tis the only reason, Mistress Gwynne, I do assure you. I imagine one gutter brat would be adept in consoling another of her kind."

Nell smiled. "How true, m'lady. But I had thought that you and I would have more in common. When one whore speaks to another, they generally comes to understanding each other." The diamonds on Barbara's wrist flashed a blue-white fire as she lifted a threatening hand. But Nell only settled herself more comfortably in her chair. "If you was thinking o' landing me a clout," she remarked calmly, "I could promise as you'd regret it. Aye, regret it bitter, you would. I wouldn't think nothing o' pulling out every bleedin' hair you got; leave you plucked bald, I would, and after that I'd bash your teeth down your perishing throat. Be a real pleasure to oblige, m'lady, indeed it would."

"You—you filthy little trollop!"

"Trollop, yes m'lady, but not filthy. Bathed meself all over just this mornin'." Nell gave an elaborate yawn, masking it behind her hand. "That being so, 'twould seem to me as that nasty smell what we was talking of must be acoming from you."

Barbara's furious eyes belied the coldness of her words. "So you bathed in joyous preparation for the King, I make no doubt?"

Nell chuckled. "Well one never knows how one's luck is running, do they, m'lady?" Her eyes swept over Barbara, noting the firm white breasts rising from a low-cut bodice, the diamonds at her wrists and throat, and the luxuriant red hair held back from her face by a little diamond-sewn cap. "Wouldn't do you much good, would it, m'lady, not if you was to bathe yourself in perfume every five minutes? They do say as the King's lost interest in you. Sad, that is, ain't it, m'lady, and you so lovely 'n' all."

Barbara's precarious hold on her temper snapped. "Close your damned mouth!" she shrilled. "Get out of my sight. Go!"

"Can't," Nell said, beaming at her. "I was told to wait in here. Looks like *you'll* have to go, don't it?"

"For whom are you waiting?"

"Ah!" Nell said, winking at her. "It could be as the King'll be sending for me. . . . Or, it could be my lady Angel. Which one o' 'em do you think it'll be, m'lady?"

"The gutter brat undoubtedly. Think you the King would have aught to do with such as you?"

"Well as to that, dearie, I wouldn't be a bit surprised.

215

He's already bedded Moll Davis, and a score of others."

"Moll Davis, at least, has some pretensions to being a lady. She is——"

"But then, you see, it could be that our Charlie likes to dirty himself up a bit with the likes o' me. I ain't had no education, I grant you, but I does know how to hold a man, and to make him feel like he is a man, which some, what ain't standing very far from me, don't."

"How dare you!"

A hard glint came into Nell's blue eyes. "You listen to me, me bleedin' fine Countess of Castlemaine. I got a friend in the Palace, and, no, I ain't talking about Angel. My friend is a gentleman, and I ain't telling you his name. He told me how you been treating Angel. Sneering at her, calling her names, and her just lost her man. Why, if I was Angel, I'd smash your bleedin' head in!"

"I am quite sure that my lady Benbrook, once she has recovered from her grief, will remember her earlier up-bringing, so you need have no fears for her."

"You heartless sow!"

"Oh come, we do but bandy words, Mistress Gwynne, and to no purpose. I assure you that, should I wish to emulate your insulting behavior, I would emerge triumphant." Barbara turned away from her and swept over to the door. "Such conduct would be unseemly in myself. But, Mistress Gwynne, your bad manners are well suited to yourself."

Her lace and satin gown rustling, Barbara left the room, closing the door behind her with a slam.

"Bitch!" Nell said aloud. "If she thinks she'd emerge triumphant, then she don't know Nellie Gwynne!"

Nell turned her head as the door opened again. A tall, white-wigged manservant, the brass buttons on his red and gold livery glittering, stood in the doorway, gazing at her in polite inquiry.

"Mistress Gwynne?" he asked, bowing.

Nell sprang to her feet. "Aye, sir, that's me right enough."

"Er—yes." The man's eyebrows rose superciliously.

216

"Pray to follow me, Mistress Gwynne. My lady Benbrook will see you now."

"That's nice. Get along, then. I'll follow after you."

As the footman's rigid back led her down one deeply carpeted corridor after another, Nell's attention was diverted by the crystal and gilt and red and gold luxury all about her. She stooped once to sniff at the purple and bronze and white of the banked chrysanthemums lining either side of the corridor, and then was forced to run and catch up with her guide.

The footman stopped before a door. Tapping on it, he waited until a low voice bade him enter. Opening it, he ushered her inside.

Nell stopped short on the threshold. Her eyes, round with wonder, stared at walls draped in ivory silk; here and there the silk was held in place by crystal chandeliers. She saw a glittering expanse of floor, strewn with rugs of gold, of green, of rose and of silver. The furniture was so carved and gilded, so lavishly inlaid with mother-of-pearl, that for a moment she was quite overwhelmed.

Angel was seated on a silver-draped couch by the window, her lovely hair gleaming bright in the afternoon sunshine. Standing beside her was the King.

"Mistress Gwynne," Charles said, striding forward. "I am happy that you have come."

"Your Majesty!" Nell fell to her knees, her eyes looked up admiringly at his tall, purple and black clad person. " 'Tis an honor to be here." She placed her hands between both of his, smiling, as he clasped them. "There is nothing Your Majesty may ask of me that I would not be willing and happy to do."

"Is it indeed so?" The curls of his long black wig touched her shoulder as he bent toward her. "Then may I ask that you rise from that plaguey uncomfortable position, sweet Nell?"

Her heart jerked into an uneven rhythm. She stared into his somber eyes. She saw his faint, slightly cynical smile, and she grinned widely, showing small, perfect teeth. "Aye, Your Majesty." Nell bent her head and pressed a kiss upon his thin, jewel-laden fingers, then she rose quickly to her feet.

Angel was looking in their direction, but Nell had the feeling that she did not really see them.

"My lady Benbrook," Charles said, taking Nell by the hand and leading her forward. "Here is Mistress Gwynne come to pay you a visit. She hath a ready and saucy tongue, as you well know, and mayhap can entertain you."

Angel rose slowly to her feet. "Nell," she said, her eyes expressionless in the pale set mask of her face. "I am—am glad to see you."

"Nay, that you're not," Nell said impulsively, "and small wonder." She caught Angel's hand in hers, pressing it warmly. "But you will be, for I have such stories to tell you. Just wait until you hear them."

Angel put her other hand to her throbbing head, her fingers massaging her temples. She did not wish to hear stories; all that she desired was to be alone. There were plans she must make, and those plans included Nicholas. Where he went, she went. Oh surely, if there were a God, he would not part them forever? She thought of her physical discomfort of the last few mornings, her ceaseless nausea of body and spirit. The longing, the never-ending longing to die was a hunger in her. To be with Nicholas, her love, her darling! Oh God, forgive me for doubting you. Let me die, please let me die!

"Did you hear me, Angel?" It was Nell's voice again, an imperious blast of sound.

"Yes," she said aloud, "I heard you."

Nell's eyes misted. Gently, she released Angel's hand. Without support, it dropped heavily to her side. *Why,* Nell thought, *she is like somebody already dead. She's not Angel, she ain't but a lifeless figure clad in a splendid gown of white and silver.*

"Listen, Angel," Nell said in a low urgent voice, "I ain't going to say nothing about being sorry, 'cause you already knows that I am. Being sorry don't change noth-

218

ing, do it? You've got to get your spirit back. You've got to fight life in the way what you used to."

"Yes, of course," Angel said, her lips curving into a mechanical smile. "Yes, Nell, I will."

Nell bit her lip. "You ain't listening to no one, are you? Would m'lord Benbrook like to see you like this?"

A quiver passed over Angel's face. The raw pain inside her stabbed deeply, savagely. Just the single mention of his name started that flow of inner tears. Nicholas! Nicholas! It was like bleeding, like a slow dying! Too slow. Oh Christ, in Your mercy, make it stop! "Don't!" she said in a choked voice, turning blindly toward the window. "Oh don't, Nell!"

Charles, with a swift look at Nell, went to Angel's side. "My lady," he said, putting an arm about her shoulders. "Would you care to be alone with Mistress Gwynne?"

She looked at him with her expressionless eyes, seeing his dark, tender face, the concern in his melancholy eyes, and for the first time she displayed a spark of feeling. "Nay," she took his hand and held it tightly. "I feel—I feel safer when you are with me. Can y—you understand that?"

"Aye, m'lady, I think so."

Her lips twisted into a painful smile. "If 'twill not inconvenience you, Sire, please remain."

"Of course." Charles bent closer to her. "Later, if you would care to see him, I have another visitor for you. 'Tis Alex Barrymore, Angel. He is most concerned for you."

Oh no! Angel drew in her breath sharply. Would he talk of Nicholas? Would he expect her to talk of him? "Alex?" she said faintly. "Alex, here?"

"He will be arriving later. Mrs. Sampson has insisted upon being with you. I think it would be for the best, so I bade him bring her to the Palace."

Angel's hands clenched. Poor Mrs. Sampson, who had loved Nicholas to the exclusion of all others. In Angel's own pain, she had completely forgotten the housekeeper.

"I will—will be glad to see her, Sire. Poor lady, she must be suffering."

"Mayhap, then, you can console each other."

Bitter, half-hysterical laughter shook Angel. "There is no consolation I can offer her, none that she can offer me. But, Sire, why do you bid her come here? I shall be returning to the house in St. Bernard's Square very soon."

The house in St. Bernard's Square? Charles felt a tightness in his throat. Not home, then? Nicholas was not here, and so, to Angel, it was not home. Almost whispering, he said, "Nay, you will not be returning there for some time. I deem it best that you stay here, you and Mrs. Sampson, until you are able to take up your life again."

She made no reply to this.

"Angel," Charles said, turning her toward the sofa, "We are neglecting Mistress Gwynne."

He led her forward. Seating himself, he drew her gently down beside him. "Come," he said, looking at Nell, "will you not be seated?" He patted the place on his other side.

Again Nell became conscious of the uneven beating of her heart. "Thank you, Your Majesty," she said, sitting down.

Charles put an arm about Angel's waist and slid the other about Nell's. "'Tis little enough time I have for peace and friendly conversation, that I cherish the moments." His fingers lightly squeezed Nell's waist. "What have you to say for yourself, Mistress Gwynne?"

Nell hesitated. She saw the smile on the King's lips, Angel's white face, and for a moment it seemed to her to be heartless to just sit there and chatter. But Charles seemed to sense her thoughts. "M'lady Benbrook has endured too much silence," he said in a low voice. "If you can do aught to entertain her, Mistress Gwynne, then I pray you, do so."

"I will, Your Majesty." Nell took a deep breath, adding in a voice that shook slightly, "But I like best to be called Nell, if it please you, Sire."

220

Charles smiled into her eyes. "It does please me. Nell, it shall be."

Involuntarily, Nell moved closer to him. Charles looked at her for a long moment, then, as if unable to help himself, he lifted his hand, his fingers toying with a lock of her honey-blonde hair. "There is much I would say to you, Nell, but now is not the time. My lady and I would hear some of your more audacious stories."

"Your pardon, Sire." Angel started out of her thoughts.

"Nell Gwynne's voice is loud and commanding to the attention. You will listen, pretty Angel, even though it be against your will."

With a sudden movement, Angel pressed her face against the King's shoulder. She closed her eyes, trying desperately to pretend that the shoulder was Nicholas's.

Charles was infinitely touched. "We are listening, Mistress Nell," he said in a voice roughened by emotion.

Nell was by nature coquettish, but as her fingers smoothed the velvet of his sleeve, her feelings were in a turmoil. There was nothing light in the emotions he stirred. She remembered the ball, the feel of his lips against her own, and it was with great difficulty she prevented herself from gasping aloud. Why, Nellie Gwynne, she said to herself, so that's why you haven't been eating and sleeping. That's why you've been crying every night because he hasn't sent for you. Nell Gwynne, you fool, you've gone and let yourself fall in love with Charles Stuart, the biggest rake going! In the name of all the saints, you're in love with the King of England!

Angel was sitting upright again, and her eyes, fixed on Nell Gwynne, were no longer expressionless, but full of knowledge. "Oh, poor Nell!" Angel said.

Nell flushed scarlet. "Poor Nell, nothing!" she retorted fiercely, her eyes avoiding the King's. "I don't know what you mean." Collecting herself, she flashed them both a brilliant smile. "Have you heard what that precious Sam Pepys did during the worst of the fire, Sire?"

"Nay, tell me."

221

Nell chuckled. "Well, Sam was that afraid of losing his possessions, that he stowed 'em all away in a cart sent to him by his friend. Never took no thought of his wife and his relations, he didn't. Can Your Majesty guess what he did next?"

The corners of Charles' mouth twitched. Samuel Pepys' many exploits during the fire, and this one in particular, had been relayed to him, but since Angel had the appearance of listening, he was prepared to hear it again. "Pray tell us."

" 'Twas in the small hours of the morning that the friend sent the cart," Nell went on, her eyes dancing. "Sam, after loading up, and still clad only in his nightgown and nightcap, clambered up on the cart and rode away to his friend's house in Bethnal Green. I seen him meself, Your Majesty. There was Sam, his nightgown flying in the wind, and them short hairy legs o' his ashowin'. He had his wig clutched tight in his hand, his mouth was set all grim, and his eyes was adarting around like he expected to have his precious pots and pans stolen at any moment."

Charles gave a stifled laugh.

"There was fire all about him, and people astrugglin' and screamin' and acursin', but Sam never took no notice o' them." Nell, with an apologetic look at Angel, dissolved into helpless giggles. "J—j—just as he thought he was safe, a c—c—cinder fell on the wig what he was holdin' in his hand, and b—b—bur—burnt it all up. And Sam shouted, 'A plague on it, that's the third wig gone up in f—flames.' "

Nell wiped tears of laughter from her eyes. "I did hear as he buried his treasures in his friend's garden, and—and two more wigs with 'em."

"Which the worms will undoubtedly eat," Charles said, joining in her laughter. "You have a refreshing way with a story, Mistress Nellie."

Contrite, Nell said, "Oh, Angel, I'm ever so sorry. I didn't mean to—" she stopped short, her mouth agape, for Angel was laughing too, wildly, helplessly.

"Hush," Charles said, drawing Angel close against him. "Hush, my lady."

Feeling her body shaking, Charles was reminded of his own words to Nicholas: *I myself have seen men laughing while the tears still fell from their eyes.*

"I'm sorry, S—Sire, so—so sorry." Angel pulled away from him. Sitting up straight, she pushed her hair away from her hot forehead. "Why am I sitting here laughing like a fool, when—when my Nicholas is no longer here? Why, why!"

It was such a bitter cry of anguish that Nell's face whitened. "I'm ever so sorry," she whispered, "it's all my fault."

"No!" Angel reached across and caught Nell's hand in hers. "I am to blame. I should not impose my misery on others."

"Nonsense!" Nell said sharply. "It's not that way at all, Angel, and you know it. I did but—"

"It *is* that way," Angel said simply. "No matter how fond you are of another, their grief can grow tedious." She looked at the King. "That is why you must allow me to go away, Sire."

"Nay," Charles said harshly. "I will not allow it, Angel. Let us speak no more on the subject."

Long after Nell had gone and the King had taken his reluctant leave of her, Angel sat motionless, staring before her. Outside, the light had dimmed, and long shadows lay across the floor. A servant entered the room, taper in hand, and began lighting the candles. She did not move. The man, giving her a soft pitying look, wondered if she saw him at all.

But Angel was vaguely aware of light and movement, and she murmured, not knowing what it was she said. She was still sitting there, still straining to listen to the echos of Nicholas's voice, when the door opened once again and Mrs. Sampson came hesitantly into the room accompanied by Alex Barrymore.

"Angel!" Mrs. Sampson's voice split the heavy silence. "Why are you sitting here alone?"

223

Angel felt a hand on her shoulder, another hand, cold and trembling, tipped up her face. "Mrs. Sampson!" she said. "I had—had forgotten you were coming."

"Aye, I'm here, and Mr. Barrymore with me. Sampson's here, child. She'll take care of you now."

Angel stared up into a face that was withered, gaunter than she remembered, into pale-blue eyes, washed paler still by constant tears. Mrs. Sampson would take care of her? But she looked too ill to do anything but take to her bed. Angel remembered the secret she had been guarding, the meaning of the nausea that attacked her every morning. She had meant to say nothing to anyone. Nicholas's child, she had vowed, would never be born. Long before that she would be dead. But now compassion flooded through her for this broken old woman standing before her. With the first real warmth she had felt since Nicholas's death, she said impulsively, "Aye, you must take care of me, Mrs. Sampson, for I—I am —going to present you with another M—Master Nicholas."

For a moment there was complete silence, then, weeping, Mrs. Sampson slumped heavily down on the sofa. "My dear, dear child! Oh I shall indeed take care of you. Think of it, my lad's child! My Master Nickey's boy!"

"It—it may be a girl."

"Nonsense! Master Nickey would never allow it." Mrs. Sampson's quivering lips firmed, and her eyes glowed with a new light of resolution. "You know well you should be in your bed, Angel. We'll take no chance with our lad, will we?"

I will give her the child, Angel thought. *Nicholas's son. No one could love him more. But for myself, I have no wish to live.*

"Angel, you are pleased, are you not?" Mrs. Sampson's gnarled hands gripped together. "We will take care of Master Nickey's son, you and I together, won't we?"

"I—I—yes, Sampson."

"You called me Sampson!"

"I'm sorry. I did not mean—"

Mrs. Sampson cut her short. "I'm not. 'Tis Master Nickey speaking through your lips, 'tis the way it should be." The housekeeper seemed to have taken on a new strength. "Aye," she said, rising briskly to her feet, "call me Sampson, Mistress Angel. I'll leave you with Mr. Barrymore now, with whom you have not yet exchanged a word, you naughty wench. But you must not be too long, for I shall want you in your bed very soon."

"There is no need to fear." Angel smiled at her. "The child is not due for many months."

Mrs. Sampson's heart hurt her for a moment. Angel's bright smile, which had always been so full of the zest of living, was now but a pale reflection, and nothing awoke in those eyes of hers. "All the same," she replied more sharply than she had intended, "I intend to see to it that you have a care of yourself."

Her shoulders held stiffly to still her own trembling, Mrs. Sampson walked across the room and jerked open the door. "Thank you, sir," she said quietly, looking at Alex. "Thank you for bringing me. I am happier than I have a right to be, since receiving Mistress Angel's news."

She turned her head and looked at Angel. "No one could take the place of my Master Nickey, never think it!" She hesitated, her pale lips twitching, then added almost imploringly, " 'Twill never be the same again, but we will have Master Nickey's lad, and that is something I have long prayed for."

"Yes," Angel answered her softly.

The door closed behind the housekeeper. For the first time since he had entered the room, Angel turned her head and looked fully at Alex.

He was standing a little distance from her, the candlelight shining on his immaculately dressed fair hair. He wore a jacket and breeches of dark blue satin, a ruffled stock held with a plain bar, and a double fall of lace at his wrists. The dark blue cape that fell from his shoulders, swinging casually as he moved, was lined with white satin. His shoes were plain, embellished with carved buckles. There was something about his attire, something

225

less flamboyant than usual, that reminded her for an aching moment of Nicholas, who had always been the nighthawk among a gathering of gaudy peacocks.

"Mr. Barrymore," Angel said, rising to her feet, "pray to forgive me. I have been rude."

"Nothing of the sort, my lady." Alex went to her quickly. "I understand, believe me." The sapphire on his finger glowed with a blue fire as he took her hand in his. "I fear that I am intruding."

She looked into his eyes, dark blue, warm, slightly narrowed in that curiously intent scrutiny of his. "Nay, Mr. Barrymore, you could not intrude. You were—were Nicholas's friend."

"I had that honor, but I am still his friend. Yours, too, if you will allow it." He bent his head and pressed a kiss upon her fingers.

He had not relegated Nicholas to the past, then? No, he sought to keep him alive, even as she did. Her hard-won composure suddenly crumbled. "Aye," she said, the tears streaming down her cheeks, her cold hand trembling in his, "you are still his friend. Thank you for that."

Alex knew that he had said something of supreme importance to her, but he could not think what it might be. With a rare tact, he said nothing, he simply drew her into his arms and held her very gently. The touch of her sent a quivering along his nerves. Without thinking, his arms tightened about her.

Angel stiffened, then relaxed with a little sigh. "Alex," she said, drawing away from him, "why do you not tell me, as they all do, that I must not cry?"

"That would be foolish of me, Angel, would it not?" He drew a kerchief from his sleeve. "You will cry for a long time, I fear," he said in a low voice, dabbing at her wet cheeks, "and there will be no one who can help you. In grief there is an isolation, a place where you cannot be reached. I know."

"You have known grief, Alex?"

"Who has not at some time or another?" He tucked the

kerchief back into his sleeve. "Aye. Different to yours, but none the less profound. I lost my father and mother to the plague. And later, from a different cause, the girl I was to marry."

"I'm so sorry!"

He saw that her eyes had changed. They were wider, softer. He wanted to say to her: *I loved my parents, but I did not love Anne. I was fond of her, but it was a pre-arranged marriage. 'Tis you I love, Angel, and will always love. You, who have nothing left to give me, who may never have anything to give!* Aloud he said, "Time has enabled me to grow a hard shell over my grief. I pray that it will do the same for you."

She shrugged, and there was hopelessness in the gesture. "I thank you for the thought."

He smiled ruefully. "Perhaps 'tis best that I leave you now," he said, taking her hand again.

"No!" The word was out before she could stop it. She did not want him to go, not yet. Quite suddenly there was a gentle warmth about him, a steadfastness that subtly upheld her. While he stood before her, he could somehow hold the terror of loneliness at bay. Listening to his comforting voice, she could tell herself that Nicholas was only around the corner. Soon he would be with them, because Alex was here, because Alex, in some curious way, made her believe that. It was insane, she knew, but for all that she wanted him to stay. She looked down at the long sensitive fingers holding fast to her hand. "Don't go," she said, forcing herself to speak quietly.

There was a dryness in his throat, and he swallowed convulsively. "If you need me, Angel, I will stay." He heard his uncontrolled voice with surprise. He was a fool! He would frighten her. "You must know, m'lady," he went on, his voice steadying, "that I will always be near if you need me. Will you promise me to remember that?"

Loving Nicholas so deeply, she could not fail to recognize love when she saw it looking at her from this man's eyes. Alex! In love with her? But he must not be! She didn't want to hurt this gentle man, but she could never love anyone else. She must not keep him with her for her own selfish purposes.

Alex had seen the sudden flaring of recognition, and he smiled at her with an effort. "It's all right. I know what you would say, Angel, what you feel you must say, but please don't. I fear that I am not a very good actor, else would you not have known my feelings. I love you, Angel! Aye, I might as well put it into words. But you must not fear, for after this I will never speak of it again."

"But you must not love me, Alex. It's—it's no use."

He said nothing to this. She let him lead her to the couch, and deep inside her she heard Nicholas's voice, brusque, impatient. *You must not love me, do you hear? I forbid it!*

"Angel," Alex said, seating himself beside her. "Had you not seen the truth for yourself, you would have known nothing. Let it not make a difference to our friendship, I beg you." He took her hand, holding it in a loose clasp. "As I have already told you, I will never speak of it again." He hesitated. "Not, that is, unless you give me permission to do so."

"I never will, Alex. It is best you know it. I'm very sorry."

"Don't be sorry, I understand." His finger rubbed her palm gently. "Remember only that I am your friend. If ever you should need me, then no matter where I may be, I will come to you."

"But if I never want you, Alex, what then?"

"It will make no difference to our friendship, will it?"

She stared at him for a long moment. *Such a gentle love,* she thought. *It is not love as I know it, as Nicholas knew it.* Perhaps, after all, Alex was fortunate to be spared such an experience. "No," she said at last, "it will make no difference." She put her hand to his cheek. "Thank you, Alex."

As though her touch had stung him, he drew back quickly, and then rose to his feet. He laughed lightly. "You touched me as my mother was used to."

She sensed his hurt. "You are going now?"

"If you will permit it." He bowed to her, and she saw the bright glitter of his eyes before he lowered them. "Mrs. Sampson has issued her orders, and if one is wise, one does not lightly disregard them. 'Tis bed for you. As for myself, I will see you tomorrow, Angel."

Dumbly, she watched him cross the room, and she was seized with an unreasoning terror. "Alex!" she cried out as he opened the door. "You w—will come back?"

"Nicholas is nearer to you when I am here, is it not so?"

"Yes, yes!" She wrung her hands together, color flooding her pale face. "I do not know why it should be so."

He smiled at her. "Yes, Angel, don't you know that I will always come back?"

He left her then, and she was alone in the silence of the room. She looked at the draped walls, the candles in their silver and crystal sconces, the glittering floor that seemed to heave upward to meet the carved ceiling, and she had the feeling that she would be crushed between them. She was drowning, dying! And only God could know how she longed for that death! Her heart steadied. Dying? she thought bitterly. Nay, she would not be that lucky! Her love was lost to her, and another love she did not want had been offered in its place.

Her hands clenching, she sprang to her feet and began to restlessly pace the room. She wanted oblivion, she thought, her head whirling with grief and fear. Would Nicholas be there at the end of the long darkness? Would he take her in his arms and swear to her that they would never again be parted? If that was so, if Nicholas did indeed await her, and all of eternity stretched out before them, golden, glorious, with no more grief, no more parting, then what did she want with life? She began to laugh hysterically, tears sliding down her face.

The high sounds of her clamoring grief drowned out the opening of the door and the quick brisk footsteps approaching her.

"Angel!" Mrs. Sampson's harsh voice exclaimed. "Stop it at once! If you carry on this way, it will be bad for the child."

Angel swung round to face her. "The child, the child! Can you not think of me?"

"Now you are being selfish. Aye, you are, and Master Nickey would be the first to tell you so."

"No, no, Sampson, don't you understand? I want to die!"

"Nonsense!" The old woman's face quivered, then fell suddenly into slack folds of fear. "I have had enough of death," she said in a low shaking voice. She moved nearer, her hands held out entreatingly. " 'Tis Master Nickey's child, and I want that boy!"

Angel stared at her, the tears still glistening on her cheeks; then, with a moaning sound, she fell to the floor, her arms clasping the housekeeper about the knees. "Afterwards, when it is all over, you must help me. You have a knowledge of herbs. You can help me to die!"

Mrs. Sampson stood very still. "You will be the mother of Master Nickey's child. If that is not enough for you, then you must go your own way."

Angel heard the coldness in her voice. She looked up, seeing the old woman's face through her blinding tears, cold, austere, and unyielding. "Help me!"

"Nay. You must do that for yourself."

"Sampson! You don't understand. If I take my own life, it may be that—that Nicholas and I will not meet again!"

"So you do have some religion." Mrs. Sampson stooped down and forcibly removed the clinging arms. "I am tired of these dramatics, my lady. I am an old woman, I am full of my own grief, and very tired. If I can live through this, so can you. When you have come to your senses, I will be waiting to serve you." She turned away.

"Damn you!" Angel screamed after her. "Damn you for a cold and unfeeling woman!"

Outside the door, Mrs. Sampson leaned against the wall and closed her eyes. She felt spent, it had cost her much to speak to Angel so coldly. *Help her,* she begged silently. *Somebody must help her. It is much too much to bear!*

The sound of footsteps and voices roused her from the

half-stupor into which she had fallen. Startled, she opened her eyes. The King was approaching, and beside him, holding the King's arm, was the blind poet, John Milton.

Mrs. Sampson felt a faint warmth stirring the ice inside her as she curtsied. The King was so kind. How like him to take the trouble to escort this man who had once spoken out so harshly and boldly against his martyred father.

"Mrs. Sampson." The King came closer to her, concern in his face. "You would be the better for your bed, I think."

" 'Tis good of Your Majesty to concern yourself. Aye, I am quite tired. 'Tis the strain of my own grief and that of my lady's combined."

Milton, who had been listening intently, his head held to one side, said swiftly, "Might I interrupt Your Majesty?"

"Please." Charles murmured.

"I would ask Mrs. Sampson how fares my lady Benbrook?"

Mrs. Sampson looked at the puckered scar on Milton's cheek, and his heavily bandaged neck. Doubtless, she thought, his injuries were the result of the fire. "She does poorly, Mr. Milton," she answered. "Mayhap it sounds overly dramatic, but I would say that her heart is broken. And now that she is with child, and she so uncaring, I know not what is to become of her."

The King started. "You are sure of this, Mrs. Sampson?"

"Your Majesty did not know?"

"Nay. But Od's Fish! This news makes the grief a little easier to bear."

"But not for my lady, Majesty."

"I have hopes that she will feel differently when the child is placed in her arms. Especially if he bear the slightest resemblance to my lord Benbrook." The King turned to Milton. "I will escort you into my lady's apartments, and then I will take my leave. Doubtless you will wish to speak to her alone."

Milton flushed as the King took his arm. This man is kind to his erstwhile enemies, he thought, and he has great warmth and charm. If his father had been possessed of one half of the son's brilliant personality, then 'twas no wonder the royalists had fought and died so stubbornly in his cause.

Had he perhaps been wrong in his outspoken denunciations? Nay! He hardened again. These Stuarts had an insidious lure that might well make a man forget his previous convictions. His mouth curled in a sardonic smile that mocked at his moments of doubt. Why, he himself, exposed to this particular Stuart, might well find himself roused to a blaze of patriotic fervor. His arm held by the King, who, like his father before him, was the enemy of all that he believed in, he was led into the presence of my lady Benbrook.

"My lady Angel," the King said in a gentle voice, "here is another friend come to see you." He hesitated, wondering if he should make mention of the news Mrs. Sampson had imparted. But seeing Angel's weary and tear-streaked face, the trembling of her hands, and the wildness of her eyes, he decided to refrain. "I will leave you to escort Mr. Milton to a chair, my lady, for I must be on my way."

"Thank you, Sire," she answered him in a dull voice.

After the King had left the room, Milton was the first to break the silence that had fallen. "Angel!" His hand lifted helplessly. "Angel, poor child!"

"John!" Angel ran forward and cast herself into his arms. "What am I to do? I can't go on without him!"

His arms closed tightly about her, his voice murmured soothingly. Just so had he once held his Serena, and, in the person of this young girl, he could almost believe he held her again. He would never now put into verse the romance of my lord Benbrook and his Angel, for the ending must be too tragically reminiscent of his own lost love.

Later, seated on the wide couch with Angel, fallen asleep from sheer exhaustion, still held in his arms, Milton wondered why he himself troubled to go on living.

Serena was dead, and without her he would never again experience real joy. It was true that he found a kind of ecstasy in his work, but without that very special one beside you, even that was not enough. Elizabeth, his present wife, was kind, and she endeavored to make him comfortable, but they were really two strangers living together in uneasy amity. She had never understood the compelling urge of that surging torrent of words inside him. When, out of lonely desperation, he had spoken to her of his innermost thoughts, it seemed that she could only giggle nervously and make one of her small inane jokes. He was fifty-eight years old. He had a wife who meant nothing to him. He had three daughters, and he understood them not at all. They, with their light minds, were alien to him. They had no love to offer him, but for this he held them blameless, since he had given them none. Mayhap 'twas because they reminded him too vividly of their mother, a woman he had grown to detest. The home in Bread Street, willed to him by his father, and which had provided him with a small income, had been reduced to ashes. He had only his work left, which he would always cherish, but apart from that, certain poverty, and a wife and three daughters to provide for.

He rested his hand on Angel's soft hair. The Fire of London had robbed this child too of all her dreams and hopes! His mind went back to the horror of that time. He heard again the roaring of the flames, the crashing of timbers, the anguished screams of the people. Somehow, in that great press of frightened people, he had become parted from his companions. He had stumbled through those fiery streets, a blind man who felt the searing heat against his flesh, but who saw only the eternal blackness. He had not cried out for help, for he knew his cries would go unheard. Milton in the inferno, he had thought, for even then he could not keep his mind from playing with words. Milton meets the flaming angel of death!

It was Samuel Pepys who had found him. Sam who had attended to the great gash in his cheek and had soothed his seared neck with unguents. And oh the safety and joy he had felt in his presence, and in the sound of that irascible voice!

"What the devil did you think you were up to," Pepys had snorted indignantly, "reeling along the streets like some infernal tosspot?"

Now that he had this peppery little man to provide the light in his darkness, he could afford to smile. Tosspot? He who took only the occasional glass of wine?

"That's right, smile!" Pepys' voice had rumbled on. "God's gracious belly! I tell you to your face, Milton, you might have been killed if I hadn't happened along. And here's me with my property burnt to cinders and not a decent wig to clap upon my head, forced to attend to a cursed drunk!"

"But I am not drunk, Sam," he had protested mildly.

"Well if you ain't drunk, you're mad. Aye, that's it, mad as a hare in the springtime."

Angel stirred in his arms, scattering his thoughts. "John." He winced at that new painful note in her voice. "Forgive me, I had not meant to fall asleep."

"Apologize not, Angel," he quickly reassured her. "Sleep as much as you can, 'twill be good for you."

"Will it? But I do not want to do good to myself. I want only to find my—my—"

"You want only to find your paradise regained. I know, child, I know." He felt his mind stirring to fertile life with the words he had just uttered. Aye, mayhap one day he would write of a paradise regained. But could either of them return to lost happiness? Was it possible that in time they would pass from purgatory into a bright and carefree world? He doubted it, life was not long enough, but it was at least a hope to cling to.

His arms tightened protectively. "Angel, if you will have it so, I would like to be your friend."

"But you are my friend, John, and have been from the moment we first met."

That first meeting, he would never forget it! "Benbrook's Folly," once again he heard the Earl's drawling voice with its underlying hint of dry amusement. Nay,

Angel had been Benbrook's joy, as Serena had been his. He bent his head and dropped a kiss on Angel's hair. "Then am I content, dear child."

In the months that followed, John Milton was to hear much from Angel. She was always unfailing in her welcome, and her voice expressed joy in his presence, but the Angel he had hoped to come to know better had vanished. To his intently listening ears she sounded bright and hard. Her cynical observations upon life hurt him, for, cynical himself, he could not bear to hear it in one who had reminded him so poignantly of his lost love. She was not Angel, she was not Serena, she was a stranger. Why then, in the face of this conviction, did he have the certain feeling that Benbrook's Angel was not lost? All that she was, all that Benbrook had taught her to be, did but hide behind a barrier of intolerable pain. It was ironical that he who dealt in words could not find those that would release her and bring her forth from that hiding place. Mayhap, some day, he constantly told himself, someone would release her, and the old Angel would emerge. She would be scarred, as he was scarred, but she would be quiet, lovely, gentle of manners; because these were the qualities Benbrook had instilled in her, and the way he wished her to remain.

ANGEL SAT BESIDE THE QUEEN, HER HANDS idle, her violet eyes, always so darkened now and shadowed with memories, staring into space. The scarlet embroidery silks with which she had recently made a pretense of working lay in neglected tangled skeins across her lap, making a vivid splash of color against her white gown.

It was quiet in the room. The Queen's little group of ladies worked diligently at their embroidery, their heads bent. Angel, by her very presence, seemed to subdue their spirits. Catherine sighed, wishing, for once, that the brash Countess of Castlemaine would enter and intrude her noisy personality upon the uneasy silence that had fallen.

Catherine flushed faintly. She was the Queen, and it was for her to set the tone of the small circle. Yet somehow, when she encountered Angel's bleak eyes, the words of reproof that sprang to her tongue were stifled. Even Joachimo, the King's dwarf, but recently come to Court, was affected, his bubbling spirits nipped as if by frostbite. He sat very still in his small chair, his bowed legs dangling, his eyes, usually bright with malice, now mournful, fixed on Angel's face.

Catherine glanced at the silks in Angel's lap. It looked like blood, she thought, shivering a little, like streaks of blood against snow. What was Angel thinking of, she wondered. Was she, in her mind, wandering somewhere with Nicholas? She gave little thought to the child she was to bear next month, in June, that much was certain.

Against her will, Catherine found herself remembering her own pregnancy, which had begun with such joyful happy anticipation and had resulted so tragically in a violent miscarriage. She glanced at the bulge just below Angel's silver girdle, and her wistful envy became mingled with apprehension. Eight months now since my lord Benbrook's death, and during that time Angel had swung from heavy brooding silences to wild storms of weeping, to feverish, brittle, almost hysterical moods of gaiety. Catherine's eyes flickered uneasily. She could not help wondering if the chronic apathy and bitterness might not afflict the child.

Joachimo, as though he sensed the Queen's thoughts, turned his eyes to her face, his thick lips turning upward in a derisive smile. Catherine glanced away quickly, staring out of the window. The little man always made her feel uncomfortable, and to her shame, filled her with repulsion. Outside, the trees foamed with their burden of pink and white blossoms, and the slight breeze that drifted through the half-opened window was laden with their fragile perfume. The sky was like blue silk, decorated here and there with fluffy, gold-tinged white clouds. A beautiful day, Catherine thought. To her, May was a season of rebirth, of new hopes, of bursting vibrant life, but somehow she could not take her usual pleasure in the thought.

"Madam?" The dwarf's shrill voice caused Catherine to start violently. "Have I your permission to address you?"

"You have, Master Joachimo," Catherine answered, collecting herself. She bent her head over her embroidery, her eyes avoiding his excited working face.

"I would know the gown Your Majesty plans to wear for tonight's banquet."

" 'Tis a strange question, Master Joachimo."

The dwarf cackled, the sound shrill and ugly. "That I may bring you flowers to enhance your beauty, Madam."

He sighed, his eyes flicking swiftly to Angel's still face. "Ah, Madam, you must be beautiful, if only to assuage the King's grief at the departure of Mistress Frances Stuart. The lady, unfortunately, is married, and even now the King's eyes turn with love and a wish for consolation upon my lady Benbrook."

This outrageous speech brought a gasp from her ladies. Bright angry color flooded into Catherine's face and released her from her frozen horror. "How dare you speak so, Master Joachimo!" she gasped, her hands clenching in her lap. "You are impudent!"

Joachimo cackled again. "But the King thinks me to be vastly amusing. He has told me more than once that I lighten his dullest hours. Why, when Mistress Frances Stuart left the Court to become my lady of Lennox and Richmond, His Majesty was most upset. He shouted at the lady, saying, 'I hope I may live to see you ugly and willing, Frances Stuart.' 'Twas I who consoled him with my japes and pranks."

"The King shall hear of this," Catherine said in a choked voice. "Leave this room at once!"

"Madam, I live to please you." The dwarf sprang down from his chair, his tiny feet hitting the floor with a thump. "But why do you not find me amusing, as His Majesty does?" he said in an aggrieved voice. "I have brought much laughter to this Court, and I do assure you, Madam, 'tis not my intention to be insolent." His eyes went to Angel's face again. "I love you, Your Majesty, Joachimo loves you, and does but seek to protect you from those who would betray you."

"You filthy little toad!" It was a violent exclamation from Angel.

Horrified, Catherine watched as Angel rose from her chair and advanced upon the little man. Her face was white, her mouth a tight straight line, and for once her eyes were alive, blazing with murderous rage. "How dare you make your slimy lying insinuations to the Queen!" she shouted.

Catherine started from her chair. "My lady Benbrook,"

she said in a quivering voice, "I must ask you to control yourself."

Angel was deaf to the Queen's voice. The horrified shrieks of the ladies failed to penetrate. Her hand shot out and lashed the dwarf round the face.

"Protect me, Madam, I beg you to protect me!" Joachimo shrieked. Again and again she hit him, only ceasing when Joachimo collapsed in a moaning heap at her feet. He flopped over onto his back, his orange-clad legs flailing the air. "My lady Benbrook does but seek to stop my mouth. I have seen her, Madam, I have seen how she looks at the King! She would betray you if she could, she would, she would—!"

He broke off, screaming, as Angel's foot caught him in the ribs. "Liar!" She spat the word at him. She swung round to face the Queen. "Madam, he lies."

" 'Tis not necessary to tell me that, my lady," Catherine said in a quiet voice. "We will not dignify it by discussing it."

Angel glimpsed the pain in the Queen's eyes, and her anger died away. "I did but seek consolation, Madam," she faltered. " 'Twas but a wish for a momentary forgetfulness. A few smiles, a jest or two, but no more. I pray you to believe me!"

"I do." The Queen's hand touched Angel's arm briefly. She came closer. "I trust you, Angel," she said in a whisper. "Now," she went on in a louder voice, "you will leave this room. Master Joachimo. Your behavior will be reported to the King, together with my urgent request that you be banished from this Court."

"But she lies, I tell you." Joachimo's voice rose to a wail as he scrambled painfully to his feet. He limped over to the door. "She is nothing but Benbrook's filthy whore! My lady Castlemaine has said so."

Catherine dared not look at Angel's face, but her own anger shook her like a violent storm. "Never let me set eyes on you again, Master Joachimo," she said in an icy voice. Her ringed hand caught at the back of a chair, her fingers digging into it for support. "You shall be severely punished for this, I promise you!"

Joachimo's derisive smile curled his lips. "I shall be banished for a time, Madam," he said, opening the door, "and that will be punishment enough. But I will return. His Gracious Majesty cannot do without the laughter that I alone can provoke." He bowed and left the room, closing the door gently behind him.

"Madam!" Lady Mary Turner's cry broke the quivering silence that had fallen. "My lady Benbrook is ill."

Angel's face had drained of all color, and there was a blue tinge to her mouth. Her swollen body jerked in a spasm of pain. She gasped, her fingers digging into her stomach. "I—I believe that the child is coming."

"Oh no, Angel, 'tis too soon!" Distracted, her lips trembling, the Queen turned to her ladies. "One of you fetch the physician at once. Hurry, please."

In the general confusion that resulted, the opening of the door went unnoticed. "What is it, Madam?" the King's voice said loudly.

"Sire!" The Queen started forward. "My lady Benbrook's time has come."

The King looked startled for a moment, then he said in a voice which he strove to make authoritative, "Calm yourself, Madam. All will be well."

Catherine was not to be consoled. She wrung her hands together, looking at him with anguished eyes. "But 'tis too soon, Sire," she faltered, "and well do I know what it is to lose a child."

"We will not lose this child, I promise you." The King patted her comfortingly on the shoulder. "Let us have no premature mourning." Passing her, he went to Angel's side. "My lady?" he said softly.

"It—it is time, Sire."

A quiver passed over the King's face. "Od's Fish, I can see that it is." His arms went round her, swinging her from the floor. "I will take you to your apartments."

241

"Nay, Sire," Angel tried to protest. "I must—must beg Your Majesty not to concern himself."

"You may beg all you please, my dear lady Benbrook," the King said grimly as he strode over to the door, "but the fact of the matter is that I *am* concerned. This is friend Nicholas's lad you are bearing, and therefore of great moment to me. Damn, if the physician does not do his job well, I'll deliver the boy myself!"

It was generally known that Charles Stuart had little use for royal tradition, save where it was politically expedient to observe it, but the sight of him striding along the corridor with Lady Benbrook in his arms, her bright hair spilling over his sleeve, was a sight that the frilled and perfumed ladies and the satin-clad and jeweled gentlemen would long remember.

For his part, the King was only aware of the woman in his arms. Her drawn, pain-twisted face excited his strong compassion, and his attitude was that of a distracted husband. He felt that Nicholas walked by his side, approving, as he spoke to her in a low, soothing voice. The lazy, good natured Charles Stuart was seriously concerned for the welfare of his friend's wife. She was too apathetic, too unconcerned with life, too willing to die. His arms tightened spasmodically about her at this last thought. His face, though he was not aware of it, had lost much of its color, there was a churning sickness in his stomach, and his brilliant smile was subdued to something that was almost a nervous grimace. Nevertheless, he continued to repeat steadily over and over again, "There, sweetheart, there, there! All will be well, you have my word."

Angel heard him through the pain racking her convulsed body. She only knew that the arms upholding her were strong, the hard flat shoulder comforting against her hot cheek. She struggled for courage and composure, and some impish humor, long buried, made her say in a faint voice, "Od's Fish, Sire, we must hurry, else will the child be born in the corridor."

"Nay!" Charles stumbled, almost dropping her in his

242

agitation. "Say not so, my lady," he begged. "We are almost there!"

The pain, subsiding for a moment, gave way to a sharper agony. Nicholas's child was about to be born, and her dear m'lord not here at her side! She glanced up into the King's swarthy face, forcing a smile to her lips. "I did but jest," she consoled him. "B—but why do you fear, Sire? I—I have it on good au—authority that you have been present at many a birth."

"This birth is different to any other. It is Nicholas's child, and that says it all, does it not?"

"Aye." Angel closed her eyes. "Dear Majesty," she whispered, "you are so very kind!"

His heart twisted as he saw the tears sliding from beneath her dark lashes. "Don't!" he begged her. "God's precious life, Angel, don't cry! Soon your child will be here, Nicholas's child."

She made no answer to this, and Charles breathed a hearty sigh of relief as they came in sight of the apartments.

Word had evidently been sent ahead, for Mrs. Sampson was at the door. She dropped a flustered curtsy as Charles entered with his burden. "Sire," she began, "I did not expect—"

"Never mind," Charles said, smiling at her. "My lady Benbrook is in urgent need of your attention." He laid Angel gently on the wide canopied bed. "Where is the physician?" he went on, straightening up and glancing about the room. "Why is he not here?"

"He has been sent for, Your Majesty. I am expecting him at any moment."

Charles frowned at the leaping fire in the grate. " 'Tis monstrous hot in here. 'Tis like summer outside. What need have you for a fire?"

"My lady must be kept warm, Your Majesty. Birth is a long and arduous job."

"Not this time, I fancy," Charles said, glancing down at Angel. "The child is due at any moment. I will leave you now, madam. Take good care of your mistress."

"You may depend upon it, Sire," Mrs. Sampson said, accompanying him to the door. "This child is very important to me."

"He is important to everyone, it would seem," Charles said in a low voice, "except, perhaps, to his mother."

Mrs. Sampson shook her head. "I know what you would say, Sire, but it will be different when the child is here."

"I hope so." Charles took her hand in his, squeezing it gently. "We have been through much with your mistress, have we not? Friend Nicholas found her, then lost her, then found her again." "Aye." Mrs. Sampson's eyes dimmed with the tears that came to her readily now. "Master Nickey lost her, but 'twas you who found her, Sire."

"So I did." Charles tried to speak lightly, but there was a deep seriousness in his eyes as he gazed steadily at the woman. "And are we to lose her again, Mrs. Sampson?"

"Nay, Sire," Mrs. Sampson said, her lips tightening. "Not if I know it."

"Excellent." Charles dropped her hand. "Then I will depend upon you."

"You may do so." Mrs. Sampson peered closely at him. "But you, Sire," she ventured, "you are not looking very well. Is there something I may do for you?"

"Nothing, thank you." Charles smiled slightly. "You may put my appearance down to the pangs of expectant fatherhood, which I am assuming in the absence of friend Nicholas."

Mrs. Sampson's eyes softened. "God bless you, Your Majesty. On behalf of Master Nickey, and my lady, I thank you. It would seem to me—" A moan from the bed caused her to turn sharply. "Sire, I think that I had best attend my lady."

"I think so, too. But where the devil is that plaguey physician?"

ANGEL'S BODY FELT LANGUID AND HEAVY, but now, at last, there was no more pain. The child had been born, someone had told her. A healthy child, the same voice had said with some satisfaction. Her brow wrinkled with a faint far-off anxiety. Was it her child? A boy or girl? Why couldn't she remember? It seemed to her that the voice had told her the sex of the child. Her head turned fretfully on the pillow. It was no use. She could remember only Nicholas, only Nicholas!

She lay perfectly still, her eyes closed. There were other people in the room, but although they were talking, she couldn't make out the words. Nicholas was speaking to her now, his voice sharp and stern, drowning out the others. "Mistress Dawson, hold your back straight, if you please! Are you practicing to be a hunchback?"

"No," she said, holding out her hand in appeal. "No, Nicholas, dear m'lord! Don't look at me like that. Don't leave me!"

His hand was taking hers, she could feel the strong warmth of his clasp. "Hush," he said in a low voice. "Hush, my lady."

She frowned, puzzled. But Nicholas was angry with her. She could see the tight compression of his lips, the dark impatience of his eyes. Guttersnipe, guttersnipe, will you never learn? Why then did he speak to her so softly, so gently? She moved restlessly in the bed, feeling

245

the damp clinging of the sheets, and now a terrible suspicion entered her mind. "Go away," she said sharply. "You're not Nicholas, you're not!"

"Angel!" a woman's voice now, harsh, imperative. "Open your eyes. 'Tis the King who speaks to you."

Absurd! What had she to do with the King? Laughter welled up, clogging in her throat, making her gasp for breath. She was a guttersnipe, ignorant, uneducated; Nicholas had said so. And once, long ago, she had been Newgate bait. Long ago? Was it? No, for there was Jim Gibbons standing before her. She could see his heavy brutal face, the implacable cruelty of his mouth, the coiled whip in his hand. He was going to flog her! Not again, oh dear Christ, not again! With a strangled cry, she flung up her arm, trying to shield her face. "Nicholas! Don't let him flog me, don't!"

"Angel!" It was the woman's voice again. "Open your eyes, you're dreaming."

It was no dream, no dream, Jim Gibbons was there! But she must obey that urging voice, she must open her eyes. With an effort, she forced her heavy lids open. Someone was bending over her. Not Jim Gibbons, another man, a man with long dark hair. She looked down at his slender fingers which held her hand in a cool grip, fingers laden with flashing rings. She blinked, dazzled. Her eyes traveled upward again, concentrating on the thin sardonic face hovering above her, the dark compassionate eyes. Beneath a narrow mustache, his full lips opened in a warm smile. Angel felt her lips trying to make an automatic response, but they were too cold, too stiff, too disobedient to her will. She stopped trying, tears of fear and frustration misting her eyes. "Who are —who—you look like—" she broke off, shaking her head. "I'm s—sorry, I can't remember."

"I look like the King," the man prompted. "I am the King, Angel."

"You cannot be," she said firmly. Ridiculous! Why should he try to deceive her? Her eyes wavered, fastened themselves on a point beyond him. "The King would not

246

talk to such as I. I am—I am Angel Dawson, I—" She
stopped, memory prodding with painful fingers at her
clouding mind. Yes, she was Angel Dawson, but they
called her by other names. Strumpet, gutter brat! The
red-headed woman, the beautiful woman with the hard
eyes and the petulant mouth—perhaps she could remember her name if she tried, but she was too tired—the
red-headed woman had called her the King's brat. Joachimo's face whirled before her, ugly, venomous. "Benbrook's whore!" Aloud, Angel said, her voice taking on a
sudden strength, "I am Benbrook's whore."

She felt the fingers on her hand tighten in a convulsive
grip. Frightened, she tried to pull her hand free.

"Sir Robert," somebody said, "why do you just stand
there? Od's Fish, there must be something you can do!"

"Nothing." It was a slow ponderous voice that answered. "I beg you to forgive me, Sire. It would seem
that she does not wish to live, and against that I am helpless. I am afraid that my lady Benbrook is dying."

"I will not let her die! Do something, man! Anything!"

"I cannot give her back her will to live, Sire."

"You can try, damn you!"

Angel closed her eyes again. She felt a small secret
sense of triumph for this unknown woman. Lady Benbrook was dying, Benbrook's whore was dying. She
clutched the words almost desperately, tossing them finally into the helpless confusion of her thoughts. But
she? Surely she was my lady Benbrook? Nicholas! Oh,
Nicholas! As though his name released something within
her, she surrendered herself to the savage twist of pain
that recollection brought. As suddenly as it had come, it
ebbed, leaving her in a dark silence, in peace. Of course,
she remembered now. She was Lady Benbrook, the woman made out of the ragged cloth of Angel Dawson. She
was Nicholas's wife, his wife! And she was dying. "I'm
glad," she said, the faint thread of her voice echoing in
her mind. "Dear M'lord, I'm so glad!"

Nicholas was there. She saw him clearly against the
screens of her tightly closed eyes. He was advancing to-

247

ward her, his hands held out in greeting. His rare smile touched his lips, and his eyes were dark and tender. She saw the dim luster of the pearl pin that fastened his lace cravat, the careless swing of the cloak that fell from his shoulders. "Brat," he said. "My brat!" His finger caressed her cheek. "Hurry, hurry!"

"I'm coming." Was that her voice? That hoarse croak? "Oh dear m'lord, I'm coming!"

Wind blew his cloak, sending it swirling about her, enfolding her, even as his arms were doing. "I've been lonely without you, brat."

She felt light and free now. She put her arms about his neck, saying with a small laugh, "Don't you know, dear m'lord, that even Heaven could not hold us if we were not together?"

"I know, I know."

She could hear the cry of an owl. "Do you hear that owl?" Nicholas said. " 'Tis loud in its hooting, is it not?"

"Dear m'lord, I am not interested in owls."

"Then in what, my lady Benbrook?"

"In you, my love. In you, and our son."

"Our son?" She could feel Nicholas stiffening against her, drawing away. "My son! I had forgotten him."

"My son! My son!" she echoed his words. "I will get him. I will show him to you. Only don't leave me, Nicholas, don't! Take me with you!"

Mrs. Sampson looked at the King. "Did you hear her, Sire? She is calling for the lad."

The King turned toward the satin-draped crib. "Yes," he said in a shaken voice.

"Perhaps if she saw him, Sire?"

The King stooped and picked up the small, warm bundle, smiling a little at the sleepy, protesting whimper. "Good morning to you, lad. Would you greet your King so pettishly?" He glanced at Mrs. Sampson. "By God, but this little rascal is friend Nicholas all over again!"

"Yes, Sire, he is. Oft times it is hard to tell until their features are fully formed, but he is very like to my Master Nickey."

248

The King heard the break in her voice, and he said very gently, "He is indeed. And will grow more like to him, I vow, as time goes on." A glint of excitement lit his eyes. "If my lady would look at him. If she would see that, in this lad, she has regained her Nicholas, then mayhap she will recover."

Angel heard the words. For a moment she lay very still, fighting the urge to return to the arms that awaited her. It seemed to her that she saw the small Nicholas, whom Mrs. Sampson had loved and cherished. She saw him afraid, crying, small arms clinging in desperation to the housekeeper. She saw him sickened by the lust of his mother. Saw him growing up, aloof from life, embittered, unbending, afraid to love, to trust, and she could not bear it. The cry that came from her lips startled the King. "Give him to me," she demanded. "Give me my son!"

Her eyes were open, shadowed still by approaching death, but seeking, hungry. "Give him to me," she said again.

The King approached the bed, smiling. "Madam," he said, depositing the child into her arms, "I present unto you Nicholas, the fifth Earl of Benbrook."

"Nicholas!" Her shaking arms hugged the child close. "My little one! My boy!"

"I believe, Sir Robert," the King said, turning to the physician, "that your job has been done for you." A loud wail from the bed caused him to grin. "From the sound of him, the fifth Earl of Benbrook is going to be fully as assertive as his father, and, I doubt not, with his demands, is already commanding his mother to recover."

Sir Robert Fleming nodded somewhat gloomily. He was a humorless man at best, and he thought the King's remark heartless and in the poorest of taste. The lady was dying, he still believed that. The King might put his faith in miracles, but he did not. "I hope you may be right, Sire," he said in his slow, precise voice.

"Of course I am right." The King waved an impatient hand. "Why must you leeches always be so gloomy?"

Seriously affronted, Sir Robert drew himself up stiffly.

"I am a competent physician, Sire, and, in my methods, am known to be well ahead of my time."

"Ah! And you like not to be called a leech." The King, with a last glance toward the bed, strode over and linked his arm through the other man's. "Oh come, Rob," he said cajolingly, smiling, "cast off your offense. Let us leave my lady Benbrook alone, shall we? She has just discovered something new and wonderful." He urged him toward the door. "Will you walk with me for a while?"

Sir Robert was not proof against that smile, and in that he was in accord with the majority. The man was a rogue and a lecher, for all that he was the King, but damn, when he exerted himself to please, there was something about the lazy Charles Stuart that was completely disarming to the most suspicious of men—women too, for that matter. Sir Robert chuckled inwardly. Would to God that they flocked about him as they did about the graceless Charles Stuart!

"Very well, Sire," Sir Robert answered, a reluctant smile appearing, "if it be your pleasure. But Lady Benbrook still has great need of my attention."

"Of course, of course," the King answered, opening the door, "I know it well. But plague take me, Rob, if I ever saw such a fellow as you. So serious, so dedicated, so cursed prosaic."

"I am supposed to be, Sire." There was faint reproof in the physician's voice. "Would you have me any other way?"

The King eased him through the door. "If I am stricken, I would not want you laughing your fool head off. You are right, Rob, right in every respect. I wonder you have anything to do with such a popinjay as myself."

"Sire!"

"I am laughing at you, Sir Robert. Aye, I am. My lady Benbrook will recover, and a new life will take shape before our eyes. What more could one ask for?"

"Hmm!" The physician stroked his bearded chin. "As

to the condition of my lady Benbrook, we must wait and see."

"You are cautious, too," Charles said, laughing. "I like that in you, very much."

"So you should, Sire. It means I will be cautious with your own health."

Mrs. Sampson stared at the closed door for a long moment, before turning back to Angel. "Is he not a little sweeting?" she said at last.

"He is Nicholas," Angel said, her eyes on the baby's face. "Oh, Sampson, he is Nicholas!"

"Aye." Mrs. Sampson's eyes were faintly troubled. "He is like to Master Nickey, and doubtless will grow more like him. Yet he will have his own character, Angel, and I beg you to remember that."

"Yes, yes! Leave me for a while, Sampson. I would be alone with my son."

"Leave you?" Mrs. Sampson said, aghast. She put her hand to Angel's forehead. "But, child, you still burn with fever. It is best that I stay."

"Only for a little while, Sampson, please!"

There was a long silence, and the woman's disapproval could be felt. "Very well," she said at last. "I will give you five minutes only." She hesitated. "You will be careful with my lad?"

"I will be careful."

Angel heard her footsteps crossing the room, the soft closing of the door. There was a haze before her eyes, and the tiny weight in her arms seemed unbearably heavy, but she held on to her burden with desperate arms. "I cannot come to you yet, I see that now," she whispered. "Our son needs me. But pray God, dear m'lord, that my life will be short. He will have Sampson. He will have all the love he needs."

The last words, though she was not aware of it, were uttered pleadingly, as though she was begging Nicholas's unseen presence to understand and condone. It seemed to her then that Nicholas came to her. She did not see

251

him, yet she knew he bent over her, almost, she felt his kiss on her mouth, warm and living. She smiled. "Dear m'lord, if I may quote the King, I present unto you Nicholas, the fifth Earl of Benbrook."

Clearly in her ears, she heard his voice. "I love you, Angel. Damn you, I love you!"

SEEN THROUGH THE THINLY SWIRLING WHITE mist, Whitehall Palace looked oddly unreal, like a child's drawing of a building, the outlines dubbed in with dark wavering lines. Although it was only four o'clock, light was reflected behind every window, small islands of comfort in the raw chill of the November afternoon.

Alex Barrymore looked at the bare, dripping trees. Then, shivering, he drew his cloak tightly about him, hunching his shoulders together for warmth. He turned quickly to the woman who stood by his side. "Why did you not send one of the servants to seek my lady Benbrook, Mrs. Sampson?" he inquired, his voice tinged with that slight bitterness that the mention of Angel could inspire of late. "If she is foolish enough to wander about the grounds in this infernal weather, there is no reason why you too should subject yourself to a chill. I suggest that you return to the Palace at once." He smiled at her in an effort to soften his words. "I imagine that, as always, the little lord Benbrook will have need of your services."

"He is in M'Zeli's charge for the moment," Mrs. Sampson answered. "Ever since the boy returned to the Palace, he has taken great joy in my lord Benbrook, and I would sooner trust him than the women." She paused, biting nervously at her lip. Alex Barrymore was often at the Palace, for his friendship with the King had deepened. She had known he was coming this afternoon, and she had deliberately waited for him at the King's private entrance. But she felt ashamed that she was using the knowledge that he loved Angel to impose upon his good nature. It was bad enough that Angel, while relying on Mr. Barrymore for companionship and understanding, should treat him in a cavalier manner. He was always there in the background, and had been ever since Master Nickey's death, warm, steady, reliant, trustworthy. Why could not Angel turn to him, give him back some small measure of love, instead of raising her eyes higher to a place where they had no right to be?

"I'm sorry, sir," Mrs. Sampson resumed hastily, "and I regret to impose upon you, but I know you understand Angel. She is always wandering off these days, and it worries me. 'Tis true I could have sent a servant after her, but servants, as you must be aware, are ever ready to gossip. She will listen more readily to you."

Alex looked at her closely, his eyes narrowing in thought. "There is something to gossip about, then? I have the feeling that it is not her wandering that worries you so much."

"I—I— Angel has changed, Mr. Barrymore, and I know you have remarked it for yourself. She has—has become light of manner, and indifferent to the gossip about herself and the King. I would have said it is because she doesn't care what becomes of her, but sometimes I think she has entirely forgotten about Master Nickey, and her son." Mrs. Sampson drew a deep quivering breath. "I fear she is becoming as bad as my lady Castlemaine."

Nay, he'd not believe it, 'twas impossible! Alex tried to ignore the pain her words brought. "That is nonsense, Mrs. Sampson, and you know it well." He spoke with sharp rebuke. "The manners, morals, and conduct of my lady Castlemaine are, and ever will be alien to her. She adores the boy. I know, for I have seen the expression on her face when she is holding him. As for my lord

254

Benbrook, she is as far from forgetting him as I am from forgetting her!"

He had not meant to say those last, revealing words, and almost instantly he regretted them. He was a man of reserve and pride where his deeper feelings were concerned, and he recoiled from the pity his remark must undoubtedly provoke. It did not occur to him that the shrewd old woman had long since seen through his pretense.

"I know you love her, sir," Mrs. Sampson said eagerly. "But does Angel?"

Alex stiffened for a moment, frowning. "I can keep nothing from you, it seems. Aye, Mrs. Sampson, she knows."

"I'm sorry, sir. Would that Angel could see you in a different light. As a man who cares for her deeply and would look to her happiness."

"Don't be sorry," he answered lightly. "I shall doubtless get over it. Or I will attempt to do so."

"Angel leaves her mark on a man, I know." Mrs. Sampson shook her head. "I never thought to say this," she went on soberly, "loving Master Nickey as I did, but I wish Angel would marry you. You would make her a fine husband, and be a father to Master Nickey's son." She paused, glancing at him anxiously. "But there, my tongue runs away with me."

"Nay, Mrs. Sampson, I am in complete agreement with your views, but it is of little use to discuss them. I imagine that my lady Benbrook is a woman who loves once, and only once."

"I'll not believe that. There are many different kinds of love, you know, sir. I don't doubt that she will never feel again as she felt for Master Nickey, but when she loves again, I am in great hopes that she will choose you, sir."

"Nicholas was right, you are an interfering old woman." Alex smiled at her. "But I love you for it. However, I fear that I am too dull for her."

"Not you, sir!" Mrs. Sampson's mouth tightened indignantly. "There is always laughter when you are about. I have even heard the Queen say that she is happy when you appear, for you make her laugh and forget her troubles."

" 'Tis indeed gracious of her."

Mrs. Sampson sighed heavily. " 'Tis little cause the poor lady has for gaiety, I know. What with, if you'll excuse me for speaking plain, that Nell Gwynne, to say nothing of the behavior of my own mistress. The Queen trusted Angel, even loved her, I think, but now, when she looks at her, there is something in her eyes that makes me shiver. It is as if she cannot believe that Angel would betray her, and yet, despite herself, she is coming to believe it."

Alex stared at her, and before the anger in his eyes, her own dropped. "You forget yourself, Mrs. Sampson, do you not?" he said coldly.

She looked at him again. "Aye, but nonetheless, sir, I have this feeling that if Angel is not now the King's mistress, she soon will be."

"I'll listen to no more. I will find my lady Benbrook. I daresay she has not gone far." Alex turned from her abruptly. "Go in now, please," he said, beginning to walk away, "else will you take a chill."

Reluctantly now, Alex walked along the winding path which glittered with a hard frost through the lifting mist. Dwarf bushes, lifeless and brown, lined the path on either side, shedding their mournful burden of water drop by drop. He was angry with Mrs. Sampson, perhaps because he feared her words were all too true. It was as though the woman had drawn aside a curtain and revealed to him another Angel, a stranger. His heart ached dully as he remembered her with Nicholas. Where had she gone, that lovely girl with the soft bright eyes, the demure but spirited manner? Had Nicholas's death been hers, in that his passing had erased her completely?

He had last seen her two nights ago, on the occasion of the Honors Ball. He had not understood her that night, and so he had tried even harder to reach her, to break through her brittle crust of gaiety. Only later, when Mrs. Sampson had told him of that first memorable Honors Ball, attended by Nicholas and Angel, had he understood what it must have meant to her. Angel had been clad in a low-cut gown of vivid blue lavishly trimmed with swags of silver lace and glittering with jewels. There had been hectic spots of color in her cheeks, her voice had been too loud, too shrill, far removed from those beautiful low tones he was accustomed to hearing.

Alex stopped short on the path. Now he came to think of it, she had danced too often with the King. She had laughed with, and flirted with him outrageously. He had thought nothing of it at the time, perhaps because he was too concerned with his own misery. As for Charles himself, he had had eyes for no one but Angel. Even Nell Gwynne, the latest object of his capricious fancy, had been neglected.

Alex walked on slowly, feeling a heaviness that was at one with the dismal day. His hands clenched. He loved her, and he would go on loving her though she became mistress to a dozen men; but she was Nicholas's Angel, surely she would not allow herself to become just another in a succession of royal mistresses? Angel was something rare and precious, a bright being. Let the Castlemaine and others of her kind disport themselves in the King's bed, but not Angel!

He came to the end of the path, and turning to his left, he saw her seated on a bench set in a grove of trees. She was clad in a fur-trimmed cloak of dark green, the hood fallen back to show bright windblown hair. Her hand holding the cloak about her looked faintly mauve with the cold, and she was shivering. Alex started toward her, but stopped again as he heard the King's deep voice.

"My lady Angel," the King was saying, and Alex noticed a slight hesitation in the usually confident voice, "will you not give me a kiss to seal our bargain?"

Concealed behind the wide trunk of an oak tree, Alex stood very still as he waited for Angel's reply.

"Aye, Charles," Angel said lightly, half-mockingly, "you may well call it a bargain. I doubt not that my presence in your bed will gain me many a coveted honor."

Charles was silent for a moment, then he said protestingly, "I did but jest when I called it a bargain, and well do you know it. I love you, Angel. Od's Fish! How many times do I have to tell you?"

"But of course you love me, Sire," Angel said, laughing. "And in exactly the same way as you once loved Bab Castlemaine, as you love Frances Stuart and Nell Gwynne. I am not such a fool as to think there will not be a host of others after me." She put her hand lightly over his mouth, stemming the words he would have spoken. "Ah, Charles Stuart, look not so. You believe yourself to be sincere, I know, and therefore must I forgive you your self-deception."

Charles took her hand from his mouth and carried it to his lips. "Minx!" he said, kissing it lingeringly. "You have ever misjudged me. I love you, and I will be telling you so when I am old and gray."

"There is no need to commit yourself, Sire. When you are old and gray, I will have long since vanished from your life."

The King's lips curled in his wry smile. "Too late, my lady. Under this wig I am already gray." His arms went round her, drawing her close against him. "You would not leave me, Angel, would you? I can make you love me, I know that I can!"

Angel put her hands against his shoulders, as if to restrain him. "Many women have loved you, dear Majesty," her voice came softly to Alex, "but I must claim to be the exception. You cannot force my love, so I beg you not to try."

"I see," Charles answered stiffly. "Then why, my lady, if you are so sure that you cannot love me, have you consented to become my mistress?"

"But you know the answer to that, Sire. My King has conferred a great honor upon me. Need I say more?"

"You are needlessly cruel," Charles said, his arms tightening about her. "The honor, as you call it, means little to you, I see that. But I have always wanted you, Angel, and if it means swallowing my pride, then this perforce I must do, for I have no intention of letting you go."

"No need to talk of letting me go, Sire. Have I not said that I will share your bed? Once, do you remember, you wished me to wear your ring." She paused, looking at him intently, then, her voice hardening, she went on quickly. "I wore your ring in innocence then, did I not? I will wear it again, if you ask it of me, this time with full proud knowledge."

Charles released her abruptly. "Not, I think, with pride, Angel. Say rather that the new Angel will wear it in arrogance and defiance, perhaps in delight of the scandal. But you may be assured that I will never ask you to wear it." He looked away from her, staring at the frozen ground. "When I offered you the ring, I did not know of the love between yourself and friend Nicholas. I have suffered much over that affair, and that must be my defense. Have you forgiven me for the deception?"

"But of course, Sire."

"Your reassurance comes too quickly," Charles said in a low voice, "and you say the words without fire." He turned to her again, catching her hands in his.

Angel laughed lightly, and Alex, hearing her laughter, felt a tremor of uneasiness. It was such a mournful sound, devoid of heart and mirth. "Ah, Sire," she answered the King, " 'tis all behind us now, is it not. I don't hate you or resent you. In truth, I feel nothing." She leaned closer to Charles. "Strong emotions are always so fatiguing, are they not?"

The King's hands touched her lightly at first, then roughly. "And the emotion of love? Do you also find that fatiguing?"

Her face clouded. "But we do not talk of love, do we, Sire?" She bent her head forward and kissed him lightly on the mouth. "Love for me is dead, I pray you to let us leave it at that. But fondness for yourself remains,

259

Sire. I feel for you as I have ever done. Is it enough for you?"

Charles studied her for a long moment. "If that is all you can truly offer, then I must make it enough." His voice took on cynicism. "As you know, my lady Angel, I have always wanted you. And as well myself as another, eh?"

"As you say, dear Majesty." She looked at him through half-closed lids, inviting his kiss. When he made no move toward her, she said huskily, "Kiss me, Charles. Don't let me remember the past. For these few moments, make me forget!"

"I wish that I could make you forget, sweetheart, but I cannot, and I know it." He drew her into his arms, kissing her eyes, her lips with a kind of desperation. "Angel, oh, Angel!" he said between kisses. "I do love you. I beg you not to doubt me!" He kissed her again, a long hard kiss. "You may laugh if you will, but 'pon my soul, I love you to distraction!"

Alex turned away, seeing her unmoved face. The King may as well have clasped a log of wood in his arms, so obvious was it that she felt nothing. Why then had she consented? Was it because she felt the need to be loved, even though she had nothing to give in return? The light and frivolous Charles Stuart would leave little impression on her life. Was that what she wanted, to be adored, but to remain untouched within herself?

Alex stumbled a little. What of himself, he thought, recovering himself. He, too, had offered her love. But perhaps he was distasteful to her. He must be if she could turn from him to the King. Charles was charming, but he was the King and, as such, he could only fit Angel into a small part of his life. Alex's thoughts turned heavy and confused. It might well be that he himself was too serious, too earnest and open in his love and his intentions. It could be that she, wishing no serious entanglements, had chosen the King for this very reason.

Angel's quick ears were attracted by the sound of Alex's footsteps, incautious now, scuffling through the fallen leaves. She stiffened in the King's arms and stared after his retreating back. A fugitive ray of sunshine, peering momentarily through the clouds, touched his hair to gold, and she was aware of a curious softening. Alex! She was surprised at her sudden emotion, and now it began to twist inside her, harsh and hurting. How long had he been standing near? Had he heard? How shameless, how faithless he must think her. She had a desire to call after him—*I'm sorry, Alex, so sorry. Forget what you heard, it means nothing. Oh, Alex, give me time. Let me once be at peace with myself and I will try to love you.*

The King's lips touched her hair, and the impulse passed. She was a fool! Nicholas was gone, and because of this, nothing would ever matter again. There was only this meaningless moment, but meaningless or not, she would grasp it. She was a woman, not a nun. Alex would love her if she encouraged him, but he would want her all his own. Charles, unless she was vastly mistaken in him, would not. No, he was too cynical to expect anything save perhaps her loyalty. Charles would make her laugh, and God knows she needed to laugh.

Angel felt a stabbing pain in her temples. She put her fingers to her forehead and massaged the pain. Could she forget the Queen? Catherine had always loved and trusted her. Could she now bring herself to betray that trust? She must speak, say something, anything, before it was too late.

"Sire," she began.

"I think I know what you would say, my lady, but don't." Charles raised his head and looked at her, his dark eyes clouding. "You think of the Queen, I know." His thin fingers touched her cheek, trailed caressingly downward. "My nature is such that Catherine is bound to be hurt, greatly though I regret it." He laughed suddenly. "Better you, who are gentle and understanding, than another who will not be."

Angel stared at him. What twisted reasoning was this? Did it never occur to him that he could be faithful if he tried? She looked into his lean dark face, his smiling eyes, and she sighed. As well ask the sun to stop shining as to demand fidelity to one woman from the Stuart. He was right. Better herself, who would never seek to humiliate Catherine. Her own reasoning was twisted, she knew. She should get up from this bench, tell him that she would have nothing more to do with him. Aye, even though he be King, he could not force her to his bed, but did she really want to go on in her old dreary way? It was something, was it not, to be the mistress of the King of England? After all, she was really very fond of him.

"Little Puritan." Charles' arms closed about her, holding her suffocatingly close. "You would be my mistress, yet you would not be. Be done with your doubts, for I want you, Angel, and I intend to have you."

"Do you, Sire." Her voice choked in her throat as his lips crushed down on hers. She felt the heavy beating of her heart, and against her will she felt her own lips responding to his urgency. He was exciting, overpoweringly attractive, he was the King, and he wanted her. Her thoughts raced feverishly. She had much to gain, little to lose.

After a long moment, Charles raised his head and looked at her steadily. "Od's Fish, my lady, I think that I do not need to coax you more." He shook her gently. "Do you dare to tell me it is not so?"

"You—you are the King. The King is always right."

A faint frown appeared between his eyes, and his arms dropped away from her. "Don't play with me, Angel," he said with a hint of impatience.

"I would not dare, Sire." Obeying a sudden impulse, she held out her arms to him. "I am cold, Majesty. Cease your scowling and come back to me."

Surprisingly, he ignored the gesture. He rose from the bench, pulling her up with him. "Time enough," he said gently. "You have given me my answer, and I am well content." He hesitated, then added, "Shall it be tonight, my lady?"

Bright color stained her face. "Yes, Sire." Avoiding his

eyes, she hung back a little. "But I pray you to allow me to stay here a little longer."

"Nay," he said firmly. He put an arm about her shoulders and urged her forward. " 'Tis cold out here. I would have you bonny and willing, not weak and wailing and afflicted with a chill." He squeezed her shoulder. "Charles Stuart's bed, you will find, is a pleasant battleground, but 'tis not a restful place for an invalid."

Her laughter rang out. "God's teeth, what a way to describe it! But who will be the victor, think you?"

"Why, sweetheart, both of us, of course." His laughter mingled with hers. "I have failed in many things, my lady Angel, but never yet, I vow, in the act of love."

They walked in silence for a few moments. When the King spoke again, his voice was grave, compelling her attention. "I will not ask for your love, Angel," he said slowly, "but this I will say. No matter what comes of this delightful escapade between us, I will always care for your son. Friend Nicholas's child is also mine, and so do I look upon it."

" 'Tis good of you, Sire." Angel's eyes were wide and dark with pain, and her mouth trembled. "But the welfare of my son is my own affair. I believe my—my lord would have it so."

"We will say no more about it for the present," Charles answered firmly. "However, if a King may be said to adopt a son, this I have done with young Nicholas. I would have you know that his welfare will always be close to my heart, and to the Queen's."

Angel glanced at him quickly. "Doubtless, Sire," she said, her voice shaking, "the Queen would prove to be a worthier mother than myself."

"What mean you by that, my lady?"

She stopped short on the path and moved closer to him. "Your Majesty, I have given much thought to my son. I love him, God knows I love him! But I believe he would be better off without me."

"Hush!" He caught both her hands in his and held them tightly. "What nonsense is this?"

She shook her head despairingly. "Your Majesty, I am a nobody, a nothing. I was what my lord made of me, but now he is gone, and once again I am nothing. I am not worthy to bring up his son. Better by far if I go back where I came from." She looked at him imploringly.

"My lady, I had never thought to call you a fool; don't make me change my mind."

"Sire, you don't know what goes on inside me."

"Perhaps that is as well. But you are Nicholas's mother, and you will not run away from your responsibilities."

"Do you think that?" Angel's face flushed. "I love my boy. I love him with all my heart. But I am no good for him."

"Now I will call you a fool." Charles' face was tight and stern. "Surely, my lady, your mind must be deranged."

"Perhaps it is. I don't know, Sire. With my lord gone, it is like wandering in a fog. But I think of my son, I think of him all the time."

"Then continue to do so, but sensibly." He drew her along the path. "Angel, you would not leave the child?"

She caught the note of anxiety in his voice, and somewhere deep inside her a resolve was formed. "And if I did, Sire," she forced her voice to lightness. "What then? *What then, Sire?*"

"Why, he would be brought up as my own son, of course. But never think that I would not find you and bring you back to him." His hand tightened on hers. "You will not leave. You understand me, Angel? I absolutely forbid it!"

"Yes, Sire, I understand you." She could feel the resolve hardening, but she added meekly, "I will stay, Your Majesty, if I believe my presence in my son's life is good and desirable."

He looked at her sharply. "There is no question of that."

"If you say so, Sire."

"I do say it." With the swiftness characteristic to him,

his mood changed. "But there, we will say no more about it, eh? We will think only of tonight, my lady."

"Yes." She looked at him with wide blank eyes. "As you say, Sire."

IT WAS LATE 1667, AND THE WAR WITH HOLland which had plagued the country for many years had come to an end—but to such an ignominious end that England, it was generally believed, would never again be able to hold up her head in pride. Though still in victorious possession of New York, she had lost the island of Surinam, and a general unrest was felt throughout the country. Parliament, with irritating insistence, began to demand explanations of the fiasco from the King. They lashed out in anger, saying that the country's resources were down to a minimum, and much of the money that should have gone into the war against the Dutch had been expended on the King's mistresses and his rakehell friends. After the first shock, however, the people were willing to discount the rumors and believe that the popular King Charles had brought them through the war in triumph. After the disastrous fire of London, the King had displayed the utmost compassion and care. He had obtained shelter for his subjects in various ways, and had provided them with food and coal, had seen that the injured and elderly were cared for, and had been to them as an anxious father. When he had a medal struck proclaiming his victory over the Dutch, there was a new wave of rejoicing. Bonfires were lit in the still gutted streets of London.

Despite the confidence of the people, there was an air

of strain in Whitehall Palace itself, and a whole new crop of rumors prevailing. The Queen was pregnant again, but little faith was put in her ability to carry the child to full term. My lady Benbrook was said to be on cool terms with the King; having graced the King's bed once, she had declined to do so again. The Countess of Castlemaine, with her usual ill nature, said, "If the guttersnipe refuses further honors from His Majesty, it is doubtless in an attempt to wash clean her stained conscience."

Adding to the King's ill humor came the news that Louis of France had refused permission to Henrietta Anne, the King's favorite sister, to sail for England. It was also said that the King's plans for the reconstruction of a new and better London went poorly. He was too ambitious, his schemes too grandiose. Plans had been presented by Doctor Christopher Wren, John Evelyn, and Robert Hooke, but these too had had to be temporarily set aside, owing to the wrangle over private property rights and, once again, lack of money.

Most staggering news of all, the indignation and the outcry against the Lord High Chancellor, Edward Hyde, the first earl of Clarendon, was assuming staggering proportions. He was blamed by Parliament for the disastrous war. It was Clarendon, they declared, who had brought about the sale of Dunkirk to the French, thus weakening his country's position; Clarendon who in his usual foxlike way had encouraged the King's marriage, knowing well that Catherine of Braganza was barren, and believing that this cunning move would secure the throne for his daughter's children. But Clarendon's enemies roared that Anne Hyde's children would never ascend the throne of England. Sooner than let this happen, the King would be encouraged to rid himself of his useless Portuguese wife. Clarendon, the wild rumors flew, had desired to make himself more powerful than Parliament, therefore he must be stripped of all dignity; he must be impeached.

His numerous enemies, and my lady Castlemaine in particular, gloated openly over the downfall of the old man. "Clarendon insulted me vilely," she remarked to all who would listen. "I shall not rest until I see him ruined!"

However, despite his tribulations and the aching of his faithful old heart, Clarendon, in his gratitude for past favors, believed in the King. Had they not written thus of Charles Stuart?—

That merciful King who has pardoned more
Than all our Kings e'er pardoned before—

It was true, Clarendon told himself, that the King was often short-tempered with him. His own code was so rigid, and perhaps he was too outspoken to suit the independent King, but Charles would stand by him.

To save Clarendon from the inevitable impeachment, Charles had prorogued Parliament for the time being. But nothing could really save Clarendon, and Charles knew it. When the Chancellor refused to surrender the Great Seal, the symbol of his office, to the Duke of Albemarle, the King decided that it was time to send for him.

The air of strain made itself more evident as the hour of Clarendon's arrival drew nearer. At ten o'clock precisely, Clarendon was ushered into the King's closet. The old man was already distressed, since he had had to run the gauntlet of a crowd of hostile ladies and gentlemen before reaching sanctuary. Now, as he stood stiffly before the King, he eyed with sour disfavor the two women, one carrying a small baby boy, seated beside Charles.

"Your Majesty," he said, bowing, "I had understood that our meeting was to be conducted in private."

"And so it is, Ned, so it is." The King surveyed him, his brows lifting. "Will you not make your bow to my lady Benbrook, to her son, and to Mistress Nell Gwynne?"

"Your pardon, Sire." Flushing, Clarendon made his bows. "My lady Benbrook," he murmured. "My lord Benbrook." He looked at Nell Gwynne, his faded blue eyes narrowing slightly. "Good morning to you, Mistress Gwynne."

Angel inclined her head, smiling at him. But Nell jumped to her feet, and, picking up the dark-haired little boy, approached Clarendon, a wide friendly grin lighting her face. "Pleased am I to see you again, my lord," she said in her loud coarse voice. "I wish you well, I do indeed."

"Thank you, Mistress Gwynne." Clarendon cursed the tears that rose to his eyes. He must be weak indeed if he could be undone by a few kind words. He looked at the child, the smiling dimpled face. "How he grows, my lady," he said in a low voice. "He is a fine boy."

As though sensing he was being spoken of, the little boy put out a tiny hand to touch the Chancellor's face. Clarendon, his heart melting, took the hand in his and held it gently. "God preserve your innocence, my little one," he said huskily. "May you grow in mercy and charity, for there is a sad lack of it in the world today."

Moved, Charles cleared his throat loudly. "Ladies, you are dismissed. You, too, young Nicholas." He waited until they had left the room, then he turned to Clarendon. "I pray you to sit down, Ned, my old friend."

Gratefully, Clarendon lowered his bulk into a chair. "My enemies may curse me, but I pray that Your Majesty will ever regard Edward Hyde as your friend and most loyal subject."

His lean dark face troubled, the King seated himself. "So have I ever thought you, Ned," he said gently, "and so will I continue."

"God be praised for that!" Clarendon said, his eyes intent on the King's face. "Your Majesty," he resumed in a choked voice, "tell me how I have failed in my duty toward you?"

Quick distress showed in the King's eyes. "Nay, Ned, you have not failed me. Never did King have a better servant, for you have ever served me with your heart as well as your mind. I am well pleased with your long years of service."

"You do not believe that I have plotted against you, Sire, or that I have worked to ruin my country?"

"I do not."

Clarenden sat up straight in his chair. "Then why, Sire, did the Duke of Albemarle come to me and ask me to surrender the Great Seal?"

Charles smiled ruefully. "You are direct in your questions, Ned. Then I must be as direct, I suppose. Forgive me, my friend, but I cannot save you from impeachment, when the Commons meet again. I believe in you with all my heart. But there is only one way you may save yourself. You must resign."

Clarendon's face went gray, and his lips trembled. "Resign, Sire! But I have ever been a faithful servant to the House of Stuart. I am innocent of wrongdoing."

"I do not doubt you, Ned. I do but seek to preserve your good name and your fortune. If there was anything else I could do, I would do it, I beg you to believe me, but matters have gone too far. Nothing will soothe the Commons but your resignation, but with it in hand, they will be ready to promise me anything. If I am to be stripped of my good servant and friend, then I will see that they provide well for him."

"Your Majesty is gracious." The Chancellor's lips curled bitterly. "I believe you because I must, Sire. For if I could not depend upon the word of Royal Stuart, then the world has no place for me, and I would be better dead. If my resignation is the only way, then I will do it."

"God bless your wisdom, Ned."

The interview was over. Shakily, Clarendon rose to his feet, wincing a little with the pain of his gouty feet. "Your Majesty," he said, bowing. "I trust it will not be long before we meet again."

"That I can promise you." Charles held out his hand. "Nay, Ned," he said, when the old man attempted to raise it to his lips, "don't kiss it, shake it."

Clarendon's tears dripped onto the King's slender hand, as he gripped it firmly. "May God bless and keep you, Your Majesty!"

The door closed behind the Chancellor, and Charles

271

sat down slowly. *I am the King, yet have I become a pawn in this dirty game. Forgive me, Ned, there was no other way!*

Once more Clarendon walked through the double line of jeering courtiers. He held his head high, avoiding their eyes, and tried not to limp too obviously. Just before he entered the courtyard, he encountered Lady Benbrook and Mistress Gwynne again, between them, holding their hands, the young Lord Benbrook. As he came toward the door, Lady Benbrook and Mistress Gwynne sank into a deep curtsy.

"You must make your bow, Nicholas," he heard Lady Benbrook's soft voice saying.

Clarendon turned. The little boy was looking at his mother uncomprehendingly, but, as she placed her hand upon his back, he chuckled, and allowed himself to be bent forward.

Gravely, Clarendon returned the bow. "I thank you, my lord Benbrook." He looked at Angel. "He is very like his father, my lady," he added gently. "How old is he?"

Angel's lips trembled, but she firmed them quickly. "Seventeen months, my lord."

"How quickly time passes." He smiled at her. "What of yourself, my lady?"

"I am quite well, thank you, my lord."

"I am pleased to hear it." Clarendon bowed once more, then, opening the door, he entered the courtyard.

Outside, more hostile faces stared at him rudely. "There goes the traitor!" somebody said.

"Traitor?" Barbara Castlemaine's voice cut in. "He is worse than a traitor. Thank God the old fool is finished!"

Clarendon looked into her flushed triumphant face, and into the faces of Lord Arlington and Mr. May, who stood beside her. "My lady?" Clarendon replied. "Are you so sure of that?"

"Aye, I'm sure." Barbara put her hands on her hips, her blue eyes contemptuous. "You cannot hide it, it is written in your face. I for one am thankful to be rid of you, you doddering old man!"

272

Clarendon's hands clenched. "Madam," he said quietly, smoothly, "I regret to remind you, but if you live, you too will grow old."

Barbara stared at him, the color draining from her face. There was fear in her voice as she cried out, "Go! Get out of my sight! I have always hated you, always!"

"I know," Clarendon said. He bowed to her mockingly, then, his head held high, he walked toward his waiting carriage. Alex Barrymore, his fair hair uncovered to the morning sun, was waiting for him.

"My lord," Alex said as he stopped before him. He held out his hand to Clarendon. "I have not the words to tell you of my emotions. If there is anything I may do to aid you, I pray you to say the word."

Clarendon shook his hand heartily. "Nothing, Alex," he said huskily. " 'Tis sufficient for me that you believe in my innocence."

"I do, my lord, you may believe it." Alex looked across at the crowd assembled in the courtyard, and his lip curled scornfully. "Pay no heed to the ignorant fools," he added urgently.

The old man smiled. "Why then, if you recommend it, I won't. You're a good lad, Alex, and I hope you gain your heart's desire."

Alex looked at him questioningly.

"Think you that Clarendon is blind, as well as a fool? You are in love with my lady Benbrook, are you not?"

"And if I am, my lord?" he answered stiffly.

"No need for that tone. I am an old man, and I have my privileges." He put his foot on the lower step of the carriage. "Help me up, lad, my gout is painful today."

Alex hefted him up into the carriage.

"My advice to you, young Mr. Barrymore, is to go after her."

" 'Tis not as easy as you make that sound, my lord."

"Nonsense! She's a woman. All women need to be loved, don't they?"

"Perhaps," Alex muttered unenthusiastically.

Clarendon settled his heavy bulk upon the seat, closed

the carriage door with a firm hand, and leaned his head out of the window. "A woman who has been loved will go after love. Once they've tasted it, they can't do without it. And if you don't let her know how you feel, you'll lose her to another. I know it. You mustn't let that happen, lad."

"You don't understand, my lord."

"An old man understands many things. Have you told her you love her? Lately?"

"No, my lord."

"Then pray do so again, before it's too late. I have a feeling about her, and I don't like it."

Alex gripped the door handle. "What do you mean?"

"She doesn't look well. There was nothing odd in her manner, but her eyes, lad, her eyes are strange. And desperation can make people do strange things."

Clarendon smiled bitterly. "I have already made a fool of myself. You would not have Clarendon add to his long list of errors, would you?" He held out his hand again.

"Tell the man to drive on, Alex. And may God speed your efforts with my lady Benbrook."

Alex watched the carriage out of sight, then he walked slowly back to the Palace. There was fear in his heart, and a burning urgency to talk to Angel. Perhaps at the ball tonight, he told himself.

As he passed Barbara Castlemaine and Lord Arlington, Barbara hailed him in a loud voice. "Do look at these verses, Alex, they are most amusing. This is a copy of the one found pinned to Clarendon's gate."

Alex disliked Barbara Castlemaine, but he glanced politely at the paper she had thrust into his hand. He frowned as he read—

Three sights to be seen,
Dunkirk, Tangier, and a barren Queen.

"Most amusing, my lady Castlemaine," Alex said coldly.

Barbara looked at him, her blue eyes malicious. "I

thought you would think so, Alex. Here is another one for your edification. Read it."

> *God bless Queen Kate,*
> *Our sovereign's mate,*
> *Of the royal house of Lisbon;*
> *But the devil take Hyde,*
> *And the bishop beside,*
> *Who made her bone of his bone.*

Alex crushed the paper in his hand and threw it to the ground. "Thank you, my lady."

"Ah, Alex, Alex," Barbara laughed in his face. "Will you not try my bed tonight? I'll wager I can warm you, which is more than the puling guttersnipe can do. Her time is taken up with mourning her lord, and with comforting blind Milton for the loss of his own love. Bah! She wants only ghosts and senile old men about her." She laid her hand on his arm, her voice suddenly serious. "I have given you the invitation many times before. Is it not time you availed yourself of it?"

"You are very beautiful, my lady, or so I have heard it said." Firmly, Alex removed her clinging fingers. "But for my part I find the paeans of praise hard to understand. You will excuse me, I am sure."

"Damn you for a fool then!" Barbara cried after him as he walked away. "If your heart is in the gutter, you'll get muddy, just as my lord Benbrook did. Go then, and may you rot in hell!"

Laughter greeted her vicious words. Coldly angry, Alex entered the Palace.

Barbara rejoiced in the laughter she had roused. Her loud voice grew yet louder as she allowed herself the luxury of one indiscretion after another. "I vow and declare," she cried out, "the Angel must enjoy the maulings of old men. First 'twas the King. Though mayhap he was not senile enough for her, for scarcely had the royal body rolled from hers, than she abandoned the sheets while they were yet heated with passion." She smiled, an ugly

275

light flickering in her eyes. "And, good friends, she never returned. Now 'tis Milton who occupies her, and I dare swear, because of this strangeness in her, that she does more than comfort that poor miserable old man."

"Art saying that the King is old, Barbara?" Lady Caroline Palmerston inquired sweetly.

"Nay," Barbara answered with a trace of uneasiness. "Didst not hear me say that he was not senile enough for the Angel's tastes?"

"You place a very slight definition between, so your meaning was clear, I think." Lady Caroline smiled widely. She could not keep the note of triumph from her voice as she added, "And what of yourself, my lady Castlemaine? If the Angel prefers senility, which I doubt, you, it would seem, prefer beardless boys quite young enough to be your sons."

Barbara's face went scarlet. "Why, you skinny evil-tongued bitch! Think you that I am not aware of your pitiful ambition to enter the King's bed?" She laughed. "I believe he had rather cuddle himself up against a skinned rabbit. I tell you now that you will never—"

She broke off with a gasp as a hand grasped her arm. "You are once more proving yourself to be a fool, Bab! I think you have said more than enough, don't you?"

"Say you so?" Barbara glared into the Duke of Buckingham's eyes. "Take your hand from my arm, or I can promise you that you'll be sorry!"

"I think 'tis you who will be sorry." The Duke's eyes surveyed the smiling audience. "Cursed if I think you have a friend among the lot of 'em."

Barbara was soon to find out the truth of his comment. Her words, as the Duke had known they would be, were reported to the King, who sent for her.

Barbara, ushered into the King's presence, glanced at his stormy face, and her heart sank. "Sire," she murmured, dropping him a curtsy.

His dark eyes were cold, and between the folds of thick dark hair his face was unusually stern. He was clad in scarlet velvet. His three-tiered white silk collar was

276

edged with a ruffle of lace, as were his wide, gold-braided cuffs, the double flounce of lace that decorated his breeches was held at the knee by jewelled garters. Now, as never before, Barbara felt the force of his compelling personality.

The King began without preamble. "My lady, various remarks of yours have come to my ears which have displeased me greatly."

" 'Tis not like Your Majesty to pay heed to malicious gossip," Barbara said daringly.

"You are right, my lady. But the veracity of your informants satisfies me. Your tongue has never been honeyed at the best of times, but it did at one time strive to employ a modicum of discretion. Now, it would seem, you have not only maligned my lady Benbrook, you have also maligned me. Were you in my position, what think you would be fitting punishment?"

Recovering from the moment of panic occasioned by his words, she was relieved to feel all her confidence come surging back. He might send her away, for she had no doubt that that was what was in his mind—and indeed he had done so twice—but he would soon call her back. Others might take her place in his bed; but he could never really forget his Barbara; she was in his blood. Forgetting that he had not sent for her in a very long time, she gave him a caressing smile.

"Sire." She ran forward and took his thin ringed hands in hers. "Do not be unkind to your Bab, I pray you!"

He drew his hands away. "Seek not to cozen me, my lady. 'Tis too late for blandishments. I regret that I must tell you this, but I have long thought of sending you from me." He smiled, and she saw the cynicism in his eyes. "Though not, shall we say, without fitting rewards for your long years of—er—devotion. I have purchased Berkshire House for you. You will remove there tomorrow. Your pension of twelve thousand pounds a year will continue as before."

"Sire!" Still she could not believe that he meant it. "Do not send me away from you. I will die without you!"

"I doubt that, Bab. Pray spare me these absurd protestations of your undying love."

She stared. Never before had he spoken to her in quite this way. Was there nothing she could say or do that would bring a return of his old smiling good nature? "You wrong me, Sire!" Her voice rose as she strove to impress him with her sincerity. "You know that I love you, Charles. You know it!"

He shook his head. "Nay, Bab, you have ever loved only yourself."

Tears brimmed in her eyes. Now it seemed that she was to lose him, she told herself that she had ever adored him. Feeling ill-used, she said in a breaking voice, "Am— am I then to be forbidden the P—Palace?"

Charles frowned uneasily. Plague take it! Why must she cry? He hated to see a woman in tears, and even a rapacious bitch such as Barbara had proved herself to be could still move him. His natural kindness reasserted itself, though he remained determined. "Nay, 'tis not as bad as that. You may visit as often as you please. Should you sometimes have the desire to stay for a week or two, then I promise you that you will always find your old apartments in readiness."

She was temporarily defeated, but she made a mental resolve to be more often at the Palace than at Berkshire House. Not so easily, he would find, would he be rid of her. "But you are done with me, is that what you would tell me? Nay, dearest Majesty, tell me that I have misunderstood you!"

Warmth moved inside him. Done with her? Perhaps not quite. In her gown of cream satin, banded with emeralds at the hem, the bodice, and the cuffs, she looked appealing, and the dim light coming through the windows was kind to her. His eyes lingered on her face, framed by the flamelike hair. He looked at her high, firm breasts, cunningly revealed rather than concealed by the specially designed bodice. He said rather breathlessly, "Not entirely done with you, Bab. I will visit you at Berkshire House."

278

Barbara should have felt triumph at this, but she did not. She knew him so well. He might be moved to desire now and again, but his attitude told her that his decision to send her away remained final. She fought to control her rapidly rising anger. But how could this be? How could he so easily send her from him, she who had once held his whole heart?

Her every inclination was to rail at him, to slap him hard in the face, but some spark of caution still lingered. Her beauty was waning—her mirror told her that—neither could she be said to be in the first flush of youth. She thought of her growing desire for young and penniless John Churchill. He was willing to oblige her, he had said so often enough, but he would not enter her bed unless she could supply him with the money he so urgently needed. She must have her pension, then, and 'twould not be wise to jeopardize it. Then too, there were the children to be thought of.

Barbara sighed deeply and said in a tear-thickened voice, "Sire, what of our children?"

"Your children will be cared for, as always."

She did not like the emphasis he had placed on the first word. Angry color scorched her face. "Why do you say my children? Are they not also yours?"

His eyes narrowed slightly. "I would inform you that my infatuation for you did not turn me into a fool. Some of the children are mine, I admit it, but I do not claim them all. Not, at least, in my mind. However, you need have no fears for their welfare, as I have said." He turned away, his temporary desire having left him. "That will be all, my lady Castlemaine."

"Charles! Please!"

He kept his eyes stubbornly averted, afraid that even now he would soften toward her. Nay, he'd not look into her face and find himself wheedled once more. "You may go," he said firmly.

He heard the sharp hiss of her indrawn breath. "How dare you do this to me!" she screamed at him. "Christ's body, how I hate you!"

He turned quickly. "My lady," he said icily, "you forget to whom you speak!"

"I forget nothing!" She stared at him boldly, but she knew that she looked at the King now, not her amiable lover. Against her will she found herself intimidated by his haughty mien. She must not go too far. There was John Churchill to think of, and she wasn't getting any younger. She dropped him a sullen curtsy, then, turning, she flounced from the room.

The forbidding expression left Charles' face. Wearily he sat down on the window seat. He had always hated scenes, especially those that involved women. Barbara could now stir him only to a faint desire, but after all, he had once loved her very much. So that he might have Barbara all to himself, in those early days of his Restoration, he had bought her husband Roger Palmer's compliance by granting him the Earldom of Castlemaine. With Palmer out of the way, he had assured himself that Barbara's firstborn, Anne Fitzroy, was his own, though he had had occasion to be faintly suspicious of my lord Chesterfield. Her second child, Charles Fitzroy, he had also acknowledged. After that, there was reasonable doubt that Barbara's pregnant condition was due to himself, but nonetheless he had claimed the child as his own. If Barbara behaved herself, it might be that he would make himself responsible for any subsequent children. Perhaps he owed her that. Except for her violent temper and her greedy demands, she had been very sweet, very exciting in those early days. But then the scenes she so constantly made, her arrogance and her rudeness began to pall on him. Aye, on the whole, he was not sorry that he had finally banished her. That she would return to the Palace, and frequently, he did not have the slightest doubt, but she could no longer claim his direct protection.

Charles drummed his fingers against the windowpane. Once out of his sight and established in Berkshire House, it might be that she would take on a new enchantment for him. He found himself hoping so. He missed the throbbing excitement that Bab had once inspired in him. Was it possible that she could resurrect it again?

He got up and began to wander restlessly about the room. He was not old, he was but in the prime of his life, and yet quite suddenly he felt old, jaded, and inexpressibly sad. He missed the old days. Ah, if only he might have them back again! If only he might turn and find friend Nicholas at his side! Nicholas with his dark steady eyes that always held a faintly mocking gleam. He had always been so strong, so sure, so devoted. He was annoyed to find that his eyes were stinging. By Christ, how he missed the rogue! It seemed to him that with Nicholas's death, life had begun to take on a sour aspect. Nothing was the same and never would be again. His thoughts turned to the Queen. Whoever else might desert him, through death or otherwise, Catherine and her love would always be there. Sometimes the very intensity of her love had annoyed him, but he needed it now. Aye, he needed to feel loved and wanted, as only she could make him feel. He had a longing for her quiet tenderness. Catherine would love him even though he became a crownless pauper tomorrow. Catherine! He would go to her now.

Barbara, after her first bitterness had passed, found that she was enjoying her new home. Careless now of her reputation, she let it be known that Berkshire House was open to any youth who might care to partake of her lavish hospitality—provided, of course, that he was prepared to accommodate her in the bedchamber. She had a craving for youth these days, and the younger the better. Her favorite was still John Churchill, and because she was able to provide him with those luxuries he thought to be his due, he came back again and again.

The King, having heard the fresh crop of scandals surrounding her name, was inclined to discredit them. Barbara, for all her faults, was not without a certain dignity. No, he did not believe that she had taken to robbing the cradle. It was on his third visit to Berkshire House that he found that Barbara had lost even that dignity that he believed her to have.

The King was a little surprised at the flustered air of the manservant who admitted him to Berkshire House, but it was only a passing surprise, for his thoughts were on Barbara. "Where is my lady Castlemaine?"

"In—in her bedchamber, Your Majesty."

"You may return to your duties. I will announce myself."

"But Your Majesty, I think—"

Charles did not hear him. He was already climbing the stairs.

The man stared after the King. Christ have mercy! he thought. The King on his way, and John Churchill snuggled in my lady's bed!

Outside the door of Barbara's bedchamber, Charles paused to smooth the lace at his throat. He had been right. Barbara, by her absence, had taken on a new excitement for him. He put out his hand and turned the handle.

"Don't stop now, you fool!" Barbara was saying, "Thrust deeper, John, deeper! Ah, that's right!"

Stunned, Charles stared at the tangle of limbs on the bed, at Barbara's flushed face as she incited the youth on. He was about to retreat, but the slight sound he made caused John Churchill's head to turn.

"S—S—Sire!" Churchill stammered. Withdrawing himself from Barbara, he leaped from the bed. "Sire," he began again, snatching at the sheet and attempting to cover himself. "I m—most earnestly beg your f—forgiveness!"

Charles saw the fear and dismay in Barbara's face. "I forgive you, sir," he said coldly, his eyes returning to Churchill's agitated face. "I know that you do but earn your bread." He stood aside from the door. "You may leave us."

"Yes, Sire, thank you." With trembling hands, the boy snatched up his clothes. Edging past the King, his face was scarlet with shame and embarrassment, his eyes

282

haunted by fear of what this might mean to his soaring ambition.

"You need have no fear, lad," the King called after him. "The episode is forgotten and forgiven."

"And am I also forgiven?" Barbara said. She got up from the bed and came to stand before him.

The King's eyes flickered over her naked body, and he felt not the faintest stirring of desire. "You are still beautiful," he drawled. "But are you not putting on a deal of weight?" He found himself ashamed of the thrust, but it was not without foundation. Bab was becoming decidedly fleshy.

"What!" Outraged, Barbara stared at him. Then, her expression changing, she said in a softer voice, like one sure of herself, "I asked if you had also forgiven me? I would know your true feelings toward me, Charles."

"My feelings?" It cost him an effort to smile, but he did so. "Why, madam, I do believe that I am completely indifferent." To his surprise, he realized that his words were true. Od's Fish! He *was* indifferent, and had been so for a long time. "You need not fear retribution," he went on, "for there will be none. But this much I do ask of you, for your own sake, that you will so live in the future as to make the least noise about it that you can. Other than that, you may love whom you please, for I care not."

After he had taken his leave, Barbara sat down on the side of the bed and began to cry. Her tears were of anger, not sorrow. Even now, so she believed, she had but to crook her finger and Charles would run back to her. But how had she come to be so careless? Usually she bolted the door. Should John Churchill ever find the courage to return—and she intended to make it hard for him to resist—his price for his services would be higher. An opportunist herself, she could recognize this ruthless quality in another. Aye, he'd make her pay, but she cared not. He satisfied her as an older man could not.

Strolling toward his carriage, the King asked himself what was to become of Barbara? Had she indeed sunk so

283

low that she must now entice boys into her bed? Devil take it! he thought, as the coachman assisted him into the carriage. Next she would be soliciting lads of six or seven!

As the carriage proceeded on its way, he dismissed thoughts of Barbara. Settling back, he allowed his mind to play with the pleasant picture of the Lady Joan Fernside. If he mistook not the signs, his conquest of her was certain.

WILL CHIFFINCH, THE KEEPER OF THE BACK-stairs, sometimes known as the Royal Pimp, came out of his lodgings and began wearily to ascend the narrow flight of stairs that led to the King's apartments.

It had been a tiring night, Will mused, rubbing at his aching head as he climbed. What a terrible scene that Lady Castlemaine had made when she had caught the King caressing Nell Gwynne. Those vile words she had used had been enough to curdle a decent man's stomach. But the King had only smiled and answered her in that lazy way of his. However, it had been enough to reduce her to angry tears. And serve the bitch right, too, Will thought, with a sudden surge of indignation. What right had the Castlemaine to make a scene? Royal Charlie had been finished with her for some time. Time she realized it. She was losing some of her looks, was the Castlemaine, and putting on a deal of flesh.

And as if one scene hadn't been enough, Nellie Gwynne had had to start one too, later, when entering the King's apartments once more, she had found him closeted alone with Moll Davis. But Nell had no need to go around uttering her threats to poison poor Moll. The King was tired of Moll, and he was planning to send her into retirement. Moll would have a decent pension, of course, for it was Charlie's way to do the handsome thing. That was doubtless what kept him poor, and the country too.

But for all that, Will thought fondly, never was man more loved by his people.

Will paused at the door that led into the chambers. There were certain exceptions, though, he had to admit. Lady Benbrook, for instance. She was fond enough of the King; it showed in her eyes, her smile. But since that one time in his bed, she had held herself aloof.

Even though the King himself showed no offense, Will resented the slight to his master, but he thought he knew the reason for the lady's reluctance. She loved the Queen, and she had suffered torments of conscience over that one episode. She wasn't like the other curled and perfumed and bejeweled whores. She had made her mistake, but she was a faithful heart and, more important, a genuine lady.

Castlemaine was always saying that my lady Benbrook had once been a gutter brat and a prisoner in Newgate. But then, it delighted her to spread malicious stories about the Angel, as Lady Benbrook was popularly known. Will felt a familiar pang as he thought of Lord Benbrook. He had been hard to understand, it was true, and sometimes his imperious manner had been enough to chill one, but for all that, Lord Benbrook did not hold him to scorn because of the work he did for the King. He had spoken to him casually and goodnaturedly, with that faintly mocking gleam in his eyes. Aye, his death had been a dirty shame, and a great blow to the King. It was said that my lady Benbrook had loved him too well, and, some said, was slowly dying of her grief. Small wonder that she had refused further advances from the King.

Will flung open the door and stepped across the threshold into the royal apartments. He stood there looking about him, feeling his usual pride in his confidential position with the King. The Queen might dislike him, but if it came to that, he did not particularly like the Queen. He knew all of the King's more intimate secrets, and he was the guardian of that highly sensual and personal life, which was a lot more than others, even those close to the King by ties of blood, could boast.

Will liked the way the apartments were arranged, and he took pleasure in them now. It was all so convenient and it made his job a lot easier. To one side of the large room was situated the door which led into the apartments occupied by the Queen, and on the opposite side, those of the Queen's maids of honor. Just ahead of him, through a scrolled and gilded door, were the King's apartments. From the small antechanber leading off of the King's bedroom, descended the flight of stairs up which Will had led many a beautiful masked lady; these stairs had the added convenience of leading directly into Will's own lodgings. There was another flight of stairs, the one which he had just ascended, but these were never used by the King on his secret assignations.

This arrangement wasn't the only thing that caused Will satisfaction. His own lodgings opened out onto the Thames, and to a small landing. From this landing the King would often take boat, usually with a beauty procured for him by Will. And Will, beaming with pride, warmed by the King's friendly smile, would see them off. When the King eventually returned, it was Will who saw that all was clear before ushering his master up the stairs.

At the sudden opening of the white and gold door to his left, Will turned his head quickly. Frances Dixon, one of the Queen's maids of honor, swept into the large room, her green and silver skirts rustling about her.

Will's heart raced. Frances was very lovely. Her blonde hair gleamed with pale silvery lights, her mouth was very red, full and sensual, and her eyes had the flash and sparkle of dark green jewels. She was but lately come to Court; her young son, the Honorable James Dixon, held the position of page to the King. From the moment he had set eyes on her, Will had cherished a secret affection for the tall and slender lady. Now, seeing the bright color flushing her usually pale skin, he started after her impulsively. "Has aught occurred to distress you, Mistress Dixon?"

Frances stopped short and turned to face him. Her

287

eyes, as she studied the rotund little man, were frankly contemptuous. "Naught that would interest you, Master Pimp," she said in her clear, clipped voice. "The Queen is distressed, therefore am I likewise. But 'tis not your job to aid the Queen in her distress, is it, but to further the demands of your lecherous master."

Will looked at the face framed and shadowed by the winged pearl cap, and his heart turned over. If he could not have her for himself, he decided, then the King would doubtless enjoy her. "Neither is it your place to speak ill of the King," he said roughly. "His Majesty is but human, and if the Queen cannot bring him satisfaction, then he is forced to look elsewhere."

Frances stared at him, her green eyes cold with anger. "You really are a vile little man, are you not!"

Will grinned widely. "You know I speak truth, and if it comes right down to it, you yourself would not say nay to the King's arms, nor would you blush unduly if he gave you a tumble in his bed."

Frances had a sudden picture of the King's lean brown body twined with hers. She saw the dark slumberous eyes, and almost could feel the touch of his slim jeweled fingers caressing her. Involuntarily, she trembled with delight at the prospect. But she would not let Chiffinch read her unspoken desires. "You, sir, are a pimp and a spy!" she said haughtily. "The Queen suffers, and still you make your coarse jests."

"A jest, Mistress?" Will said, his brown eyes narrowing. "I do not speak of the Queen, but of yourself. Would you not care to become first in the King's affections?"

Frances laughed scornfully. "With the King, 'twould be difficult for any woman to know how she ranked."

"Nay, Mistress Dixon, with you, it would be all or nothing. His Majesty, who has a strong sense of humor as well as an appetite for beauty, would be the first to appreciate that."

"Aye, until the next beauty came along. But I am concerned with the Queen, not with myself. Tell me, how did you persuade my lady Benbrook to His Majesty's bed?" Seeing his look of utter dismay, Frances smiled slowly, tauntingly. "Ah yes," she went on, enjoying her small triumph, "this knowledge has but recently come to Her Majesty's ears, and so I go now to bring Lady Benbrook into her presence. I cannot tell you the pain it has caused the Queen. She believed Lady Benbrook her true friend."

Will stared into her slightly slanting, enigmatic eyes. "It happened many months ago. Had she been less of a friend to the Queen, she would have continued the liaison. She entered it of her own free will."

Frances had never cared for her own sex, but inasmuch as she was able, she had a fondness for Lady Benbrook. She was intrigued by the secrets that seemed to lurk in her eyes, and by her apparently undying love for a dead man, a strong emotion of which Frances was not as yet capable of experiencing. Will Chiffinch's last words had given her an unpleasant shock. " 'Twas undoubtedly your machinations that brought it about. You cannot deny it."

Will shrugged. "You may think ill of me, if it pleasures you to do so. But I will return good for evil. You are very beautiful, and you will make a rare ornament for the King. Therefore shall I bring you to His Majesty's attention, and a pox on the consequences?"

"A pox indeed," a drawling voice said from behind them. "But the consequences between myself and such beauty can only be pleasurable. How say you, Will?"

Chiffinch spun round. His face a dull red, he bowed. "Your Majesty," he gasped, his eyes apprehensive. "I did not hear you approach."

"I believe you, Will," the King said pleasantly, his smiling eyes on Frances.

"Your Majesty." Frances, a slight smile on her lips, curtsied before him. "We did but jest. It meant nothing."

The King moved closer, put both hands to her small waist, and assisted her to her feet. "Well now, I must confess that I am woefully disappointed." He moved yet closer, his breath fanning her flushed cheeks. Frances felt a mounting excitement as his eyes, warm, intimate, gazed into hers. "You do not care to be brought to my attention?" the King said, a caressing note in his voice.

Frances' nerves tingled, but she said haughtily, " 'Tis your turn to jest, I see, Sire."

His long finger traced the line of her lips. "Nay, lady, I do not jest."

I am dreaming this, Frances thought wildly. " 'Twould depend upon many things, Your Majesty," she answered huskily.

"On what, lovely one?"

Why didn't he stop touching her, why didn't he move away? He was too overwhelming, too exciting. "Why, Sire," she said at last, "upon how often you chose to give me your attention, and—and upon the care you took of me."

Laughing, Charles put a velvet-clad arm about her shoulders. "You are a bold wench. Aye, as bold as you are beautiful. You shall have all of my attention."

Frances tilted her head arrogantly. "Sire, I do not believe that I have expressed a wish to share your bed."

His arm drew her tightly against him. She felt his lips touch her cheek. "Have I not told you that you shall have all of my attention?"

"And you mine, Sire," Frances said, succumbing. "And my attention you'll long remember, I vow."

"Aye," the King exclaimed in delight, "I believe you."

Coming back to the present, Frances shot a look at Will Chiffinch. "Forgive me, Sire, but 'tis not the time or the place."

"You dare rebuke me, Mistress Dixon? Pay no attention to Will. He knows me well. At times like these, he becomes part of the wainscoting."

"I am glad of the reassurance, Sire," Frances said, recovering her poise. "But it might be that the Queen or some of her ladies will enter."

Charles nodded his head gravely. "I know of a very private place."

"Sire, I cannot," Frances said, resisting his efforts to

draw her in the direction of his apartments. "The Queen has sent me to deliver a message to my lady Benbrook upon a matter of some urgency."

"Chiffinch will deliver the message."

"But, Sire," Frances' protesting voice was weaker. "I am in attendance upon the Queen."

"I will make all right, Mistress Dixon, have no fear."

Avoiding Chiffinch's eyes, Frances walked beside the King. His light touch upon her arm seemed to sear through the thin silk of her sleeve. Her heart raced, and unconsciously, her body was already prepared for his onslaught. Her son wished to become a physician. Through her association with this remarkably attractive man, she would see that he achieved his heart's desire and would have honors and lands to go with it. But Frances was aware that her surrender to the King was not entirely altruistic. Quite suddenly the men she had known paled into insignificance. Here was her man, and though he be King, she'd not let him go without a fight.

Just before she passed through the gilded door and into the King's apartments, Frances caught sight of Chiffinch scuttling away. Then she forgot him, forgot everything but the man before her. The King's hands helped her to disrobe. He flung her garments impatiently aside, then his lips were on her body. Naked, she stood before him, her fair hair tumbling about her shoulders, her eyes gleaming with sensuous delight. It was she who led him over to the great bed, she who invented and improved upon the love play.

"By God's shining eyes," Charles groaned, as he claimed her for the third time, "never was there such a woman!"

Her long white limbs twined themselves about him, her body jerked spasmodically. "And never, I vow," she breathed in a spasm of aching delight, "was there ever such a man!"

Some time later, when they lay quietly side by side, Frances raised herself on an elbow, and looking down at the peaceful figure of the King, she quoted softly—

Here lies our sovereign lord, the King
Whose word no man relies on,
Who never said a stupid thing,
And never did a wise one.

Charles smiled at her dreamily. "So you quote Rochester's words, eh? I will answer you, as I answered my lord
Rochester—'My discourse is my own. My actions are my
ministers'.' Dost satisfy you, sweet Frances?"

Frances laughed. "I know not. May I rely upon your
word?"

"When I say I love you, that you may!"

"Ah!" Frances lay down, snuggling close to him. "I
believe you not, dear Majesty," she said, taking his hand
and raising it to her lips, "but your words have a wonderful ring."

Charles picked up a strand of her hair and pressed it
to his lips. "But I am a man who never said a stupid
thing, and that, too, you must remember, minx, when I
tell you that I love you."

Frances smiled. "I'll remember, Majesty, if you will
love me now."

"What again, sweetheart? By God, but you are insatiable!"

"But not too much for you, I trust, Sire?"

"Impudent baggage." Charles' lips teased her neck.
"Nay, never have I known the woman who was too much
for me."

Frances was still for a moment, then she said demurely, "Not even my lady Benbrook, Sire?"

"We will not discuss her, if you please," Charles said
coldly, his body stiffening. "My lady Benbrook is in a
class apart."

"I pray your forgiveness for offending you."

Realizing that she was angry, Charles said soothingly,
"Have my words removed your ardor, Frances?"

"By no means, Your Majesty."

Charles gave a light laugh. " 'Twas my vanity I was
preserving," he said ruefully.

Frances drew a little away from him, looking into his face with curious eyes. "How so, Sire? What need has the fascinating Charles Stuart to preserve his vanity?"

Charles stroked her soft cheek. "What I tell you now must never go beyond this bedchamber. You understand?"

"But you need tell me nothing, you know."

"Yet, for the salving of my conscience, and my lady Benbrook's reputation, I am prepared to tell myself that there is one lady, at least, who knows the truth. My lady Benbrook occupied this bed. 'Tis also true that I laid beside her and held her in my arms, but—" He paused for a moment, his smiling eyes on Frances' expectant face. "But, Mistress Dixon, nothing happened between us."

Frances' eyes went wide. "Do you tell me that the Angel, under all that beauty, is without passion, without feeling?"

"Nay, but the fire and the passion and the love are given to one dead man. I am not the man to awaken her." He sighed. "I envy the man who does."

Frances frowned. "I am a woman, too, and like you, vain. Let us not talk of Lady Benbrook now."

Charles' lips hovered above hers. "However, before we close the subject, I must tell you that if I were prepared to wager, my money would be on one man for the awakening of the Angel. Alex Barrymore."

Frances half closed her eyes, picturing the tall, elegant man. He wore his clothes with such an air, and there was a languid grace to all of his movements; if not prepared to look below the surface, one might very well dismiss him as a court dandy. Frances, an intelligent woman greatly attracted to him from the first, had looked deeper. She had easily recognized his quiet, hidden strength, the certain things that could cause his sleepy-lidded smiling blue eyes to turn cold with anger. But she had also seen the love in Alex's eyes whenever they rested upon Lady Benbrook, and she had reluctantly discontinued her pursuit, knowing it to be quite useless.

293

Frances, whose sophisticated air hid a strong streak of romance, gave a little shiver of delight. What kind of intense, exciting lover would Alex Barrymore make? In the bedroom that elegant man of fashion would disappear. Those slender bejeweled fingers of his, she rather thought, would caress gently but firmly, awakening passion in an unresponsive body. Mayhap she was wrong, but she thought not. She had not made a study of men for nothing. Aye, the King was right. Alex was the very man for Angel. For all his affable smiles, his gentle and unassuming manners, Alex might well be ruthless if crossed, and a very dangerous adversary to any man in his way. Were Lady Benbrook to look at Alex, really look at him, she might find that an exciting and pleasant surprise awaited her. "But speaking of the Angel," she said, her eyes narrowing in thought, "is she not paying a deal of attention to the importunings of Count François Duval?"

The King pressed her head against his shoulder. "Aye," he said, his fingers playing with her breasts, "but I doubt that the French popinjay will make a lasting impression."

"He is very handsome, Sire."

Charles agreed with ready generosity. "And a cursed adventurer. He is land poor, and, if I mistake not, is looking for a rich wife."

"There is a lack of warmth in your tone, Sire."

Charles tweaked her breast, bringing a faint startled cry from her. "To speak truth, I detest him."

"And yet, Sire, he is allowed the freedom of your Court."

Charles grimaced. "François, curse his hide, is a great favorite with the ladies, and in particular with my sister. When he arrived from France, bearing messages from Minette, he was thus assured of my hospitality."

Frances nodded. "The Princess Henrietta Anne, or Madame of France, as I must remember to call her, would have been grieved had you given him a cold reception."

Charles smiled. "She has the very devil of a temper, that sister of mine. But let us not talk of the Count," he

294

went on, his voice dropping to a husky caressing note. "There is a ring I would have you wear, little one. A ring that will make you irrevocably mine."

"Ah yes." Frances smiled at him knowingly. "It brands me your mistress, does it not?"

"It does. But it is given only to very special ladies. It means that other men may not touch." He kissed her again.

Frances touched his face, stroking it gently. "I would that I were your only mistress, Charles, and I would that I could remain so forever."

She did not see his faint smile as he buried his face between her breasts.

ALEX BARRYMORE STOOD BEFORE THE LONG mirror, a critical frown on his face as he examined the set of his dark blue satin jacket. Fashioned over a stiffened material, it fitted his broad shoulders without a wrinkle, buttoned tightly at his lean waist, and flowed smoothly over his hips. His lace cravat, fastened with a narrow silver bar set with sapphires, was lightly starched and dazzlingly white against the severe blue, and a two-tiered ruffle of lace edged his wide cuffs.

Sir Anthony Carstairs, lounging in a chair, his plump legs thrust out, was resplendent in scarlet satin trimmed with quantities of beige lace, each scallop edged with a gold binding. He sighed audibly and waved a heavily ringed hand. "I must say, Alex," he complained, "that the cut of your breeches causes me acute pain. Why so cursed plain, eh? One would think that you were studying to become a damned Puritan."

"Scarcely a Puritan, Tony," Alex said, raising his tawny brows in good-natured mockery. " 'Tis more a question of revolt against the frills and furbelows."

" 'Tis good enough for the King, so it should be good enough for you."

"The King has somewhat moderated his attire, it seems to me."

"Ah well," Lord Anthony said, winking, "it might be

that the influence of my lord Benbrook lives on." He stared at Alex's fair hair, eyeing the plain ribbon that bound it, with strong disfavor. "Not even a wig, curse it!" he grumbled. "Nor even a sprinkle of powder for the ball tonight?"

Alex looked at the towering wig adorning Sir Anthony's head, and grinned. "I wonder, Tony, that you can walk beneath that monstrosity."

" 'Tis the latest style," Lord Anthony answered hastily. "It came from Paris, and I'll not hear a word against it." He stretched his arms above his head and yawned widely. "Speaking of Paris, when does François Duval plan to return to France?"

"I have no idea." Alex's voice took on a sudden chill. "The Count does not confide in me."

"No, he wouldn't, would he?" Lord Anthony twisted the ring on his middle finger. "He knows well your feelings concerning my lady Benbrook."

"We will not speak of my lady Benbrook."

Lord Anthony looked up, startled. "Damn, Alex, you sounded just like Benbrook. He had that same way of snubbing a fellow."

" 'Twas not my intention to snub you, Tony. 'Tis merely that I do not wish to discuss the lady."

A look of indignation clouded Sir Anthony's plump features. "Now here's a pretty thing, Alex," he burst out. "I came here to warn you there's something afoot, old lad, and I'll wager it concerns the Angel. But if you'll not even listen, what's the use of going on."

Alex's sleepy blue eyes became very intent. "Yet you will go on, Tony," he said in a quiet voice.

" 'Tisn't what I know, exactly. 'Tis more what I suspect." Lord Anthony drew a small fan from his sleeve and, opening it, began to fan himself. Seeing the kindling of Alex's eyes, he hastily snapped it shut and returned it to his sleeve. "I suspect that the Frenchman, Buckingham, and the Castlemaine are devising some sort of plot against my lady Benbrook."

"What sort of plot?"

"How do I know? 'Tis a feeling I have, and you know my feelings, Alex."

"Bah!" Alex clenched his hands impatiently. "You come here blathering a lot of vague rubbish and choose to call it a warning."

"My feelings are not to be sneered at," Lord Anthony said, aggrieved. "My lady Benbrook has changed lately. Where she once flirted with the Frenchie and was kind to him, she is now damned cold and indifferent."

"I am happy to hear it."

"Ah, but Duval doesn't like it. He's after a rich wife, everyone knows that. He's taking this new attitude of hers hard, I can tell you, and he's forever got his head together with Buckingham and Castlemaine."

Alex sat down in a chair, drumming his fingers on the arm.

Lord Anthony eyed the drumming fingers with some trepidation. He well knew that it did not do to take Barrymore at face value. He had once witnessed a street brawl between Alex and a gang of ruffians, and he knew that Barrymore was really two men in one: the sleepy-eyed good-natured fellow, and another, with eyes that reminded him of two steely points of fury. He himself, seeing Barrymore's predicament, had done his best to aid, but it was Barrymore, almost single-handed, who had vanquished the ruffians. His sword flashing and thrusting with lightning rapidity, his cloak swirling about him, but in no wise impeding, he had sent them off howling for mercy. And when one of the ruffians, recovering some of his courage, had flung himself into the fight again, damned if Barrymore hadn't thrown his sword aside and set about him with his fists. Near broke the fellow's jaw, he had.

Lord Anthony moved uneasily in his chair. Barrymore could be a very dangerous fellow if aroused. He said slowly, "Perhaps 'tis foolish of me, but I suspect that they mean to do my lady Benbrook a mischief."

Alex got up from the chair. "I see," he said, looking thoughtfully at Lord Anthony.

"Do you? Well it's more than I do, then. I suspect,

that's all. You're an odd fellow, you know. I'd expected you to become excited."

Alex smiled at him gently. "I regret to disappoint you, Tony. Without proof, 'tis senseless to become excited, is it not? And now be off with you. If it will relieve your mind at all, I will keep a watchful eye on the Frenchman." The smile in his eyes deepened. "Aye," he went on softly, "a very watchful eye."

Lord Anthony lumbered to his feet and made his way over to the door. Pausing, he grinned cheerfully at Alex. "I'd far rather be in bed than attending this bloody ball. What or whom are we honoring tonight?"

"Nothing in particular," Alex said, shrugging. "Though I have heard that Christopher Wren and Robert Hooke intend to present yet one more set of plans for the rebuilding of London."

Sir Anthony puffed out his fleshy lips in disgust. "I tell you, Alex, the streets are a disgrace. It has been two years since the fire, and little or nothing has been accomplished."

"Oh come, Tony, you exaggerate. Much work has been done."

"Aye, perhaps, but I choose to disregard it. 'Tis such shoddy work."

"I cannot agree with you. For buildings that are not intended to be permanent, the work is adequate. But I have the feeling that tonight's meeting will result in the final plans for a new and spacious and permanent London. So take heart, Tony."

"That's all very well, but a fellow scarcely dare venture out lest he splash himself with mud to the very belly. In the old days I expected it, but now, hoping for improvement, I do not expect to get myself fouled from foot to chin."

Alex laughed. "To the belly, I thought you said."

"Never mind." With a gloomy wave of his hand, Sir Anthony went out, banging the door behind him.

For some moments after he had gone, Alex remained

deep in thought. He was inclined to discredit Carstair's warning, if such it could be considered. Sir Anthony was a kindhearted and generous man, but his wagging tongue and overactive imagination had been responsible for a good many scares and countless rumors.

In a deliberate attempt to distract himself from thoughts of Angel, he turned his mind to the condition of the London streets. In the two years following the fire there had been, as he had remarked to Sir Anthony, some work done. London's mean little streets had been widened in preparation for the clean-lined spacious houses and shops they hoped to build. Some houses had already been built, and accommodation of a reasonably comfortable nature had been provided for the working populace. But all this had taken much time. Also, since one house was forced to accommodate at least six families, the people, with good cause, were constantly complaining and sending petitions to the King. It was going to take many years and much money to rebuild the city that the King planned. But eventually, Alex was certain, it would come to pass.

Alex pictured London as it had been before the fire. Disease had constantly stalked the narrow streets, and the open gutters had created a poisonous effluvium over the whole of the city. The gutters were still there, but soon perhaps they would be abolished to make way for a newer idea in sanitation. The stalls of the hawkers had crammed Newgate Street, the Stocks Market, and the crossing roads of Cornhill and the Poultry. Lumbering carts, their wheels rimmed with iron, tore up the cobbled surfaces of the streets, for the cobbles were set in mud and bound with inferior materials. There were no pavements, and people who attempted to cross the street were in dire danger of being crushed beneath the cart wheels. But despite the misery, the poverty, the cramped living conditions, and the all-pervading stench, London then as now exercised its own fascination.

Alex stared about the luxurious room, with its white and gold drapes, the vivid tapestries covering the walls, the colorful rugs strewing the white marble floor. He, at least, could not complain of discomfort. Nevertheless, he found life in Whitehall Palace confining. Soon, he decided, he would leave London and take up his residence at Edgehill, his country estate. He would breathe clean air again, and he would leave behind him the petty plots and the scandals. He would immerse himself in the work of the estate, and he would forget Angel.

Alex smiled ruefully. Nay, he was a fool. He could never forget her. He had so many mental pictures of her, bright and beautiful, glowing with love. Bereaved Angel, her face white and strained, her eyes lifeless. Angel kneeling by Nicholas's grave, tears falling from blank eyes, fingers clawing at the earth that covered him, as if she sought to tear him from his very grave. He could hear her laughter, forced, unreal, he could see her smile that never quite reached her eyes. Angel, telling him that she could never love him, that never again would she love any man. And finally, Angel with her child. The love she had given to Nicholas was all poured out on the boy. Whenever young Nicholas was near, her eyes followed him everywhere. Let him take the slightest chill, and she was immediately distraught. Alex sometimes wondered if she regarded him as a son or as her own lost Nicholas, growing up to become once again her love.

Nay, he'd not leave London. Angel was here, so here he must remain. If she could not love him, then perhaps he could aid her, could, in some capacity, become a vital part of her stormy and troubled life. Someday she might need him. He smiled thinly. What a poor thing he had become. But still, he would rather be in the background of her life than not there at all.

Alex rose hastily as he heard sounds from the adjoining room. Soames Patrick, his valet, was about to enter, and he was not prepared to hear a further tirade on his mode of dress, the careless way he splashed his boots with mud, tore his cloak, and in general, in Patrick's opinion, behaved like a ruffian of the lowest order. In Patrick's presence, he felt like a seven-year-old being lectured by a sternly censorious father. With a look at the opening door, he made his escape.

Entering the ballroom, he blinked his eyes in the dazzling light of the hundreds of candles in their silver and crystal sconces. The dancing had not yet commenced. Alex made his way past great banks of flowers, their mingled scents heavy and cloying, vying with the heavier perfumes surrounding him. He strode past groups of chattering ladies and gentlemen, vividly dressed and bewigged. The gentlemen's jewels, he noted, outshone those of the ladies. Once or twice he heard his name called, but he did not stop, contenting himself instead with a smile and a wave of his hand.

He found the King seated informally at a small table. Beside him, their wigged heads bent over a large square of parchment, were John Evelyn, Robert Hooke, and Christopher Wren.

"The plan is good," the King was saying. "At last, gentlemen, we are in full agreement. London shall rise in beauty and majesty." He broke off as Alex approached the table. "Alex," he said, smiling, "come, sit on my other side."

"Your Majesty." Alex bowed. Avoiding the King's indolently outthrust legs, he sat down in the chair indicated.

Charles' eyes held a twinkle as he looked at Alex. "I will not say you are a colorful sight, my friend," he murmured, "but curse me if you don't do your tailor credit."

Alex smiled. "So I had hoped, Sire." He looked at the King's jacket of light green velvet. The full sleeves were slashed with silver. There was a ruby-studded flow of silver lace at his throat, and his legs were encased in green stockings threaded with silver. Circling each knee was a wide black garter decorated with a red rose. His breeches were of silver tissue embellished with four tiers of green lace, the last flounce ending just above his knees. His square-toed shoes were green, with green ribbon bows thrust through diamond buckles, and heels that were high and red.

"Well, Alex?" the King said. "You are staring at me

303

very intently. What is your judgment on my attire?"

"Very becoming, Sire. You also are a credit to your tailor."

Charles smiled. "My thanks, sir. Though I don't believe a word of it." He looked at the three men. "You have met?" he inquired of Alex.

"Indeed, Sire. On many pleasant occasions." Alex glanced about him. "I do not see the Queen, Sire. May I ask if she intends to grace us with her presence?"

"The Queen is indisposed." Charles said shortly.

Alex, seeing his frowning brows and the tight line of his mouth, said with genuine concern, " 'Tis nothing serious, I hope."

"The child bothers her. She carries it badly."

The three men, who had been chattering to each other, fell silent and turned grave eyes on the King. "I pray, Sire," Robert Hooke said, his thin rubicund face falling into melancholy lines, "that Her Grace will carry the child to full term."

"And I," Christopher Wren and John Evelyn said simultaneously.

"As do we all, gentlemen," the King said, sighing. "I would give much for a good strong heir."

A footman approached the table. "Your Majesty," he said, bending over the King. "A messenger awaits you in the anteroom. The gentleman has ridden from Somerset House. He gave me to understand that the matter was urgent."

The King paled slightly. He rose quickly from his chair. "I pray you to excuse me, gentlemen."

He walked quickly away, following behind the footman.

John Evelyn sniffed in disgust. "Her Grace, the Duchess of Lennox and Richmond is at present residing in Somerset House," he said, giving a meaningful look to the other men.

Christopher Wren nodded. "It would seem that the fair Frances Stuart still retains her hold on the King's affections."

John Evelyn smiled. "I had thought that the two latest objects of his esteem were Nell Gwynne and Frances Dixon."

Wren picked up the parchment and rolled it carefully. "Why, so they are," he answered Evelyn. "But Frances Stuart has ever had a strong fascination for him. At one time he believed himself to be sincerely in love with her. Rumor had it that he intended to make her Queen of England. He was genuinely brokenhearted when Frances eloped to marry the Duke of Lennox and Richmond." He tapped the parchment thoughtfully against the table. "The only other beauty to take such a strong hold on his heart, as far as I know, is my lady Benbrook, and she, gentlemen, refused to sleep with him after the one time."

"Once was enough with Old Rowley, eh?" Robert Hooke remarked, laughing.

"Aye," John Evelyn put in. "The lady is of a delicate frame, and no doubt could not endure the plungings of the stallion."

Alex Barrymore said nothing, but his eyes resting on the men's faces were very cold. "Excuse me, please," he murmured politely, rising.

Christopher Wren stared after him. "Damn us all for fools!" he exclaimed. "I had forgotten Barrymore's feelings for my lady Benbrook."

"I too," Hooke said. He looked troubled. "Did you see his eyes?"

Evelyn nodded. "They were like a winter sea. I have hitherto regarded Barrymore as nothing more than an elegant fop, but now I am not so sure. He would make a bad enemy, I think."

Christopher Wren snorted. "A fop? Barrymore? Where are your eyes, John? There's iron beneath that quiet exterior, and 'twould be advisable not to forget it. As for my lady Benbrook, she is wasting her time with the Frenchman. She should look to Barrymore, who, in some of his ways, reminds me of Benbrook."

Hooke laughed. "Not his ways. His dress perhaps."

"Nay, his ways. Study him, you'll see what I mean."

As Alex approached the door, the same footman came forward. "Sir," he said, "the King desires to see you. This way, if you please."

Surprised by the summons, Alex followed the footman into the anteroom. He found the King pacing up and down, the expression on his face quite distracted.

"Sire," Alex said, going toward him, "is aught wrong?"

The King clutched at Alex's hands. "Everything is wrong. Frances is ill of the smallpox, mayhap dying!"

Wondering why the King had chosen to honor him with his confidence, Alex said quietly, "You must not worry, Sire. Frances Stuart, as I remember her, is of a robust constitution."

"Damn, Alex, she is little and frail, and you know it. You do but seek to console me. The pox will kill her, I know it!"

Alex looked at him wonderingly. Never before had he seen the King so wild-eyed, so entirely lost to all sense of dignity. Charles was behaving like an about-to-be-bereaved husband. "You sent for me, Sire," he said after a moment. "What may I do for you?"

A change came over the King's face. "Aye, Alex, I sent for you. It may be, if the Queen feels well enough, that she will attend the ball. I rely on you to amuse her. She has ever been fond of you, and is never happier than when in your company."

"But happier in yours," Alex said swiftly. "You are not leaving, are you, Sire?"

"I must. Frances needs me. The messenger tells me that she calls for me in her delirium."

"Is it so, Sire?"

"Aye, over and over again. Charles, Charles, Charles!"

Alex looked at him steadily. "The Duke of Lennox and Richmond is likewise named Charles, Sire."

"She would not call to him," the King snapped, his face hardening, "she detests the man. She married him to spite me, as I well know."

"In that case, Sire, should the Queen decide to attend the ball, I will do my best to entertain her."

"I knew you would. I'll not forget this, Alex."

"And if she should inquire for you, Sire?"

"You may say that I am closeted with Wren and the other two, and must not be disturbed. The Queen is very understanding of such matters."

"She must be, Sire," Alex said dryly.

The King glanced at him sharply. "What are you thinking, Alex? Od's Fish, but you're a cursed puzzle!" Recovering himself, he forced a smile. "Go now, and send Wren and the other men to me. I do not desire the Queen to see them."

"But naturally, Sire." Alex made his bow and departed. "Frances!" the King muttered to himself. "Frances, dear love, I'm coming to you!"

After he had led Wren and his companions to the King, Alex looked about him, hoping for a glimpse of Angel. She did not always attend the balls unless commanded, preferring instead to spend her time with her son. But he saw her almost at once. She was standing a little distance from him. She looked beautiful in her gown of white satin and lace. Diamonds sparkled about her slender throat, and her bright hair was coiled high on her head and fastened with a small coronet of diamonds and emeralds. By comparison, Barbara Castlemaine in an artistically draped gown of gold tissue looked slightly blowsy and overdressed. Standing beside Angel, magnificent in black satin and crimson lace, stood the Count François Duval, a perfect foil for the Duke of Buckingham, who was clad in cream satin looped with gold braid and with a high gold collar. Alex was surprised at the presence of the Duke of Buckingham and the Countess of Castlemaine, for he knew Angel detested them. But, judging from the laughter, they were apparently on the best of terms with each other.

As Alex drew near, Angel hailed him with that forced note of lightheartedness which had such a painful effect upon him. "Alex, I have been watching you. I was wondering when you would deign to join us."

Barbara Castlemaine gave a trill of laughter as Alex

307

bent over Angel's hand. "Lud! Is not Mr. Barrymore a somber sight? Really, Alex, I am disappointed in you."

"But I am not," Angel said quietly. " 'Tis my opinion that he looks quite outstanding." She glanced at the Count, then at Buckingham. " 'Tis the fashion, I know, but I dislike to see men in frills, their fingers loaded with jewels, and reeking of perfume."

"The lady has spoken her mind," Buckingham drawled. "I declare, Duval, I am quite cast down. Are not you?"

"But yes." Duval's teeth gleamed in his dark handsome face. "And are you also disappointed in me, *cherie?*" His eyes, warmly ardent, lingered caressingly on Angel's face.

Angel made no reply, and Duval, shrugging, turned to Barbara. "Well, my lady Castlemaine, shall we let the very excellent Alex share the joke?"

"Yes indeed," Barbara replied. "I vow that he will be most diverted." She turned a sparkling eager face to Alex. "Sir, you are no doubt aware of the Lent parade, in which the workers chose to demonstrate a grievance. They declared, if you remember, that there were far too many bawdy houses in London."

"I remember," Alex said, nodding.

Buckingham laughed. "Never shall I forget the King's reply. 'If they feel there are too many bawdy houses, why then must they visit them?' 'Twas quite amusing, was it not?"

Barbara flung the Duke an impatient glance. "Do be quiet, Buck. I dislike to be interrupted." She turned to Alex again. "It seemed that the workers did not understand this abundance, especially after the fire; neither could they understand why some of these brothels belonged to the Duke of York. Poor James, though he be the King's brother, I see no reason why he should not enjoy himself. Anyway, not content with pulling down many of the brothels and administering a sound whipping to the whores, they now dare to complain because some of their leaders were hanged."

"Impudent of them," Alex said softly. "I wonder they dared."

Barbara flushed. "I do not admire sarcasm."

Alex scrutinized her with his intent and slightly narrowed gaze. "I crave your pardon, my lady," he said at last. "Do go on. Or is that the extent of the joke?"

"No," Barbara said sullenly. "There is more." She stared at him, then her face gradually brightened. "Ah well, Mr. Barrymore will always be Mr. Barrymore, will he not?"

"Always," Alex agreed. "Will you not tell me the joke?"

"Aye. Well, as a result of this riot, a pamphlet was delivered to me. It was called 'The Poor Whores' Petition.' They addressed me as the Countess of Castlemaine, the illustrious and eminent Lady of Pleasure. In it, they called me the head of the order of whores, and asked for my help in their distressed plight. Was it not shockingly impudent of them, Mr. Barrymore?"

"Quite indiscreet," Alex said gravely. "But I am impatient to hear the joke."

"That is the joke." Barbara saw Alex's slight smile. "I am no whore," she said, glaring at him. "Therefore it is a joke."

Buckingham choked, and Barbara whirled round to face him. "Are you laughing at me, Buck, you fool?"

Buckingham dabbed delicately at his eyes with a lace-trimmed kerchief. "I was thinking of your reply to the pamphlet, Bab. You are no whore, you say, yet methinks your reply branded you one of their order."

Barbara tapped a menacing foot. "Explain yourself, sir."

"Willingly." Buckingham looked at Alex. "Bab's reply is the real joke, though she sees it not. 'Give no entertainment without ready money,' she told them, 'lest you suffer a loss. For had we not been careful in that particular, we had neither gained honors nor rewards, which are now, as you know, both conferred upon us.'" Buckingham dabbed at his eyes again. "My cousin is a fool, Barrymore, but so very beautiful that one needs must forgive her follies."

"Mr. Barrymore does not think me beautiful," Barbara said, her blue eyes spiteful. "Imagine, Buck, he had the insolence to tell me so to my face."

Buckingham whistled. "I admire your courage, Barrymore. I had thought that only I had that much temerity."

"But you are blind, *mon ami,*" Duval put in. His dark eyes swept admiringly over Barbara. "The Countess is of a beauty quite superb." He looked at Angel. "There is only one whom I know to rival her." His voice dropped to a softer note. "Or, perhaps, to surpass her."

Alex straightened from his lounging position. His face imperturbable, he extended his hand to Angel. "You are looking heated, my lady Benbrook. Would you care for some fresh air?"

Angel placed her hand quickly in his. There was understanding of his motive in her eyes, Alex thought, and perhaps just a little relief in the way she squeezed his fingers. Angel, he knew, was not really at home with court functions. "Why yes, Alex," she said. "I would like that."

"Too late," Buckingham said. "The Queen has just made her entrance."

"Angel," Duval whispered urgently. "You will remember that you have promised to meet me after the ball? There is a matter of some importance that I must discuss with you."

"If I am not too tired," Angel answered him indifferently, "I will come."

"But this matter cannot wait. It is of the importance to me, you understand?"

"Very well," Angel said shortly. "I do not understand why it cannot wait till morning, but, if you insist, I will meet you."

Alex heard the whispered remarks, but they did not register. His anxious eyes were on the Queen. Always fragile of appearance, tonight Catherine was looking positively ill. What had induced her to put in an appearance? Was she reluctant to disappoint the King?

Catherine advanced toward them with her regal step. The plumes decorating her dark hair nodded as she passed the line of bowing men and curtsying women with scarcely a glance. She was clad in bright pink, the wide skirts and the low-cut bodice lavishly sprinkled with diamonds. More diamonds glittered in her ears and about her neck. The rosy color of the gown made her delicate skin seem very sallow, while its cut emphasized rather than concealed the prominent bulge of her stomach. There were dark stains beneath her eyes, Alex noticed, and her hand holding the spread fan was trembling. As she passed Angel, her step seemed to falter. Recovering herself, she gave her a cold glance, then passed on to the chair on the gold-draped dais.

Angel felt the hot color flooding her face. Catherine had not forgiven her, then? She had not realized how much she had cherished the Queen's friendship, until it was withdrawn. She remembered that interview with the Queen as if it had happened only yesterday.

Catherine had been alone when Angel had entered the room. Her eyes had been hard and cold. "My lady," she had said without preamble. "Perhaps you have guessed why I have sent for you?"

"No, Madam."

"A certain matter has been brought to my attention, my lady Benbrook. A matter involving yourself and my husband, the King. Do you know to what I refer?"

And then Angel knew. Catherine had not sent for her to scold her for some trifling fault. She felt sick with guilt as she stammered, "M—M—Madam, I—"

"Do you know why I have sent for you?" Catherine repeated in a hard voice.

"Yes, Madam, I believe that I know."

"Is it true? Have you indeed become my husband's mistress?"

"No! No!"

"What foolish lies are these?"

"Madam." Angel's voice, as it always did when she was most agitated, took on a sullen note. "I tell you that I am not lying."

"You were seen to enter the King's bedchamber. You were seen in his bed."

"No one saw us, no one!"

"Ah, then it *is* true. Just as you have betrayed me, my lady Benbrook, so now you betray yourself. I would have expected such conduct of others, but not from one who called herself my friend."

Angel's fingernails dug deeply into her palms. "Let me explain, Madam."

"Can you? Then pray do so."

"I was lonely and frightened, consumed with my grief. But even so, I know there is no excuse for me. I—I told the King that I would become his mistress." She stopped, seeing Catherine's wince of pain. "Madam, I pray you not to look so," she cried desperately. " 'Tis no secret that His Majesty keeps mistresses."

"As you say," Catherine said in a lifeless voice. "Go on, please."

Angel said on a swiftly indrawn breath. "I was in his bedchamber. I lay by his side, but, and I beg you to believe me, Madam, nothing happened between us."

Catherine's heart twisted painfully. Nothing? her heated thoughts ran. Her Charles, with his slender elegance, his charm! No woman could resist him! "Nay, I do not believe you."

Angel stared hopelessly at the Queen. Catherine, she knew, could see the King in only one light. She had even confided that she believed the King to be more sinned against than sinning. Poor Catherine, who did not realize in her doting love, how pitiful was her belief in the lecherous, goodhearted Charles Stuart. "Madam," she said hoarsely, "when it came to it, I could not betray you, or myself."

"Poppycock!" Catherine's hard-held dignity was betrayed into a flash of primitive anger. "I am expected to believe this farrago of nonsense?"

Angel felt her knees trembling beneath her, but she stiffened them. She did not know this Catherine with the flashing eyes and the clenched hands. The normally gentle curves of her mouth had hardened into cruelty. "I wish you would believe it, Madam," she said at last. "Before God, I swear 'tis the truth!"

"Do not swear before God, my lady, lest he punish you." Catherine's eyes held Angel's. "You are a liar and a false friend!"

Angel's long-buried savage instincts stirred, and for a fleeting moment she wanted to retort as once she would have done, but Nicholas's rigid training went deeper than she knew. Swallowing the impulse, she said quietly, "No, Madam, I am a true friend, and no liar. But if you believe this of me, then naturally I must leave Whitehall Palace at once."

"Ah! You know well, my lady, that the King will not permit it."

"I believe that he will, Madam. I will go to him and explain."

Angel was surprised at the panic that showed momentarily in the Queen's eyes. "No," Catherine said in a hard voice, "you will not go to the King. I wish him to know nothing of this interview."

"But why, Madam?"

Catherine looked away, a painful blush crimsoning her cheeks. "I will tell you only this, my lady Benbrook. I have my reasons, and I do not care to explain them. You will stay in the Palace until such time as your visit is cordially terminated. As for myself, I shall have to endure your presence, I suppose."

" 'Tis not necessary, Madam. The King will understand. And I am more than willing to——"

"You may go, my lady Benbrook."

Angel hesitated. She wanted to say something that would bring back the Queen's affection and trust, but she dared not. Curtsying, she left the room.

Outside, she stood motionless, unconscious of the people passing by who stared at her curiously. She was remembering the fear in Catherine's eyes. Could it be that she feared a repetition of the King's anger, which he had shown to her when she had demanded the dismissal of the Countess of Castlemaine? Angel felt trapped. The interview that had just taken place was known to her ladies, and they had not, in the past, proved particularly loyal to the Queen. No, only her continued presence would give the lie to the gossip that would inevitably result. Angel felt a pang of pity for the little Queen, so torn between her love of her husband and her fear of losing the casual affection he showed her.

Recalling herself to her surroundings, Angel gazed round the huge glittering ballroom. She had been so lost in her thoughts that she had failed to notice the commotion that had arisen.

" 'Tis the Queen," Barbara Castlemaine said, her eyes glittering with excitement. "The Queen is ill!" She smiled. "Doubtless 'tis the child arriving too soon. If it should be so, then I win my wager with Buck. I knew she'd not carry him to full term."

"I would not count on it, my lady Castlemaine," Angel said coldly.

"Nay, Bab," the Duke of Buckingham said, his smile mocking. "I vow you are too impetuous, coz." He looked at Duval. "Barrymore is already at the Queen's side. It would perhaps be as well if we showed a like concern."

Duval shrugged. "I do not understand this lack of ceremony, 'tis too informal for my taste. In the French Court things are conducted very differently."

"Ah, my fine French friend," Buckingham drawled, linking his arm in Duval's. "The English are all heart, the French all hard practicality."

"Practicality has nothing to do with it," Duval retorted, allowing himself to be led away. "We talk at cross purposes, Buckingham."

"Lud!" Barbara exclaimed. "I do not see the King. I vow he will be quite brokenhearted should the Queen lose the child." She chuckled. "Three sights to be seen,

Dunkirk, Tangier, and a barren Queen.' Dost remember that most amusing jingle, my lady Benbrook?" Without waiting for an answer, Barbara picked up her skirts and hurried after the two men.

Angel followed her quickly. Pushing her way through the crowd of spectators about the dais, she saw the crumpled figure of the Queen. Alex Barrymore was bending over her, chafing her hands.

"Madam," he was saying in a low concerned voice, "I beg you to lie still. I have sent for your physicians. All will be well."

Angel saw the tenderness in his face, and something within her moved in response. For the first time she was seeing him without the shadow of Nicholas hanging over him, as a man, a man who loved her. This new warm feeling was shattered at a gasp from the Queen.

"The child!" Catherine gasped, looking up at Alex with terrified eyes. Her fingers tensed about his hand, her nails digging convulsively into his flesh. "Mother of God, help me, I am losing the child!"

Horrified, Angel saw the dark spreading stain on the Queen's skirt. "Alex!" she said, bending close to him. "We cannot wait for the physicians. You must carry the Queen to her apartments. I fear she is suffering a miscarriage."

"A miscarriage!" the onlookers took up the cry.

"No!" It was a cry of pure agony from the Queen. She looked at Angel, naked hatred in her eyes. "Don't come near me! I will have my child. I will not lose him. Not this time, not this time!"

The onlookers fell back as Alex, lifting the Queen, strode forward. A silence fell upon them as they watched; even the music was stilled. From behind flower-decked galleries, the musicians craned their heads as the Queen, her loosened hair tumbling about her feverish face, her body arching upward in a spasm of such strong agony that Alex almost dropped her, was borne from the room. Even Barbara Castlemaine looked subdued, and it was some minutes before she turned to the Duke of Buckingham, demanding in a high triumphant voice that he pay his wager.

"*Mon Dieu!*" Duval said. "What a country! What a people!"

Angel said nothing. She was temporarily isolated by her thoughts, unaware of the whispering tongues, the covert glances of those who had witnessed the Queen's look of hatred.

To Alex fell the unpleasant task of informing the King that the Queen had miscarried.

Charles' tan faded to a sickly hue. "Poor Catherine!" he said in a broken voice. "Poor England, for now I know there will never be an heir to the throne."

" 'Tis not the end, Sire," Alex said comfortingly. "Do not despair."

"The Queen is not destined to bear children. I feel it!" Charles slumped into a chair, staring bleakly before him. "This is not like you, Sire," Alex said hesitantly. "Does Charles Stuart so easily admit to defeat?"

"Aye, I do," Charles laughed bitterly. "Even the Stuart cannot fight a woman's barren heritage." He glanced up at Alex. "There is yet more on my mind. I am possessed of a knowledge that I truly cannot bear."

The King hesitated, and Alex said in quick sympathy, "Tell me, Sire, if 'twill ease you."

" 'Tis Frances," the King whispered, his dark eyes haunted. "The physicians fear that she is dying. Little Frances, my dear and only love!"

Alex stared at him, fighting his anger. At a time like this, he dared speak of Frances Stuart! He thought of the Queen as he had last seen her. Her agony over, she had been lying drained and listless in her great bed. To him, whom she honored with her confidence, she had spoken of the King, of his grief when he heard of the loss of the child, his disappointment, his possible anger with her, who had again betrayed her duty to King and country. In vain had Alex assured her of the King's love and sympathy. Catherine had turned her face into the pillow and wept. Wept for herself, and for this man who now spoke of Frances Stuart.

In a tight controlled voice, Alex said, "Physicians do wonderful things these days. I feel sure that they will not allow her to die."

"'Tis in God's hands, not the physicians'." The King put a shaking hand on Alex's arm. "Even if they save her, it may well be that she will be disfigured by the pox! Think of it, Barrymore."

"'Twill be most unfortunate," Alex said dryly. "But should it be so, I feel sure that the Duke will comfort the Duchess in her affliction."

The King heard the slight emphasis in Alex's voice, and he drew his hand away. "You attempt to reproach me, Alex?"

"Nay, Sire. Why would I do that?"

"I know not." The King sighed. "Unless it be that you have ever been a damned bold knave. If called upon, you strike with a swift rapier and an equally swift tongue." He smiled wearily. "Alex," his face suddenly sagged into lines of grief, "when Frances left me to marry that dolt, I shouted at her, and I cannot forget my words. I said to her, 'I pray that one day you will be ugly and willing.' Before God, if Frances is disfigured, those words will ever haunt me! 'Twill be my punishment whenever I look at her dear face!"

Alex moved impatiently. He knew the King well enough to know that a disfigured face would revolt him. He would be kind enough, for Charles, despite his faults, was remarkably tender-hearted, but his love for Frances Stuart would suffer a swift change. It was to his sovereign's tender heart that he now appealed. "Sire, I fear that Her Majesty is quite broken with grief. After the physicians left, I spoke to her. I believe she fears your anger."

"What nonsense is this?" Charles stood up slowly. "She shall have my loving sympathy and my support in her grief. But my anger, never!" He strode over to the door. "'Pon my soul," he said, pausing there, "to look at your

317

face, Alex, one would think that you were husband to the Queen." He grinned. "She confides in you overmuch, sir. Be careful that I do not challenge you to a duel. I would assuredly, save that your blade is too cursed quick."

Still grinning, he went from the room. Alex shook his head. The mercurial Charles Stuart, he ever amazed him.

Following after the King, Alex heard a soft voice call, "Sire! Sire!"

Charles stopped short as Nell Gwynne hurried toward him. "Well, Nell?" he said, placing an affectionate hand on her bright hair. "What ails you?"

Nell bobbed a swift curtsy. "May I speak with you, Sire?" She nodded her head toward the room he had just vacated.

"Aye. Do come along." Charles took her hand, nodding to Alex as he passed.

"Well, Nell?" the King repeated, closing the door of the small private room. "Speak quickly, for I am in a monstrous hurry."

Nell Gwynne looked about her, as if fearing that somebody might be lurking there, then she picked up her rustling lavender skirts and flew into his arms. "Oh, Charlie boy," she said, as she felt them close about her. "Oh, my Charlie boy, I'm sorry about the babe, God's truth, I am!"

The cynicism ever present in the King's eyes faded as he looked at Nell Gwynne. "And is that what you wanted to tell me, wench?"

"Aye." Nell's hands crept upward. "Aye, my own darling, Charlie boy," she said, her fingers caressing his face softly. "That, and to tell you that I love you!"

The King caught her hands in his. "I believe you do, Nell," he said, kissing her palms. "I believe you really do."

"Never doubt it, Sire. Why, I'd die for you, I would!"

She was like a flame in his arms, a small, bright-haired, starry-eyed flame. She was lusty, bawdy of tongue, but by God, she made life worth living. He thought of her quips, her pranks, her imagination in the art of love, and his mouth went dry. He did not think of the Queen, or of Frances Stuart as he pressed her close against his body. "Nell," he whispered, "it has been a most disastrous day, and I am in sore need of comfort."

It was Nell who recalled him to his duty. "I know, my love, my darling, my Charlie boy, and I will comfort you, but first remember Her Majesty, who is in like need."

"I stand reproved, dear Nellie."

Nell giggled. "Nay, Nell Gwynne'd not reprove the King of England, lest he decide to take her head clean off her bloody shoulders." She winked at him. "And wi'out a head how could she love you and love you and love you!" She drew her hands gently from his, allowing them to wander.

"Mistress Gwynne," the King gasped, trying to control the spasmodic shuddering caused by her wandering fingers, "your head I could doubtless do without, but not these cursed magic fingers of yours, not this remarkably sinuous body that rides so well beneath mine." Stooping, he kissed her partially exposed breast. "Neither could I do without these rounded baubles that are so artistically attached, and fit so well within my hand." His shuddering increased, and his eyes smoldered. "God's life, Nell, forbid me not, for I would have you now!"

Nell looked back at him with hot and slumberous eyes. She drew the laces of her bodice aside. "The baubles move, Your Majesty," she said in a choked voice, "and may easily be withdrawn from their snug little nest." Her breathing quickened as heat flushed her body. "Will you not withdraw them, giving to each a kiss of farewell and a promise to visit them with your lips at a later date? But not too much later, dear Majesty, else will poor Nellie burst asunder with the force of her desire!"

She stood very still as he bared her breasts. He bent his dark head, touching his mouth to her thrusting hardened nipples. She felt his lips close gently about them, and her body, in sympathy with his own, began a violent trembling. "I must have you now, Nell, I must!"

She felt drowned, swollen with desire, but if she allowed

319

him to take her when his first duty was to the Queen she knew that he would reproach her later. With a great effort she managed to push him away. "Later, my love, my King!" With shaking fingers she drew her bodice back into place, rearranging the lace. "Nellie shall have new sweets for her Charlie boy, she promises him. Aye, your Nellie still has sweets in her body that you've yet to taste."

"Do not talk to me as if I were a child, Mistress Gwynne," Charles snapped. In his disappointment, a small streak of cruelty rose to the fore. His hands flashed out, ripping the lace, his fingers crushed her breasts as he jerked them forth again, "Now taste my sweets, Mistress Gwynne!"

His tongue darted like a flame, his hands caressed, driving her into a frenzy. "Shall it be later, Nellie love, shall it?"

"No!" she sobbed, pressing herself hard against him. "No, now, Charlie, now!"

"Nay." He drew back. "Now 'tis your turn to wait, Nellie." With a calm he did not feel, he walked over to the door and opened it. "I will visit you later. Be ready, or by God's beard, I will really be tempted to lop your head from your shoulders!"

IT WAS THREE O'CLOCK IN THE MORNING when Alex Barrymore at last reentered his apartments. Although he knew Soames Patrick, his manservant, to be meticulously correct in the observance of his duties, he had given him leave to retire to bed after the midnight hour. He was therefore surprised to find the man awaiting him. Patrick was fully dressed in dark brown jacket and breeches; his linen looked as fresh as if he had but recently donned it, his cravat neatly tied, but his gray hair had lost its usual well-brushed smoothness, and looked as though he had repeatedly passed agitated fingers through it.

Alex, looking at him curiously, made a mental note to allow the man to wear the powdered wig which, it seemed, was his most ardent desire. At the same time he could not help wondering which particular peccadillo of his Patrick was about to expose. In his own domestic realm, the man was inclined to be something of a tyrant. However, since he had proved himself to be invaluable with the wardrobe, and had given up his hope that his master might one day return to his erstwhile flamboyant mode of dress, many of his more irritating habits could be overlooked.

"Well, Patrick," Alex said in his soft, deceptively lazy voice. "What have I done now?"

"Sir," Patrick said, his face working, "my sense of what is fitting has been outraged."

"Ah!" Alex smiled. "You intrigue me, Patrick."

"Sir," he answered, wringing his plump white hands together, "I refer to the lady. 'Tis not fitting that she should enter a gentleman's apartments at this advanced hour. I have remonstrated with her, you may believe me. I have in fact used all of my not inconsiderable powers of persuasion to dissuade her from staying, but to no avail. I was courteous, sir, though there are some who, knowing the lady's background, would not have been. But the lady was not to be moved."

Yawning, Alex sat down on a chair. "Patrick, am I to understand that one of your lovelorn wenches has secreted herself in here?"

Patrick stiffened and gave Alex an affronted look. "No, sir, if you please, you are to understand nothing of the kind. I, having been disappointed in marriage—my wife, as you are aware, took it in her head to run off with a cursed groom, hoping you will pardon the roughness of my speech—and that being so, 'tis scarce likely that I would look with favor upon one of the members of that extremely untrustworthy sex."

Alex hid a smile. "I regret, Patrick, that you have such a soured outlook on life."

"Thank you, sir. But if you will allow me to make my point, I would tell you that I have a downright hatred of all females. Speaking in all humility, sir, I would beg you to remember that."

"Why so I will, Patrick, if 'twill soothe your ruffled feathers." Smiling, Alex looked down at his fashionably shod feet. "If 'tis not one of your wenches, then pray to enlighten me as to the identity of this mysterious lady."

"There is no mystery about it, sir. Only a person of low upbringing, which this lady is, could have behaved so. 'Tis my lady Benbrook."

Alex looked up sharply.

"I could not forcibly remove her," Patrick continued in a pained voice, "it not being my place to do so. I therefore urged her to wait in the small sitting room. It is beyond my comprehension, sir, the airs these low-type females give to themselves."

Patrick started nervously as Alex rose abruptly to his feet. "Patrick," Alex said in a drawling voice, "I must beg you never to refer to the lady in such manner again. Should you do so, I will take my knife in my hand and I will cheerfully slit your fat throat!"

The smiling blue eyes were suddenly like ice, and Patrick felt a touch of fear. Then, observing Mr. Barrymore to be smiling again, he thought perhaps he had imagined it. Drawing himself up, Patrick said coldly, "I am sure I did not mean to give offense, sir. If I have been guilty of doing so, then I beg your pardon."

"Patrick, you can have no conception of how deeply you have offended me. If in the future you have occasion to refer to my lady Benbrook, I trust you will remember this conversation. I should regret to lose you, Patrick, for you are a truly admirable fellow."

Mr. Barrymore's smile was amiable, and the distressingly hard note that had momentarily crept into his voice was quite gone. He was once again the good-looking, soft-spoken, though vacuous young man he was accustomed to serving. But just for a moment it had seemed to Patrick as though another and altogether different personality had looked out at him from those icy eyes. Those eyes were sleepy now and Patrick, rebuking himself for his foolish fancy, allowed a note of severity to creep into his voice. "I trust, sir, that you will be discreet."

"Curse discretion!"

"Come, sir, this is not like you!"

"Is it not? You have been with me—how many years, Patrick?"

"Seven, sir. I believe that I know you, sir, and a nicer young gentleman I never did work for."

"But you see, Patrick, I am not at all—er—nice. Though 'tis obliging of you to consider me so."

"I think you are, sir, though there are times when you can be somewhat misguided."

Alex turned away, and Patrick said hastily, "I pray you to remember, particularly at Court, that discretion must be observed at all times. If you will leave the door open whilst conversing with her—her ladyship, I will remain on guard. I will not have it said of me that I was lax in protecting my master's reputation."

Alex shrugged, then strode toward the door of the sitting room. "Patrick," he said, "you really must allow me to tell you that you are a fool, but a well-meaning one, I make no doubt. You may go to bed."

"Bed? Nay, sir, if you will pardon me. I could not rest easy."

"To the devil with you, then!"

Alex lifted the latch and entered the room. "Go to bed," he said again, and closed the door firmly behind him.

Angel was lying on the blue and white satin striped couch. She was sound asleep. Alex bent over her. She looked, he thought, like a weary child dressed up in an adult's finery. She was so small, so wonderfully and delicately made. One arm trailed to the floor, the hand relaxed in sleep. He could see the delicate tracery of blue veins beneath the soft white skin. If Patrick could have seen the look in his eyes then, he might have been forced to reverse his entire opinion of this man whom he served.

Alex knelt by the side of the couch. "Angel!" The jewels upon his narrow hand glittered as he stroked back the hair from her forehead. "Wake up, Angel!"

It was as though she had only lingered on the edge of sleep, for instantly she started wide awake. She stared into his face, seeing the finely drawn features, the blue eyes that held a different look somehow, a curiously exciting look. His blond hair gleamed in the candlelight, and she put up her hand and touched it lightly. "Alex, here you are at last. I had not meant to fall asleep. I am so sorry." She sat up quickly. "Pray forgive me."

"It matters not, my lady," Alex said, rising to his feet. He waited until she had swung her legs to the floor, then he sat down beside her. "As always, I am delighted to see you. But that you should be here at this hour worries me. Is aught wrong?"

"Is the hour so very advanced, then?" Angel looked down at his hand resting upon his knee. "I should not be here, I know," she said slowly, "but I felt that I had to see you."

"Did you, my lady? Why? I am the King's most unwilling guest, for I have a great longing to terminate my stay and return to my own home, but in all the time I have been here, you have not once sought me out."

"I know." Angel's eyes came up slowly to meet his. Her voice trembled. "I—I felt that I had to come. S— sometimes I feel so lost, so—so bewildered. Tonight, when I saw you bending over the Queen, it was as if I were seeing you for the first time. Truly seeing you. There was a—a strength about you. Th—the kind of strength that Nicholas once gave to me."

Her mouth quivered, and Alex said quickly, "Dear, my lady, you must not be afraid to speak his name."

"Must I not? But Alex, it hurts so much!"

"Of course it does." He took her hand and held it lightly in his. "Speak his name, Angel, say it often. For when you do so, Nicholas lives again. He lives because you remember him. He is here in this room now, because you spoke his name."

"You—you really believe that?"

"I do, Angel. You must believe it too."

Tears misted her eyes. "I will try to believe it, Alex. I must believe it, else I could not live!" She was silent for a moment, then, like someone forced to say words against her will, she hurried on. "When I—I saw you bending over the Queen, saw the expression in your face, the—the tone of your voice, I felt that I had to come to you. It was as though N—Nicholas was urging me to do so. As though he was telling me that only with you would I be safe and—and secure. Only with you would I come alive again, and feel that I truly b—belonged to this world."

Alex did not answer at once. "Perhaps I was wrong," she burst out. "Perhaps there is no place for me with you, or with any other man."

"There is a place for you," Alex answered huskily. "And if you decide that place is with me, I would be—be grateful." He put a finger in his white lace cravat, easing it. It was suddenly too tight. He wanted to tear it free in order to ease his breathing. Did she know what she was saying? Perhaps not. He would be gentle with her; now was not the time to force an explanation.

Watching her expression, Alex said carefully, "You will always be safe with me, my dear. I pledge it. As for the rest," he went on lightly, almost casually, "you must know that I have ever thought, from the first moment I set eyes upon you, that you belonged with me."

No! Angel wanted to say. You must not say that. I belong with Nicholas, only with Nicholas! Suddenly, as though her thoughts had indeed brought him into the room, he seemed to be standing there before her. "I love you, brat!" Nicholas's voice said in her ear.

Shivering, she shook her head. It was her imagination, her longing. Nicholas would never again be with her.

Alex was looking at her. She wanted to deny her own words, to tell him that she belonged with Nicholas. With him, and no other man. But even as she thought it, her contrary heart urged her to take that blond head and hold it close to her breast. Hating the stiff unfriendly sound of her voice, she said slowly, "Whatever I may have said, I do not love you, Alex. I would not w—wish you to—to m—misunderstand."

"I promise I will not, my lady Benbrook," Alex answered her almost formally. "I am aware that you do not love me. But you do trust me, perhaps even like me a little. Is it not so?"

She searched his face. Was he laughing at her, mocking her? Ashamed, she turned her face away. He put a gentle arm about her, and she stiffened. "I think I understand, Mr. Barrymore. But do you hold me to be of so little account that you may freely embrace me?"

"Now it is once again Mr. Barrymore, eh?" The smile had left his voice. She moved, and his arm tightened about her. "Nay, Angel, you little fool, do not pull away! Whatever you may be thinking, you are wrong. I will always love you. But if you cannot accept that, then will you not consider my embrace, unwelcome though it is, as a token of my friendship?"

She looked at the grim set of his lips, and once again she was reminded of Nicholas. "I—I will consider it so."

Angel looked down. She stared at the lace that spilled from his sleeve, the dark blue glow of the sapphire upon his finger, and she felt her mind whirl in painful confusion. His touch brought a warmth, a stirring of her frozen feelings. She realized then that she wanted him to kiss her. She wanted to feel his thin and elegant body pressed close to her own. Unconsciously, she let herself relax against him. What would it be like, she wondered, to see those lazily smiling blue eyes turn hot with a passion that would match that which was so suddenly burning her? Her hand clenched. Had not Nicholas once called her a trollop, a wanton? She had not been so then, but perhaps she was now. It might be that she should not only have lain with the King; perhaps she should have answered his urgings and allowed him to make love to her. She had wanted Charles, she remembered, even as she now wanted Alex. Her heart began to beat rapidly. Alex's face was very near to hers. She could smell the light lavender fragrance of the lotion he used, the clean, healthy odor of the breath that fanned her hot cheeks. Was he going to kiss her?

"Alex!" She turned swiftly in his arms. Meeting his intent and narrowed gaze, she felt hunger leap up anew. It was a terrible and urgently burning hunger, but it was not just passion. No, she felt for him a kind of love, and she wanted to tell him so. Was it possible that she could belong to this man as she had once belonged to Nicholas? *And still do,* a voice said inside her. *Don't you know that you will always belong to Nicholas?* She ignored the voice. She would listen to it later. But she must love, she must be loved!

"Alex!" She took his face between her hands. "Alex, I know not what I want. But this is what I feel at this moment." She pressed her lips to his.

Alex kissed her back, then he drew gently away. "You know well that I love you, my lady," his normally assured voice was trembling slightly. "But for all that, I would not have you use me as a substitute for Nicholas. But if you will only allow it, I believe that you could love me."

"No!" she said. "No, Alex!"

"Aye, I know that you could. Not as you loved Nicholas, with all that glory and fire, but with another kind of love that would strengthen with the years, believe me."

"It may be that you are right," she said, sitting up straight, "but how will I know it is love? How will I recognize it?"

"You will know. I can wait, for I know this feeling you have for me is the beginning of love."

"Is it? But," she blurted out the words desperately, "how can I love two men? I still love Nicholas! He is not dead for me! He never will be!"

"I know," Alex said in a low voice, "you love him, you will always." He bent his head and kissed her lightly on the lips. "Why, Angel, think you I would have it otherwise? Think you that I would endeavor to take his place? If you do, then you do not know me. We will build a new love, and that love you will give entirely to me."

"Alex, there are things about me that you should know, things, perhaps, that could turn you from me."

"Nay, love. I know all that I should. That you were once Newgate bait. Aye, Angel, even that."

She blinked at his calm use of the term. "Who t—told you?"

"The King. Living in the Court as we do, how could you think I would remain in ignorance of your story?" He smiled at her. "That would be asking a little too much, would it not?"

"Yes—yes, I suppose so."

His finger touched her lips. "I know, too, that you were referred to as 'the King's brat.'" He laughed. "We will give them another name, Angel. If you will try, if you will let me love you, they will call you 'Barrymore's brat.' Barrymore's much loved, much adored brat. Well, Angel, will you marry me?"

She saw the teasing light in his eyes, and she found herself laughing. "Then 'tis a decent proposal you offer to me?"

"How could it be otherwise, my lady Benbrook?"

Angel got to her feet. "You must ask me tomorrow. I can't tell you now. I must think." She smiled. "The hour must be disgracefully late, and lest Patrick suffer a fit of apoplexy, it is best that I leave now."

"Curse Patrick," Alex said, rising too. "Do you promise to give me your answer tomorrow?"

She looked at him soberly. "Yes, tomorrow. And now I really must go." Her smile reappeared. "Despite the advanced hour, sir, I have a rendezvous with another lover."

"Have you so?" He contemplated her for a moment. "Go, then, baggage. But know this. If I really thought for one moment that you meant it, I'd never let you go."

Baggage! Nicholas had often called her so. She felt the sharp thrusting of pain. Day and night he was in her thoughts, in her dreams, her aching heart! Alex was smiling. Let him believe she jested. It did no harm. Duval was waiting for her; in his way, he had helped to lift her spirits, and for that, she felt, she owed him something, but he was not and had never been her lover. He had said that he wished to see her on a matter of urgency, and knowing Duval, she did not doubt that he would be waiting. She frowned. The Frenchman with his dark handsome face, his polished charm, his reputation as a practiced lover, fascinated some women. But she had seen through him from the very first. He was not remotely to be compared with Alex.

"You look troubled, Angel."

"Do I?" She forced a light laugh. "Nay, Mr. Barrymore, all is well."

He came closer to her. "You do not care for the name of Alex?"

"Aye. But I will use it, dear Mr. Barrymore, when the mood moves me."

"I am happy to hear it." He held out his arm. "Come, my lady Benbrook. I will accompany you to your apartments."

" 'Twill not be necessary," she said quickly. "Naught can happen to me in the corridors of Whitehall Palace."

"I am sure of it," he said firmly. "Nonetheless I will give myself the honor of accompanying you."

She bit her lip, swallowing the impulse to tell him of the prearranged meeting with Duval. She opened her mouth to speak, then closed it again quickly. Duval's matter of urgency might well be a further plea that she marry him and sail with him to France. It would be better, therefore, if she did not involve Alex. She had been given several glimpses of late of the iron beneath his lazy manner.

Alex, she knew, did not like Duval, but then neither did the King. Duval was not a man's man. Buckingham, it was true, had shown the Frenchman some slight semblance of friendship, but doubtless there was motive behind it. With Buckingham, one could almost rely on the motive being there. She'd let Alex escort her to her apartments. At the most, it could only delay the meeting a few extra moments. Duval, if she was not mistaken, had many gaming debts, and mayhap he needed money to pay them. Well, she had plenty of that if Duval needed it, but she would tell him once and for all that she had no intention of marrying him. Having made up her mind, she laid her hand on Alex's sleeve. "Sir, I accept your escort."

"Good of you," Alex said, leading her forward.

The Duke of Buckingham stood by the couch, smiling down at Barbara Castlemaine, who was reclining at her ease. "Think you the brat will meet with Duval, Bab?" he asked.

Barbara yawned, hiding the yawn behind a heavily jeweled hand. "Do sit down, Buck. You know that I cannot bear to have you loom over me."

"Your pardon, m'lady," he said with heavy irony. He seated himself. "There, is that better?"

She smiled to herself as she watched the meticulous way he lifted the stiff satin skirt of his jacket and arranged the folds carefully about him. "Why, dear Buck," she cried, "art turning into a dandy?"

Unmoved, he studied her with his cold blue eyes. "And what of yourself, cherished coz? Art studying to become known as the fat lady of Whitehall? You must know that you have added considerable weight to your dainty frame."

Barbara glared at him. "And if I have, you insolent swine, what business is it of yours? You yourself are not as elegant as you once were."

"How true, little coz," Buckingham said, sighing. "But on me, you see, my increased girth is arranged more attractively."

"Damn you, Buck, 'twould pleasure me to rip your insolent face to ribbons!"

Buckingham smiled. "I am sure of it, Bab. However, should you be foolish enough to attempt it, you know quite well that I would break your arm."

"Bah!" Barbara relapsed into brooding silence. After a moment, she said, "If you have come here to quarrel with me, it will avail you nothing."

He grinned. "Nay, Bab, you misjudge me. I have come for the pleasure of your company, which, as you know, stimulates me like a draft of strong wine."

"Liar! Fool!"

He surveyed her smilingly. "Would it soothe you if I tell you that I have also come here to question you about Duval and the brat? Will she meet with Duval, think you?"

"She has promised," Barbara answered sullenly, "and if the guttersnipe can be said to have a virtue, it is that she always keeps her word."

"Unlike you, eh Bab?"

Angry color flooded Barbara's face. "Has anyone ever told you how extremely unpleasant you are?"

"Frequently, my dear. There is yourself, and you are never backward. There is also my wife. In the intervals between her blind adoration of my so charming self, she rouses herself to tell me of the many flaws in my character."

"But I have heard differently. It is said that you have at last managed to kill your wife's love. That she now looks with favor upon a certain gentleman of your acquaintance."

Buckingham's eyes narrowed dangerously. "Bab, you will hasten to change the subject. Now then, where has Duval arranged to meet the Angel?"

Pleasantly aware that she had managed to penetrate Buckingham's guard, Barbara smiled amiably. "In the most romantic spot I know. In the Queen's Retreat."

Buckingham lounged back in his chair, stretching his legs comfortably before him. "The meeting place was your suggestion, I imagine, Bab?"

"Naturally."

"Naturally," he repeated, managing to imbue his tone with a wealth of meaning. "I have told you before that you are a fool, Bab. You know well that the Queen's Retreat is forbidden to all save the Queen and her ladies."

"I know it. But you grow overcautious, Buck. Who is likely to see them at this hour?" Barbara picked up her fan from the couch. "They will not be there long enough for it to matter," she said, fanning herself lazily. "And, since it is your own plan, you know that Duval will simply abduct the brat, should she still refuse to marry him."

"Aye," Buckingham said, frowning, "and I need no reminder." He stared thoughtfully at Barbara. "Nonetheless, coz, there are times when your malice amazes me."

Barbara shook her head unbelievingly. "Your own malice, if I may point it out, is not slight, you know. I gain only the reward of her absence from Court. While you, the mighty Duke of Buckingham, should your plan go smoothly, will gain a considerable monetary reward."

"How tiresome of you to point it out," Buckingham said smoothly. "However, a point well taken. Duval will, I know, be duly grateful. Mine was the plan, as you said, but I trust you will spare me the actual details. I leave such things to my inferiors."

Barbara stared at him with hard eyes. "Nay, why should I spare you? 'Tis my belief that the brat will refuse Duval. Therefore he will take her back to the haunts that she originally came from. No one will think of looking for her there. She is a gutter brat, and she will go back to the gutter, until such time as she realizes that her reputation is hopelessly compromised. Then, I think, she will come to the conclusion that it is best to marry Duval. You left it to me, and you could not have left it in better hands. I have arranged all."

"Dear Bab, my own hands would have been better. But no matter, I must simply entertain the hope that you have not bungled it too badly."

"Can I help if you, lazy fool that you are, were too much involved in your pleasures that you must leave it all to me?"

Buckingham smiled. "No, Bab, that, I admit, you cannot help. But have you also arranged where the Angel is to be lodged?"

"I have." Triumph was in Barbara's answering smile. "You will like this, Buck. She is to be lodged next door to a bawdy house." Seeing his expression, she hurried on. "Nay, you need not worry. I was most discreet. The old hag who keeps the lodging house was very far from recognizing me. Even had I not been plainly dressed and veiled, I doubt that she would have done so."

He laughed. "Perhaps you are right. One would not expect the great Lady Castlemaine to frequent such a district." He shrugged. "'Tis scarce justice, is it, that the one-time whores of our gracious King should while away the rest of their lives in perfumed and silken luxury? But so it is, by the grace of our generous and beloved monarch."

Barbara's eyes smoldered. "I am no whore, Buck! Do you hear me?"

"Clearly. And I am becoming rather tired of hearing it."

"And there is another thing I would say to you. Do not class me with the women the King has discarded. Soon he will return to my bed, I know it."

"Do you indeed? Let us return to the matter in question. Duval intends to keep the Angel there by force?"

"Naturally. Did not you yourself advise him to do so?"

"Did I? I have forgotten."

Barbara's hands clenched. "Oh no, Buck! Think you I do not see your little game? If aught should go wrong, I will see you are judged as guilty as I."

Buckingham gave her an injured look. "Why, Bab, I did but help to clear an obstacle from our path. I have talked myself out of many an awkward situation." He smiled at her. "I feel sure, since you are fully as adept as I, that you will be able to do the same."

She stared at him. "You intend to deny all knowledge of this affair, should it come to light?"

"Naturally. As for laying the blame on your shoulders, if, as you insist, you are still beloved of the King, he would refuse to hear aught against you, would he not?"

"Damn, Buck, you sicken me!"

He nodded pleasantly. "But tell me, my clever Bab, since you have arranged the details of this matter, is it likely to go wrong?"

"Of course not," she said sulkily. "But I like not your attitude."

The Duke pressed the tips of his fingers together and contemplated them thoughtfully. "Tell me," he said slowly, "is Duval, should he find himself facing unforeseen difficulties, likely to implicate us?"

"No. If anything should go wrong, I have arranged passage for him to Spain."

"Why Spain?"

"Now your own stupidity is showing, Buck. Think you,

if the Angel and Duval disappear at the same time, that inquiries would not be made at the French Court?"

"I see. Yes, I see."

"He will lose himself in Spain, until such time as he deems it safe to return to France," Barbara concluded with some complacency.

"It may well be that you excel in intrigue," Buckingham answered, unmoved. "But you seem to have forgotten one very little but important point. Duval may not implicate us, but the Angel most certainly will."

"She will not, because she will not know we have had anything to do with it. Duval has promised to take all the blame, if blame there be. Our names will not be mentioned before her in any connection."

"No?" Buckingham's tone was cynical. "All the same, in the end I will doubtless be forced to call upon my wits to extricate myself. But I will come through, I believe, and without a stain upon my character. Regarding Duval, do you then, who are usually the most wary of women, trust him so implicitly?"

"But of course not," Barbara said in some surprise. "Who in their right mind would?"

Buckingham raised an eyebrow.

"Like you, Buck, I too have my spies. I know many things about our handsome Duval he would not like anyone to know. When you left the planning to me, I wrote down my knowledge of Duval's many unsavory activities. I then took the paper to him. I was willing to help, I told him, but only if he would append his name to the paper, it being an admission that all the things I had written down were true."

Buckingham stared at her, then he began to laugh softly. "I see you are a true Villiers after all. My congratulations, Bab."

"So I should think."

"However," Buckingham went on as though she had not spoken, "whatever else I may think of the Angel, I have never thought her a fool. The four of us have been much together of late, I am sure you will admit. The

Angel does not exactly love you, coz; neither is she disposed to look with much favor on my so fascinating self. Might it not be that she will fit all the pieces together?"

Barbara nodded. "Aye, she might indeed. But it will be her word against ours. She will have no proof."

"And the King, though he is noted for his championship of the oppressed, would require proof, rather than wild accusations." The Duke sighed. "My mind should be at ease, and yet, Bab, I know you, you see. Something is bound to go wrong. I am perfectly willing to gamble, but I fear that we are once again overlooking something—the Angel's earlier upbringing might cause her to consider being compromised with Duval as quite unimportant. In other words, she would have two choices. Marriage with Duval, or a scandal attached to her name. Angel, I believe, will choose the latter."

Barbara smiled. "Nay, Buck, the brat has a son now. For his sake, she will consider her reputation to be of supreme importance."

"Why, Bab," Buckingham said admiringly, "can it be that I have misjudged you? There are times when you can be very clever indeed."

"One woman, you know, generally knows another. Should the brat be tempted to throw her reputation aside, she will find herself remembering Benbrook's mother and the effect that the woman had on his life. She will not want the same thing for her own son."

"Not just clever," Buckingham drawled, "but brilliant."

Barbara lifted the spread fan to her face and looked at Buckingham over the top of it. "Think of it Buck. With every day that passes, Benbrook's son grows more and more to look like his father. He must not be haunted and embittered as was his father, the brat will tell herself."

The Duke's cold blue eyes studied her intently. "I wonder why you hate the Angel so much."

Barbara said hastily, "In any case, as I was saying, the brat will marry Duval, you need have no fear on that score. You, Buck, will be considerably enriched by the grateful bridegroom. The cream of the jest is that it will be my lord Benbrook's money that will add comfort to your life."

Buckingham considered this. "To say nothing of the sweet serenity it will afford my many creditors." He smiled slowly. "Aye, 'tis fitting. Benbrook ever hated me."

"Hated you?" Barbara looked away from him. Suddenly she was remembering the Earl of Benbrook's austerely handsome face, the yearning that she had had for him. Had those dark eyes ever looked upon her with softness or desire, Barbara told herself, she could have loved him utterly and completely. "Nay, Buck," she went on, "I will admit that my lord Benbrook had many reasons to hate you, yet he did not. You were beneath his notice, you see. He was merely indifferent."

"As he was with you, do you mean, Bab?" the Duke drawled. "Indifferent, and worse still, unutterably bored in your presence."

Barbara snapped the fan closed. "Be quiet!" she shouted, flinging it at him.

"Ah, you do not like to hear the truth, do you?" Buckingham rose to his feet, picked up the fan, then, bowing, restored it to her. "I see that you do not care to be reminded of my lord Benbrook's indifference. But for one smile from Benbrook, Bab, for the touch of his lips, his hands upon your body, you would have done anything, well, almost anything, eh coz?"

Barbara sat up straight. Her eyes glittered dangerously. "Yes, anything! Are you satisfied now?" She leaned forward. "I would have slit your throat, the King's, had my lord requested it of me. I would have left this Court, and I would have lived in poverty, if it had to be, if only he would have allowed me to follow after him!"

"Do you know, Bab, your self-deception never ceases to astonish me. Why, if you loved him, would you consider doing this thing to the woman he loved?"

"For exactly that reason, because he loved her, not me! I hope she suffers! I hope she dies!"

Buckingham's smile was taunting. " 'Twas not love you

337

felt for Benbrook; do not, I beg of you, delude yourself. Nay, 'twas lust pure and simple. Strip the Countess of Castlemaine of her comforts and her jewels, and you would find your supposed love soon lost." He waved his hand impatiently. "Had Benbrook been a poor man, had he in actual fact asked you to follow him into poverty, you would quickly have grown to hate him. There is your love. Face it."

"I would have hated another man, perhaps, never him!"

"I pray you not to become hysterical," Buckingham said coldly. "Strange, I myself have always considered Benbrook to be a surly swine. Upon my soul, Bab, I cannot think what there was about the man to so fire you. To so fire any woman that came near to him, it seems."

Barbara turned her face away. "Perhaps because his coldness was a challenge. Perhaps because men like Benbrook are rare in this or any age. If that is not enough for you, then 'tis little use my explaining further. Suffice it to say, Buck, that you haven't those qualities that made him rare. Now, if you please, leave me. I want to rest."

"I understand, dear coz," Buckingham drawled, walking over to the door. "I will leave you alone with your poor broken heart. When do you plan to return to Berkshire House?"

"When I choose, and not before."

"I see. By the way, I have heard it said that you are now indulging yourself with a young rope dancer." He opened the door. "But are you not a little old for him? Just a little, shall we say, overblown?" He smiled his malicious smile. "But fear not. As long as you have money enough to repay him for his sacrifice, it may well be that he will never desert you."

Barbara stared at him, naked hatred in her eyes. She sprang up from the couch and rushed toward him. "Get out, you swine, get out! By God, I'd like to kill you!"

"We will postpone this discussion to another time, my lady." Buckingham stepped swiftly through the doorway.

"You know, Bab, you really must learn to be sweet and gentle, for I fear 'tis all that is left you. Your admirers are dwindling fast." He shook an admonishing finger. "Do you also wish to lose me, your own sweet cousin?"

Barbara slammed the door in his smiling face.

Laughing to himself, Buckingham proceeded slowly along the corridor. Nearing his own apartments, he was struck with a sudden thought. How fared Duval with his courtship? It might be, if he kept carefully out of sight, that he could hear what transpired.

Walking in the cool darkness of the grounds, Buckingham trod cautiously. He had no wish to be seen or heard. Should Duval, in his desperation for a rich wife, be forced to abduct Angel, the Duke of Buckingham had no wish to be connected with the matter.

Reaching the high walls of the Queen's retreat, Buckingham concealed himself behind some high bushes growing close by and prepared to listen. At first he heard nothing, and he wondered if the Angel had failed to arrive and Duval grown tired of waiting.

Seated on a bench in the Queen's Retreat, Angel stared impatiently at Duval. When, she wondered, would he get over the paroxysm afflicting him? For the last five minutes he had sat beside her, his hands covering his face, his shoulders hunched in abject despair. She was growing weary of trying to console him.

"François," she said, trying again, "I am truly sorry if I have hurt you. Such was not my intention, please believe me. But I must repeat that I have no wish to marry you. Not now. Not at any time. You are in need of money. I am willing to give it to you, within reason, of course, but that is all."

"Oh, my lady!" Duval moaned, moving at last. "How cruel you are!" His hands dropped heavily, and he turned a ravaged, tear-stained face toward her. "Think you, my lady Angel, that it is your money I want?"

"Yes," Angel said simply.

"Mon Dieu!" Duval cried, clutching at his carefully dressed hair. 'How then am I to convince you? Oh,

cherie, my *cherie!* How can you say this thing to me, François, who loves you to the distraction?"

"Very easily," Angel said dryly. "Have done with this playacting. I am no simpleton, you know."

Buckingham grinned to himself, feeling a stir of admiration. God's bones! Benbrook himself could not have put it more succinctly. She knew Duval for what he was— a handsome fortune-hunter and nothing else. Or, as Bab had once put it, a French fribble. Buckingham almost found himself regretting his own part in it, but he shrugged the thought aside. It was too late for regrets. Duval, if he knew anything about him, had the carriage waiting. The next move was up to him.

Duval clutched at Angel's hands. "Have pity on me, *cherie!* I pray you to look long upon your François, and when you have looked, to reconsider."

Angel drew her hands away. "I have looked, and I will not reconsider. I see no point in discussing it any further. Goodnight, François."

"Ah, *non, non!*" Duval sprang to his feet. When she made to pass him, he barred the way. "You must not say goodnight. *Non,* you will not say this to me!"

Angel's heart gave a frightened jump. The moonlight was full on his face, and she could see the feverish glitter of his eyes. He looked distracted, she thought, and capable of anything. "Move aside, François, if you please."

"But me, I do not please. I will not take your refusal for your final answer. You will marry me, you will see!"

"Perhaps I am a little too English to appreciate this superb show of drama," Angel answered coolly. "I repeat, I am sorry for your disappointment, but I find you becoming excessively boring."

Buckingham's grin widened. It might be Benbrook speaking through her lips. The arrogance of her! The icy reproof in her voice! Aye, the little guttersnipe had learned her lessons well. Benbrook was to be congratulated on his expert tuition.

Duval's hands opened and closed. A vein in his temple

began a heavy throbbing. "Again I must beg you to reconsider," he urged in a hoarse voice.

"And I have told you that I will not. Now, will you allow me to pass, or must I call to the guard?"

"You will not call, *cherie*." Duval brought a clenched fist from behind his back. "*Non*," he said, hitting her on the point of her jaw, "you will call to no one."

Buckingham moved away unhurriedly. As he got nearer to the Palace, he quickened his footsteps. So it was done. There would be a pretty furor when it was discovered that Angel was missing. Suspicion, he felt sure, was bound to turn on Bab and himself, for they had made no secret of their dislike of Benbrook's Angel. That they had changed toward her in the last few weeks, becoming almost ostentatiously friendly, might count in their favor, but he rather doubted it. The suspicion would still be there. But, until approached with a direct question, he would keep his own council and a still tongue in his head. Bab must be forced to do the same. She liked to boast, to give mysterious hints, and she had always been damnably indiscreet.

Letting himself into his apartments, the Duke thought for a moment of Alex Barrymore. The man could perhaps be difficult, being so obviously in love with the Angel. Buckingham had heard it said that Barrymore did but hide his true self behind a mask of smiling languor and would make an extremely dangerous enemy if crossed, but the Duke discounted this. Nay, Barrymore was naught but a fop; there was nothing to fear from him.

The Duke smiled, much to the relief of his man, who had hurried forward prepared to disrobe him. The Duke allowed his man to divest him of his satin jacket. Barrymore of the elegant movements, the sleepy eyes, and the slow drawl. The most the man would do, when he found the Angel missing, would be to sigh and mope. God save my lady Benbrook if she relied on Barrymore to be her champion.

In high good humor, the Duke laughed out loud and gave his manservant a friendly thump on the back, so startling the man that he dropped the jacket. Bending to retrieve it, he made feverish apologies, though for what, he was not quite sure. Still, the Duke of Buckingham became easily enraged. One did not take liberties with him, or advantage of his occasional bursts of good humor. Brushing the jacket, the man wondered what particular piece of skulduggery had brought forth this most unusual laughter.

With the unconscious Angel in his arms, his dark cloak concealing her white gown, Duval moved swiftly from one patch of shadow to another. Once, when a patroling guard passed nearby, he was forced to stand very still, his heart beating uncomfortably. The guard moved on and disappeared around a corner, leaving Duval to stumble the remaining way to his carriage. Angel was slight, but by the time he had deposited her on the seat, he was perspiring profusely.

"I am ready," Duval called softly to the coachman. "Drive on, if you please. Hurry!"

The man looked down at Duval. "No, sir. This here's dirty work what you're adoing, so I ain't hurryin'. Least I ain't till I get the rest o' the money what you promised me."

Duval scowled, but since it was dark, and Duval only a vague outline, the scowl did nothing to intimidate the coachman. "You will get your money, fellow. Have I not promised?"

"That's as may be, and I've known o' promises to be broke. No, sir, I'll take the money now, or we stays right here."

Muttering under his breath, Duval groped in his capacious pocket until he found the leather money bag. "Here." He held the bag up to the coachman. "Now whip up those horses."

"Ah," the coachman said, shaking the bag. "Now that's different, that is."

"Will you hurry, fool!"

The man grunted. "I don't take to being called a fool, sir. Never did like it."

"Very well then. I apologize!"

"Thought you might. Now don't you get to worryin', sir. After I count me money, I'll hurry all you please."

Fuming, Duval was forced to wait while the man carefully counted out the money. "Are you satisfied?" he said, when the man made preparations to depart.

"Tolerably so, sir, though you done me out o' one coin. I'll have it when we get there, eh?"

"Good of you," Duval hissed.

"I'm good to them what is good to me," the man said in an unmoved voice. "Now then, sir, get in. We're off."

Duval jumped into the carriage. Sitting down, he drew Angel into his arms and held her closely against him. He sighed. She was surely the most beautiful girl he had ever seen. A great pity that she could not love him. Had she been prepared to marry him, he would have given up the way of life that had led him to this sorry pass. He would have made her a loving and satisfactory husband. Filled with self-pity, really believing he could reform, Duval stroked Angel's soft bright hair. It had not been his idea, this abduction. He was not bad, as, for instance, the Duke of Buckingham was bad. But he needed money, therefore he had allowed himself to be easily led.

Duval frowned uneasily. He knew himself for a coward, and it would not be easy, that moment when she opened her eyes and realized what he had done. He was beginning to dread the thought of that confrontation. There was something about Angel that both infuriated and disturbed him. It was that way she had of looking at him. He could swear it was a pitying scorn he saw in her eyes. Angry blood heated his cheeks. No woman had ever scorned him. They had been only too happy to receive his caresses. There had been one girl, Simonette, who when he ceased to love her had drowned herself in the river. Nevertheless, Angel was different than any he had known, and that look of hers had the effect of subduing his self-importance, of making him feel infinitely small. Who was the girl, that she should look at him so? She was beautiful, it was true, but before my lord Benbrook had decided to educate and groom her, she had been a street waif! A gutter brat! She had made one brilliant marriage; surely she should be happy to make another. After all, was he not from one of the finest families in France? Conveniently forgetting that that same family, despairing of his excesses, had long ago decided to disown him, Duval began to work himself into a self-righteous rage.

Duval laid Angel on the opposite seat. Sitting down again, he took a deep steadying breath. In the past, he had found that when he grew enraged, he was not responsible for his actions. There had been the scandal of Marie Dupré's death, for instance. Marie had died of stab wounds. Awakening in her bed, he had found her cold in death. Fortunately, he had managed to get away unobserved, but he believed that he, himself, in one of his rages, had inflicted those wounds. When the scandal broke, his father had accused him of the crime. But, because Etienne Duval could not deliver his only son to justice, the matter had been hushed up.

He must force himself to be calm and cool, or else the game would be lost before it had properly started. It would be exactly as the Lady Barbara and the Duke had said. His vanity stirred. After all, she was a woman. He knew women well. In the end she would find herself quite unable to resist him.

Well pleased, Duval smiled. If she did not fight him, he would be good to her. If she displayed a becoming meekness, he was prepared to become that incredibly dull thing, the faithful husband. *Mon Dieu,* but he would earn her fortune! Who else in his circle of friends would be prepared to give up so much for the sake of one woman?

They had left the Palace behind them now. Duval, about to relax, started violently. Once before he had imagined he heard running footsteps, but now he knew it was not imagination. The footsteps were clear now. His heart racing, Duval drew the leather curtain aside with trembling fingers and peered out into the darkness. Yes, someone was running behind, gaining on them! He heard a voice cry out—"My lady Angel! Wait! Wait!"

Duval dropped the curtain. "Go swiftly!" he shouted to the coachman.

"Bleedin' foreigners!" the man said audibly. "Always gettin' so excited. Always awavin' o' their arms and ashoutin' their heads off."

"I told you to go swiftly," Duval cried. "Did you not hear me?"

"Can't help it, can I?" the man replied. "What with you ayellin' your lungs out, all London can hear you."

"How dare you speak to me so! If we were in France, I would have you whipped!"

The man guffawed. "Ah, but this here is England, in case you've forgot. But right, sir, you wants swift, you gets swift. Here goes!"

To his relief, Duval heard the crack of the whip. The horses, surprised at this outrage, went plunging forward in a burst of terrifying speed.

Duval sank back against the cushions of the rocking carriage. Leaning forward again, he held Angel steady with one hand while, with the other, he wiped his sweating forehead. The horses kept up the pace. But Duval's heart did not resume its normal beat until long after they had left the running figure behind.

M'ZELI BOWED AGAIN BEFORE SOAMES PATrick. Looking at the man with inscrutable eyes, he repeated as he had done several times before, "I must see the lord. It is imperative that I do so."

"Is it indeed," Patrick answered, his voice heavy with sarcasm. "Well you can't." He snorted. "Another thing, Mr. Barrymore is not a lord, as well you know."

"It matters not," M'Zeli said softly. "It is my way to call him so. I pray you to tell him that I am here."

Patrick stared at him. The insolence of the lad! From the way he spoke and behaved, one would think him to be a king at the very least, and for a black boy to give himself such airs and graces! "Now you look here, Pip—" Patrick blustered.

"I beg of you to forgive the interruption, sir. But I am now known as M'Zeli."

"All right, then," Patrick said, glaring at him. "M'Zeli, Mr. Barrymore is sleeping. He wouldn't thank either of us for disturbing him."

For the first time since he had entered the room, M'Zeli showed signs of agitation. "I will see him now!"

Patrick drew himself to his full height. "I will thank you to leave these apartments. Heathens like yourself may not feel the need to sleep. But white people do, I assure you."

M'Zeli inclined his head. Then, with a faint smile, he walked past the man. "I go to see the lord."

"Oh no you don't!" Patrick caught at his arm, bringing him to a standstill. "You're asking for a clout around the head, lad, and I'm the very one to give it to you."

M'Zeli looked at the hand upon his arm. "I pray you not to do that," he said solemnly. "Please to remove your hand, sir. If you do not, you will be sorry."

"Well!" Patrick gaped at him. Recovering himself, he shouted, "I'm removing *you,* that's what I'm removing. Come along, boy. Out with you, I say!"

"Patrick," a sleepy voice called from an adjoining room. "Is that you making that infernal racket?"

Patrick started in consternation. "Now see what you've done!" he whispered to M'Zeli in a furious voice. "You've awakened him. If he does not get sufficient sleep, he can be very trying indeed!"

M'Zeli smiled. "It was my intention to awaken him. Now, if you will remove your hand, I will see the lord."

Patrick's hand dropped. "You'll do nothing of the sort. If you don't get out now, I'll—"

"Patrick," the voice demanded, "why are you mumbling to yourself?"

"I'm talking to the lad, sir. The black lad insists upon seeing you."

There was a pause. "Is it you, M'Zeli?"

"It is, lord."

"Bring him to me, Patrick."

"If it is your wish, sir." Red-faced, frowning, Patrick ushered M'Zeli into the bedchamber.

"Light the candles, Patrick, please."

The man hastened to obey. In the soft yellow glow, Alex blinked at M'Zeli. "Well?" he said.

M'Zeli glanced at the hovering Patrick. "Lord," he said, a note of apology in his voice, "I regret to disturb you. It would be my desire, if you would be so kind, to speak with you alone."

"Of course. You may leave us, Patrick."

"Very well, sir," Patrick answered stiffly. "But before

348

I go, I wish to make a protest. This lad has been very rude and insulting to me."

"It may be so," M'Zeli said, "for I was greatly agitated. But if I have offended, then I ask forgiveness."

Alex laughed. "There, Patrick. A very handsome apology indeed. Are you satisfied?"

Patrick sniffed. "I will have to be, will I not?"

"The thought comforts me excessively," Alex said dryly. "But I pray you, Patrick, to return to your bed."

Defeated, Patrick bowed, and retired with dignity.

M'Zeli looked at the man in the satin-hung bed. This man was not as the lord Benbrook, M'Zeli thought. He was not forbidding as the other had been. The lord Benbrook had exuded strength and determination. He had frowned often, it was true, but if one looked beyond the frown, it would be noticed that the lord's dark eyes held a smile. He had hidden his true self behind a stern façade. Only the King, the lady Angel, and his own humble self had been permitted to look beyond at the real man. The lord Barrymore hid, too, but his was a lazy and smiling façade.

"I am not deceived, lord." M'Zeli spoke his thoughts aloud. "You are not as the people of the Court believe you to be. You have courage. You will punish the offender, this I know."

Alex's eyes narrowed slightly, then crinkled in amusement. "But surely you have not disturbed my sleep to tell me this?"

"No, lord. I have come to tell you that the Frenchman has abducted my lady Angel."

"What!" Alex sat up straight. "Explain yourself!"

The drawl was gone from the lord's voice now, M'Zeli noted. It was hard and compelling. "I am permitted to walk in the grounds before retiring," M'Zeli said. "I saw the Frenchman enter the Queen's Retreat."

"The Queen's Retreat?"

"Yes, lord. It is forbidden, I know. But enter it he did. It was not for me to interfere or to reprimand, so I continued my walk. So it was that—"

"Damn it, M'Zeli," Alex said in exasperation, "get on with it, can't you? What of my lady Benbrook?"

"So it was," M'Zeli continued, "that I did not see my lady Angel enter. On my way back to the Palace, I stumbled over a stone. I fell, and hit my head against a tree. When I came to myself again, I got to my feet and leaned against a tree for support."

"M'Zeli," Alex's voice was dangerously quiet, "I regret my impatience, but you don't suppose you could hurry this a little, do you?"

M'Zeli saw the grim set of Alex's jaw. "I saw my lord, the Duke of Buckingham, returning to the Palace. It was a little later when I saw the Frenchman go by. He had the lady Angel in his arms."

"He did?"

"Yes, lord. He was carrying her. I must have been dazed. I did not immediately realize that the lady Angel was unconscious, or that he might be carrying her away against her will."

"When you did realize?"

"The Frenchman had placed her in a carriage, and it was driving away. I ran fast, but I could not overtake them."

Alex lay back against the pillows. "So you saw the Duke of Buckingham?"

"I did, lord." M'Zeli looked at him impatiently. He was not responding as he had hoped. "The lady Angel would not go with the Frenchman willingly. I know well that she despises him."

The bleak look that had entered Alex's eyes cleared. "That remains to be seen, does it not?"

"No, lord," M'Zeli said firmly. Again his calm deserted him. "You will find my lady Angel?" he cried. "You will punish the Frenchman?" He stopped and looked appealingly at Alex. "My lady Angel was lost once before. She was gone for a long time. I suffered, even as my lord Benbrook did. I would not wish it to happen again."

"M'Zeli, were you ever young?"

"I am young in years, lord. But I believe that I was born old."

"So I am inclined to think."

"You will find my lady Angel?"

Alex smiled. "Why yes, lad. I might possibly make an attempt, my persistent young friend. If things are as you say, or believe them to be, then yes, I will undoubtedly punish the Frenchman. Are you content?"

"Yes, lord."

"I am happy to hear it. Pray leave me now."

M'Zeli looked at him incredulously. "But surely you will require my help? Surely you—surely you would not return to sleep?"

Alex turned over on his side. "Would I not?"

"But this I—this I cannot believe!"

"Then damn you for an impertinent young cub," Alex said without rancor. "But to answer your question, no, I would not return to sleep. Are you satisfied now?"

"I am." M'Zeli's solemn face split into a grin. "I knew that I was not mistaken in you."

Alex's tawny brows rose mockingly. "I will try my best to justify your confidence in me."

M'Zeli's grin faded as he came a step nearer. "You smile," M'Zeli said, peering into his face. "Yet if I were your enemy, there is that in your face and in your eyes that I would greatly fear."

"You have far too much imagination, lad. Will you go now, or shall I call on Patrick to remove you?"

"It will not be necessary, lord," M'Zeli said with dignity.

Outside the door, M'Zeli stood still for a moment. No, he thought, it was not my imagination. I saw what I saw. I would not like to be your enemy, lord, I would not like it at all.

Alex lay very still in the bed. M'Zeli's words came to him again—*"I saw my lord, the Duke of Buckingham, returning to the Palace."* And Anthony Carstairs had said, *"I suspect that the Frenchman, Buckingham, and the lady*

351

Castlemaine are devising some sort of plot against my lady Benbrook."

Alex rose from the bed and dressed swiftly, not troubling to call Patrick. "I think, my lord Duke," he said softly, "that I will pay you a little visit."

THE DUKE OF BUCKINGHAM TURNED REST-lessly in his bed. Something was disturbing his sleep, he thought, opening one eye reluctantly. Had he dreamed it, or had he heard somebody crying out? It had sounded remarkably like that fool Grimshaw's voice. Grimshaw, his manservant, had ever irritated him, and if it had now got to the point where the irritation followed him into his dreams, then the sensible thing to do would be to dismiss the man from his service. He listened intently for a moment, but not a sound disturbed the silence. Deciding that it must have been a dream, he shrugged, closed the eye, and settled down again. The Duke pulled the covers up over his shoulders, and burrowed his head into the pillows. Very soon a light snore issued from his lips.

He did not hear the opening of the door. Something cold touched his neck. Muttering a curse, the Duke flopped over onto his back.

"Do not move quite so violently, my lord Duke," a soft voice cautioned, "else will my knife sink into your throat. That would be a pity, for we have not yet conversed together."

The Duke lay rigid. Fearing to move, he kept his eyes closed, but his brain was active. He knew that voice. Or did he?

"Open your eyes," the soft voice bade. "I have lit the candles that you may better observe your visitor."

353

The Duke's eyes flew open. The man bending over him was fully dressed in dark gray jacket and breeches. A gray cloak swung from his shoulders, and his face was partly shadowed by his plumed hat. There was sufficient light, however, to enable the Duke to see his eyes. They looked cold, almost deadly, in complete contrast to the smiling lips.

"Barrymore!"

"Even so, my lord Duke." Alex seated himself on the side of the bed. "That is more comfortable," he said, crossing one leg over the other. "It fatigues one to stand overlong, do you not agree?"

Despite himself the Duke was conscious of a thrill of fear. Instantly he tried to belittle it. Who could possibly fear Barrymore? "What the devil are you doing here at this hour of the night?"

Alex looked surprised. "Can it be that you have grown into slothful habits?" he remarked amiably. "It lacks only an hour to full daylight."

"Curse the daylight and you too! Why are you here, you fool?"

"I desire to have a word with you, of course. Why else would I be here?"

The Duke looked at the knife held negligently in his visitor's hand, and he swallowed the heated retort he had been about to make. "Barrymore," he said, his eyes narrowing, "is it possible that you have come here to threaten me?"

Alex nodded. "I commend you on your astute grasp of the situation."

The Duke opened his mouth. "Grimshaw!" he bellowed.

"A very pleasant fellow, Grimshaw," Alex murmured, smiling. "But a little too officious, I fear. He will be unable to answer you."

"He will be unable to—why? What do you mean?"

"He became rather noisy. It occurred to me that he might awaken you. I regret it exceedingly but I was forced to silence him."

"Silence him? What in plague have you done?"

"Nothing too drastic. I have merely rendered him unconscious. I have no doubt that he will be grateful for this temporary respite from his troubles."

Alex leaned closer to the Duke. "Do you know, Buckingham, I think it best to advise you against that nightcap. It doesn't suit you in the least. We must try for harmony, must we not? The puce color clashes with your complexion. I never wear caps myself. They are said to bring on premature baldness."

The Duke snatched the cap from his head and flung it from him. "You must be mad, Barrymore. As for Grimshaw, he will get a permanent respite. He shall be dismissed from my service."

"Ah! Then I cannot help but feel that I have done him a great service. He will live to bless my name."

"Will he so!" Breathing hard, the Duke clenched his hands together. "I don't know what you are up to, but I do know you'll pay for this impertinent intrusion. Put that knife away and get out of here."

"In due time, my lord." Alex looked at him admiringly. "But such fire, such fury! I myself have not the energy for strong emotions." He lifted the knife and examined it through half-closed eyes. The blade glittered in the candlelight. "A handy little weapon," his drawling lazy voice went on. "But you know, my lord, I have ever deplored violence, and this weapon is too often employed to violent purpose."

"Bah! For the last time, Barrymore, what is it you want?"

Lowering the knife, Alex smiled down at him. "A simple answer to a simple question."

"What is the question?"

"I pray you, friend, do not bark at me so. You are liable to overset my nerves. Where is my lady Benbrook?"

The Duke's heart jumped. "How should I know?" he answered in a hoarse voice. "Why do you ask me?"

The smile left Alex's lips. "Where is she, Buckingham? Where is Duval?"

Duval! So he knew! How? Speechless for once, the Duke gaped at him. Without the smile, Barrymore looked grim, purposeful, dangerous. The Duke felt a return of his earlier fear. He looked at the glittering eyes, the tightly set lips, at the face he had deemed feminine rather than masculine. That face had taken on harsh craggy lines. He saw now that it was a strong, rather ruthless face. Why had he never noticed this before?

"I don't know, Barrymore," he managed at last. "I don't know where my lady Benbrook or Duval are."

With an economy of movement, Alex laid the knife blade against the Duke's throat. "But you will search your memory, will you not, my lord? 'Twill be a great pity if I am forced to slice your throat. The sight of blood has ever turned me faint. But if needs must, I will force myself to the distasteful task."

Damn the fellow, he was a maniac, a dangerous man masquerading behind a mask of smiling good nature.

The Duke moistened his lips. "Aye, I know you'll use it." He stared into the hard blue eyes. "I'm seeing you for the first time, Barrymore. I have no idea of the lady's whereabouts. No idea at all, curse you!"

Alex relaxed the pressure on the knife. "No," he said. "I don't advise you to move, my dear fellow."

"I'll not lie here tamely and submit to this!"

"Will you not? Too much movement might very well cause my hand to slip, and that would be unfortunate." Alex looked thoughtfully at the knife. "But it may well be that I proceed in the wrong direction, Buckingham." He removed the blade from the Duke's throat. "Knave and charlatan though you undoubtedly are, I had forgotten that you are possessed of courage."

"Remember it in the future," the Duke panted, glaring at him. "And be sure that I will demand satisfaction for this episode."

"Will you? No, m'lord, I think not."

"You are quite wrong! Will you leave me now?"

"Nay. We are just getting to know one another," Alex said reproachfully. He looked at the Duke, and now the expression in his eyes was almost dreamy. "Do you remember a few nights ago, Buckingham? 'Twas the time we played cards together. As I recall, you lost to me rather heavily."

A cold feeling crept over the Duke. "Why—why do you refer to the matter?"

"I will allow you to guess, m'lord."

"But you would not—I mean, surely you do not intend to call in your notes, do you?"

"Clever lad! I do indeed."

"But it would ruin me! Why, damn your hide, you promised to give me time!"

"Unfortunately, m'lord, my memory is not all that it should be."

" 'Twould not be the act of a gentleman!"

"True. But I must bear the burden of public censure."

"Barrymore, you can't do it! You must not!"

"I can and I will," Alex said, beaming upon him. "May I ask if you have quite grasped the situation, m'lord?"

"You're bluffing, Barrymore."

"Why, Buckingham, you move me! Your trust in me is positively childlike." Alex scratched his chin with the tip of the knife. "If you refuse to pay, you will be branded as unsporting, a man who cannot be depended on to pay his just debts. In other words, my dear Buckingham, you will be ostracized."

"Give me two months—one month then, curse you! I'll raise the money somehow!"

"It pains me deeply to refuse you. However, if you would call upon my good nature, you might start by telling me where my lady Benbrook is."

The Duke glowered at him. "I cannot. I don't *know,* Barrymore."

There was a long pause. "Strange as it may seem," Alex said slowly, "I believe you, Buckingham. Nevertheless, you know who has knowledge of her whereabouts. Don't you?"

The Duke turned his face away. "Aye," he said sullenly.

"Who?"

"Either way I face ruin," the Duke answered unsteadily. "But the one I can talk myself out of. The other I cannot; it is a debt that touches upon my honor."

Alex smiled. "You have great faith in your powers of eloquence, I see."

"Oh yes, Barrymore, I can do it. Try to prove that I told you of the plot against my lady Benbrooke. It will be your word and m'lady's against mine."

"So it will. However, I intend to return and administer to you the thrashing you so richly deserve."

Trying to hold on to his dignity, Buckingham said loftily, "I am well able to defend myself, sir. Can you say the same?"

"Why yes, I think so. I am judged to be moderately capable with a sword, with fists or—" Alex paused significantly— "or with a horsewhip, my lord. And now, if that is quite clear to you, pray proceed to tell me of this plot."

The Duke began to speak. Mindful of the increasingly dangerous glitter in Barrymore's eyes, he talked at great length, excusing himself as he went. When his voice finally faded into silence, Alex said simply, "How fortunate that I also hold the notes of the lady Duchess."

The Duke laughed. "I'll wager you'll not find Bab easy to deal with."

"But I am sure you will help me to persuade her, will you not?"

Defeated, the Duke nodded. "Even if I do help you, you could still call in the notes."

"My dear Buckingham," Alex said in a gently reproving voice, "you must not judge me by yourself. I will give you the necessary time to redeem yourself. And now, please favor me by rising. We will go together to the apartments of my lady Castlemaine."

Buckingham got slowly from the bed. "You may be sure that matters are not finished between us."

Alex sighed. "How you do distress yourself, and all to no purpose. Of course they are not finished, my dear fellow. Have I not given you the assurance that I will return to give you a thrashing? Really, Buckingham, you might listen!"

"By Christ! I'll kill you for this!"

Alex smiled. "Now I'm really glad you mentioned that last. I have been meaning to tell you that, should I find that harm has come to my lady Benbrook, I will of course be forced to kill you." Alex shivered. "I pray you not to put me to the trouble. I dislike to kill."

Buckingham stared into his smiling face. Barrymore had uttered the words in his usual lazy tones, thereby robbing them of any particular significance. Buckingham felt his confidence come flooding back. "Why, you popinjay! Think you to defeat Buckingham in swordsmanship? I am thought to be highly skilled. Rarely, except in my younger days, have I been defeated."

Alex blinked sleepily. "I am acquainted with your progress, as who is not? But though I am greatly averse to bragging, there is always the question of a greater skill, is there not?"

"We shall see!"

Alex stood aside to allow the Duke to precede him. "So we will," he murmured. "So we will."

ANGEL STARED UP AT THE CRACKED AND DIS-colored ceiling. Duval had brought her here, to this incredible place! Did the fool think that his absurd histrionics could force her into a distasteful marriage? If so, she would speedily disillusion him. François Duval, after Nicholas! It did not bear thinking about. Her eyes wandered to the door. Where was Duval? What was he doing? She would see that he was punished for this outrage!

Her head was still swimming a little. When it cleared she would go in search of Duval. But perhaps she need not encounter him at all. It was a feeble hope at best, but if Duval was off on some errand, maybe she could simply walk out of the door. Last night—was it only last night?—when he had brought her to this dismal place, she had been too weak to resist him. Her head and her jaw had ached excruciatingly and she had felt very ill. All she had wanted then was to lie down. After Duval had left her, she had managed to stagger across the room and try the door. It had been locked then and doubtless it still was. But now, apart from the swimming sensation and a slight feeling of nausea, she was in full possession of her senses. She would be forced to wait for Duval to put in an appearance.

She moved on the bed, trying to brace herself to rise. She wrinkled her nose in distaste as the disturbed mattress puffed forth a sour and disagreeable smell. I have grown soft with rich living, she thought. At one time such smells would have meant nothing to me. I would have accepted them because they would have been part of my everyday existence.

Her arm began to itch and she scratched it automatically. Lifting it, she examined the minute red spots made by bedbugs. Those little bites were the mark of every slum child. Once, long ago, her own arms and legs had been covered with them.

"Long ago?" Angel whispered. "Nay, my Nicholas, not so very long ago. And yet without you, my darling, a lifetime away!"

She closed her eyes and tried to conjure up Nicholas's dark, handsome face. She found that she could not hold the picture clear. Another face persistently intruded— Alex Barrymore's, with his deceptively gentle manner, his sensitivity, his love of the arts and of all things beautiful. He fitted ill into the oft times coarse and bawdy atmosphere of the Court, and she had no doubt that before long he would request the King's permission to return to his own home. She was surprised at how desolate that thought made her feel, and she concentrated instead on the enigma of the man. Alex pretended to be a lamb, and yet she, perhaps more observant than others, knew him to be more of the lion. Quite suddenly, despite the plight in which she found herself, Angel wanted to laugh. Was Alex gentle? Yes, she believed so. But it was the man who lived beneath the gentle and civilized exterior that she needed now.

"Alex," Angel said softly, "will you not send that carefully hidden man to my aid?" She smiled at her foolishness. If Alex knew where to seek her, he would come. But Duval would have hidden his tracks, and she had only her wits to rely upon.

Angel sat up on the bed. Shading her eyes against the bright sunlight streaming through a narrow window, she took in her surroundings. Like the window, the room was narrow and filthy. The ceiling was low, the walls stained from the constant seeping of water, the splintered wooden floor covered with a thick layer of dust. Mingled with the dust were litterings of crumbs—the residue of many past meals—pieces of torn-up paper, and the whitened droppings of rats and mice. The room was scantily furnished: the bed, one chair, and a stand set with a basin and a jug with a cracked lip.

The sight of the jug reminded her that she was very thirsty. Hoping that it might contain some reasonably clean water, she swung her legs from the bed. A rustling from the corner of the room attracted her attention. She watched, frozen, as a rat emerged from a hole in the wall. The sight was the more horrifying because, in common with most people, she had believed that the fire of London had effectively destroyed the vermin.

Rats! Filthy and obscene things! She had always feared them. They had infested Newgate Prison—would she ever forget?—and it was the boldness of the rats that had heralded the coming of the plague.

Shuddering, she drew her legs up again. Could nothing destroy the creatures? They had survived plague and fire, and she had no doubt that they could survive flood and famine too.

The rat was in the center of the room now, its long ugly snout poking among the rubbish on the floor. Hysteria gripped Angel, and the never-to-be forgotten nightmare was there in the room with her. Newgate! The plague! The death cart with its piled-up corpses—"Bring out your dead! Bring out your dead!"—Herself, still living, thrown on top of those putrefying corpses and on her way for burial in a communal grave! Nicholas, her Nicholas, suffering, dying!

"No! No!" She leaped from the bed and hurled herself at the door. The rat, alarmed, darted into his hole. "Let me out!" She battered at the door with frantic fists.

" 'Ere, you there," a hoarse voice shouted. "You shut up that row!"

There was a shuffling of feet outside, then the grating of the key in the lock. The door opened to admit a small skinny woman attired in a shapeless black gown, a stained apron, and a pair of men's shoes. The upper of the left shoe had torn away from the sole, exposing dirt-rimmed and calloused toes. Upon her yellowed white hair was perched a frivolous bonnet. This confection of lace and ribbons and flowers looked grotesque above the thin and wizened face. Staring at this apparition, Angel felt her terror recede.

"What's all the 'ollerin' about, eh?" the woman demanded.

Angel clasped her still trembling hands together. "The door was locked. I—I wish to leave."

"You do, do you? Frenchie says as you ain't ter go nowhere. 'E says you got ter stay 'ere."

"You may tell Mr. Duval that he is quite mistaken." Angel drew herself up and looked haughtily at the woman. "Now, if you please, stand aside."

The woman laughed, showing one or two broken and yellowed teeth.

"Who'd you think you are then? Listenin' ter you, one'd think you was the Queen o' England."

"I am—I am Lady Benbrook."

The woman was not impressed. "I knows who you are all right. Frenchie tol' me." She pointed a thin finger at Angel. "You ain't a real lady. One o' us you were. An' one o' us you still are. So don' you go givin' me none o' your 'igh an' mighty airs."

"I tell you that I am Lady Benbrook!"

"Knows that, don' I? Ain't I jus' says as I knows it? I tol' Frenchie as I wouldn' lock up no real swell. But seein' as you're one o' us that's different, that is."

"I pray you not to be a fool!" Angel snapped. "Whatever I was, whatever I am now, it won't make one speck of difference. You will still be severely punished."

The woman seemed shaken for a moment, but she recovered quickly. "I don' believe you. Frenchie says as it's all right, 'cause it ain't like you're a real swell, see." She put a hand to her head and touched the dainty bonnet. "Brung me this, did Frenchie. Ain't it lovely?"

Angel stared at the woman. She was obviously feeble-minded, and Duval had turned her condition to his advantage. It would do little good to argue with her. Unconsciously Angel's eyes measured the distance to the door.

The woman, intercepting the glance, began to shake with laughter. "Frenchie says, if you try ter get away, that I'm ter tell you as me 'usband's below. Strong, is my Tom. Soon bring you back, 'e would. Aye, an' give you a clout ter go on with."

Angel's shoulders sagged. "Where is Duval?"

"'Im? Sleepin' on me bed, 'e is. Made a proper ol' fuss 'n' all, 'e did. Says as me bed ain't clean," the woman said indignantly. "Ain't clean! Me what puts me beddin' out to air ev'ry single day. Washes that beddin' ev'ry six months, I do. Fit for 'Is Majesty, is me bed. An' I don' want no Frenchie tellin' me as it ain't!"

Feeling a sudden kindling of hope, Angel said softly, "I am afraid that Mr. Duval is very rude." She hesitated. "Will you tell me your name, please?"

"Whafor?"

"Because I should like to know your name."

The woman appeared to be thinking this over. After a moment she said, "You talks ter me better'n what 'e does, even if you ain't no better'n me. I don' min' tellin' you me name. Mist'ess Pegley, tha's me."

"And a very nice name, too." Angel moved a step nearer. "Mistress Pegley, if you do a favor, I will see that you are well rewarded."

Mistress Pegley thought this over, too, then the gleam died out of her small brown eyes. "No, I ain't goin' ter 'elp you," she said, shaking her head. "Frenchie says as 'e's goin' ter marry you. It'll be 'is money then, won' it? Aye, 'e'll 'ave it all."

"Mistress Pegley," Angel exclaimed, starting forward. "If you would but—"

A look of terror flickered in the woman's eyes. She let out a shriek. "No!" she shouted, clapping her hands to her head. "Don' you touch me bonnet! I's mine, it is. I's the firs' pretty thing what I ever 'ad! Frenchie, 'e says as it makes me look as gran' as one o' them Court ladies. 'E says as it makes me look proper rav— rav—" She broke off, looking helplessly at Angel.

"Ravishing," Angel supplied.

"Tha's it, tha's what 'e said. I's mine, is this bonnet, an' you can' 'ave it, see!"

"I won't touch your bonnet, Mistress Pegley." Angel turned away. "Mr. Duval is quite right," she said gently. "You look charming."

"Do—do I? Tom, me 'usband, 'e's blind, 'e is. So 'e can' never tell me if I looks nice."

Angel turned back to her. "Your husband is blind?"

"Aye. 'Ad 'is eyes put out some years ago. Caught stealin' 'e was. Still 'n' all, ol' Noll never 'ad no right ter give an order what was goin' ter punish 'im so crool." Her eyes narrowed cunningly. "But don' you go thinkin' as me Tom couldn' stop you if you was ter try 'n' get away. Proper wonder is me Tom. Even if 'e can' see, there ain't no one what can get pas' 'im."

"But you can get past him?"

Mistress Pegley bridled indignantly. "O' course I can. Knows me, don' 'e? Times when 'e's sleepy an' ain't thinkin' straight, I only 'as ter say ter 'im—'I's me, you bleedin' stupid puddin'.' Le's me by then, 'e do." The woman looked down at her feet. "Loves me, do me Tom," she continued bashfully. She wriggled the dirty toes. "Even I can' get pas' 'im if 'e don' wan' me ter. But mos' o' the time 'e's jus' like a baby. Depen's on me, do me Tom."

"I'm sure he does." Angel thought quickly. Perhaps she could appeal to the woman's love of finery. "Mistress Pegley, if you can arrange to help me, I will give you this gown."

"That un'! That un' what you're awearin'!" The woman drew a deep quivering breath. "I ain't never 'ad nothin' like that give ter me. Lovely is that gown!"

"Help me," Angel said eagerly, "and the gown is yours. I'll wear one of your old gowns. Will you do it?"

366

"Well I don' know. The Frenchie give me 'usband money, an' Tom, 'e won' wan' ter give it back."

"But I will give you money, too," Angel urged desperately. "More money than Duval can give."

"I doubt that," Duval's voice said from the doorway. "And Mistress Peg knows that I intend to give her many new and beautiful gowns."

Mistress Pegley was not to be appeased. "I never 'eard you comin', Frenchie," she said truculently. "I don' like no one ter go creepin' roun' me 'ouse like a perishin' cat. Things like that upset Tom proper, they do."

François Duval advanced into the room. "Do not call me Frenchie," he said in a hard voice.

"Oh? Well then, don' you call me Mist'ess Peg. Pegley's me name, not Peg."

Duval waved his hand in her direction. "Leave us."

The woman glared at him, then, mumbling under her breath, she departed.

"Well," Duval said turning quickly to Angel, "and how is my beautiful Lady Benbrook?"

Angel looked at him coldly. He flushed under her steady gaze. "How do you expect me to be?" she answered.

Duval's white smile flashed. "Ripe and willing, *cherie*," he said softly.

"Then I am sorry to disappoint you. François, can you not see that this thing you have done is very foolish? You must know that you cannot force me into marriage." She hesitated, then added quickly, "However, if you will let me go now, I am prepared to overlook your conduct."

Duval shook his head. "You are most amiable, madame, but I fear that I cannot let you go. We are to be married tonight. After that, we set sail for France."

"I can only think you have taken leave of your senses," Angel said, staring at him. "I pray you not to be so ridiculous!"

Duval seated himself on the edge of the bed. "But for

all your protestations, *cherie,* you will find that you will be eager to marry me."

"What do you mean?"

"You have a son, have you not, my lady Benbrook?"

"Do you intend to persist in talking in riddles? Of course I have a son. What of it?"

"The father of your son, my lord Benbrook, suffered greatly from the scandals attached to his mother's name, did he not?"

So that was it! Angel felt a coldness creeping over her. "I see." She turned blindly to the window. "Yes, I begin to see."

"I thought perhaps you would, madame."

Angel did not answer him. What would Nicholas have her do? Would he, for the sake of his son, expect her to submit tamely to this man's demands? Or would he have her fight? From far off she seemed to hear Nicholas's voice saying, as he had said once before, "You have fire and spirit and courage, brat. Had you been other than you are, I could not have loved you half so well."

"Well?" Duval said softly. "Have you decided, my lady Benbrook? Are we to be married? Or do I tell the world that you came to me of your own free will? And that I, trying to protect your reputation, offered you marriage, an offer which you brazenly refused? Shall I also tell them of the many lovers of which you boasted?"

"Fight!" Nicholas's voice urged. "Fight him, brat!"

"Well?" Duval said again. "If you love your son, madame, you would not wish him to suffer for his mother's misdeeds, would you?"

Angel turned to face him. "His mother's misdeeds?" she said calmly. "Name them, François."

He frowned. "You still do not understand, m'lady. Except for that one episode with the King, I know you to be almost tediously virtuous. Lies will serve me here, not the truth." He got up from the bed and went toward her. "Come, my darling," he said, putting his hand on her arm, "I will be a very good husband to you. Marriage with me will be a blessing, not a punishment, you will see."

Angel looked at the hand upon her arm, then she reached out and calmly removed it. "I love my son," she said softly, "but I will not protect him with lies and deceit." She shrugged. "Concoct your scandals if you must, François. Later, when my son is old enough to understand, I will tell him the truth. He will believe me."

"Will he indeed!" Duval's face flushed scarlet. He saw the smile on Angel's lips. Damn the filthy little slut! Did she dare to laugh at him, Duval? His fists clenched. He was about to reply, when a sound arrested his attentions. He glanced across at the door, then, as softly as the cat to which Mistress Pegley had likened him, he was across the room and wrenching open the door. Mistress Pegley, fairly caught, almost fell into the room.

The old woman blinked nervously at the infuriated Duval. She gave a slight titter. "Don' look like the lass wants ter marry you, do it, Frenchie?"

It was too much! Duval lifted his hand and lashed her across the face. "Get out of here, you old hag!" he shouted.

The force of the blow had knocked the little bonnet from her head. Slowly she stooped and picked it up. "I's the only nice thing what I ever 'ad," she whispered, "an' you've gone an' made it all dirty." Tears ran down her seamed cheeks. "Hag means ugly, don' it?"

Duval glared at her. "It does. Now get out of here!"

"But I ain't ugly, not when I'm wearin' me bonnet." She touched the blue ribbons with a gnarled finger. "You—you says as I looked as gran' as a fine Court lady. You says as I looked lovely in it."

Angel could bear no more. She walked across to the old woman and took the bonnet from her trembling hands. Gently, she placed it upon the snarled white hair. "There," Angel said. "'Tis my opinion that you look grander than a Court lady." She smiled. "Indeed, Mistress Pegley, you look quite beautiful."

The woman raised tear-filled eyes. "I knows I do. You can' wear a bonnet like this un' an' not look it, can you?"

"It would be quite impossible, Mistress Pegley."

"Tha's what I thought." The woman nodded at Duval. "I don' like 'im, for all that he give me the bonnet. You're nicer than 'im, even if you ain't no lady."

Duval took a threatening step forward. "Will you force me to throw you out?" he shouted.

"It's my 'ouse, ain't it?" the woman muttered, backing to the door. Opening it wide, she went out. " 'E's mad, 'e is," she said from the comparative safety of the landing. "Me 'usband won' like it when I tell 'im what you done to me. No, 'e won' like it none at all."

Duval slammed the door in her face.

Looking at him, Angel was inclined to agree with Mistress Pegley. Duval did look mad. His face was red and congested, and there was an odd look in his eyes. "I have given you my answer," Angel said trying to speak calmly. "Now, if you will move aside, I will go."

Duval shook his head. "You will marry me, my lady. If you do not, I promise to make you very sorry."

Angel forced a smile. He looked very strange, so strange that she was frightened of him. "Then I will be sorry, François," she said in a placating voice. "Come, let us not quarrel. I have told you that if you are in need of money——"

"It will not be enough, my lady Benbrook. I need more, much more than you would be willing to give. Marriage is the answer to all of my problems. I have said you will marry me, and so you will."

Anger swept aside her fear. "It is as though we were characters in a very bad play. You say that I will marry you, and I say that I will not. Will not, François, under any conditions or for any reason! Do you understand me?"

He couldn't believe that she meant it. "Not even for the sake of your son?" he said in a strained voice.

"Not even for his sake. I can protect my son from

gossip, make no mistake about that. I will leave England if I have to."

"But—b—but they told me," Duval stammered. "They said—"

"Who?" Angel said sharply. "Who told you?"

"I—I have f—forgotten."

Duval felt that his head was about to burst. Was he going to have one of his fits? But he could not, must not, not with her contemptuous eyes watching him! Useless to tell her that, when the fit left him, he was as sane as any man. She would not believe him. He clenched his fists tightly together. Beads of perspiration started out on his forehead. The perspiration was running down his face now. He could not hold on. He was slipping, slipping down into that terrifying flame-shot black abyss. Laughter shook him. It was funny, very funny the way he had been deceived. Gone were his dreams of affluence. There was nothing he could say or do that would frighten the lady Benbrook into marriage. They had lied to him! The lady Barbara had lied, Buckingham had lied! All of them, all! The laughter strangled in Duval's throat. What was left to him now? A debtors' prison, or, as his father had once threatened, incarceration in an asylum for the insane. But he wasn't insane! No, no! The fits were only temporary. They always passed.

"François! What is it?"

That was her voice. The lady Benbrook's voice. She was laughing at him. He could see the laughter in her eyes. He stared at her, hoping to intimidate. Now her face was wavering, breaking, it was reforming into Simonette's face. Simonette was crying, begging him to love her again. She was so cloying, so clinging! *Mon Dieu!* But he was so very tired of her. Brutally, he told her so. "Never let me see your face again, Simonette. The affair is finished!"

Angel backed away from him. Who was Simonette? Why was Duval looking at her in that terrifying way? His eyes made her think of the insane eyes of the Bedlamites!

"François," she said in a hesitant voice, "you are mistaken. I—I am not Simonette."

Not Simonette? Was she lying to him? But no, how could she be Simonette? She was dead. For love of him, she had drowned herself! He could see her white dead face now. The slime of the river befouling her long blonde hair. Simonette, Simonette, forgive me!

Duval looked at the woman standing before him. What a stupid mistake to make. Of course it wasn't Simonette, he could see quite clearly that it was Marie Dupré. His rage caused him to tremble violently. He was remembering the night when he had been unable to love her. He had been tired, that was all. But Marie had taunted him, called him impotent. She had said— had said— Ah, now he remembered. She had said, "You are not a man, my so handsome François. You are only a spoiled little boy. Leave me. Run home to your mama. I will find a real man to share my bed!"

Marie was just like all the others! Always taunting, always laughing at him!

"Leave me," Marie was saying, "Stand aside, François, I wish to go home."

So she would not be warned. He would show her what it meant to defy Duval, to laugh at him! Marie was dead, he had murdered her. But she would not stay dead, she had come back to life. He would kill her again and again if needs must. "Don't laugh at me, Marie! I can bear anything but your laughter!"

"In the name of God, François, what is wrong with you? I am not Simonette, I am not Marie. I am Angel! Don't you recognize me? I am Angel!"

Duval smiled. So she was afraid of him, afraid enough to lie. Angel, she called herself. She was a highly paid prostitute, and the name Angel fitted her ill. "Wait, Marie." He fumbled in his pocket. "I have a little present for you."

"François! You're mad! Put that knife away!"

"You're afraid of the knife, aren't you, Marie? You're afraid that I will kill you again." The blade flashed in the sunlight as he lifted it. "I will kill you again, Marie, I will! You're not a woman. You are a foul and stinking disease! You should not be allowed to live!"

"François! No! No!"

He took a step toward her, then another. She wasn't laughing now! He could see her white face, her terrified eyes, the tumbled red-gold hair. Her gown was torn. Had he done that? No matter, it would be her shroud.

Angel pressed herself against the wall. Duval was between her and the door, she could not get past him. Was this the way she was going to end? She thought of Nicholas, of her son, and there was a weeping inside her. "I wan' ter be a lady," she had told Nicholas. Nicholas had made her into a lady. He had given her his love, his name. She had loved Nicholas with all her heart and soul. She would always love him! Why was she thinking of the past? Duval was closer now. But she could not elude him, she knew it. She would fight for her life, for her son, and for Alex. A pulse hammered in her head. Yes, yes, for Alex. She wanted him, needed him. She loved him! Duval was stretching out his hand. She could not escape him. He was insane, and he was going to kill her. She opened her mouth. "Alex! Alex! Help me."

Her screams mingled with the screaming in Duval's head. The noise, the shrill ugly sound of terror! It was mounting to a crescendo. He could not bear it! He must stop her screaming, he must! Perhaps then the screaming in his head would stop.

Duval grabbed her hair. "Stop that noise, you bitch, you dirty little slut!" He shook her so hard that her head snapped backward and forward. "Stop it, Marie!"

"I—I—I am n—not M—Marie."

The white terror in her face, her distended eyes, pleased him. He began to laugh. His hand slipped lower, touched her neck, her breast. "I'm going to kill you again, Marie, again and again!"

Marie was raising her own hand. Surprised, Duval pulled back a little. Was she going to touch him in tenderness? Was she trying to buy back her life with caresses? Duval made a howling sound as a fiery pain struck his cheek. She was clawing at his face with her nails, gouging at his flesh, hurting him! He must stop the pain, he could not bear it. Blood was running down his face. The fiery darts struck again and again, aiming for his eyes. But she was the one to die, not he! He moved in closer, pinioning her hands. Now her body was arching forward, touching his own. Her beautiful body! Her diseased body! Whore, whore, dirty whore!

"Oh dear God! Don't, François, don't!"

He liked to hear her beg for her life. It made her insults less, it made the burning pain in his face less. He flung her to the ground, laughing as she gave a despairing scream.

"Marie!" He knelt by her side. "Why will you not stay dead? Why, Marie, why?"

He could see her eyes, enormous and violet-blue in a stark white face. He leaned closer, trying to peer into their depths, trying to see the true Marie. Was she full of pain and sorrow? Was she sorry that she had insulted François Duval? He pressed his body close to hers, the warm struggling body that he soon must still.

Trying to throw him off, Angel struck at his face with her nails. It was a silent fight. She could not speak or cry out, she was dumb with horror. The hand holding the knife was close to her face now. Terror gave her another burst of strength. She grabbed for his hand and sunk her teeth deeply into his flesh.

Duval swore, but he did not release his grip on the knife. With his free hand he struck at her face. The blow seemed to drain the life from her. She was very still beneath him. Her eyes were blank now. Empty eyes, so empty! He found himself remembering the time when he had loved her. And she? She had loved him too. She sold her body to other men, but she had loved him. "Marie!" he whispered. "Marie!"

She did not speak or move, she only watched him with those empty eyes. "Do you remember when we loved each other, Marie? Do you remember the poem I used to quote?"

There was no response. Suddenly he was very angry with her, angrier than he had ever been. She had said he was not a man. She had laughed at him! But she would listen to his poem, he would make her listen! Before she died she would remember that sweet long ago when he, above all other men, had been first in her life. "Marie! Listen to my poem of love. Listen! Listen!"

He waited again. Still she did not answer. His fury was such that it was like a gigantic explosion in his head. "It's our poem, Marie! You will listen, you must!" He began shouting the words into her still and unresponsive face—

Pity the man whose heart you hold
Whose love in these few words is told
Pity the man who dares to care
Not knowing whether you'll be there.

Run to me, darling, look in my eyes
The promise they hold never lies
I promise a love that falters never
Come to my arms, stay there forever!

The woman beneath him moaned. "Please!" she entreated him. "Oh, please!"

Duval shook his head. "No more, Marie, no more! You'll never hear our poem again."

There was a startled gasp from behind them. "Wha's goin' on?" a rough voice said. " 'Ere you, Frenchie! What you adoin' wi' the lass?"

"Get out!" Duval snarled. "Get out of here!"

"Help me!" Angel managed to whisper. "H—help m—me, Mistress P—P—Pegley!"

"Tom!" the woman shrieked. "Get on up 'ere, lad. The Frenchie's akillin' o' the lass!"

Duval heard lumbering footsteps on the stairs, a voice demanding, "Wha's that you say, Bessie girl?"

375

They wouldn't stop him, Duval thought. She deserved to die. She had laughed at him, and he couldn't bear her laughter. He lifted his hand and struck downward. The knife entered just below her right breast, grating on bone. Duval stared at the bright spreading stain dyeing the front of her white gown. "Now you'll laugh no more," he muttered. "No more, Marie!"

Alex! Nicholas! The names echoed in Angel's brain. Too late for us, Alex, too late! She was falling, spinning downward into darkness.

"Oh Christ, Tom, 'e's killed 'er! The bleedin' loonytic 'as gone an' killed 'er! Get 'im, Tom lad. Don' let 'im do nothin' more!"

Duval felt hands fumbling at his shoulders, rough hands that dragged him upward. "What you gone an' done, eh?" A man's voice growled. "What you done ter the lass?"

Duval pushed the man's hands away. He felt both surprised and outraged. Why were they looking at him so? The man's face was red and congested. There was fear in his sightless eyes? Duval was vaguely interested. He had not known that blind eyes could have expression. He looked at Mistress Pegley. The old hag was gaping with terror. "What is the meaning of this intrusion?" Duval demanded. "My lady Benbrook and I desire to have a private conversation."

"You gone an' killed her," the man said. "Bessie says as you 'ave."

"Look at 'er!" Mistress Pegley shrilled. "Look what you gone an' done ter 'er!"

Duval did not look down. He began to shake violently. No, he did not want to look down. He was afraid, so afraid. The woman was staring at him, the man looked dangerous. He would have to look down, he could see no way of avoiding it. Very slowly his eyes went to Angel's still body. His eyes widened with horror. No, no, he could not have done that. *"Mon Dieu!"* he whispered. *"Mon Dieu!* What is this thing that you have done?"

"It ain't what we done. I's what you done, you murderer!"

Why did they call him that? He could hear his father's voice in his ears—"You're insane! The best thing for everybody is to have you locked away where you'll be unable to do any more harm. You killed that poor unfortunate girl!"

"No!" Duval put his hands over his ears. He must drown out the sound of his father's voice.

"Murderer!" the woman was saying. "Bleedin' murderer!"

"I did not do it," Duval said hoarsely. His hands dropped and he looked at the woman appealingly. "I would not do such a thing! I could not!"

"Look at your 'ands then. O' course you done it."

Duval looked. He winced as he saw the blood on his hands. "But it was not I," he said again. "You must believe me. How could you think I would kill her?"

"You 'ear 'im, Tom?" Mistress Pegley screamed. " 'E's tryin' ter put the blame on us! We'll 'ang, lad, 'e'll see to that! We'll 'ang!"

The woman backed through the door, then, turning, she ran down the steep stairs. " 'Elp! 'elp!" she shrieked. "The Frenchie swell's gone an' killed a lass!"

Her screams faded into the distance. Duval became conscious of the throbbing silence in the room. "My lady!" he said brokenly. He fell to his knees. "My lady Benbrook! No, no, this cannot be!" He placed his shaking hand on Angel's body. "Holy Virgin! What have they done to you!"

"She dead, is she?" the man's voice cut in on his agony.

Duval raised his head and looked into the blind eyes. "I—I cannot tell."

"Try then an' see if you can feel 'er 'eart beatin'."

Once again Duval placed his hand on Angel's body. After a few fumbling moments, he said in a stricken voice, "I cannot feel it!"

Again there was silence in the room. "You look 'ere, Frenchie," the man burst out, "We ain't takin' the blame

377

for what you done, so don' you be thinkin' it! You'd bes' think o' a way ter get rid o' the body."

Duval stared at him. "But I could not have killed her," he said in a low voice. "Don't you see that? I could not destroy such a beautiful creature."

"Tha's as may be. You done it, tha's all I know."

Mistress Pegley's shrill high voice came to them again. "In there, sir!" she was shouting. "Aye, tha's me 'ouse. 'E's done 'er in, sir. The Frenchie's gone an' done 'er in!"

Duval rose to his feet. Listening to the swift light footsteps on the stairs, he knew intuitively that the death he had always so feared was very near. He took a deep trembling breath. Better death, better a million times, than an asylum for the insane. He could face it now. He had two choices; he chose death.

Alex Barrymore paused in the doorway. Duval heard the swift intake of his breath as he saw the figure on the floor. For a fleeting instant Alex's eyes rested on Duval, then he crossed the room and knelt beside the lady Benbrook.

Duval's strange calm deserted him. Suddenly he found himself terribly afraid. He clenched his hands and tried to stop the shuddering of his body. He was afraid of the weak and idle, the luxury-loving Barrymore! But it was Buckingham who had judged him so. And Buckingham lied, as he had always lied. Duval put a shaking hand to his mouth. Barrymore was to be his nemesis, he knew it, he felt it! Had he not seen the look in the man's eyes? Holy Mother, I pray you to protect me! Death comes clad in gray, he thought wildly. In gray, not black, as he had always believed. Hysterical laughter shook him, and though he fought for control, he could not stop the mad spiraling sound. "In gray, by God!" he shouted.

Alex was only dimly aware of Duval's laughter. In an agony of fear, he bent over Angel. Her head had fallen sideways and her bright hair veiled her face. The ornate jeweled handle of the knife flashed red and green in the sunlight. He looked down at his hands. There was blood on them, her blood! Scarcely knowing what he was doing,

378

he wiped his hands on the front of his jacket. Staring at the rusty smears, he thought, this is a nightmare from which I must shortly awaken. I cannot be kneeling by Angel and watching her life blood drain away!

Mistress Pegley, panting, came hurrying into the room. She cast one scathing look at the laughing man, then she hurried to Alex's side. "'Ark at 'im!" she cried indignantly. "Laughin' fit ter bust 'imself, 'e is. 'E's a looney all right. I ain't never seen one, but I know tha's what 'e is. What I say is—" She stopped short, staring. "Oh sir, I think I seen 'er breathe! Look there, sir! Ain't that breathin' what I seen?"

"Yes," Alex said after a moment. "Yes, she is breathing. But I believe—" his voice broke. "I b—believe she is dying."

Mistress Pegley's hand touched his shoulder in an awkward gesture of consolation. "Don' say that, sir. She's alive ain't she, an' tha's what counts." She came nearer and stared closely at the girl. "'er 'ead's turnin', sir," she said in an awed voice, "an' 'er eyes is openin'!"

Angel's eyes opened slowly, reluctantly, as though the effort was too much for her feeble strength. Clouded with pain though they were, she recognized Alex. "A—Alex!" Her lips writhed as she fought to bring out words. "N— n—need y—you. I—I w—want—"

"Hush, love, hush." Tenderly Alex smoothed the hair back from her face. "I'll always be close by when you need me. Don't be afraid, my darling."

"Am—am I d—dying?"

"No, no!" Alex said quickly. He forced a smile. "You know well, my lady Benbrook, that I would not allow it."

"D—don't lea—leave m—me."

"I must. But only for a very little while. I'm going to get help."

Her lips moved in a faint smile. "I love y—you, Alex." She drew in a sighing breath, then her head fell sideways again.

She loved him! Had he actually heard her say those words?

An outraged shriek from Mistress Pegley broke in on Alex's thoughts. "Tom, lad," she shouted to her silent husband. "I don' know what's 'appenin', or 'ow it's 'appenin, but there's an 'eathen black astarin' at us from the doorway. An 'eathen black right 'ere in me 'ouse!"

Tom grunted, but said nothing. Alex turned his head and looked without surprise at M'Zeli. "So you followed me."

M'Zeli came forward. "I did, lord. I thought you might have need of me." He looked with hard eyes at the hysterical Duval. "It would seem that my lady Angel's murderer finds her death amusing."

The words were said tonelessly, but they had the effect of sobering Duval. "Keep away from me," he muttered. "Don't you come near me!"

M'Zeli's words were not toneless to Alex, he had caught the underlying menace. He rose to his feet. "Stay with my lady Benbrook," he said sharply. "I will be back very soon. And, M'Zeli, you may safely leave Duval to me."

"I hear you, lord. I am content that it should be so." M'Zeli looked at Angel, his eyes full of sorrow. "He shall not go unpunished, my lady Angel, the lord's words have told me so."

"Barrymore!" Duval cried as Alex passed him. "You have no proof that I killed her! The black boy has no proof! Will—will you take the word of these people? Their word! Bah! It is nothing."

"I will take their word," Alex said, turning to face him. "I believe them."

Duval found himself staring into those icy implacable eyes, and his nerve broke. "Very well then, I did it!" he cried. "The word of those people will not be taken against mine. You can prove nothing! Nothing!"

A muscle twitched at the side of Alex's mouth, and the look in his eyes changed to one of hating fury. "I do not need proof to kill you!" He lifted his arm and smashed the back of his hand against Duval's sneering mouth. "Don't try to run from me," he said, grasping the front of Duval's jacket and pulling him close. "Don't try it! I'll find you wherever you go. I'm going to kill you, Duval. Remember it!"

Alex released him, and Duval staggered back and collapsed to the floor. "I'm sorry," he babbled, his eyes on the gray-clad figure going out of the door. "I didn't mean to do it, Barrymore! I couldn't help it. Don't you understand?"

Duval covered his face with his hands, sobs shaking his body. He felt helpless. He couldn't run, as every instinct urged him; his legs were too weak. Even were he to try it, the black boy would stop him. He dropped his hands and looked fearfully across the room. Mistress Pegley had hold of her husband's hand. Her mouth was trembling, and the little bonnet was awry. For once she had nothing to say. The black boy, kneeling at his mistress's side, had his back turned toward him. Duval noticed that he had a knife in his belt. His gaze became concentrated on the knife. He knew now what he was going to do. Still staring, he rose slowly to his feet.

Mistress Pegley gave a convulsive start as Duval hurled himself forward. " 'Elp!" she screamed. "Oh, God save us, 'e's agoin' ter murder us all!"

M'Zeli turned swiftly, but not swiftly enough. Duval was already backing away from him, the knife clutched in his hand.

M'Zeli got to his feet. "Give me the knife," he said, holding out his hand. "Give it to me!"

"Keep away!" With his back pressed to the wall, Duval felt safer. Confused fragments of memory whirled through his head. Was it always like this just before you died? He saw the faces of his parents, so concerned and sorrowful. He had put the sorrow there. He saw his sisters and his brothers running together, laughing. Simonette, with her white dead face. Marie Dupré, her beautiful body mutilated by stab wounds. Last of all he thought of Angel, so still, so dead! But he hadn't meant to do it! No, he had not! Barrymore, his gray-clad nemesis. He need not expect mercy from him, but he did not want mercy, he wanted only to forget.

The black boy, who had stopped, was advancing again, his hand still held out. "Give me the knife," he repeated.

"No! No! No!" Sobbing, Duval gripped the hilt tightly with both hands. Without a moment's pause, he thrust the blade violently into his own stomach. He stood there swaying for a moment, then the floor seemed to tilt toward him. With a gasping cry, he fell heavily forward.

M'Zeli was still again. He looked at the fallen man, his face impassive. Unheeding of Mistress Pegley's screams and the bewildered shouts of her husband, he walked over to Duval. M'Zeli stood over him, his hands folded before him. "It is well," he said after a moment. "You deserved to die. My only regret is that I could not be the one to kill you."

Blood dribbled from the corner of Duval's mouth. "N—not dead y—yet," he whispered. He choked, then tried again. "For—forgive me."

"I, M'Zeli, do not forgive you. In the past, many of my people have died violently. Some of them, before they died, begged for forgiveness. Their crime was usually trivial, and so they did not know why they should have to die so violently. But still they begged, hoping in this way to obtain the white man's mercy." He touched Duval with his foot. "No, I do not forgive you, and I extend to you that same mercy the white man extended to my people."

Duval did not hear his words. He was dead.

"The lass!" Mistress Pegley cried. "She's movin' again."

M'Zeli turned abruptly. "My lady Angel!" he cried, running to her side. "Help will soon be here." He got to his knees and peered into her face. "You must not despair, for I will help you!"

Angel did not respond. After a moment, M'Zeli looked up. "Do not stand there, woman," he snapped at the pale and frightened Mistress Pegley. "Come here. I wish you to hold my lady still. I do not know of a way to stop this bleeding, but still I will try. I cannot watch her die and do nothing. It may be that your white God is watching over her, and it may be that he will show me the way."

Mistress Pegley cast a flinching look at Duval's sprawled body. "Ain't you got no 'eart? What 'bout 'im alyin' there? What 'bout folks adyin' all over the place, tha's what I'd like ter know?"

M'Zeli heard the hysteria in her voice, and he said sharply, "My only concern is with my lady." He gave her a long, meaningful look. "Questions will be asked of you, Mistress. You will be asked why my lady was here in this house, and how it came about that you aided the Frenchman in his criminal act."

" 'Ow'd I know it was wrong, eh?"

"You knew. It can be proved that you knew. Now come here."

"Don' you go givin' me no orders, you black imp of Satan!"

"If you do not immediately obey," M'Zeli said grimly, "I will show you that I really am an imp of Satan!"

" 'Ark at 'im," the woman appealed to her husband. "I don' like 'im talkin' ter me like that."

"Never min' that, Bess. You do like 'e says. We ain't wantin' no more trouble." Tom Pegley scratched his head. "We got 'nough o' that, I'm thinkin'."

"I ain't wishin' the lass no 'arm," Mistress Pegley said, glaring at M'Zeli. "I thought as you knowed that. But I don' like you talkin' ter me like that."

"Don' you take no notice o' Bessie," Tom Pegley said soothingly. "She's frightened, she is, an' tha's 'er way o' 'idin' it."

"Hold my lady still. I will, as I have said, try to stop the bleeding."

"What 'bout the knife? Ain't you goin' ter take it out?"

M'Zeli shook his head. "Nay. I believe it would be fatal. It might be, if I removed it, that the blood would flow in greater force."

"It'll kill 'er sure if you don' take it out."

"I think not." M'Zeli looked up at the woman. "My lady is not likely to move. I believe that she is too weak."

"You says for me ter 'old 'er."

"I know. But it might be better if you brought me some hot water and a clean cloth."

Mistress Pegley rose to her feet. " 'Ot water?" she said blankly. She looked at her husband. "Shall I get it for 'im?" she asked.

"O' course," he answered. He turned his face in M'Zeli's direction. "You'll 'ave ter give your orders a bit slow like. Poor Bess ain't too bright."

Mistress Pegley rose to her feet. " 'Ot water?" she said blankly. She said uneasily. "What you doin' ter the lady, sir?"

"Nothing harmful, I assure you. I have found that the pressure of my fingers in the area of the wound seems to slow the bleeding a little."

"Tha's good, ain't it, sir?"

"I pray so."

"Listen," Tom Pegley said. "I can 'ear someone acomin'. Look, sir, Bess an' me, we never meant no 'arm. I'd be 'bliged ter you if you would put in a good word for us."

M'Zeli heard Alex Barrymore's voice on the stairwell and a slow deep voice answering back. "If my lady dies," he answered Pegley, "you will be punished for your part in it. If she lives, it may be that I will try to aid you in some small way."

"M'Zeli," Alex Barrymore said, striding into the room, "how is she?"

M'Zeli rose to his feet. He looked first at Alex, then at the tall burly man beside him. "The gentleman is a physician?" he inquired.

"Aye. But how is she, M'Zeli?"

"She is alive." M'Zeli bowed his head and turned away. "It is all I can say, lord."

THE PALACE WAS BUZZING WITH EXCITEMENT, speculation, and gossip. So much was happening, and so swiftly.

François Duval, the handsome, the gay, who had apparently abducted my lady Benbrook, had died violently by his own hand. Etienne Duval, François' father, acquainted with the tragic news, had requested that the body of his son be sent to France for burial. The Pegleys, also part of the plot, had been thrown into prison. In her apartments the lady Benbrook lay near to death. She had lingered like this for several days, and the hope that she would recover was rapidly fading.

Shortly after my lady Benbrook, more dead than alive, had been carried into the Palace, the King sent for the Duchess of Castlemaine. What had been said on that interview there was no way of knowing. But when she emerged, her enemies—of which she had many—had gleefully noted that except for the hectic spot of color in each cheek, her face was paper white, and she was trembling violently. She had now retired to her estates near Windsor. It was hoped, by her detractors, that this time the King would never see her more.

A clue to that interview between the King and the Duchess of Castlemaine was given when Alex Barrymore had publicly accused the Duke of Buckingham, my lady Castlemaine's cousin, of harmful conspiracy against my lady Benbrook. The Duke, making light of the charge, had scarcely bothered to answer. But he had, in his turn, accused Barrymore of insulting him. He had then challenged him to a duel.

Accepting the challenge, it had been noted that Barrymore looked quite unlike the smiling, good-natured man they were accustomed to seeing. His lips were a tight line in his gaunt face, and those nearest to him had decided that, from the dangerous blaze in his eyes, the Duke had best look to himself. The onlookers could not believe what they were hearing. But those who had believed Barrymore to be a fop and little else now asked themselves if they could possibly have been mistaken. It was known by some present that Barrymore had a certain skill with the sword and was, perhaps, fully as expert as the Duke. Tentative bets were made, many of them running in favor of Barrymore.

Barrymore, with his next words, had shattered the sporting spirit. "My lord Duke," he had answered, "you have challenged me. Therefore the choice of weapons is mine."

Sneering openly, the Duke made him a little bow. "Of a certainty, Mr. Barrymore. What is your choice?"

Excitement again rose to fever pitch when Barrymore, holding up his jeweled hands, replied, "I choose fists, my lord Duke. The winner is afterwards allowed to flog the loser with a horsewhip."

At these astounding words, the Duke seemed taken aback. Then he smiled. "Interesting, my dear Barrymore, decidedly interesting. The horsewhip I approve, but the use of fists is decidedly plebeian. However, 'tis a choice that might have been expected of you, I suppose. The sword, as you must know, is the choice of gentlemen."

"I know it well," Barrymore had answered. "Therefore my choice should be particularly suited to you, my lord Duke."

Dark color had stained the Duke's face, and for a few tense moments his hand had lingered over the hilt of his sword. Mastering his rage with a supreme effort, he had snapped, "I accept, Barrymore. It will pleasure me greatly to knock you down. But afterwards, when I make use of the whip, I pray you not to whine, or to cry unfair, for 'tis your own choice."

"You need have no fears," Barrymore answered, bowing. "But naturally, my lord Duke, I must request the same of yourself."

Fresh bets were made by the sporting element. But this time the odds were heavily in favor of the Duke. Barrymore was tall and slender of build, but he appeared to be well-muscled. Those in the know, however, opined that he was not sufficiently muscled to beat the much heavier Buckingham.

The King, hearing of the proposed duel, expressed his strong disapproval. But it was only a token disapproval, and most of them knew it. This was later borne out when the King, forgetting he had spoken out against the duel, wagered his brother, the Duke of York, that Barrymore would win. The Duke of York looked slightly taken aback at the King's choice, but he eagerly accepted the wager.

What followed would remain forever, in sporting minds, as a classic event. Buckingham fought gamely, but again and again he was felled. The audience was in a perpetual gasp. Was this Barrymore, this merciless fighting machine? Despite his own injuries, and they were numerous, Barrymore seemed untiring. His fist pulped Buckingham's lips, broke his nose, and closed one eye. When Buckingham sprawled to the ground for the last time, Barrymore was heard to say, "I will withdraw the horsewhip if Your Grace so desires."

"Be damned to you!" Buckingham shouted. "Use your whip! You've won, haven't you?"

"My lord Duke," Barrymore's reply came clearly to the audience, "I do not like you, but I have to admire your courage. I will use the whip, if you, likewise, use yours."

The Duke, glaring at him, said loudly, " 'Twas the winner who was to handle the whip, not the loser."

"And I have said that we will both handle the whips. Come, do you accept?"

"I want no favors from you, curse you!"

"And you will receive none. I propose, however, to give you an equal chance."

"Very well, I accept." With some effort the Duke rose to his feet and stood there swaying. He wiped the blood from his face with the tail of his silk shirt. Spitting the blood from his mouth, he said jeeringly, "I have no doubt that you consider yourself to be quite magnanimous, Barrymore."

The audience strained to hear Barrymore's reply. "Since my every instinct is to kill you, Buckingham," he answered, "yes, you might say that I am being extremely magnanimous."

The whips were brought to the fighting area and formally presented to each man by Lord James Warwick.

The first blood was drawn by Buckingham. The whip caught Barrymore in the face, opening a gash down his left cheek. Nor was this Buckingham's only victory. Barrymore's shirt was hanging in ribbons, and great bleeding weals crisscrossed his back before he struck the final blow that brought Buckingham to his knees. Barrymore stood there for what appeared to the onlookers to be a very long moment, then he flung the whip from him and limped painfully away.

Buckingham had been a sorry sight. But though he had fought gamely, it was noticed that the King regarded him coldly; but he had joined in with a will when the crowd cheered Barrymore. Could it be, they asked themselves, that the charges made by Barrymore had some element of truth in them?

It would seem so. As the unfavorable reports on my lady Benbrook's condition continued to arrive, so the coldness of the King's manner toward Buckingham increased.

On this day, when it became known that the King had

sent for Buckingham, the men stood around in little groups and discussed what this might mean. Was Buckingham guilty? Was my lady Benbrook sinking? Was she, perhaps, already dead? Barrymore's face might have given them the answer, but Barrymore was in the sickroom, as usual. If the lady be dead, and if Barrymore had spoken truth, then it might be said that Buckingham had been involved in a conspiracy to murder. It was a fact that Duval, who was apparently a madman, had attacked my lady Benbrook, but it was Buckingham who had brought about the situation. Buckingham and, they did not doubt, the Duchess of Castlemaine. But it yet remained to be proved, of course.

There was a heavy silence in the small anteroom whither the King had summoned Buckingham.

The King, standing by the window, his back toward the Duke, had not spoken for the last five minutes. Buckingham, his face still showing the marks of that disastrous fight, looked uneasily at the tall, scarlet-clad figure. What was Charles thinking of? Was he convinced that Buckingham had had no part in the abduction of my lady Benbrook? Why did the King not speak?

"Sire," Buckingham began, "Might I ask—"

The King turned to face him. "You may ask nothing, my lord Duke. But you will listen."

"I came here prepared to do so, Sire," Buckingham answered sullenly.

"I like not your tone," the King snapped. "Insolence has become second nature to you, has it not, my lord? But I warn you now that I will not tolerate it!"

It was rare for the King to display temper, and Buckingham was dismayed. "Your Majesty, nothing has been proved against me. You have only Barrymore's word. Surely, Sire, you will not condemn me without proof?"

"Without proof?" The King's eyes narrowed. "Supposing I were to tell you that I have proof? What then, my lord?"

Buckingham's brain whirled in confusion. Duval was dead, so he could not speak against him. Bab, with unusual caution, had continued to deny her involvement in the affair. Could it be that Duval had mentioned their names to the Angel? It might be, of course, but the Angel was desperately ill and unable to speak.

"Well, my lord," the King said coldly, "what have you to say?"

Buckingham thought quickly. He had always been a gambler, and he would gamble this time. "Sire, you could not have proof. I am innocent. Therefore there are none to speak against me."

"Not even my lady Benbrook?"

"Not even my lady. If she has told you that I am involved, she lies!"

The King's lip curled contemptuously. "Worry not, Buckingham. My lady Benbrook has not yet spoken. But I know in my heart that you are guilty, as is my lady Castlemaine. I have marked your malice toward my lady Benbrook. It is not my policy to condemn a man unfairly. But, if it be possible, I will obtain that proof. In the meantime, my lord Duke, you are dismissed from this Court. You will retire to your estates in Gloucestershire, and there you will stay until such time as I see fit to recall you."

The Duke caught his breath in dismay. Gloucestershire! That dreary place! So it was to be the manor house, was it, and the unadulterated company of his wife? Nay, it was not to be borne! Without pausing to think, he burst out, "Sire! You are unfair!"

"You forget yourself, my lord!"

The flame in the King's eyes should have warned him, but still he persisted. "I am innocent, Sire!"

"We have given you a command, my lord Duke. We expect it to be obeyed."

The Duke's heart sank. When the King spoke thus formally, and with him it was as rare as his former display of temper, it meant that he would listen to no appeal.

"Then, Sire, I will obey." The Duke bowed. "You are the King, therefore it is not for me to protest your decision, however unfair that decision might be."

The King caught his breath. "You have ever been an insolent rogue, Buckingham. You speak of proof. What of the proof of the heart, the mind, the senses?"

"Unfortunately, Sire, that kind of proof would be inadmissible in the eyes of the law."

"Which is most fortunate for you, my lord," the King said curtly. "I, however, choose to be guided by what I know in my heart to be true. You may go."

Buckingham bowed again. "Then I will take my reluctant farewell of Your Majesty."

The door closed behind him. The King turned back to the window. It was not like him to act without proof, and Buckingham, knowing this, had doubtless believed himself to be quite safe. But he had heard Barrymore's story, and he believed it. The sight of my lady Benbrook lying in her bed, so small and still, so white, her lovely hair dulled with the perspiration of approaching death, had hardened his suspicion of the Duke's guilt. In the past Buckingham had, he was sure, been guilty of many crimes, but always, it seemed, the complaining party was unable to produce proof. This time, though, he was determined that the Duke should not escape punishment.

Charles sighed. He could not, of course, banish the Duke forever, nor could he command him to stand before a jury of his peers to answer for his part in this shocking affair; not, that was, without the necessary proof. But a long banishment of many months might be the most appropriate punishment, for Buckingham became easily bored. The quiet of the Gloucestershire countryside was not for such as he, and Buckingham, daring and insolent as he undoubtedly was, would not dare to disobey his royal command.

The King drummed his fingernails against the windowpane, his thoughts turning to the young Earl of Benbrook, who was constantly inquiring for his mother. He had been told that she had gone away for a time. No one had as yet the heart to tell him that his mother was already in the Palace but she could not see him. He was too young to understand, and death to him would be only a word, but it was quite evident that he sensed something was wrong. It might have been the hesitant, evasive, not too cleverly contrived answers given to him by Mrs. Sampson, Nell Gwynne, and various ladies of the Court, or it might be something inside himself, for young Nicholas had ever seemed older than most lads of his age. The Queen had tried to comfort him, but without success. Forgetting her animosity toward my lady Benbrook, she had taken the boy upon her knee and explained that, though his mother could not be with him for a time, she loved him dearly and was constantly thinking of him.

M'Zeli had also failed. Resourceful though the boy was, he could not lie convincingly, nor could he charm a smile from young Nicholas. The fact was that the boy had grown very quiet of late. He would sit motionless for a long time, making no attempt to play with his toys. The eyes he turned on the King, his constant visitor, were the dark, solemn, and watchful eyes of his father before him.

The King shook his head. It pained him deeply that he seemed to read hurt in those eyes, too. The boy was sensitive, perhaps too sensitive—again like his father. But he loved his mother dearly; he must wonder why she did not come back to see him. Only yesterday, Mrs. Sampson had told the King, Nicholas had fallen down and cut his knee quite badly. Instead of crying, as most lads of his age would have done, he had closed his eyes against the tears and bit his lip. "When my mama comes," he told Mrs. Sampson, "I will show her my knee. Then I will cry."

Thinking of this, Charles smiled ruefully. He was the King of England, and he had faced many dangers, but it seemed that he had not the courage to tell a little boy that his mother was very ill, that it might be that he would never see her again. *Poor lad! I fear you will cry very soon.*

Charles turned abruptly from the window. Plague take it! My lady Benbrook could not recover, of that he was certain. In her last moments, might it not be that the sight of her son would comfort her? And was he such a coward that he could not take Nicholas by the hand and say to him, "I am taking you to see your mother, little friend. She is very ill, so you must be careful to smile."

There was a lot of friend Nicholas in the lad, and 'twere better that he be temporarily distressed than to grow up with the idea that his mother had abandoned him.

The King walked slowly along the corridor, absent-mindedly acknowledging the bows of passing courtiers and the curtsies of the ladies. It might be that I make too much of this matter, he thought. The lad will be told the date of his mother's death. He will see her grave. So how can he possibly believe that she abandoned him? Charles frowned. But the Court had ever been a hotbed of gossip. There were plenty of malicious tongues to tell the boy of his father's story. They might be motivated by spite, envy, or dislike, but those tongues could, if they wished, paint a lurid and damaging portrait of my lady Benbrook. A guttersnipe, they might call her, a thief, a sometime prisoner of Newgate who had managed to worm her way into the Earl's affections. It might be that the boy would choose to believe his friends, and that he would turn on his informants and give them the lie. But once Nicholas senior had got an idea into his head, it had been cursed hard to dislodge it.

Outside the door leading into the nursery, the King hesitated. Then, lifting the latch, he entered. Nicholas was seated on the floor beside Mrs. Sampson's chair. He was rattling stones in a can, a device of Mrs. Sampson's which he seemed to prefer to his many expensive toys. The King looked wistfully at the boy, wishing, as he had done many times before, that he was his own son.

"Sire!" Mrs. Sampson jumped hurriedly to her feet. "Forgive me, Sire. I did not hear the door open."

Charles smiled. "A terrible crime, mistress. I must think of a fitting punishment." He looked at Nicholas. "Well, little friend, and how do you do this day?"

"Master Nickey," Mrs. Sampson instructed him. "Rise to your feet and bow to His Majesty. Come now, there's a good lad."

The boy's solemn dark eyes inspected the tall King. He liked this man with his vivid clothes, his jewels, his long dark hair, his merry laugh, and his kind eyes. He put the can aside, rose slowly to his feet, and made the King a deep bow. He glanced at Mrs. Sampson, who was mouthing words. "I am well, Majersey," he said.

"He cannot manage 'Majesty' as yet," Mrs. Sampson explained. "But he's a good boy. A very good boy."

"You do not have to tell me that, mistress," Charles said. "My lord Benbrook and I understand each other well." He held out his hand to Nicholas. "Do we not, my friend?"

Nicholas came closer. Placing his hand in the King's, he said, "Go now and see Mama?"

"Ah," the King said, laughing. "You have read my mind, my lord Benbrook. That is exactly where we are going, to see Mama."

"Mama!" Solemnity fled the dark eyes; they were bright with joy. "See Mama!" he said again.

"Sire!" Mrs. Sampson exclaimed. "Pray to forgive me, Your Majesty, for speaking out. But— but is it wise?"

With his eyes on the boy's face, the King saw some of the joy fading. The little hand pressed his anxiously. "Mama!" there were tears in the voice.

"I think, mistress," the King said gently, "that it might be the wisest thing I have ever done."

"But, Sire!" Mrs. Sampson twisted the corner of her apron with agitated fingers. "She is— I mean, my lady is so ill. She might not recognize him. Great damage could be done to the lad."

"I think not, mistress." The King stooped and lifted the boy into his arms. "I think, wherever my lady may be wandering, that the son of her Nicholas will call her back."

"God grant that it be so, Sire!"

"God grant!" the King echoed. He put his face against the boy's soft cheek. "Nicholas, do you know what it means to be very ill?"

The boy drew away that he might look into the King's

face. For a moment he seemed puzzled, then he smiled. "Hurts," he said, putting a hand to his stomach. "Nickey ill."

"That's right." The King smiled at him. "You are a clever lad, are you not? Well, Nicholas, your Mama is very ill."

Nicholas's lower lip trembled. "Mama hurts?" he inquired.

"Aye, lad, Mama hurts. She hurts very much. But I believe she would like to see you."

Tears filled Nicholas's eyes and ran down his cheeks. "Nickey stroke Mama. Make her all better."

"I do that to him," Mrs. Sampson explained. "It seems to soothe him when he has a little ache in his stomach."

"Now, Nicholas, you must stop crying. Mama, though ill, will want to see you smile. Will you do that, lad? Will you smile for her?"

Nicholas considered this. Then he nodded. "Smile," he said, suiting the action to the words.

With his tear-wet cheeks, that smile seemed to the King to be infinitely pathetic. He was about to take a child to see a mother who might well be already dead. The King's arms tightened about him. "Then we will go now, shall we Nicholas?"

"Go," Nicholas repeated, nodding his head vigorously. "Go to Mama."

Mrs. Sampson, her face distressed, held out her arms. "Shall I take the child, Sire?"

"No, mistress, I will carry him."

"Walk," Nicholas said, wriggling in his arms.

"Aye, I know you can walk," the King reassured him. "But we will get to Mama sooner if I carry you."

The boy subsided instantly. The King said softly to Mrs. Sampson, "Come with us, mistress. It may be that the lad will have grave need of you."

"Oh, Sire! Surely my lady will live?"

"That is in God's hands."

"Yes, Your Majesty."

And so the King, carrying the young Earl in his arms,

strode swiftly along the corridors that led to the apartments of my lady Benbrook. There was fear in his heart, fear for the little boy, fear for himself. For if God did not spare Angel, something bright and lovely would disappear from his life. The last link with friend Nicholas, save for this little one, would be gone. It might be that he would not live to see the child grow into the man. Trying to dismiss his gloomy thoughts, the King lengthened his stride.

Those courtiers and ladies who marked the King's rapid progress, Mrs. Sampson hurrying along behind him, asked themselves what it could mean. The King's face was unusually grave. He was staring straight ahead, and he seemed not to notice their low and respectful obeisances. Was my lady Benbrook already dead? Why else would the child be exposed to such a melancholy scene?

The news rapidly sped through the Palace. The words, "my lady Benbrook may well be dead," were soon transmitted to "my lady Benbrook is dead!"

The Queen hid her face in her hands and wept, recollecting those times when Angel had been very dear to her. Had Angel really betrayed her? Or had her own overwhelming jealousy, her sense of shock that it should be Angel of all people, caused her to close her ears to the truth? It might well be so. But how tragic, with my lady Benbrook lying dead, that only now should she seek to question and excuse. Oh, if only Angel had lived, she would have sent for her! She would have told her that she believed her, and that all would be between them as it once was. It was too late now!

The Queen's hands dropped. "My poor little friend!" she said.

The Queen's ladies drew back as she rose with a rustle of silken skirts. "Come, ladies," the Queen said, turning her pale face to them, "I ask that you join me in prayers for the soul of my lady Benbrook."

Alex Barrymore, for once absent from his vigil in the sickroom, likewise heard the news. He could not believe it! And yet had he not sat by the bed and watched the remorseless ebbing of Angel's life? His face turned very white, and there was a great sickness inside him. Like a man stricken with sudden blindness, he groped his way back to the apartments of my lady Benbrook. He could no longer hope for a miracle. God help him, he must now look upon her for the last time! He did not know that he was crying. Those who saw his tears looked hastily away. They, too, had heard of the death of my lady Benbrook, and they were embarrassed to witness such bitter grief.

Angel wandered in a hot and delirious world. There was pain in her body, burning savage throbbing pain. She was alone in her terrible world, so alone! Sometimes, though, when the pain subsided slightly, it would seem to her that she heard voices. Alex's voice, the King's, Mrs. Sampson's, Nell Gwynne's, and once, so she believed, the Queen's. Hope would surge, it might be that she was not alone. She would cry out to them, trying to hold them, to bring them closer so that she might grasp their hands and pull herself out of her frightening world, but she could not hear her own voice. How then could they hear her, how could they help her?

Images sprang out at her, images etched in flame against the trembling blackness. She saw Duval, his face contorted, his eyes blazing with madness. Screaming, she fled from him, but she could not escape. She was so afraid. She wanted Nicholas. Where had he gone, her love, her darling! She stumbled along, helplessly seeking, and then suddenly Duval was gone, and Nicholas stood in his place. He looked so tall, so sane, such a cool and wonderful vision. She ran to him, her arms held out. "My dear, my love, wait for me!" But it seemed that Nicholas could not wait, for already he was disintegrating. "No, dear m'lord, don't go! In the name of God's mercy, wait for me!"

She could still hear his voice. "I love you, brat! My little one, my darling!"

"Wait, Nicholas! Wait!"

"Nay, Angel, I cannot! Find Alex."

Alex! His name echoed in her mind like a roll of thunder. She must find him; Nicholas had said so. She would be safe then, he would not let Duval harm her. Alex! I need you!

She had cried out to him, but he did not answer. Had he left her too? No! She could not be left alone and desolate for the second time. "Don't leave me, Alex! Oh, don't! Don't!"

The pain seemed to be subsiding, and now she could hear voices again. Not muffled as they were before, but so clear that they hurt her ears. Someone was sobbing, was saying in a broken voice, "Oh thank God! I had heard that she was dead. Pray to forgive me, Sire. I did not mean to break down."

"Ask no pardon of me, Alex lad," the King's voice answered, "for I greatly fear that I am in like condition."

Angel's fingers twitched in feeble protest. *Don't cry, love! Not for me!*

"Her hand moved!" came the King's excited voice. "See! It moved again. Does it seem to you, Alex, that she is looking a little stronger? Or is it perhaps my own wishful thinking?"

"I cannot tell, Sire. But I pray God that you might be right."

A soft hand was touching her cheek. "Mama," a small voice said. "Wake up, Mama!"

"Be careful, lad." Alex's voice. "Do not go too near Mama. We wouldn't want to disturb her, would we?"

"Ssh!" the small voice said. "Mama a'seep."

"Yes, Nicholas, she's sleeping."

"Od's Fish, Alex! Look at the expression on her face. Can it be that she knows the boy is here?"

"Sire! Her eyes are opening. Look, she's smiling!"

"There's no time to go to pieces, Alex lad. Call in the physicians. By God, what a time for me to send them from the room! And while you're about it, you may tell that plaguey long-nosed priest that I don't think my lady Benbrook will be needing his services."

"But, Sire, what if 'tis only a temporary improvement?"

"Have *faith,* lad! Have *hope!*"

Now Angel could hear hurried footsteps, a blur of voices all talking together. A door opened, then closed. The walls of her black world were fast fading to gray. She could see dim shapes. Someone was bending over her. A cool cloth touched her lips, her forehead. It was such a delicious sensation that she wanted to beg them not to take the cloth away. But her lips were difficult to manage; so was her tongue, she could only shape two words. "Nicholas! Alex!"

"Mama!"

Angel saw her son's little face through a mist. That little face that was so like Nicholas's. With a tremendous effort she brought out a third word, then a fourth. "B—baby! M—m—m—my b—baby!"

"God's precious body! Look there, Alex. Now I know she's returning to us!"

"Yes, Sire! Yes!"

"Od's Fish, lad, don't stand there gaping. Take her hand, talk to her! Do I have to tell you everything?"

"No, Sire!" Alex laughed, the sound of his laughter shaky and uncertain. "This much at least, I had thought of for myself."

Angel felt a firm warm hand taking hers. Her eyes strained through the mist. It was thinning now. She saw Alex's white strained face, his heavy eyes. He looked so terribly tired. "A—A—Alex!"

"Yes, my darling, it's Alex."

He had answered her. He was really there! She tried again. "I w—w—w—want—"

"No, darling, don't talk any more. Save your strength."

Why not? She *wanted* to talk, she wanted to tell Alex not to go away. He was her strength. She needed him, loved him! Yes, she did love him, she knew that now. Not as she had loved Nicholas; she loved Nicholas passionately, deeply and enduringly, and that love would never die. But she loved Alex in another, quiet tender way, a lasting way, and that love would endure, even as her love for Nicholas. How strange that out of the fevered jumble of her mind these thoughts should emerge so clearly. Suddenly she was afraid that if she did not voice her thoughts, Alex would go away and leave her. For so long he had loved her, but she, grieving for Nicholas, had not heeded him. To the last day of her life she would mourn Nicholas, but did Alex know that it would not lessen her love for him?

Her eyes were stinging. She must not cry, else would she not be able to see his dear face. *I love you, Alex, I want to tell you so, but I have not the strength. Have I left it too late to tell you that I love you?*

"Don't cry, love. I'm here beside you. See, I'm holding your hand."

Alex's voice! It was as if he knew her secret fears and he was reassuring her. Dearest Alex! His hand, his firm, warm and blessed hand was grasping hers tightly. Her throat worked, and then she was bringing out her difficult words, "I—I—I—I—I—love you, A—A—Alex!"

Alex blinked the mist from his eyes. He turned his head and looked appealingly at the two physicians standing at the other side of the bed. "Will she—will she live?"

Sir Benjamin Meadows looked at his colleague, who nodded. They conferred together for a few moments, during which time the King grew very impatient.

"Well, sirs," the King cried, "what is your verdict? Have you nothing better to do than mumble in your beards and make people anxious?"

"I believe, Sire, that the lady may have a fair chance of recovery," Sir Benjamin said slowly. " 'Tis really too soon to tell as yet." He put his hand on Angel's forehead. "The fever appears to have gone," he went on, looking at Alex. "It might be, providing there is no relapse."

"Might be, may be!" the King said impatiently. "Cannot you be more certain?"

Sir Benjamin drew himself up. "Forgive me, Sire," he said coldly. "I am not God."

"And damned fortunate it is for us that you are not. Of all the fumbling, cloud-brained idiots! Never did I see a bigger pair of knaves!"

"Sire! Pray forgive me, but I must protest. My colleague and I have worked to the best interests of my lady Benbrook."

The mercurial King's mood changed instantly. "Of course you have." His charming smile flashed. "Forgive me, I am a dolt. You may call me so if you wish."

Sir Benjamin looked shocked. "No indeed, Sire. I would not dream of doing so."

Mrs. Sampson, who had been looking on, moved nearer to the bed. "There, lad," she said, putting her hand on Alex's rigid shoulder. "You have heard Sir Benjamin. He is very hopeful. Now come, come, you really must pull yourself together."

A faint smile touched Alex's lips. "One can always rely on you for the bracing speech, can they not, Mrs. Sampson?"

A tear fell on Alex's hand, and he looked up startled.

"Aye, lad," Mrs. Sampson said dryly. "When I speak harshly 'tis for your own good. My lady will need your strength."

"And she shall have it." Alex looked at Nicholas. "We will both give her our strength, will we not, lad?"

Nicholas smiled shyly. Edging closer to Alex, he hid his face against his shoulder. Alex's arms went round him. "We are going to be great friends, you and I."

Nicholas nodded, but he did not look up.

"And what have we here?" the King said. "Art deserting me, friend Nicholas?"

Friend Nicholas! Angel felt a quick stab of pain. The King's name for her Nicholas. And now he was bestowing it on her son. She moved her head. "S—Sire."

The King bent over her. "Yes, my lady?"

"Th— thank you."

"For what?"

"For s—so many th—things."

"No more talk, my lady," Sir Benjamin said sternly. "You must not exhaust yourself."

Angel was content to remain silent. They were all with her, her loved ones. Even Nicholas was here. She could not see him, but she sensed his presence. Alex was holding her hand. The King was smiling. Little Nicholas, withdrawing himself from Alex's arms, came to hold her other hand. And Mrs. Sampson, clicking her tongue disapprovingly, was attempting to straighten the bed covers. But Angel knew that the disapproving face she wore covered love, and she was happy in that knowledge.

"M—my dear on—ones," she said. "All—all m—my d—dear ones."

"Not quite all," the King said. "The Queen is not present."

Angel looked an inquiry. "The Queen has been very anxious," the King went on. "I know that she would want me to give you her love. Until, that is, she is present to give it herself."

Angel closed her eyes. She fell asleep, her smile still lingering on her lips.

WITH HER HAND CLASPED FIRMLY IN ALEX'S, Angel awaited their turn to walk down the long carpeted aisle to where the King and Queen were seated. The ceremony attendant on such functions was always wearying, but tonight Angel did not mind. She felt light and gay. She was happy in a way she had never thought to feel again.

Alex looked very handsome, she thought proudly. His plainly cut jacket and breeches were, save for the frill of lace at his neck and cuffs, devoid of the lavish ornamentation that decorated the costumes of the other men, and were suited to his lithe, elegant figure. His blond hair shone in the light of the myriad candles, and his lazy blue eyes were smiling.

She looked away. Her two men! Nicholas had always dressed severely, wearing his own hair rather than a wig, and he had disdained the frills and furbelows then currently in fashion. Alex, who once had been a slave to fashion, had, either by choice or an inherited natural good taste, followed in Nicholas's footsteps. Angel smiled to herself. Despite the severity of his clothes, the appellation of "fop" still clung to him. Tonight he looked more than usually distinguished. He stood out from the other men. Even the King, clad in amber satin trimmed with silver lace, a fountain of lace falling from his wide cuffs, his jeweled fingers flashing multicolored fire, could not, in her opinion, compete with him.

Angel looked about her, and she felt some of her bubbling good spirits deserting her. This occasion, the lights, the scent of flowers and perfume, the vivid gowns of the ladies, the jewel-trimmed satins and silks of the men, the music playing softly from behind the flower-hung galleries, could not help but remind her painfully of another occasion. The aloof and coldly dignified Earl of Benbrook had not loved her then; or if he had, he had not been ready to admit it to himself. Angel bit her lip, trying to shake memories from her. She must not think of Nicholas now, but how could it ever be otherwise? She loved Alex, she was pledged to marry him. And somehow she felt that Nicholas, who in life had been so possessive, would not resent her love for Alex. She believed this sincerely, and she was happy in the knowledge. It was a new love, a different love, but nonetheless sweet for all that.

She is thinking of Nicholas, Alex thought. She has never buried him, not really, not in her heart, and she never will. But the thought did not stab him as once it would have done. A smile touched his lips and his fingers tightened about Angel's. He would not change her if he could. For if part of her was given to Nicholas, the other part was his, and would so remain, finally and forever.

My lady Benbrook and Alex Barrymore were beginning their slow approach. With that part of his mind that was not occupied with greeting his guests, the King thought of Angel. She was still frail from her bout with death, but she was looking particularly beautiful in her gown of soft blue silk. Pearls were threaded through her hair, and bright loose curls bobbed on her shoulders. Diamonds edged the numerous flounces of her skirts, studded the heels of her blue slippers, and flashed from her fingers. The King remembered when he had encountered her in the corridor. She had already been dressed for the ball, and he had thought then that the diamonds were no less bright than her eyes. His lips twisted in his faintly cynical smile. How poetical he was becoming. But somehow Angel, as lovely and as delicate as a spring flower, had ever managed to bring out this side of him. There was still desire mixed with the poetry. Aye, he admitted, he did desire her still, and he always would. But he had learned to control that desire. Once, without meaning to do so, and without knowledge of the Earl of Benbrook's feelings toward the girl, he had hurt both Angel and Nicholas with his determined pursuit. His desire had turned their lives upside down and had all but shattered them. No more, though. He must force himself to remember that Angel was sacrosanct to Alex Barrymore. Alex would soon be marrying her and removing her from Court life, and when Angel was gone, the temptation would be removed. Charles smiled warmly at a plump lady in cherry-red satin who had just curtsied before him. The smile so flustered the lady that she dropped her fan and her small jeweled purse. She recovered the articles and retired in great confusion.

A rustle of skirts caught the King's attention, and his nostrils were teased with a familiar and excitingly heady perfume. He turned his head and glanced with appreciation at the beautiful Frances Dixon. Her silvery blonde hair was caught back from her face with a wide silver band studded with emeralds. Her green and silver skirts swayed with her movements, and the low-cut bodice seemed scarcely adequate to confine her small, pert breasts. Her green eyes flashed a question as they met the King's.

Charles nodded to her. *Trollop*, he thought. But Frances could pleasure him in bed as no one else. Barbara Castlemaine, now in temporary retirement at her estates near Windsor, had perhaps been Frances' equal. But he no longer felt the smallest desire for Barbara. Her hold on his senses had been broken.

Smiling with satisfaction, Frances Dixon turned away. The King would send for her tonight. Her flesh tingled at the thought, and heat flushed her body. Anticipation caused the nipples of her breasts to stand out darkly against the flimsy material of her bodice, and already she could feel the dryness of desire parching her mouth. A passing servant, bearing a tray with goblets of wine, paused as Frances hailed him. Frances took a goblet from the tray and drained it greedily. The servant stood there with bowed head, his eyes on the prominent nipples straining against her bodice. Frances replaced the goblet, and the servant passed on. Charles! Frances thought. Tonight she would lie in his arms and rediscover the ecstasy, the pulsing excitement of Charles Stuart.

The Queen had her eyes on Frances Dixon, too. *How can you, Charles! How can you be so faithless to me. I love you with my body, my life, my heart and my soul. I even love you above God! Why is it not enough for you?*

Nell Gwynne, her hands clenching on her orange skirts, glared at Frances Dixon's slender back. *God rot the hussy! One of these days I'll kill that bitch. Charles loves my body, it pleases him. I amuse him. I make him laugh when he's sad. Aye, and I'll keep him longer than you will, you silver-haired whore!*

Forcing a smile, the Queen nodded graciously to Lady Margaret Beresford. Lady Margaret's smile to the Queen was shy, almost timid. But the Queen noticed that her dark eyes were bold as she took the King's hand and pressed a kiss on his jeweled fingers. Another one, the Queen thought bitterly, who was anxious to tumble into the King's bed. Had she not seen that inviting look in the eyes of countless other women when they looked upon the King?

The lady Margaret was moving aside, surrendering her place reluctantly to my lady Benbrook and Alex Barrymore. The Queen smiled as Angel dropped in a low curtsy before her. She was so glad that the breach between Angel and herself had been healed. Hurt and seriously displeased by what she believed to be Angel's treachery, she had forced herself to be cold. But she had been unhappy in the doing, for, despite everything, she could not help but be fond of Angel. The years had made many changes in Angel, but she was pleased to see that the look of brooding unhappiness had left the girl's eyes.

"My lady Benbrook," the Queen said softly. "How beautiful you are looking."

The King nodded to Alex and then turned to Angel. His dark eyes were warm and soft as he took Angel's hand in his. "You are indeed beautiful, my lady," he remarked formally. "I echo the Queen's sentiments."

"I thank Your Majesties. You are most gracious."

The King smiled. "How stiff and remote is the Angel," he said in a low voice. He looked at Alex. "Is she not, my friend?"

Alex, who had barely managed to catch the words, bowed. "On such an occasion, Your Majesty, with so many eyes upon you, she could be little else."

"True." The King retained Angel's hand. "Tonight, my lady Benbrook," he said in a loud clear voice, "you will open the ball with your King." He pressed her fingers warmly.

Angel knew how much the Queen loved to dance, and she flushed scarlet. "Your Majesty," she said, shooting an apprehensive look at the Queen. "You do me too much honor."

"You are confused, my lady Benbrook," the Queen said understandingly. "The King has not yet explained to you that I am unable to dance."

"Unable, Madam?"

The Queen drew her filmy pink skirts to one side and exposed a tightly bandaged ankle. " 'Tis a recent accident, my lady. It happened just an hour before the ball. So, as you can see, I am quite unable to dance."

Angel looked at her sympathetically. "I am very sorry, Madam."

"And I, child." The Queen touched Angel's cheek lightly. "But I am feeling a little weary, and I doubt not that I shall enjoy the rest."

Angel turned to the King. "I shall be honored indeed, Sire."

"Nay, my lady, the honor is mine." The King leaned forward, sinking his voice to a low pitch again. "Are you truly honored, Angel? Do you tell me that you are not dying to dance with your Mr. Barrymore?"

She saw the teasing light in his eyes and, as it had always done, something within her responded to his vital attraction and his aura of pronounced sensuality. "I will dance many times with Mr. Barrymore, Sire," she whispered. "But when I dance with Royal Charles, it may well be for the last time."

Preoccupied with his secret conversation, Charles did not notice that the latest beauty from France was standing just behind Angel. The Queen, however, looked with dismay at the copper-haired lady with the slumberous eyes and the full ripe mouth. The expression in the beauty's eyes increased her dismay. Her hands clenched. Charles will surely become infatuated with her, she thought. And she will surely do her best to take his time and attention from me. 'Twill be an easy task. The slumberous eyes met hers, the full mouth smiled faintly. The Queen flushed. It would almost seem as if the lady had read her private thoughts.

"A good answer, my lady Benbrook," the King was saying, "and a damned tactful one. But it will not be the last time you dance with me." He raised his voice, including the Queen in the conversation. "Here is my lady Benbrook proposing to bury herself in the country forever. But you shall not entirely escape us. We do not intend to lose you, my lady." He looked at the Queen. "Do we, Madam?"

"No indeed." There was trust and real affection in the little Queen's eyes. "You must return to Court often, my lady."

"If you do not," the King added, "you will be commanded to do so. What have you to say to that, Mr. Barrymore?"

Alex's brows lifted. "What can I say, Sire? Only that I trust, from time to time, that I may be included in the royal command."

Charles' laugh rang out, startling the line of people waiting to be presented. "Rogue! And if you are not included? What then, Mr. Barrymore?"

"Why then, Sire, I shall have no recourse but to throw myself on Your Majesty's mercy."

"Will you so, Mr. Barrymore? There now, be off with you."

They moved to one side. Charles held out his hand to the French beauty, and Catherine saw on his face that look that she so dreaded to see. "Madame Damiens," Charles said softly, "we are delighted to welcome you to our shores."

He held her hand a little longer than was strictly necessary, before turning his attention to the Duke of Mulgrave. "My lord Duke," Charles said, his eyes still on Madame Damiens' smiling face, "we are happy to see you here."

Catherine smiled and nodded mechanically to each in turn, but her thoughts were far away. She caught sight of Angel again, and her eyes followed her wistfully. Alex Barrymore was so much in love with my Lady Benbrook that it was a joy to look at him. What must it be like to be loved like that? she thought. She would give up her crown, her entire fortune, and her hope of heaven to have Charles look at her like that. Aye, in just that way, that very special way!

Catherine started. My lady Deptford was waiting to be presented. "My lady," Catherine said, "we are happy to receive you." She smiled at the woman, and she did not realize that her eyes were bright with tears.

Angel drifted lightly to the measure of the dance. The King, as was his wont, was holding her much too tightly, much too close, but it did not confuse her as once it would have done. She was no longer that raw and frightened girl of long ago. She smiled at him in unconscious coquetry.

The King turned her about, then drew her close to him again. "If you look at me like that, my lady Angel," he whispered, "I shall forget all my good resolutions. Your King is but human, you know."

"Sire! We are being observed."

His hands tightened on her waist. "But the King can do no wrong. You know that, little Angel." He was teasing her again.

"Sire, the movements of the dance do not require that I be held close to Your Majesty's body."

He stopped dancing. Instantly the musicians in the gallery stopped playing. When the King opened the ball, it was unheard of for him to stop dancing. The people waiting to join in the dance smiled to themselves. This King of theirs had ever been unconventional. What now? they wondered.

"Plague take it, my lady," Charles said, smiling at her. "If I am to be denied the pleasure of holding you close, then I will invent a new dance." He turned to the watching people. "I am about to invent a new dance I hope will pleasure you. Watch closely, and then, I pray you, join in." He hesitated. "I shall call it— Ah!" he snapped his fingers in sudden inspiration. "I shall call the dance 'The Stuart's Dream.' What say you, my lords and ladies, will you follow me?"

Laughter and cheers greeted this. "Play," Charles called, waving his hand toward the gallery. "I wish for something gay and flowing."

The harassed musicians, after a moment's pause to think, began to play.

Charles drew the flushed and disconcerted Angel into his arms. Holding her pressed close to his body with one hand, his other hand holding hers, Charles began to whirl her about the room.

The audience watched wide-eyed, turning scandalized faces to each other. Why, it was unheard of! Such a dance was shocking! The ladies, embarrassed, were afraid now to look at their escorts. But there was a distinct gleam in every male eye. Despite the embarrassment, one by one they became caught up in the gay lilt and dip of the dance. With scarcely a pause, fascinated, they glided onto the floor. The dance was thrilling! Exciting! Wicked! Shocking! But remarkably exhilarating and romantic. Who but their own wicked Charles Stuart, they asked themselves, would have dared to execute such a dance? The bodies of the men responded to the excitement, and the soft breasts of the ladies, crushed close against hard male chests, showed a similar response. There had never been such a dance! There never would be again.

Catherine, watching from her chair, looked prim. But inwardly she had determined to dance The Stuart's Dream with Charles, at the earliest possible opportunity.

Madame Damiens thought—*Magnifique!* This is a dance of the heart, the senses! She thought of her own King. I will show him this new dance. He will be delighted.

The skirt of Angel's gown flew out like a great colorful bell as Charles whirled her about the room. She could feel the hard beating of his heart against her body, and she smiled into his dark eyes, laughing with excitement. Now the dance became faster. She could not breathe evenly. The candlelight whirled before her eyes in a yellow blur, her nostrils were filled with the scent of perfume and flowers, and her body, responding unconsciously to Charles', was heated with excitement. Jewels flashed in the light, hair became loosened, but nobody cared. Alex, watching, likened the sight to a glittering whirling rainbow of color.

Charles' hand held Angel's tightly. He had meant the dance to be only a rather daring joke, and as a means of getting his own way. But now he felt alive in a new way, a way he had never felt before. His blood stirred, and a pulse in his forehead began to throb. My lady Angel was not for him, and doubtless never would be. But there was Frances Dixon, there was Nell Gwynne, and Madame Damiens. He had seen the look in Madame's eyes, and he knew that she would be more than willing. There was even Catherine, his Queen, of the small but exciting body. Why, he had not shared her bed in a long time. He must do so. If not this night, which was to be given to Mistress

Dixon, there was always tomorrow. Tomorrow and tomorrow, always another tomorrow.

The dance ended. But the dancers, hypnotized by this new thrill, wanted to sample it again. Smiling, Charles led Angel from the floor. For the moment he had had enough, but he waved his hand to indicate that the dance be resumed. He paused before Alex Barrymore.

"Well, Alex," he said. "What think you?"

Alex smiled. "I have never seen anything quite like it, Sire. It is wicked, but—er—extremely fascinating."

"I thought you would think so." The King placed Angel's hand in Alex's. "I am sure you will wish to try something that fascinating."

Alex bowed. "I had formed that intention as soon as I saw Your Majesty leave the floor."

Charles laughed. "The damned plaguey fellow is full of sin, my lady Angel. I would that he were as simple and as innocent as myself."

Angel's mouth trembled into laughter. "If all were as simple and as innocent as Your Majesty, the world would become an extremely intriguing place."

"Saucy wench!" The King pinched her cheek. "Take her away, Alex, else will I be tempted to lead her in the dance again."

Laughing, the King went on his way. Alex, with a look in his blue eyes that made her heart beat very fast, took her by the hand and guided her among the dancers. Taking her in his arms and holding her very close, he said, "I love you, my wicked lady Benbrook."

"Wicked?"

"Aye, wicked to dance as you did. 'Tis the dance of the abandoned."

"But you will try it, will you not, Mr. Barrymore?"

"Aye, I will. But in future you will dance only with your husband."

Catherine smiled at the King as he approached. "Charles," she said, when he was seated. "I would greatly like to try the new dance."

"We will try it, Catherine, when your ankle is healed."

He took her hand in his. "But we need not a dance, do we, Cat?"

"We do not need a dance?" Catherine repeated. "I—I do not understand your meaning, Charles."

"You do not?" Charles' fingers tightened about hers. "Do you know, Catherine, that when you look at me like that, you're truly delicious?" He leaned closer to her. "I meant that we do not need the dance to excite us. Do we, Cat, do we?"

Color flamed in her cheeks. "No, Charles. You are the music to me, you are the excitement!" She looked into his smiling eyes, and she wished fervently that this happy moment could go on forever.

Lord Roger Melton looked at the unusual spectacle of the King and Queen holding hands. He nudged his friend, Andrew Perry. "The new dance has much to answer for, I believe. Look there, Andy. Doubtless the Queen will soon be carrying a royal heir in her body."

Andrew Perry laughed. "Though 'twill be a miracle if she carries it to full term." He nodded toward the dancers. "The Angel is in radiant beauty tonight. Do you not agree?"

Sir Roger, who had a tenderness for my lady Benbrook, looked disgruntled. "She is beautiful indeed. But why she had to fall in love with that damned fop Barrymore, I'll never know. The lady is spirited. She needs a real man."

Andrew Perry, who had witnessed the downfall of the Duke of Buckingham, smiled. "You may not believe this, Roger, but she has one." He thought of the Duke's battered face, and he chuckled. "Aye, the Duke of Buckingham found him to be damned uncomfortably real."

Sir Roger looked at him blankly. "I have been away, as you know. Perhaps you would care to explain your meaning? 'Tis my belief, Andy, that you've had too much wine." He shook his head rebukingly. "Aye, that's it. You don't know what you are saying."

The young Earl of Benbrook, with Mrs. Sampson beside him, looked through the peephole at the dancers. He pointed excitedly, then turned a smiling face to Mrs. Sampson.

"You've seen Mama. Is that it?" Mrs. Sampson said. Nicholas nodded.

"Let me see, Master Nickey." Nicholas moved obligingly. Mrs. Sampson bent down. She wiped the peephole free of the stickiness of Nicholas's fingers, and applied her eyes to the two rounded holes. "Aye," she said, "I see Mama. She is dancing with Master Alex." She stiffened suddenly. "Disgraceful!" she exclaimed. She straightened up abruptly and held out her hand. "Come, Master Nickey. Such sights are not for small boys."

Nicholas frowned, and his mouth looked mutinous, but he took her hand obediently.

Walking along the corridor, Mrs. Sampson glanced down at the boy. When he is grown he'll be my Master Nickey all over again. But I pray he will be happier, more trusting. Able to give love and to receive it.

In the nursery, Mrs. Sampson settled Nicholas in his small canopied bed. He did not protest as was usual with him. He seemed tired. "Goodnight, my lovie." She smiled down at the boy. "May God bless you, little one."

"Goodnight." Nicholas smiled at her, then he closed his eyes.

Mrs. Sampson settled herself in her chair. She was feeling her age these days, she thought. She doubted if she would live to see the boy grow up. Her eyes brooded. She had had a good life, a full life. It had been marked with too much tragedy, she had sometimes thought, but then, few lives were free of it. But somehow, through the plague, the fire, the unbearable sorrow, she had managed to survive. And so, thanks be to the blessed Lord, had Angel.

Mrs. Sampson's smile was touched with sadness. Angel! She had so many memories of the girl. Angel as she had once been, dirty, bedraggled, her hair full of lice. Her speech had been the speech of the London gutters then, but with it all she had been so very lovely! Then there was Angel defying Nicholas, screaming at him, hating him. And the Angel in love, her face glowing and beautiful whenever Nicholas was near.

Mrs. Sampson closed her eyes. She could see Master Nickey now. The way he had stood there at the foot of the stairs, looking up at the pale and fearful Angel. Not saying a word, he had held out his arms, and Angel, her face flushing to vivid beauty, had flown down the stairs and hurled herself into his arms. It was all over now, that wonderful and magical love story, but she knew that it lived on in Angel's heart. A new love had come to fill the aching void, and it was right that it should be so. Angel would never forget her dear m'lord, but Master Alex would not suffer for that.

Mrs. Sampson opened her eyes at the sound of voices just outside the door.

The door opened, and Angel and Alex entered. "Sampson," Angel said, smiling at her, "is Nicholas asleep?"

"He is. And I'll not have him awakened."

Angel went over to the bed and looked down at her son. She touched his cheek tenderly. "How like he is to my Nicholas."

Mrs. Sampson cast a swift look at Alex, but he smiled at her. "I understand, Mrs. Sampson," he said softly. "He will always be her Nicholas. But if I may be her Alex, then am I content."

Angel turned round. "Are you two conspiring against me?"

"Nay, you saucy wench," Alex drawled, "but 'tis an idea."

Angel came to him slowly. She looked into his eyes for a moment, then she smiled and put her arms about his neck. "Alex, I love you!"

"So I should hope," Alex said calmly. "Come, I am in the mood for dancing."

"Bah!" Mrs. Sampson said, when the door closed behind them. "If they call that dancing, they are sadly mistaken. 'Tis more like a sinful romp to me. I wonder the King allows it. I really do!"

IF YOU LIKED MY LADY BENBROOK, YOU'LL WANT TO READ...

THE KING'S BRAT

by Constance Gluyas   (91-125, $2.50)

The Earl of Benbrook gazed at the waif who had been kind to his dying sister. With a mixture of guilt and gratitude, he vowed to turn the street wench into a lady. It was a task that would involve him with Angel far more deeply than he guessed, and would change her far more than she dreamed! The temptestuous tale of Angel Dawson's rise from the streets of London to the court of Charles II.